The Heart Key

Robyn Braemer

Halstad House

Chapter One

Tabitha stared up at the institution style clock hanging on the drab cinder block wall though the time didn't register in her thoughts. The wall had been painted a dull gray in another decade. The small room felt cramped and smelled like a locker room. The FBI agent sitting beside her at the small, laminated table in the cramped room had just told her to start at the beginning. "Start at the beginning," she muttered to herself. *The beginning of what*? He seemed to think that she had some clue as to what he was talking about. She didn't.

In the beginning there was Tabitha, third child of four, born to Emilia and William T. Anderson. She had been the tomboy, all about horses and dogs, playing sports and reading everything that she could get her hands on. Tabitha had wanted to be a boy because boys had all the adventures. In all the books she had read as a child, boys had fun and girls didn't. She wanted to be a cowboy and ride horses on cattle drives. She wanted to hop on a barge floating down a river and live what adventures came her way. On her tenth birthday she had gotten a cowboy hat and a jackknife and was the happiest girl in the world that day. By her eleventh birthday she was writing boys' names on her notebooks instead of wishing she was a boy. Though she had acquired a horse the dream of driving cattle in the old west was barely a memory. Puberty kicked in and instilled an interest in boys in her life instead of living a boy's life at the turn of the century. Tabitha had grown up in a standard Midwestern family environment until just before she turned twelve.

Perhaps that was the beginning. Her parents had gotten divorced just before she turned twelve. Getting divorced just wasn't done in small-town Minnesota at the time. It was only as an adult that the complications of coming from a divorced home became apparent. Now parents married a lifetime was more the non-norm. So did children from stable home environments now create complications? That didn't make sense. She wrinkled her nose as she considered the ramifications. For a few minutes she forgot that she was sitting in a concrete walled room being interrogated by the FBI as she got lost in considering nature versus nurture.

The FBI agent cleared his throat. Tabitha glanced at him. The thought of doing the tired routine of beginning at her childhood made her want to giggle. It's hysterics, she told herself. Why else would she even consider her childhood the beginning? Tabitha rubbed her palms on her legs, an action to relieve the stress more than sweaty palms. She'd never had sweaty palms in her life, though she'd heard the term often enough. Tabitha glanced at her palms. So did people really sweat through their palms? Maybe it was a guilt thing. Maybe she had indeed sweated from her palms in the past and didn't realize it or remember it. Everyone probably sweated from their palms, which was why in gym in school there was talcum powder for rope climbing. That made sense even if she'd never really given it thought before. Now that she thought about it, there had been a time where she remembered sweaty palms but she couldn't exactly place the specific event, just a tickle at the back of her mind, a memory rising as a result of thinking about it. The FBI agent was scowling at her.

The beginning. Tabitha tried to focus on the task at hand. At what point did life toss something at her that would have prompted this FBI agent to grab her off the street and sit there with his scowly face? To her the beginning was being dragged into this oxygen deprived room, so institutional and mind numbing. Though there was nothing in the room to distract her eye she found it difficult to focus. She was a law-abiding citizen and found it quite shocking to be treated like a criminal. Maybe they weren't treating her like a criminal. Maybe this was how they treated everyone they yanked off the street. Tabitha actually didn't have anything to compare it to. She had never even been called to the principal's office in school. Tabitha had never done anything wrong in school to require being sent to the principal's office. If she had done something wrong maybe this would make more sense. Why did she feel so guilty when she had done nothing wrong?

Tabitha stole a glance at the FBI agent. He sat back in his chair, holding a steaming white Styrofoam cup to his face, occasionally blowing a bit to cool the coffee. Tabitha felt a bit confused because he didn't seem to *like* her. Everyone liked her. She had a pleasant face and had developed curves early so she had always had the attention of the male sex. She had the confidence of knowing she was pleasant on the eyes even if she didn't feel model or superstar material. Women also liked her. Tabitha had an easy manner and was outgoing and friendly without being intrusive. She was comfortable with herself and used to people liking her.

It was enough for her that she wasn't ugly. Tabitha had never gotten into spending hours grooming for a certain look. A shower and towel dried hair was enough for her. Tabitha was vain enough to select clothes that suited her coloring and figure, most of the time. Though she wasn't big on sweat pants she did like the comfort of baggy shirts rather than something more flattering. Clothes just weren't a priority for her. Like many people, she bought clothes that looked nice in the store but ended up sitting untouched in the closet because there were always those favorite shirts or pants or dresses that she automatically reached for all the time.

The truth was, when she did spend time at the mirror applying make-up she felt like she looked the same in the end. Lipstick intimidated her. She had a healthy complexion, large green eyes, and an easy smile. Usually people liked her. Tabitha was used to being treated kindly and warmly by everyone. Even if it took spending a few minutes in her company most people warmed up to her. This man in his off the rack suit seemed to be growing more distant and cold to her with every passing minute he spent in her company and she didn't know why.

Tabitha closed her eyes, to better concentrate when she felt the agent's gaze burning holes in her right ear. She had terrific peripheral vision, even with closed eyes. What was the beginning he was wanting? Tabitha went backwards, discarding possibilities. The strange man's house was the most likely starting spot. Then there was the gorgeous man at the art supply store. That made her smile. No, he was just a pleasant thought that jumped into her head too often all day. It had to be the meteor shower. Though she couldn't possibly imagine what it had to do with the FBI agent's question it was by far the most fascinating and unusual experience she had had recently and events seemed to be cascading from it since.

Tabitha went back to the art supply store in her mind. It was an exhilarating feeling that washed over her as she remembered. The man at the art store had taken her breath away. At the time Tabitha had been overwhelmed by the feelings washing over her but now she just felt giddy. The man at the art store made her feel flitter pated. Still, it was the meteor shower that had put her at the art store that day. The man at the art store had the most amazing eyes and a smile that made her want to smile just thinking about it. His deep voice had sent shivers through her whole body, all the way to her toes. He felt larger than life. Tabitha sighed. As so often happened when she met a man who she found extremely attractive, when he tried to talk to her she had turned into a frozen smile statue and even the smile was hard to maintain because her mouth would go dry and her lips felt like they would get stuck together if she let them touch so it was more of a grimace than a smile.

Just thinking about the encounter almost made her forget that she was sitting across the table from a scowling FBI agent in an interrogation room. Tabitha blinked when she again became aware of her surroundings. Agent Bismarck didn't look like he wanted to hear her romantic daydreams, which had nothing to do with why she was here, as far as she knew, though she really had no clue why she was here. Still, she was quite confident that the man in the art store had no bearing on finding the beginning. There must be a reason why she was here and she'd figure it out eventually.

Yes, the meteor shower was the beginning. Nothing before it could have had any bearing. Everything after that seemed to have led up to this. It would help if he could give her some more information to go on but since he hadn't she would take a shot at finding the right answer. She opened her eyes, the black clock staring back at her. That had to be it, the meteor shower.

"Technically it started with the meteor shower, I guess," she said.

The agent frowned and slowly, purposely set down the coffee cup that he was about to sip from. "What does a meteor shower have to do with the disappearance of Agent Ellis?" the FBI agent asked, an edge of impatience making his voice sharp.

Tabitha turned her gaze from the black circle on the wall to the man sitting to her right. Standing, he was average height, in his mid-fifties, and he wore his charcoal gray suit as though he lived in suits. He wore his hair cropped so short as to be shaved, the result being that it was barely noticeable that he had a receding hairline. He had very blue eyes. Tabitha thought he might be wearing tinted contacts to have eyes so blue. To her it seemed an odd sign of vanity in a man who projected an image so hard, until she considered that the short haircut might also be a sign of vanity since it disguised the receding hairline.

Tabitha sighed at how easily she was distracted. She couldn't help it. Getting to the heart of people was her thing. Some might call it a hobby. Some might call it an obsession or a waste of time. Once she felt she knew what made a person tick she just felt better. All sorts of things would fall into place once she could delve a person's personality. Tabitha had already decided that Agent Bismarck might even be a nice person under other circumstances and that what made him so upset was that he knew and liked the mysterious Agent Ellis who had somehow managed to vanish with some unknown connection to her.

He had introduced himself as Agent Bismarck when he had grabbed her arm in an iron grip as she left the grocery store. His sharp "Please come with me," had been accompanied with a quick wrist flex of some badge that she had no time to see clearly and there was no please about it. He had simply taken her arm and before she could say a word had shuffled her to a waiting car and stuffed her into the bland car driven by a bland man in another suit and driven her to this bland building with this bland room with the bland walls and bland clock.

Her single bag of groceries sat on a table against the wall in the corner. The bag had been searched and then left sitting. What had they expected to find in a bag that she had used to carry her purchases from a grocery store? It was a brown paper bag. There was ice cream in that brown paper bag sitting on the table, butter pecan. No one seemed to care about that. Tabitha expected beige ooze to come creeping out the bottom any moment. She doubted that the FBI would repay her for the somewhat expensive treat. The carrots and milk should be fine, unless they kept her all night. Tabitha tried to remember what else she had bought that might be perishable. Maybe she should ask them to put the ice cream in a freezer.

"Are you saying aliens abducted Agent Ellis?" the agent asked.

Tabitha had just remembered that she had also bought two containers of yogurt, so was distracted and caught off guard by his question. Tabitha stared at him, eyebrows raised. "Are you serious?"

"You're the one who mentioned aliens."

Tabitha took a deep breath. "I said it started with a meteor shower."

Agent Bismarck leaned closer. "What started?"

"This whole crazy whatever it is," Tabitha said, waving her arms.

"Just what is it?" Agent Bismarck asked.

Tabitha leaned back in her chair and took a deep breath before she got into a shouting match with the man. She hadn't been arrested. They had simply wanted to ask her some questions, so she had been told. Tabitha was prepared to cooperate fully, yet as the meeting continued she was becoming more and more confused. She didn't know any Agent Ellis and she didn't know what they expected her to know. There weren't questions for her to answer. There were expectations of her to supply information without any hints as to what was wanted. They seemed to be waiting for her to tell them something but it was as if they didn't know the questions either. Tabitha looked at Agent Bismarck. The man was an FBI agent. He wasn't stupid. Well, he couldn't be stupid. She was sure that was written in an FBI requirement or something.

"I don't know what you expect. While you keep jabbering at me…" she paused, seeing that his mouth tightened at the word jabbering, then decided to dive all the way in. Tabitha had never managed to hold back from saying what was on her mind and just because he didn't like it she wasn't going to stop now. "I keep thinking what changed for me lately and I would have to say it was the meteor shower. That seemed to have started a whole chain of events. If I have some connection to your agent disappearing I can only think it had something to do with the meteor shower."

"When was this meteor shower?"

"About a week ago," Tabitha said, perking up.

"A week ago?" Agent Bismarck repeated, tossing his pen in disgust.

Tabitha nodded happily at the topic. "I found meteorites." The excitement lifted her mood and her voice. It still excited her to think about it. "I remember at the time thinking how momentous a thing it was. I actually found meteorites. My brother said he knew about someone who was always looking for meteorites. There's this ad posted at the university. You know, like for selling a bike or puppies? I finally got over there to take a look and I contacted the man recently and now you snatched me off the street," Tabitha said. She tilted her head as she considered the statement. "Or off the sidewalk, I guess. Or off the parking lot. Is that a term? Snatched off the parking lot?"

"This man. Tell me about him. How does your brother know him?" Agent Bismarck said in a more calm voice, reaching for his coffee cup.

Tabitha relaxed. "He was very tall and very skinny. I would think about six foot four inches and barely one hundred sixty pounds. He had thinning blonde hair that was in need of a haircut. He wasn't really balding, just thin hair. His nose has been broken at least once, maybe twice, but probably years ago. His eyebrows are quite shaggy though facial hair doesn't seem to grow very well for him. He has rheumy eyes, so I suspect allergies."

"He struck me as someone who had a hard childhood. Maybe an overprotective mother. Maybe a neglectful mother. Maybe a mother who was abusive while being overprotective. I kind of felt sorry for the little boy still visible under the surface even though he was probably a creepy child just as he's a creepy man. Yet when it's a child it's easier to feel sympathy. I guess." She hesitated, feeling a blush creep up her face. Agent Bismarck was staring at her over his coffee cup.

"You're very observant of someone you only met once for a few minutes," Agent Bismarck said dryly, lowering his coffee cup.

"I notice things. Okay, maybe I also have a vivid imagination. But there was something wrong with that man so it had to stem from something," she said. She took a deep breath and got back on track. "I showed him two rocks I had found from the meteor shower. He looked at each one for several minutes and said he'd give me five dollars each for them." Tabitha snorted just thinking about it. "I said no."

Tabitha paused, remembering the way his eyes had narrowed when she had snorted and said she wasn't interested in selling them for such a low price. For that price it was worth keeping them herself even if they just sat on a shelf, or she could donate them to an elementary school or university. They were not as interesting as the other items she had found at the site but were still unique. She hadn't gone expecting to retire from the proceeds. Tabitha had been curious to know their market value. He was the only market she was aware of. Though she hadn't expected thousands of dollars, his offer of five dollars was more insulting than anything else.

The meteor man had been quite agitated when she had said no thanks and moved to leave. Tabitha had tried to leave. He had stepped in front of the door to block her way, clasping his hands together over his chest, as if trying to hold back from grabbing her.

"Okay," he had said, tapping his thumbs together. The meteor man was so much taller than her that when he leaned over her it made her feel like he was looming over her, quite an uncomfortable feeling. Tabitha resisted the urge to step back because she didn't want to give him the power to push her back just with his presence. "I can go as high as one hundred." He glared when she just stared at him. He added a regretful, "Each."

"I suppose you were looking for something else. Something more than a physical description," Tabitha said to Agent Bismarck. "He was creepy. He had that haughty attitude when I arrived. I had called and he said to stop by when convenient. When he gave me the address I was nearby so I said I could be there in a few minutes. He asked if I had the meteorites with me, stating very coolly that I needn't waste his time by stopping by without the rocks." Tabitha snorted again just thinking about it.

"As if I'd be so stupid to go without the rocks. That's how he is though, I think. One of those who either thinks no one else has a working neuron in their head or one of those who think no one else can do something right. Me, I'm the opposite. I always think everyone has brains in their heads that should work at the same level as, well, as everyone else."

Agent Bismarck rubbed his forehead with his fingertips. Tabitha noticed and paused. She knew that sign. She had seen that same motion over and over in her lifetime. It was the subconscious gesture of someone suffering from the brain freezing properties of her tendency to chatter a bit more than average. She didn't mean to do it. It was just what happened.

Tabitha had heard childhood tales of people "considering" what words escaped between their lips. She was sure it was a myth, although she had encountered the occasional person who seemed to pause between statements, as if they had given thought to their words before speaking. Not her. Tabitha would be the first to admit that sometimes the words spilled out so fast that she couldn't always know what she was saying until it was said. Luckily she usually meant what she said even if it wasn't always comprehensive.

"Oh, yeah," she said, remembering. "When I said I didn't necessarily want to sell what I'd brought he looked capable of violence."

Agent Bismarck looked interested. "He threatened you with violence?"

Tabitha shook her head. "No. Just a fleeting feeling of rage emanating from him, that I was thwarting him and that he didn't like being thwarted."

"You some type of genius?" the FBI agent asked.

"What do you mean?" The question confused her. Was he being serious in asking if she was a genius? If so, how had he figured it out? Tabitha quickly tried to retrace what they'd discussed but she'd already forgotten a lot of what she'd said. His tone hadn't felt genuine so she suspected the question wasn't genuine.

"Guess not."

Tabitha ignored his sarcastic comment. "Then he said he'd give me a hundred each," she said, shivering as she remembered. "He seemed to resent me not just giving them to him but he also suddenly seemed determined to have them. I took it just to get out of there. He made me uncomfortable. That's it. On the way home I ran some errands, stopped at a few stores, the art supply store and the grocery store and then you grabbed me."

Agent Bismarck frowned. "It wasn't grabbing," he said in a tone bordering on exasperation. The agent looked surprised that Tabitha had gotten under his skin. He took a deep breath and pushed the interview back on track. "You didn't say how your brother knows him."

"I didn't say my brother knows him. You said that my brother knows him. I said my brother heard that he was looking for meteorites. My brother is a grad student at the U. He hears all sorts of things."

The door opened and another man in a suit stepped inside. It was Agent Pierre. He had been driving the bland car which Agent Bismarck had pushed her into. Agent Pierre had started out sitting with them when they first arrived and then had excused himself very early in the interview, leaving her alone with Agent Bismarck. He looked like he could be a slightly younger brother to Agent Bismarck, same short hair, same suit, and same hardness, just taller and he had a pointy nose. Agent Pierre smiled at her. At least his mouth formed the acceptable shape of a smile. Agent Pierre would go into politics, Tabitha decided. Agent Pierre had that properness about him. He also smelled too strongly of cologne. Her uncle had always smelled too strongly of cologne, to hide the smell of alcohol. Whenever Tabitha smelled a man doused in cologne she thought of what smell he was trying to cover.

Agent Pierre smiled again, as if forgetting that he had already given her a smile, then sat down opposite her with his elbows on the table. He studied her thoughtfully for an excruciatingly long minute. "It's unfortunate that you were dragged into this. The man you visited this morning has been under surveillance for quite some time," Agent Pierre said in a slow, smooth voice. "He has been suspected of the disappearance of a number of people but we have no proof."

Tabitha felt goose bumps tingle along her arms and the back of her neck and shivered. Someone was walking over her grave her gramma had always said. Her gramma was full of gramma sayings. Tabitha knew that it was a primordial fear raising the hairs like some prehistoric animal. "These people. Do they go to his house to answer ads for meteorites?"

Agent Pierre considered the question, then shrugged. "Some might have."

Tabitha felt sick to her stomach. She turned to Agent Bismarck. "So you knew that. You knew that I could have been in danger and you sit there and accuse me of talking about aliens and of being involved in some mystery agent's disappearance?"

"You are involved," Agent Bismarck said firmly. He had no signs of a guilty conscience. If anything he still glared at her like she had all the answers and was holding back. "Agent Ellis reported making contact with you."

"Not everyone disappears. Definitely not a first contact," Agent Pierre said quickly, shaking his head at Agent Bismarck. "There is quite a lot of foot traffic. If we felt you were in any danger we wouldn't have allowed you to go in. At least not without warning you. We have been keeping a very careful watch. We have no reason to believe he has harmed anyone. It has just been a strange series of coincidences that brings us back to him."

"You are investigating him for making people disappear and yet here I sit being treated like a criminal," Tabitha said. "How can you let people go in there if you think they are in danger?"

"We have no proof," Agent Pierre said. He grimaced. "I don't know why I mentioned it. Except maybe to let you know how serious this is."

"No danger but you lost an FBI agent to him?" Tabitha stared at Agent Pierre in disbelief. She almost snorted at the outright lie. No idea why he mentioned it? He knew exactly why he mentioned it. He wanted to see her reaction to the information. "What makes you think I wasn't taking this serious?"

Agent Pierre frowned, looking confused and uncomfortable. "Well, you, uh, well don't seem to be taking this very seriously."

"You suspect this man of abducting or harming an FBI agent and you're sitting here thinking I have some hand in it yet you don't think I'm taking it seriously?"

"We don't know that Agent Ellis has come to harm at this man's hands. He was investigating him and vanished," Agent Pierre said. "Lots of people seem to vanish in connection with this man but we have no proof." He frowned when he realized he had blurted out information that he hadn't intended to share. Agent Bismarck glared at Agent Pierre for a split second before turning his glare back to Tabitha.

"And now you," Agent Bismarck snapped.

Agent Pierre sighed. "You are the first difference." He paused for dramatic effect. "He followed you."

"What do you mean, he followed me?" Tabitha asked. Her throat suddenly felt very dry. She tried to swallow but couldn't.

"As we mentioned, he has been under surveillance. Several agencies actually have an interest in him. When you left it wasn't long before he got in his car and followed you. Or at least tried. It seems that you managed to elude him without being aware that he was following you," Agent Pierre said. "Once it was determined that he had an interest in you, you were followed by one of our agents until we decided whether it would be beneficial to bring you in for questioning."

Tabitha stared at the clock. It was afternoon. She was pretty sure it was afternoon. She didn't think she had been in the room for more than twelve hours though at times it had felt like a long time. That meant she had only been in the room for less than two hours. The clock's hands showed half past one. The creepy guy who the FBI suspected was a serial killer had tried to follow her when she left his house, where she had been alone with him. They had lost an FBI agent that very morning. A trained FBI agent had vanished and the FBI didn't know where he was or what happened to him.

Tabitha didn't know what to feel. Overwhelmed was the closest word to describe the mind numbing, upper lip tingling way she felt. She turned her head to look at Agent Bismarck. He stared back at her with a face carved of stone. Maybe he had merely been asking her for information. She tried to remember how the interview had started but she came up blank. This was serious stuff and she had been distracted by no one bothering to tell her what they actually wanted of her. Now that they had told her she wished she had escaped the room without knowing anything beyond the fact that they wanted to know if she knew anything about a missing FBI agent.

Tabitha grimaced. Okay, maybe that had been serious enough to begin with but she hadn't fully registered that a missing FBI agent meant that he might be dead, cut up into tiny pieces and buried in a backyard or basement. Tabitha just thought it had meant that the agent was, well, missing.

Chapter Two

Tabitha had been driving along on a county road in rural North Dakota late at night when she had spotted the lines of lights streaking across the sky. She had slowed, then pulled over to the shoulder to watch the display. The click-click of the blinker continued for several minutes before she remembered to turn it off. Tabitha leaned against the steering wheel, peering up through the windshield at the falling bits of light. Some flared out quickly, winking into nothing, while others remained lit to the horizon. It was the largest shower Tabitha had seen, the closest meteor shower she had ever seen. One after another they streaked through the sky. It felt like they were right above her instead of off in some abstract distance.

Tabitha Anderson was an artist and a romantic and a woman of great imagination. More than that, she was a genius. Somehow her left brain and right brain were equally dominant. Tabitha had studied engineering in college but thought to switch to English as a major and ended up taking two extra years to finish because she stayed with engineering but kept taking classes that had nothing to do with her degree. Art flowed through her veins. Tabitha enjoyed making things. Yet she loved the challenge of mathematics and problem solving. To her it was the same thing. Art was visualization and math was theoretical. Tabitha did so well at everything she did that she literally bounced all over the place in her interests.

Tabitha also quickly grew bored with her career choices. Currently Tabitha was working as a software tester in Minneapolis and the challenge kept her interested but the urge to make pottery was growing stronger. There was something so therapeutic about sitting at a pottery wheel and feeling the clay gain its center. It was thrilling to start out with a lump of clay and watch it form into a bowl or vase or pitcher with just slight pressure from her fingers. She could get lost for hours building sculptures with clay. Tabitha also worked with wood and stained glass and painted and sewed and anything that looked fun to do. The problem she found with being an artist was that she had to sell her work and she didn't like doing that. Tabitha wanted to make things, not sit in some booth trying to sell it or make the rounds trying to get it into stores.

It was a definite paycheck every two weeks to get up every day and go into work and do a job that was most often enjoyable. Tabitha was good at the job and enjoyed the company of most of her co-workers. Tabitha felt a great sense of responsibility so she arrived at her job every day at her scheduled time, even if the urge to make a purse with the awesome leather she had just found at the leather store was stronger than reading code on a computer screen. It just felt stifling to her artistic side to be putting in so many hours a week at some rigid time schedule. It also felt scary to not have steady income so she put in the many hours a week with a rigid time schedule. Art was in her blood but a scheduled job working for someone else paid the bills.

Her artistic side wanted to stay up as late as she wanted if her muse woke her creative spirit at eleven pm. Tabitha could easily get lost in time while working on projects. Her logical side recognized that the structure and discipline of a normal job was also beneficial so she kept going to work every day and collecting her paycheck and used her free time to be creative. Between work and all her projects it just didn't leave much time for anything else in her life.

Tabitha had stumbled into the opportunity to host a creative arts television show once. She had thought she would enjoy it when she had her own television show but that hadn't worked for her either. Tabitha had been expected to do *craft* projects. She had thought she would have free rein to make whatever she wanted and gradually the reality set in as she was being pushed week after week to use specific products. Tabitha realized that she was being used to sell products. Using kits and pre-packaged products wasn't what she had hired on to do. Money came from selling expensive craft projects and supplies provided by sponsoring businesses, not from using an old Altoids tin to create a travel jewelry case or using toilet paper rolls and wire to create armatures for sculptures. Why would she promote some twenty dollar pre-made armature when it made more sense to use what was at hand?

Watching the meteor shower made her feel restless. She had itchy feet again, which happened sometimes. Tabitha would feel unsettled and need to change her life, whether by moving or changing careers. The feeling would start as an ache in her chest, almost like she couldn't breathe. Tabitha often thought it must be what migratory animals and birds felt, a driving need to be somewhere even if she didn't know where it was she was meant to be. For some reason the vastness of the night sky above her served as a catalyst to those restless feelings. Beyond the flaring bits of falling space rocks burning into dust as they went streaking across the sky were stars. It seemed somehow ironic that they formed the backdrop for the shooting star display. A meteor is so finite, an end to something. And beyond the meteors was the infinite blackness of forever.

There was no end to the stars, always more and more, twinkling bits of faraway sunshine captured in a moment of time millions upon millions of miles away, a distance so vast that it was impossible for the human mind to comprehend the distance. Far, far away, that was what it amounted to. The universe was so big and made her feel so small. With so many suns and so many planets around those suns there had to be life beyond one little blue planet in the Milky Way.

Tabitha couldn't help but think that somewhere out there were planets with someones staring up at their sky, mesmerized by so many stars on a clear summer night. Stars twinkled in the vast emptiness of space yet there were so many stars up there. She had always been fascinated with the night sky and its diamond twinkling promise of things beyond her reach. Tabitha had never had the urge to be an astronaut however. The thought of going into the vacuum of space in a tin can made her nauseas. She felt the same way about oceans and didn't understand how anyone could go out into all that deep water on a tiny little ship. Submarines were enough to give her heart palpitations.

Tabitha felt along the car door with her fingers for the button for the window and pressed it. The window rolled down with a soft electronic whir and a final thunk as it sank into the doorframe. She then shut off the car. For a few minutes the car made soft pinging sounds as it cooled, then silence surrounded her. It had rained recently and the land smelled of wet dirt and leaves. Gradually the sound of crickets serenading each other rose through the silence, increasing in volume as more and more crickets announced their presence. The meteors made no sound as they fell through the sky. That was almost sad, to watch the silent death of each meteor. Several flared into nothing directly overhead.

Suddenly she heard a ping sound and then a whack. Tabitha turned her headlights on and stared as a tendril of smoke drifted up from the ditch, visible just at the edge of the beam of her headlights. A second ping sounded and she turned her head to the right just in time to see a glowing ember of a meteor burn its way through a tree trunk on the other side of the ditch. Her eyes opened wide in amazement, half expecting the tree to burst into flames any minute. It didn't. A small tendril of smoke drifted out from the hole in the bark.

Tabitha glanced ahead again, leaning forward, chest pressing against the steering wheel, up through the windshield until her eyes ached from being stretched to the top of her sockets, just in time to see a fireball streaking straight for her car. She froze, knowing she should duck but unable to tear her gaze away. The fireball slammed into the ground twenty feet in front of her into the ditch. The car actually vibrated from the impact. Bits of gravel and dust rattled against the front of her car. A few pieces of grass floated back to the ground in her headlight beam.

"Wow," Tabitha said slowly, when she remembered to breath. She forcibly unwrapped her fingers from the steering wheel. Her heart was racing. That had been so close. There were two more pings then silence. Tabitha leaned forward and stared up and out through the windshield. The meteor shower was about over. A few more distant streaks of light silently flared across the star studded sky then nothing. It didn't take long for her to realize that there were meteorites that could be found and collected. Tabitha opened the console and grabbed the flashlight. She didn't need to check if it was working because she always maintained fresh batteries in the flashlights in her vehicles but out of habit she flipped it on to check the strength of the beam. It was strong and steady.

"They'll be hot," she said aloud to herself.

Tabitha popped the trunk from inside the car. She had been lucky to not be in the path of any of those falling rocks. That tree could have been her head. She glanced up at the sky again, looking for any more errant meteorites. Nothing. She opened the car door and felt a moment of panic when she couldn't get out of the car. Seatbelt. She had forgotten to remove the seatbelt. Tabitha released the clip, stepped out of the car and quickly shut the car door to silence the annoying, intrusive ding-ding warning chime. The crickets had stopped their singing again. Tabitha stood patiently beside the car to let her eyes adjust after the brief night blindness from having the overhead light come on when she had opened the car door. Opening the trunk immediately eliminated the benefit of doing that because it also had a light that automatically came on when she opened it.

In the car's trunk was a white plastic crate where Tabitha kept a wool blanket, glass cleaner, paper towels, and a wide variety of items that could come in handy while driving in rural areas, such as binoculars. She liked to be prepared. The ordinary windshield wiper fluid filling the standard plastic reservoir under the hood of the car was no match for the swarms of insects that could cover the windshield in no time, especially in spring or fall. Well, summer as well. Tabitha had forgotten that her miniature binoculars were in the car trunk and when she saw the case she slipped it into her shirt pocket. Tabitha paused, suddenly remembering she also had a small telescoping single lens scope. She wondered if it was in the glove box. She would have to remember to look.

There was also a cardboard box that she fortunately had forgotten to bring in to her studio a few weeks ago. Though she had forgotten repeatedly to bring it inside from the car but she hadn't forgotten it was there. The box was what she was looking for now.

Tabitha slid the box closer and opened the flaps. Inside the box were nestled neatly many handy supplies. Some she had recently purchased at the hardware store and were still in the plastic bag with the hardware store's logo on it and some she had been using to teach a friend how to do a project. Tabitha pulled out a spool of heavy gauge galvanized wire from a paper bag of newly purchased supplies and spent almost ten minutes trying to tear off the hard plastic covering. She had wire cutters and a hammer and even a small folding saw in the trunk but no scissors or knife. Contemporary packaging was a design in sadism. Tabitha tried pulling it open by finding a spot to slide her thumbnail along but it was sealed completely. She tried the claw of the hammer but it wasn't sharp enough and just marred the plastic. She tried the saw but it kept sliding along the edge. At last Tabitha found a screwdriver and stabbed the plastic repeatedly until she could bend a piece back and with a lot of swearing and twisting was able to create an opening large enough to get her fingers in and pull.

Once Tabitha managed to get the wire to slide off the spool she cut five lengths of wire about eighteen inches long. Tabitha hesitated then cut a sixth piece. She had heard five pings but an extra piece was good. Tabitha looked at the wire, shrugged and cut two more pieces. Better to have extra than not enough.

Tabitha put the wire cutters and wire back in the box, wire spool in the bag and wire cutters back exactly where they had been and grabbed a roll of masking tape. She tore off a piece and wrapped it around the end of a piece of wire, folding it over like a little flag. She did that to each piece of wire. Tabitha was starting to feel a sense of urgency, hoping that the meteors didn't cool immediately. There would be no way of finding them if she didn't have the smoke and glow. She had a general idea of the location of three of them but hadn't seen where all had hit.

Armed with her wire markers and flashlight Tabitha walked in the direction of the site of the first ping, swinging the light from her flashlight back and forth. It was actually easy to spot the smoking meteorite right away and she stuck a wire into the ground near the glowing meteorite. Tabitha visited each spot, looking for the tendrils of smoke to locate the two she had not seen hit. She found the third one when she tripped on the tall grass covering an uneven clump of dirt and landed with her hand a scant four inches from the glowing rock. The recent rain kept the grass from burning and she would have most likely not found that one. A hole in the knee of her jeans and long streak of dirt and grass stain was an acceptable cost for finding it.

Tabitha marked each spot with a wire marker and then wandered over the area a second time and a third time to make sure she hadn't missed anything. She still had one more flag. When Tabitha found nothing more she settled back into the car seat to wait for them to cool. It was quite exciting to find meteorites. She decided that that ranked quite high in the exciting things to happen in her life so far.

Agent Bismarck had stared at her as if she was hiding something. Well, in a way Tabitha was but she was certain that it had no bearing on this missing agent. Not telling the whole story was not the same as telling a lie. Leaving out details was not hiding anything. If what Tabitha had found had any bearing on some missing FBI agent then so was not reporting that the crickets had remained silent the rest of the night. Could crickets singing or not singing have any bearing on an elusive FBI agent? What she had found was something she'd never expected, a treasure. To her it was a treasure. It was called a tektite, ground around the impact site melted to glass by the impact of the meteor. Tabitha had found several of them and two even had a zircon inside, a jewel as green as an emerald.

It had still been early morning when she had started collecting her finds, after.dozing off and on in the car for a few hours. Twice passing cars slowed and asked if she was all right and she had waved them on, saying she was just resting her eyes. No one drove past after midnight. Once morning dawned and it was light enough to see she visited each marker, armed with her flashlight even though the sky had turned that early summer morning gray. If they hadn't been warm she wouldn't have even noticed that the tektites were the result of the meteor shower, just thinking they were old garbage, broken glass smoothed from time in the elements. But when her flashlight caught the tektite it changed colors. Tabitha had reached down to pick it up to look at it and been surprised that it was warm. Tabitha directed her flashlight over it and the gem inside turned purple. The first one she had found had been one with the zircon embedded inside so she started looking for more at each site.

Tabitha suspected that this Daniel Thomas knew she had been hiding something, that she had found more than two rocks. Tabitha wasn't good at keeping secrets and even though she knew the tektites were no one else's business she also knew something must show in her face that she was hiding something. It had nothing to do with a missing FBI agent though. It just couldn't. Tabitha just had a guilty face. It was like when she was a kid and had a secret that ate at her to share it with someone, with anyone.

"Look, I didn't see anyone else at the house. At least not inside. I didn't notice anyone in particular outside. I was just looking for the address," Tabitha said. She suddenly realized that they had never said how long the man had been missing. "When did your agent go missing?"

"This morning," Agent Pierre said. "Right after you left the suspect's house." Agent Bismarck scowled at him.

"When and how was I supposedly in contact with him?" she asked.

Pierre and Bismarck exchanged glances. Pierre sighed. Bismarck scowled. "When you were at the university getting the address," Pierre said.

Tabitha frowned as she tried to remember. She had talked to several people, mostly friends of her brother, just quick hellos. There was an oversized cork bulletin board in the hall full of the general chaos, birds for sale, bicycle for sale, and the like. Daniel Thomas' ad was the standard piece of paper stating that he was looking for meteorites and old maps with his phone number written vertically at the bottom repeatedly and cut into fringe so that a person could tear off the information.

There had been a man who stepped up to help her when she reached up to tear off the tab of information. The paper was hanging quite high on the bulletin board and there had been a printer in the way. For someone tall it was a simple stretch, for her it was a jump up and down stretch. The man had just stepped up to tear off an address tab and the only view Tabitha had really gotten of him was his arm. Oh, and she remembered the university logo on the front of his sweatshirt when she glanced over as his arm swung up above her and she was staring at his armpit. He hadn't said anything and her brother had joined her just then, surrounded by several of his friends, and Tabitha was left standing with a piece of paper and no clear image of the man who had handed it to her but she was sure he couldn't have been an FBI agent. At the time she had the fleeting impression that he was an engineering student. By the time the commotion calmed down the man was gone. It wasn't something she had given much thought at the time so now couldn't pull up any clear memories.

Tabitha remembered an old man asking for directions in the hall just after that but he certainly hadn't looked like an FBI agent. He looked rather confused and feeble. He was probably someone's grandfather come by to say hi or to talk some professor into passing his struggling grandchild. There were a lot of people at the university, on the grounds, in the halls. Unless he had come up to her she wouldn't have noticed an FBI agent. No one had come up to her.

"Sorry, I don't remember anyone," Tabitha said. The past events had been too much for her and she suddenly felt drained and tired. "I would like to leave now."

Agent Pierre nodded. Agent Bismarck scowled. Tabitha stood, her chair scraping loudly as she pushed it back. Suddenly it hit her, what had been said and she sat back down abruptly, the table several feet away from her now because she had pushed the chair quite a distance from the table.

"You are watching the man because people disappear and he followed me? What does that mean?" She looked back and forth between the two agents but neither said a word. "Is he a serial killer?"

"There is no evidence that he killed anyone. If there was we would have arrested him," Agent Pierre said. He stood, fumbled inside his suit jacket and pulled out a business card. He took one from Agent Bismarck and handed both to her. "Please contact us if you remember anything else or hear new information. We might be in touch with you again."

Tabitha took the business cards he gave her without even looking at them. "Isn't this terrorizing? To scare me about this man and then turn me loose out onto the street? All I did was go see a man about a meteorite."

"I'm sorry if you feel threatened," Agent Pierre said. Tabitha glanced at Agent Bismarck. He didn't look very sorry. "If we felt you were in any danger we would have warned you. Suspecting the man is one thing but we have no proof and we can't exactly intercede and confront every person he talks to," Agent Pierre pointed out in his smooth, political voice.

Tabitha nodded slowly. They were probably just trying to scare her. Well that had worked. For what good it did them. She still didn't know anything about a mystery missing FBI agent and being scared didn't jog open any missing memories. Tabitha had just visited a man who had given her the creeps and now found out that he was a suspected serial killer who was so good that the FBI could not pin any proof on him and people continued to disappear around him. If she didn't have nightmares all night it would be a miracle.

Tabitha walked to the door and out of the room in a daze. There was the vague impression of some gray hallways but she didn't really pay attention to anything around her, just let her feet go where they wanted. Her feet took her in the general direction out of the office and into the path of foot traffic flowing out of the building. Tabitha was at the street before she remembered that her bag of groceries was still sitting up in the bland room. She also had no ride back to her car. Tabitha stopped and stared up at the building she had just exited. A man walking by suddenly veered her way and she froze in alarm, her breath catching in her throat.

"Excuse me, can you tell me the time?" he asked, tapping his left wrist.

Tabitha looked at her left wrist. Yes, she was wearing a watch. She had cut down one of the tektites and used the pieces to make beads she had included in the jeweled watch band. She was quite delighted with the result. Tabitha glanced at the time and told him what her watch said. He thanked her and turned to the woman she hadn't noticed standing next to him. Tabitha heard him telling the woman with him that they had twenty minutes. The man's voice faded quickly as the couple continued along their path on the sidewalk.

Tabitha glanced at her watch. She seldom wore watches. They died quickly. She had tried everything, cheap watches, expensive watches, wind up watches, and battery driven watches and the life expectancy of them all was less than a year. It had seemed like a fun idea to make a watch band from the pieces of tektite and she was quite pleased with how it had turned out but it had been so much work that she wouldn't consider making another even if she had more of the tektite. Everything seemed to come back to the tektite she had found. She was still staring at her watch when Agent Bismarck came out the door, carrying her bag of groceries.

"There you are," he said. "I'll give you a ride back to your car."

Tabitha nodded. It suddenly felt good to not be alone, even if it was Agent Bismarck keeping her company. They rode in silence for a while. After several minutes had passed Tabitha began to relax. It was nothing she told herself. Tabitha had nothing to do with Daniel Thomas except to answer an ad. It was all a strange coincidence, nothing else. She would never see the man again and eventually this would all be but a memory told at parties after a few drinks. Even then the ordeal would lose its luster and would fade into a memory only brought back to the surface when she again encountered the FBI. What would prompt another FBI agent encounter? Selling red chickens?

The thought made her laugh out loud and when she tried to stop the laugh from escaping into public it turned into a choke. Tabitha had no intention of trying to explain to the upset FBI agent why she was laughing and knew that selling red chickens gaining the FBI's attention would fall flatter than a pancake missing baking soda.

"I really don't know what's going on," Tabitha said, trying to distract from her laughing choke episode.

"I know," Agent Bismarck said.

"I would think you'd have more luck bringing in Daniel Thomas for questioning," Tabitha said. Agent Bismarck stared straight ahead in silence. "Bringing in everyone who has contact with him instead just doesn't seem very logical."

Agent Bismarck chose not to respond. Tabitha wouldn't have been able to remain silent like that and it always amazed her that people could just sit there and not say anything, even when someone was trying to converse with you. They rode in silence for a few minutes. Tabitha wondered how an FBI agent who was watching a suspect could just vanish but one glance at Agent Bismarck's face warned her not to ask that question. Still, she could ask. No, she wouldn't. She stared out the window at the skyscrapers receding in the distance. It never failed to fascinate her to watch the sunlight play over the faces of the skyscrapers.

"I'm surprised that so much has happened today, all because I saw a meteor shower that left behind meteorites," Tabitha said to the window. She caught her reflection in the glass. She didn't look like a criminal yet she felt changed forever because the FBI had brought her in for questioning. Agent Pierre was very wrong. She did take it all very seriously.

"Look, I'm sorry," she said. "I know you do this every day but I've never even knowingly talked to an FBI agent. You sort of caught me off guard and I didn't know what this was about. If people explain things to me I can help but I can't always figure out what people want unless they say."

"We simply asked for your cooperation," Agent Bismarck said coolly.

"I thought I was giving it," Tabitha said.

They rode again in silence through the early afternoon traffic. The downtown skyline was now at their back and Tabitha continued to stare at it through the side mirror as Agent Bismarck zipped through the traffic on the freeway. It only took a few minutes before he took the ramp off the freeway and took the two turns to the grocery store.

When Agent Bismarck pulled up behind her car in the grocery store parking lot she turned to him. "I hope you find your missing agent. Agent Ellis, you said?" Agent Bismarck didn't say anything, just nodded his head once, curtly. He drove off as soon as she got out and shut the car door. Tabitha glanced around her warily. There was no sign of the creepy meteor guy or any sign if someone else was following her now. It was completely unnerving to think she was being watched by someone.

Tabitha hurried home and though she tried not to think about it, it was all she could think about. Twice she caught herself just before running a red light because she was so distracted, having to slam on her breaks to stop at the intersection. How could the FBI lose an agent? If the man was so dangerous as to kidnap FBI agents why was he walking the streets? The FBI said she'd had contact with this

Agent Ellis but how did they know that? Why would a serial killer place an ad for meteorites at the university?

Tabitha was home, on her front steps without even being aware of what she was doing, totally in a daze. She gave herself a mental shake. It was time to snap out of it. Next she'd wander into the river because she wasn't paying attention to what she was doing. She was usually quite good at paying attention to what she was doing.

"Excuse me, Miss Anderson?"

Tabitha turned, keys in her hand to unlock the door to her house. Her heart jumped into her throat when she saw Daniel Thomas standing below her at the bottom of her front stairs. Tabitha struggled to keep her face smooth when all she wanted to do was throw her bag of groceries in his face and run. The quiet neighborhood suddenly seemed deserted.

"Your address was in the phone book," he said. He tried to smile and failed. Then he frowned. "I really hate to bother you. It's just that the two specimens I acquired from you are exciting finds. By any chance are there more? And could you tell me where you found them?"

Tabitha chewed her lower lip as she studied him. He looked totally harmless. He gave her the creeps. He had given her the creeps even before finding out that the FBI was watching him. Still, if he was a serial killer it seemed that the FBI wouldn't let him run around loose. Yet they had managed to lose one of their own agents while watching him. Tabitha glanced around, over his head, out to the street. If they were watching him then they should be around somewhere even now. There were no white Acme vans parked on the street and no one sitting in any of the parked cars. She wondered if he knew he was being watched. Probably not. Maybe he didn't care. After all, he was doing a fine job of making people disappear even while being watched. She shifted the bag on her hip.

"That was all I had to sell," she said slowly. "I was up by Rugby. Coming back from a wedding. Sorry I can't be of more help."

He nodded, getting excited. "Rugby. Yes, yes, the shower about a week ago. Can you give me more information?" He looked up at her, noticing the grocery bag. "Oh, I'm sorry. This is a bad time. Would it be possible for you to meet me? My house later tonight? Say nine?"

Tabitha almost laughed out loud in disbelief. Go back to his house? It was insane. Then she hesitated. The tug of Midwestern hospitality was strong, the urge to help despite the knowledge that she could be walking into danger. He looked so non-threatening right now. If the FBI was watching him he wouldn't do anything. But no, he was dangerous even if he didn't look dangerous. The invitation to come back to his house was purely a need for him to get her back there for whatever dastardly plans he had. Tabitha wondered how he could dispose of bodies without the FBI being able to find any trace, which they would if he cut up people and buried them in his basement. She wondered if he chose his victims by having to pay more than five dollars for a meteorite. An idea struck her. Tabitha smiled, visibly relaxing.

"I might be able to do that," she said. "Let me check with my boyfriend."

He sort of smiled, looking off to the side distractedly. "That would be…acceptable."

"If I can't make it I will let you know. I should still have your number," Tabitha said.

"Okay," he said. He stood there, awkwardly shifting his weight from foot to foot for a moment, giving the impression he wanted to say something more but he never did. Finally he nodded again and turned and walked away.

Tabitha waited until he reached the sidewalk before turning her back to him and quickly unlocking her door. She felt her heart pounding as she hurried inside and immediately shut and locked the door. Tabitha glanced out the window, holding her breath until she saw him drive away. Her cat, Snooze, came running, complaining loudly. Tabitha scooped him up and headed back to the kitchen. She quickly fed him then put away the ice cream and the rest of the groceries. She didn't even look at what condition the ice cream was in. Then she walked through every room of the house, checking that windows were locked and the side door was locked.

Tabitha was digging through her over-sized handbag for the cards the FBI agent had given her when the phone rang. Her first thought was that it was the FBI but it wasn't, it was her brother. He wanted to hear how it had gone at the meteor guy's place, had she scored big enough to retire. She continued to dig for the business card while he chatted away. Tabitha found the card while he was talking and promised to call him back and tell him all about it. After she ended the call with her brother she called Agent Pierre's number. She got his voice mail. Tabitha left a message that Daniel Thomas had contacted her in person, at her house, and that if he would accompany her posing as her boyfriend she would go to the house that night. It gave her a strange exhilaration to do so. After she hung up she stared at the phone in her hand, wondering if she was demented. Hopefully he would call back and tell her it wasn't necessary and she could be done with the whole thing.

Tabitha set the phone down, still staring at it as she mentally sorted through the day's events. Somehow she had been caught up in this and it was in her nature to face things head on. If Daniel Thomas was a serial killer he needed to be stopped. If he wasn't a serial killer then he needed to go away and leave her alone. Tabitha didn't like it that he had followed her to her house just because she had gone to see him about some meteorites. He could have called or respected that she had two, sold him two, and now their business was concluded. What kind of man would follow her to her house looking for more rocks that he originally offered to pay her only five dollars for? A serial killer. A creepy serial killer. She had just volunteered to go back to the house of a serial killer.

Tabitha stayed by the phone for several minutes, expecting Agent Pierre to call her right back. As she waited she started to wonder what she was doing. It didn't actually make sense to expect a resolution because she was going to his house. It was just that she felt she could help the FBI by getting them into the house. Helping the FBI seemed like a good thing. When it became apparent no one was calling her right back Tabitha decided to do something to take her mind off the whole situation.

Chapter Three

While Tabitha waited for a call back from the FBI agent she
walked back to her studio. The room Tabitha had converted into a
studio was a large room at the back of the house. When the realtor
had shown Tabitha the house years earlier he had labeled the room
as a family room or den but Tabitha had instantly seen its potential
as a studio. Two walls were broken up with a bank of windows
which let in wonderful natural lighting. One wall had a French door
in the middle of three windows on each side, which led out to a
cobbled patio in the back yard. The other two walls were lined with
shelves filled with a wide assortment of books, square baskets, and
various containers. An old wood dining table cluttered with tools and
boxes and other miscellaneous items she was currently working on
sat near one wall of windows. An oversized upholstered chair sat in
one corner under a window, facing a flat-screen television on one of
the shelves.

Tabitha liked to use the television for background noise to help keep her aware of time passing. If she didn't have the television on she often became so involved with what she was working on that she wasn't aware of how late it had become. When late night shows came on, their familiar theme music would warn her that if she wasn't at a stopping point she needed to reach a stopping point or she would be hitting the snooze button multiple times in the morning.

Tabitha put her hand on her chest, feeling for the necklace under her shirt. She pulled the pendant hanging around her neck out from inside her shirt. Tabitha had ground down the tektite with the zircon inside it to a heart shaped pendant and attached it to a wire wrapped necklace she had made. The tektite with its embedded zircon was beautiful and when she held it up to the light it sparkled. The tektite had looked rather bland when she had found it, when not having a light shining into it, but cleaning and grinding had worked wonders. No one would ever guess it had originally been a lump of meteorite glass mottled with metal.

Tabitha dropped the necklace back inside her shirt and walked to her work bench. The bench ran the whole length of one windowless wall and shelves above the bench stretching to the ceiling held tubs and containers of all shapes and sizes and materials. There were plastic tins, plastic bins, round tins, square tins, and wicker baskets. Every container held a variety of materials; silver wire, gold wire, copper wire, gemstones, shards of glass, leather, yarn, stones. There were containers filled with tools, glue guns, crotchet hooks, awls, hammers, soldering irons, and the list went on.

Sitting on the bench was the largest meteorite she had found following the meteor shower. It was about five inches in diameter. She had kept that one because it had interesting iron looking streaks on one side. Plus it was big and she felt a special bond to it since it had come so close to taking out her car and possibly her with the car. Would Thomas be so desperate for his meteorites that he'd stop at nothing to get it? It would make more sense to simply pay a little more rather than kill people. Tabitha looked around the room for a hiding spot. Eventually she settled on a tin filled with river stones. She dumped them out, put in the meteorite, then covered the meteorite with the stones.

Tabitha pulled out a plastic bin and looked inside. It was filled with various sized shards of colored glass, mostly blues and purples. She pushed it back and pulled out the bin next to it. This one was filled with greens and yellows. Tabitha picked out several pieces, holding each one up to the light to study the colorization. When she was satisfied with the right pieces she plugged in her soldering iron and sat down to start cutting and wrapping each cut piece with copper foil tape. She was well underway on her project when the phone rang. Tabitha jumped in surprise then grabbed the phone, scrambling to set the hot soldering iron down without burning anything, including herself.

It was Agent Pierre returning her call. Tabitha quickly told him about Daniel's visit and her idea even though she had already explained in her message. Agent Pierre listened without comment then said, "You'll be picked up at 8:30. Watch for the car."

Tabitha stared at the phone then set it down. She had never had to deal with the FBI before and had never really thought that much of it but was deciding that it wasn't pleasant. A sigh escaped her. Of course they were upset that an agent had vanished and still didn't know her part in it so she could hardly expect them to be embracing. She turned back to her project. In less than an hour she had a simple glass box with metal feet and a hinged lid. Tabitha dug through several tins before finding what she was looking for. When she had first bought her small kiln for glass she had made several experimental errors. Tabitha pulled out the small lumps of melted glass and carefully arranged them in the glass box.

Looking around her room she laughed at how absurd she was being. Laughing helped relieve the underlying stress she was suddenly aware she had been feeling. It was probably paranoid to think that someone would search her house when she was gone. Mostly Tabitha just needed something to keep her mind busy while she waited but since this whole adventure had started with the meteors she felt better making them a little more secure. Tabitha picked up the glass box and carried it into her living room, setting it on the coffee table. Then she went looking for the rock she had brought back from New Mexico years ago and set it on the coffee table. It was the only rock she had that was vaguely familiar to her remaining meteorite. In fact, when she had found it she had thought it might be a meteorite.

The stage was set. It certainly looked like she felt the rock and globs of glass were important enough to display on her coffee table. What rocks would be so important except for newly discovered meteorites? And if someone broke into her house and stole them and discovered they weren't from outer space, well, then she'd know someone was breaking into her house for her meteorites and she'd deal with the rest then.

Promptly at half past eight Agent Bismarck pulled up to Tabitha's house. Tabitha was waiting and watching for him and immediately went to the car. When she saw that he was alone in the car she looked around but saw no sign that anyone else was joining them. Well, she had said she thought he could pose as her boyfriend so it wouldn't make sense for five men to show up with her at Daniel's door.

Tabitha glanced at his suit as she slid into the passenger seat and grimaced. Next to her well-worn jeans, Bjorn half-boots, and burgundy faded to pink hooded sweatshirt he looked exactly like an FBI agent. She had expected Agent Pierre. Tabitha had thought that he could pose as her boyfriend but looking at Agent Bismarck she realized that plan wouldn't work at all with the older agent. It wasn't because he was so much older than her thirty-two years. It was that she didn't think he could pretend to even like her. He smelled like cedar. The smell tickled her nose.

At five feet five inches Tabitha was average height. She had an athletic build with curves in the right places. She had always attracted male attention so she knew she was considered attractive though she didn't pay much attention to it. Tabitha realized she took it for granted. Except at times like this. She could have been a ninety year old grandma for all Agent Bismarck seemed to care. Most men said they liked her eyes, a rare green. Her hair was dark brown, almost black, with copper streaks that showed up in the sunlight. Her nose was straight and her eyebrows arched without aid. She had always been satisfied with her looks and didn't give it much thought, except today. It did feel odd to be in the company of a man who didn't seem to care at all though. Tabitha had never realized before how much she took for granted that men appreciated her company.

Agent Bismarck pulled up to Daniel's house and parked in the street. They walked up to the front door in silence. Daniel had a forced, tight smile in place when he opened the door, which quickly flickered then died when he saw her companion. Tabitha decided introductions were not necessary. There was no way she was going to blatantly lie and try to pass off Agent Bismarck as a boyfriend or uncle or other concerned male relative. If he wanted to introduce himself that was his choice. Agent Bismarck chose not to utter a word. She did think she heard him grunt some type of greeting.

"Yes, well, come in," Daniel said. Tabitha slipped past Agent Bismarck and entered the house. Daniel led them to the living room and they settled on couches and chairs. It was a very awkward moment for Tabitha. Daniel didn't look comfortable either. He kept licking his lips and giving Agent Bismarck futile, sideways glances. After several minutes Daniel said, "Yes, well, I have maps, as you can see." He gestured to a pile of paper maps on the coffee table.

Tabitha had been looking around the room since entering the formal living room. It was a large house in an affluent neighborhood and the living room was quite dramatic. She found it hard to believe he could have decorated it so well on his own and concluded that he must have hired someone or had a girlfriend with wonderful decorating tastes. He just didn't strike her as the type of man to so tastefully decorate a home. Daniel Thomas was the empty pizza box, cinder block entertainment center, and books and electronics strung out everywhere type of decorator. For him it would be function and he wouldn't have thought to find throw pillows the same teal color as the petals in the flowers in the drapes. All the wood furniture was coordinated, though not a set out of a store.

Tabitha tilted her head thoughtfully. Or maybe he had a mother who took a hand in his life still. She glanced at him. Yes, she could see him having a mother who would decorate this house so nicely. His mother would be a domineering type, that controlling overprotective type of mother who couldn't bear to have her son living like a bachelor. But her first thought remained stronger, that he hired someone to do it.

"It is a lovely home," she said. "Did you decorate it yourself?"

"What?" Daniel glanced around the room, clearly not certain why she found it interesting. "Oh, it came this way. I liked it so I left it," Daniel said.

Tabitha's eyebrows rose. It came that way? What an odd way to say it. He didn't even seem to project any pride in his beautiful home. She opened her mouth to ask him what he meant then snapped her mouth shut. She would be quiet. She would not question everything. That was her new rule. Sometimes she had to make herself rules or she would ramble away without direction. Still, it was an odd way to say it. He didn't say he offered to buy it furnished. That was so unusual anyway. He said it came that way. Tabitha scanned the room carefully, noting the quality of the furniture and approving the selections. She couldn't imagine whoever selected the furnishings willing to just walk away and leave it behind, unless he had offered a lot of money to acquire the house furnished.

Tabitha picked up a state map and unfolded it. Daniel grabbed a pen and paper, making notes and studying the map as she explained where she had been when the meteor shower found her. Tabitha had left her wire markers and noted the mile marker on the county road but she didn't tell him that, instead she gave him a more general description of where she had been, an area roughly around five miles east of her mile marker. Maybe it was a bit petty but she had no desire to help him and once said she couldn't take it back. Daniel stared at the map and notes he had made, probably seeing how daunting it would be to search such a large area. A flat expanse of nothingness covered with prairie grasses, that's what he would be searching through for some bits of rock.

"It's quite an open area," he said, sighing.

"Yes, that's why I waited for them to cool and collected them while I was there," she said brightly. Tabitha glanced around the room again. If she was right the furniture was very expensive, very old, and very high quality old. "How odd to get this place furnished. You just don't see that very often. Especially such nice furniture."

Agent Bismarck now looked around the room, frowning thoughtfully. Daniel hunched his shoulders, refusing to look at Agent Bismarck. Daniel had not looked directly at the agent even once since they'd come through the door. The agent's presence seemed to really put Daniel at odds with something. Tabitha suddenly felt very grateful to have the scowling agent at her side.

Daniel nodded. "Yes, well, it seems silly perhaps to drag you all the way back for a few directions on the map, doesn't it?" he said, setting down the notepad and pen. He glanced around the room, looking at each piece of furniture as if just noticing it now. He nodded thoughtfully, as if coming to a decision. His eyes warmed up. "But my main reason is far more exciting, you see. I am a man of research. Science is a broad field of study with so many nuances most never dream of."

Tabitha refolded the map but it didn't go back the way it had been so she unfolded it and tried again, then made new folds and set it down. The map now looked all poofy so she used the side of her hand to pound it flat. She tried not to think about the fact that it was no longer the original folding order, which meant the cover section was now the fourth page. Tabitha reached for the map to straighten it then snatched her hand back. It didn't matter. It just didn't matter that it had been folded differently. Daniel had gotten quiet. Tabitha looked up guiltily, realizing that she had tuned out what he was saying. The last thing she remembered was something about science.

Agent Bismarck sat on the couch alone, across from Daniel who sat on the matching loveseat, while Tabitha sat on an upholstered chair between the two men. Agent Bismarck looked like he was about to launch himself at Daniel. Daniel seemed oblivious, his attention on Tabitha. Tabitha sighed. If she were sitting next to Agent Bismarck she would kick him in the shin.

"This is why you search for meteorites?" she asked, forcing a smile. "Your science?"

"Yes!" Daniel said. He was bubbling with excitement. He glanced at Agent Bismarck then quickly looked right back to Tabitha. "I hadn't expected you to bring a, uh, a friend. I am a specialist. I am a specialist and I have few I can share my discoveries with. But you, you found the rocks so I am certain you can appreciate the rarity and specialness of the find."

Tabitha glanced at Agent Bismarck, who was still silently glaring at Daniel. At Daniel's last words Agent Bismarck grunted. It had seemed a good idea at the time to bring an FBI agent when meeting a potential serial killer but now she had some regrets. Daniel seemed harmless while the agent, well, he was not behaving as she expected. She wasn't quite certain what she had expected but maybe that he would excuse himself and investigate the house while she kept Daniel distracted. At least maybe he should be asking some cutting edge questions.

"I agree meteorites are interesting. I certainly found it exciting to find them. But iron is iron and rock is rock," Tabitha said with a shrug. Daniel grinned a superior grin. Tabitha felt any budding sympathy fade. He was irritating. He was creepy.

"Come, come," Daniel said, standing. "I want to show you something. It's something you have to see to appreciate and understand."

Tabitha hesitated, debating on leaving her purse in her chair, then decided to keep it with her. It felt like she didn't trust him, not wanting to leave her purse sitting alone, unguarded, but she didn't trust him. She used reasoning to explain why she was hugging her purse close to hand, that she didn't know if he'd show them out through a side door instead of the front door and if he did that it would mean she would have to come back for her purse, so it made more sense just to bring it with her at the outset.

Tabitha glanced at Agent Bismarck, making sure he was joining the tour. She had no intention of following Daniel Thomas by herself. The agent had stood and was politely waiting to follow her. Daniel led them down a hall toward the back of the house. The hall opened up to a large kitchen to the right and to the left a sitting area complete with a large television on the wall and a massive stone fireplace. The hall ended at a large sunroom between the kitchen and sitting area. There was nothing in the sunroom except bare wood floors that gleamed with polish and three walls of windows that showed a view of a wooded lawn. There was nothing visible but grass and trees as far back as was lit by floodlights along the house's foundation.

This was quite a nice house Tabitha thought again. She wondered what Daniel did for a living to afford such a nice house in this neighborhood, a nice house that came furnished with tasteful furnishings that looked like the pieces had taken a lifetime to collect and put together or paid a lot of money to someone to do the work of collecting them.

"There!" Daniel said, waving his arm in the direction of the sunroom.

Tabitha glanced at Agent Bismarck. Maybe she was missing something. He looked at her and shrugged. It was an empty sunroom. Daniel stepped closer to the sunroom and the other two automatically stepped along, though there was nothing to see any closer. Daniel was grinning from ear to ear. It looked like just a sunroom with its windows and view. The hardwood floor was coated with enough polyurethane to see the reflection of the windows but it was still an empty room. Tabitha could picture a cozy settee, offset a bit to enjoy the view but still be a part of the kitchen and sitting area. It would have to be purple to give a punch of color to the neutral all around them. Also a lot of plants and some tables for holding books would look nice. It did look odd that the room was completely empty. The rest of the house was so completely furnished that to her the only thing special about the sunroom was that it was completely bare of any furnishings, not even a rug.

Maybe it was the long day. Maybe it was the strain of dealing with creepy man and rigidly angry man, both of whom she had spent too much time with in one day but she felt a wave wash over her of just wanting to go home. It was all Tabitha could do to resist the urge to tell both of them that she had had enough, that she just wanted to go home. Instead she forced an interested smile, ignoring the feeling of homesickness sweeping over her.

Daniel laughed. "That's the beauty of it. I own twelve houses and they all contain the same thing." He walked into the sunroom, arms spread wide and a grin on his face, turning completely before facing them again. "I learned of their locations from ancient maps. Imagine my surprise when the first one worked. I've hunted high and low for more locations since. And of course the keys. You would be surprised to learn where more are located. Some buildings have held their secrets for centuries."

"I don't understand," Tabitha said, frowning.

"I know," Daniel said, chest puffing out slightly as his confidence and self-appreciation grew with his guests' obvious confusion. He felt that whatever he was showing them was beyond their grasp while he clearly knew exactly what he was talking about and it gave him an intoxicating dose of superiority.

He walked back toward them, stopping at a console table at the back of the sofa in the sitting room. He gestured for them to join him. A long glass display case sat on the table, holding various rocks. Little paper tags labeled each rock. Tabitha was surprised to see that each tag had hand written on them the name of a city followed by a slash and a comment, when expecting to see labels of rock types or something to do with geography. She only had time to read a few. The first one had written Denver/dangerous barbarian world in a childish scrawl. The second had Omaha/paradise and rich in gold written in more of a chicken scrawl.

"I think it's the structure of the space debris. Diamond versus coal. You understand? Finding the keys has so often led me to space debris."

Tabitha looked back at the case. There were three labels for Minneapolis. The first one said *Minneapolis/angry Vikings potential though*. The second one said *Minneapolis/unknown*. The third one just said *Minneapolis/*. Tabitha decided again that she was glad that

Agent Bismarck was there. Daniel had to be insane. The only reason she was staring at an empty sunroom next to a glaring FBI agent while a maniac spouted gibberish was because she had found meteorites and let her brother talk her into contacting this man in the hopes of finding out that the meteorites were worth a lot of money. The second Minneapolis label was in front of one of the rocks she had found and sold to him earlier that day. The other rock he had bought from her was nowhere in sight. Tabitha should have donated the rocks to an elementary school or high school.

"You don't see," Daniel said with a grin. "How could you?" He picked up a Minneapolis rock from the case with his right hand, then waved his left hand over the one labeled for Denver. "Normally I keep the correct rock in the correct city but there are a few I take with me. Too dangerous to not keep my eye on them." He was so excited he was bouncing on the balls of his feet. "Watch. Come closer. Yes, that's it."

Tabitha was genuinely confused. She glanced at Agent Bismarck. He made a face, a slight touch of being human after all. They followed Daniel once again into the empty sunroom. Tabitha felt the urge to be home so strongly that she almost turned and walked away but she resisted. It wouldn't be much longer and they could leave.

Daniel walked further into the sunroom carrying the rock. A sliver of light glimmered in the air then shot up and down to shine from floor to ceiling to the left of the center of the room. "It's a key.

The rock you brought opens the center zipper. But this is the one I want to show you. You like adventures, don't you, Miss Anderson? You strike me as someone who likes adventures. I made up my mind this afternoon when you were here that I had to show you the zipper. This one in particular. You and your fraternity smugness."

"Zipper?" Agent Bismarck said, eyes studying the room for hidden spotlights.

Tabitha's eyes widened. Fraternity smugness? First, she was no longer even in her twenties, which eliminated her from some college comment. Plus, he seemed to mean it as a slam against her. It made no sense. She was not smug.

"Zipper," Daniel said. "There are three in this room. The first opens to a rather harsh land. The second I just opened for the first time today, thanks to you, Miss Anderson. I am hoping that Agent Ellis will manage to give me a report." He sighed. "Sometimes people don't make it back out to report to me."

Bismarck's hand went to the bulge under his jacket. "You are telling me that Agent Ellis went through a beam of light to another world?"

"Zipper," Daniel said in a corrective tone. If he noticed Agent Bismarck reaching for his gun he chose to ignore it. "Yes, come see." He hesitated, face growing thoughtful. "It's always so hard when I make a new find. It's so exciting and no one to share it with. I always have to tell someone. All I had at first was the map and the one house. Now I have twelve houses and where the zippers are in public buildings I had to get quite creative. I wish I had the time to tell you how clever I've had to be. It hasn't been easy, that's for sure. Can't have anyone blathering about it though, can I? The first time I sent someone through it was more of a reflex but now I let them help me explore. Only to a second one though. I learned that the hard way. Maybe after a visit here you will be more willing to tell me what you're holding back. If I bring you back. I know you're holding back on me. I just don't know if you're one of them."

Bewildered by what he was saying, Tabitha edged closer to Agent Bismarck, who had turned to face Daniel. She opened her mouth, intending to suggest privately to the agent that she was ready to leave now and was totally caught off guard when Daniel shoved her in the back, directly at Agent Bismarck. Instinctively she reached out for the agent to stop herself from falling. Agent Bismarck reached up to steady her, taking two steps back and they stumbled through a beam of light.

Tabitha expected to fall against the windows and prepared to get out of the way to allow Bismarck to do whatever it was he needed to do. What Tabitha didn't expect was for the light to swallow them and send a chill down her spine. The heart pendant under her shirt suddenly felt hot against her skin. The world transformed around them. Nor did she expect to be staring at a group of men wearing leather and furs in a smoky tent where a wall of windows in an empty sunroom should have been.

The noise of laughter, shouting, and general conversation in a foreign language cut off abruptly. All heads turned to stare at Tabitha and Agent Bismarck. It didn't take long for the smoke hanging in the air to make Tabitha's eyes burn and water. And the smells! Body odor, feces, rotting flesh, wet leather, wet dog, wet horse, and wet soil lay a foundation of stench for an even more pungent odor that Tabitha couldn't place.

Agent Bismarck swore. Just one word muttered under his breath but Tabitha heard him and she had almost said the same word in unison. A large shaggy, gray dog that looked like a wolfhound slowly stood just a few feet away, hackles rising and a low growl building in volume rumbled deep in his throat as it stared at them. If it was a wolfhound it was a super-sized wolfhound. The growl was quite an intimidating sound.

Tabitha clutched Agent Bismarck's arm and stepped back away from the group of long-haired, facial-hair covered Vikings. They looked like Vikings to her. She almost sighed. This would forever stifle her romantic fantasy of the strong, noble Viking staking claim to her without a care that she was a princess in a faraway land or a favored daughter of a powerful nobleman who fought to save her until accepting that her heart's desire was to sail away with her bronzed Viking giant and create a horde of Viking babies. Not a man in that tent fit her profile of a giant, muscle-bound, clean-shaven Viking who smelled of fresh meadow grasses and leather. All she could see were men covered in hair and coated in dirt.

Agent Bismarck stepped back step by step with her, eyeing them all warily, but especially the dog. The dog took a step forward and its growl increased in volume. Two more waist-high dogs stepped out of the crowd, gazes locked on the two intruders. Still the hairy men stared in shocked silence. Suddenly a shiver ran down Tabitha's neck and the beam of light in a sunroom replaced the tent. The smell was still trapped in her nose.

"What?!" Daniel yelled in surprise.

Tabitha turned. They had come out backwards so their backs were to the kitchen. Daniel was behind them but more to the right. Out of the corner of her eye she just had enough time to see that he held her meteorite and a second beam of light shone in the center of the room, Daniel's newly unlocked zipper. Tabitha was starting to consider the possibility that these beams were more than just some light show.

Once again Daniel used her as a buffer. He grabbed her shoulder and spun her around, her purse swinging out so she automatically clutched the strap to her shoulder to keep it from being flung aside. She was still clutching Agent Bismarck's arm and instinctively held onto him to keep her feet. Then Daniel shoved her at Agent Bismarck with even more force than he had used before. Tabitha looked up to see his face, hair forming a wispy halo and his eyes wide in desperation. This time they slipped through the center beam of light. She heard Agent Bismarck curse and Daniel was yelling something about crossover impossible. It all happened so fast.

This time they both stumbled and fell forward once they stepped through the zipper. The same chill passed down her spine. The bright sunlight was blinding. Tabitha took several long strides down and down, trying to keep from falling on her face. They were on a hill, just steep enough to keep her off balance when she was already off balance. With a sigh she succumbed and plopped on her rear end to keep from rolling all the way down the hill. Agent Bismarck fell to his knees but quickly scrambled to his feet and looked around warily. This time instead of a smoky, dark tent they were surrounded by knee-high grasses laced with wildflowers on a warm spring day.

Chapter Four

They were on a hill. Below was a cobbled road leading to a small cluster of stone-walled buildings with thatched roofs to the left of their position, mostly blocked from view by a thicket of trees growing in a line up the side of the hill. The trees were tall, soaring almost as high as the tallest pines of the Northwest. Tabitha let her head fall back, wincing slightly when the back of her head hit grass and ground a bit harder than expected. A small "ow" escaped her. Staring up at the wide, blue sky Tabitha saw cotton ball clouds slowly drifting past. Breath normal, she reminded herself. Eventually her racing heart slowed to a normal pace.

Tabitha relaxed slightly. She raised her chin to look up and behind her, stretching her neck as far as she could. Agent Bismarck had recovered his senses faster than she had and he was already pacing the hill a few steps behind and above her, clearly trying to find the now vanished beam of light which Daniel called a zipper. In her view the agent was upside down as he stabbed at his cell phone buttons while he paced and searched. When the agent accepted that he had no reception he gave up on the phone but kept pacing back and forth, occasionally waving an arm, moving up the hill bit by steady bit.

It was a little difficult to see upside down but she could see that there was no longer a beam of light and they were the only ones on the hill. It seemed odd to see a grass-covered hill stretching out above them. It would probably be odder to see Daniel Thomas' kitchen behind them on the hill. There was no beam of light or any sign at all that anything but a grass-covered hill existed there. Slowly she got to her feet, watching Agent Bismarck as she brushed the grass off her clothes. The zipper was gone. Agent Bismarck searched longer than necessary to determine that there was no longer a beam of light to let them return to the sunroom.

Tabitha shivered. She resisted the urge to laugh hysterically. This was impossible. Yet here they stood, on a hill above a cobblestoned road leading to a village with straw roofs in bright sunlight when it should be night. It was so quiet. The only thing she could hear was grass rustling in a very gentle breeze and the sound of Agent Bismarck stomping and muttering. Tabitha had grown up in the country but this was quiet beyond anything she had experienced before. Even in rural Minnesota there was the sound of distant traffic.

Logic prevailed. Though there didn't seem to be any way to open the zipper, once they stepped off this hill it would be nearly impossible to find the location again. The urge to orient herself helped calm her as well. If Tabitha had something to do she wouldn't panic at the idea of being shoved against her will through a beam of light into who knew what. Tabitha did not have wire and wire cutters with her this time. She looked for the sun. It was high and to her left. She sighed when she realized that she didn't know if it was morning or afternoon. It had been night back in the real world.

Well, she would set her own rules. North was behind her, so the village was to the east. Tabitha stepped purposely down the hill, counting each stride, a little slow because she was wearing heeled boots. Her legs also felt slightly rubbery for some reason. At the road she stared to her left and then to her right. There was nothing unique to mark where she stood. She needed tools. She found a rock and tried scratching a cobblestone but it just rubbed off the dirt. Her hands trembled so much that she could barely hold the rock and she tossed it aside. The feel of dirt on her hands bothered her so she rubbed her palms on her legs repeatedly. Tabitha looked up to the top of the hill. A few trees dotted the hillside but they all looked too similar to be able to use one as a marker.

Tabitha tapped her chin with her finger as she considered options. It was a road so people could come along and unknowingly disrupt any sign she could make. She felt along the edge of the road until she found a cobblestone loose enough to pry up, then pressed three stones in a triangle into the ground and dropped the cobblestone back. Tabitha put three more rocks in the shape of a triangle in the dirt a few inches from the loose cobblestone, pressing them down into the dirt. Agent Bismarck was still on the side of the hill staring at the grass where a glowing beam of light had been.

An idea struck her. She always carried a small point and shoot camera in her purse. Tabitha dug around until she found the small case. She took several shots, first up the hill then to the village, moving her body to get a panoramic view with multiple shots. She even took pictures of the ground where she stood.

Tabitha set off towards the village, striding as purposely as she could on legs that still wanted to collapse, counting each stride. Thus she marked off the distance in strides to the nearest tree at the edge of the village. Now all she had to do was remember how many strides from tree to loose cobblestone and from loose cobblestone to the right spot on the side of the hill. Of course, none of it did any good unless they had a meteorite to open the zipper again but that was something to deal with later.

Tabitha glanced up at Agent Bismarck. He was still standing up on the hill where they had passed through the zipper, though his attention had turned to studying the buildings with a frown. The grass was trampled flat all around him. When he saw Tabitha he looked startled. She wondered if he'd forgotten that she was there, sharing his unexpected adventure. He held his right palm up and used his other hand to gesture to be quiet. Tabitha had just been going to yell up to him to ask what he thought they should do next but snapped her mouth shut.

Suddenly she heard the sound of soled shoes on cobblestone. A moment later a man appeared, walking out of the village. When he saw Tabitha he froze. Unless people in this land of cobblestone rural roads and stone huts wore FBI suits he had to be the missing Agent Ellis. Tabitha relaxed. At least one problem had been solved. They had found the missing agent who had dragged her into this mess. Tabitha frowned, remembering that Daniel Thomas had mentioned something about the missing agent. Agent Bismarck now knew that she had nothing to do with his disappearance. There was always something positive in everything, so she believed.

Tabitha had expected the missing agent to be an older man with short cropped hair and dour face. This man was only a few years older than her. He was tall and broad shouldered with a strong jaw and high cheekbones. Even from this distance he took her breath away. There was a sophisticated roughness to him that heightened her awareness of him as a man. He would attract women's gazes in any room he entered. Not only did he have a physique that made her knees weak, he had a face that drew the eyes.

The most gorgeous man she had ever met was the missing FBI agent who was responsible for dragging her into this mess. Wait. Had it really only been earlier that day? It seemed so long ago. What surprised her even more was when he suddenly broke into a run, directly at her, even as he drew his gun out of the holster so that when he reached her he was holding his gun pressed against her jaw.

"You! Are you behind this? Get me back. Now!"

Tabitha licked her lips. "Uh, you must be Agent Ellis. Let me call for someone." She took a deep breath and yelled, "Agent Bismarck!"

He winced at the volume of her voice then pressed the gun more firmly in place. "Nice try. I saw you hanging out at the university talking about Thomas. Now you're here. What game is this?"

Tabitha felt her knees knocking together, her legs shook so much. "I think I'm going to faint." She meant it. There was a roar in her ears and things seemed to grow dark. Her upper lip tingled. Then she noticed the look in his eyes. He had green eyes. That surprised her. There was a wild look in those green eyes, of fear, controlled fear, but definitely fear. It made him seem more human than the hard-core tough guy holding a gun to her head. It would take a lot to scare a tough, confident man like him. Tabitha understood that fear. She had just stepped through a beam of light into a different world. Tabitha fought back the urge to faint. She took a slow, deep breath. The ringing in her ears faded.

"I'm Tabitha Anderson. We haven't formally met. Agent Bismarck and I sort of got pushed into a beam of light. We managed to get back out but ended up here through another beam of light. Since you are still here I am guessing it won't be as easy to get out of this one."

He glared at her. Tabitha found it very disconcerting to stare into the face of the most gorgeous man she had have met while he glared at her and held a gun to her head. Compound that with the fact that she had just traveled to another world through a beam of light in someone's sunroom and it was too much. She laughed.

"Yes, I'm hysterical," she said, pushing the gun out of her face. He was so startled he let her go. Tabitha wiped her palms across her shirt, brushing away bits of grass. "We are probably on some drug trip," she said. "Yes, that is it. First the Vikings and now a hunk of FBI meat to drool over. A drug trip."

He eyed her warily. "A drug trip?"

"Do you have a better explanation for stepping through a beam of light into another world? Or maybe back in time?"

"Mind altering chemicals. Drug trip is not even a term."

Tabitha threw her hands in the air. "You understood."

"That's because I'm smart," he said, a hint of a grin tickling the corners of his mouth as he holstered his gun.

"Well, do you have a better explanation, Mr. FBI Man? Maybe something about tears in space time continuum allowing passage through different dimensions, possibly? Or maybe we're in fairyland? My literature is rusty but I think there's the stories about mushrooms growing in a circle but we were in a blasted sunroom."

He shook his head. "Fairyland is only reached in England, through rabbit burrows."

"That's Alice," she snapped. Tabitha paused. "Hey, either Agent Bismarck's totally ignoring me or he should have been here by now. Maybe only one of you can show up at the same time, like Clark Kent and Superman."

"I hate to hear which I am," he said dryly.

Agent Bismarck was standing mere feet away, back against the tree she had chosen as her marker, watching them with interest. Agent Ellis actually looked surprised to see him standing there, even though Tabitha had told him the other agent was there. The two men grinned at each other and each grabbed the other's arm as they robustly shook hands, then laughed and did the male black slap hug.

"Simon!" Agent Ellis said emotionally in greeting.

"Dane," Agent Bismarck replied in a calmer voice.

"Some rescue party," Agent Ellis said.

"Hunk of FBI meat?" Agent Bismarck said, shaking his head.

Tabitha turned red. Her face warmed as the blush spread across her cheeks. She had actually said that out loud? They both seemed to have already forgotten that she was even there. Tabitha studied Agent Ellis as the two men talked. He was quite impressive, yet likeable. Well, maybe once she got past the fact that he had held a gun to her head. She wouldn't have thought she could find an interest in an FBI agent in another dimension.

Tabitha shook her head. No. It wasn't interest. There she went getting her emotions confused again. It wasn't interest. It was an adrenaline rush at everything that led up to this moment. There was no point in confusing the increase in her heart beat and sweating palms with interest. The mixed emotions washing over her were all a result of having a gun pointed to her head after stepping through a line of light into what appeared to be another world. She had never had that happen before. She had never expected to have that happen ever. One would think that once a man put a gun to her head she would be rather irate with him but she decided to let that one go for now, allowing for unforeseen circumstances. If he ever did it again, however, that would be inexcusable.

Tabitha almost laughed out loud but settled for shaking her head in disbelief. Here she was looking at an attractive man and thinking about those long, lean legs and strong, masculine hands when she had just stepped through a beam of light into another world. It was inconceivable, yet here they were. Simon and Dane were right there, standing under a tree where most likely a garage would be in the real world. This couldn't be real.

"You checked out the area?" Agent Bismarck asked. Tabitha noted that for the first time since she had met him he almost looked happy. He definitely looked more relaxed. How he could look happy now was beyond her understanding.

"Village is deserted," Dane said.

"Thomas give you a cocky story to feed his ego?" Agent Bismarck asked, eyes scanning the area around them as they talked.

"He must do that every so often, then send the poor soul through the zipper to silence them." Dane periodically glanced at Tabitha as he talked to Agent Bismarck. "Explains why we never find evidence."

They went back and forth, comparing notes. Daniel's story was slightly different for Agent Ellis but basically the same. He had knowledge of dimensional doorways that he called zippers that unlocked with keys which amounted to meteorites of a specific chemical composition and structure. He clearly found the need to boast about his cleverness but since there wasn't anyone he could confide in he chose victims to crow his achievements to before shoving them through the zippers.

"How did you get caught in here?" Simon asked.

Dane was studying Tabitha. He looked back at Simon. "What? Oh, I was in his back yard. The missing dog routine, leash and all. He said he had found my dog. Had it in the house." Dane shrugged. "So I went in. He was clearly excited about his new zipper. Busting a seam about it."

"So you think it's real?" Tabitha asked.

They both looked at her. Agent Bismarck scuffed the ground with his mirror quality patent leather shoe that seemed to have picked up something from the Viking tent. "It's real something."

They went back to discussing the situation as if she wasn't there. Tabitha glanced at the village. That looked interesting. She decided she would explore while the men bonded. Er, shared notes. Tabitha started walking along the cobblestone road, noting how much work it would have been to lay down each cobblestone. Every city Tabitha had visited in Europe had cobblestone streets as well, in the city centres. When visiting Barcelona she almost bought a cobblestone stamped with the city seal as a souvenir but the price was almost twenty dollars, which had seemed outrageously expensive at the time. Yet later she regretted not splurging and wished she had gone ahead and bought it. What was twenty dollars in the long run?

Tabitha was curious to see how far they had gone out of town with the cobblestones. Did cobblestones indicate wealth or poverty here? These stones likely did not cost twenty dollars each. Tabitha stared out in the opposite direction of the village. The cobblestones continued until the road went out of sight into the trees and grasses. The village was first on her list, however. The cobblestones probably ended not too far out, turning into a dirt or gravel road.

"What are you doing?" Agent Ellis asked when she had gone about twenty feet in the direction of the village.

"I'm going to go look at the village," Tabitha answered as she kept walking.

"Not alone."

"You're welcome to tag along," she said. Tabitha resisted the urge to point out that he had been wandering in there alone. She strongly resisted the urge to say, "You're not the boss of me."

Both men fell into step behind her. Tabitha sort of listened to them talk as she walked. Agent Ellis had not seen anyone about, yet the village looked recently lived in. It had been quickly deserted or everyone had evacuated but expected to return because personal items were still in homes. Their discussion of possible hostiles made her snort but they ignored her if they heard her. Hostiles? Possible hostiles. That was a term Tabitha didn't want in her everyday vocabulary.

It felt real. A sense of panic threatened her. The sun felt warm on her back. Tabitha could smell the earthy musk of dirt. She felt the cobblestones under her feet. A breeze brushed her cheek, lifting her hair around her face. If it was real that meant that they had stepped through into another world. She could accept it or keep denying it. Either way she felt it was insanity. It was real. It just couldn't be real.

'So you two have met before?" Simon asked.

"Not at the university like you said," Tabitha said. She scowled at Agent Ellis. "He tried picking me up at an art store. Fed my ego with talking about my television show, how much he liked it. Now I realize it was a ploy to get information from me."

Tabitha had stopped to pick up sterling wire before meeting her brother at the university and getting the information on the meteor guy. She had been sidetracked by a display of charcoal pencils. An amazingly handsome man was walking by, studying the various papers on display as he walked. He stopped and looked at Tabitha, frowning. "Sorry, I think I know you."

Tabitha shook her head. "Sorry. No. I'd remember." This man was not someone she would forget.

He snapped his fingers. "Got it. You hosted a show. What was the name of it? I used to watch you all the time."

Tabitha felt the familiar flush warm her cheeks. He had said he watched her, not that he watched the show. For some reason amazingly handsome men who interested her turned her knees to jelly and her face into a beet and her tongue into bean sprouts. If she wasn't interested in him she would have been fine. It was the interested part that turned her into a vegetable display.

"You're even more amazing in person," he said.

For a moment she thought he was sincere. She drew on reserves and found her voice. "Uh, thanks."

"It's a shame it was cancelled," he said.

"Uh, thanks," she said.

"They must have written script for you without a live audience," he said with a grin. He held out his hand. "I'm Dane. It's nice to meet you in the flesh."

Tabitha pictured him in his flesh and her face heated to a burn. She opened her mouth to respond when the motherly saleswoman interrupted, stepping up to Tabitha as a recognized steady customer. She grabbed Tabitha's elbow and steered her toward the pressed water paint papers. "A man like that is just trouble," the woman said in a low, concerned voice. "I saw him watching you before he came in." Tabitha was used to motherly women trying to watch over her also.

Tabitha had glanced over her shoulder, peeking between the store aisles. He was already gone. How much trouble could one gorgeous man be? Maybe she would like to give a bit of trouble a try. That's what she had thought then. Tabitha had already forgotten that she had become mute when he tried to talk to her. Now she knew. He had just been trying to get information from her because she had pulled Daniel's name and number off a sheet of paper on a bulletin board. It made her angry all over again. Maybe she wouldn't so easily forgive him for pulling a gun on her. Tabitha stopped in her tracks. No. He had been at the art store before she'd gotten the number for Daniel. It had been a confusing day, made more confusing by stepping from night to day on this side of the zipper.

The village was a cluster of small houses built of stone with wooden doors and shutters for windows. They had been built around a commons area, an open green square with a well in the center. The main door of every hut opened out into the square. The roofing was almost all dried grass or straw, what wasn't thatching looked like clay tile. Tabitha took several shots of the village. Tabitha stepped up to a random house with an open door, tapping softly on the doorframe. After a few minutes passed without anyone coming to the door, or even any sound of activity in the whole village, she stepped into the building through the open door, at first only going a few steps past the doorway, feeling like an intruder. Agent Ellis had said it was deserted but it still felt odd to just walk inside uninvited. She could see two rooms with a loft above divided into separate sleeping quarters with a folding screen. The whole house was practically visible from the door.

Tabitha ventured further inside. The beds were mattresses stuffed with wool or feathers on wood frames strung with rope to hold the mattress. The first room on the main floor had some wood benches and a large table. The second room had a water pump, a stove, a table, and a cot against the wall. It smelled earthy. She went to the next house and stepped inside, Dane and Simon trailing her.

Some houses were bigger, having three rooms on the main floor, the third room being a bedroom, but basically they were all the same. Tabitha found it depressing. Some of the buildings had dirt floors but a majority had stone floors. Overall they were fairly clean. An idea struck her and she laughed out loud. Both men stared at her as if worried she was going to break.

"I just thought of something," she said. "It's deserted and what if it's a model homestead, you know, like they build for summer for tourists to show how Quakers lived or pilgrims lived, or something. Maybe we got bumped on the head and Thomas dropped us off in Maine and we just think we're in another dimensional world."

"This isn't Maine," Agent Bismarck said.

Tabitha scowled at him. "You know what I meant." Another idea hit her. "Are you guys like a special department in the FBI who hunts down x-files stuff? Is that why you're so ready to believe this?"

Simon shook his head. "Believe this? It is what it is."

"It's not a matter of believing or not believing," Agent Ellis said. "Is there anything that happened that leads you to believe that

Thomas has the technology or capability to create a deception of stepping from a room in his house to this?"

Slowly Tabitha nodded. "You're right. That is even more science fiction. This is simple fantasy."

Agent Ellis grimaced. "It isn't the right time for sarcasm."

Tabitha looked up at him in surprise. "Oh, I was serious. Think of all the folklore and legends and stories that have survived for centuries. Why do you think people believe for so long? I've always wondered if there's a grain of truth to some of the stories. I even have dreams that come true," she said. She instantly blushed. She hated admitting that to people. It had just blurted out. "I guess it could be science fiction but there doesn't seem to be science to explain this so it has to be fantasy."

"He called it a zipper. It's scientifically possible to encounter a rip in space," Agent Ellis said. "No magic. That would be fantasy. This is science."

"Opened with a meteorite?" Tabitha asked, planting her hands on her hips and glaring at him.

"Be real," Agent Ellis said with a grunt. "We live in the twenty-first century. Aren't cell phones and remote detonators magic in terms of nineteenth century? Just because we haven't yet explored the science of chemical structure opening dimensional doorways doesn't mean the possibility doesn't exist."

"I know that," Tabitha snapped back. "Which is why I'm suggesting we find a way to open it back up again."

"When did you jump from not believing to finding a way to open it?" Agent Ellis asked. Tabitha glared at him. He glared right back.

"We have to establish a plan of action," Agent Bismarck said, ending the discussion by physically stepping between them. Agent Ellis nodded and turned his attention back to Agent Bismarck. The two men talked as they continued to wander through the village, letting her lead the way. They continued to talk about exploring the area.

"I vote for finding a way back," Tabitha said.

"How do you plan on opening *it*?" Bismarck asked.

"Another meteorite," Tabitha said, glancing back at them. Both men stared at her. She shrugged. "Okay, how about a tuning fork?" Tabitha glared at Agent Ellis. "Or you could try your magical cell phone, Agent Bismarck. It seems to have worked so far."

"Bismarck?" Agent Ellis repeated.

"Yes, Bismarck and Pierre," Tabitha said, hand on hip. "I'm surprised you aren't Agent St. Paul." Agent Ellis grinned.

Agent Bismarck cleared his throat. "Actually, I would like to tell you that despite your incessant rambling, I am surprised at how often you toss out a jewel of useful information."

Tabitha stared at him. "Thank you, I think." She wasn't sure what jewel of useful information he was referring to. Tabitha was convinced everything she had said was valid. Well, currently. Tabitha couldn't vouch for everything said before coming through the zipper but she was pretty sure anything she said since coming through the zipper was valid.

Agent Ellis shook his head. "Another meteorite? That could take years. Or forever."

"We just go up to Rugby," she said. Then she thought about it and realized that not only were her wire markers not going to be there but there possibly would be no mile markers either. Still, it was a start. If this world was the same. Was it the same world? She didn't know.

Agent Bismarck's look of interest faded to a look of disappointment. "Rugby? What are the odds the same meteor shower occurred in this dimension?"

"You're right," Tabitha said, chewing her lower lip as she pondered. "But it isn't the meteor shower I have doubts about. It's finding the location of the meteor shower."

"We need a plan of action before we do anything," Agent Bismarck repeated. "We don't know where we are, who lives here, what lives here, our options."

Agent Ellis nodded. "A base camp. We need a base camp."

Tabitha stumbled and stopped walking. Something Agent Bismarck had said tickled her mind. Jewels. She glanced at her watch. When they had gone through the first zipper they had backed right out. Thomas had been so startled. He didn't seem to think it possible. If Daniel Thomas sent people through those zippers all the time and no one else had ever made it back out before then the zipper didn't stay open long enough for people to turn around and go right back out. Tabitha grinned. She might not have a meteor but she probably already had something that would open the zipper.

"Come on," she said, running without waiting for them to respond.

Tabitha slowed at the edge of the village. Movement in the trees caught her eye. For a minute she thought she had seen someone. Tabitha stopped and stared but didn't see anything.

"Did you see something?" Agent Ellis asked.

"What are you doing?" Agent Bismarck asked at the same time.

"I think I have a key," she said. "And I thought I saw someone in the trees just now."

Both men dropped to a crouch, pulling her down with them. "You saw someone in the trees? Where?" Agent Ellis asked.

Tabitha pointed in the direction she had seen movement. "Don't you think it would look a bit odd, ducking down like this?" Tabitha tried to stand and Agent Ellis pulled her back down. "What if it's just someone who lives here? This is ridiculous."

"I told you, the village is deserted," Agent Ellis said.

"Did you search that area?" Simon asked, jerking his head in the direction Tabitha had seen movement.

Dane shook his head. "Just a cursory look. I didn't want to go too far from the, uh, zipper."

They gave Tabitha strict orders to stay where she was and slipped into the trees, leaving her crouched next to a tree on the edge of the village. Tabitha put her hand on the tree trunk, brushing her palm against the rough bark. It felt real. She looked up at the leaves swaying gently over her head. Clouds scuttled across the very blue sky, light bits of cotton too high to block the sunlight. Tabitha jumped in startled surprise when Bismarck and Ellis silently appeared a few feet away. They looked very somber.

"What did you find?" Tabitha asked.

Ellis hesitated before answering. "A scarecrow."

Tabitha frowned. "A scarecrow? In trees?"

"It isn't safe to stay in the vicinity, yet we need more time before moving forward. Any suggestions would be welcome," Bismarck said to Ellis.

"Didn't you hear me? I said I think I have a key to open the zipper. We can go back."

Agent Bismarck turned to Tabitha. "You think you have something? Did you suddenly remember you're carrying a meteorite in that giant purse? I think we need to form a parameter and wait for help to arrive."

It couldn't have been just a scarecrow. These men now looked edgy, their eyes constantly moving, on the alert for anything. A scarecrow was for grain fields and gardens. They had seen something bad enough to make them want to desert the village without trying the zipper again. Even if her idea didn't work out they were better off staying with the village for now. Someone had to notice that she and Agent Bismarck had disappeared after going into Thomas' house. Of course, there would be no sign of them.

"Any chance you were wearing a wire?" Tabitha asked. Agent Bismarck looked startled, then shook his head. "So how do you expect anyone to find us?" she asked.

"You're right. No one is ever going to think to carry a piece of rock from a case to open a beam of light. But they know we went there. They'll get the info out of Thomas but it might take some time and we need to establish a secure base." Both men were continuously scanning the area around them. "Okay, tell us what you got," Agent Bismarck said.

"Well, I was thinking that both of us backed into that first zipper. But, the second time we fell quite a distance from the zipper and when I looked back and it wasn't there and you were trying to find it again I didn't try. Maybe something I have opened the first one. Remember how shocked Daniel was?"

"Maybe. He was also standing there with that rock in his hand. He said something about crossover," Agent Bismarck said.

"I must have something that opened it," Tabitha said, taking a step toward the hill.

"Again, did you suddenly remember a spare meteorite? Whatever you have, we don't know that it will open this one. It was the first beam of light that let us through and Thomas said they all open on different keys," Agent Bismarck said, taking her elbow to stop her. He held out his hand. "Give it to me and I'll try. You two stay out of sight here."

"We agreed to investigate first." Agent Ellis said.

Tabitha almost stomped her foot in frustration. "Why is this so difficult for you? We just go back up that hill, open the zipper, and go back home."

"I've been here since last night. Or rather this morning. Who knows what time of day it really is?" Dane muttered, sidetracked. He glanced at her like it was her fault that he'd lost his train of thought. "I found no way back. Don't get your hopes pinned on it. That's all. We might be stuck here quite a while," Agent Ellis said.

"So you're willing to just give up?" Tabitha asked.

"I'm trying to be realistic," Agent Ellis said. "And I'm not so sure that turning around and running out of here is the best choice right now." He shook his head. "Do you really not want to investigate? We came through a beam of light into, well, something. Don't you feel at all curious?"

"What I feel is the need to go home," Tabitha snapped. "I see you didn't stray too far from this zipper."

"It's the first rule of survival. Stay with the downed plane. Now I know no help is coming," Agent Ellis said in explanation. "Trust me, more than once I was ready to leave the area. I'd have stayed another day then headed out."

"Well, that's just stupid," Tabitha sputtered for lack of anything else to say. Agent Ellis rolled his eyes at her.

Agent Bismarck shook his head yet stared up the hill in the direction of the zipper thoughtfully. "It would be good to know if we have a ticket out of here if things get rough."

"I think we should all go up there. We go over that hill and strike out cross country. When I first came through I went to the top of the hill. It was dark then and I could see a glow. It looks like there is a sizeable town or city in the distance. The land is mostly like this, a few hills, copses of trees, and grass. We'll have cover and it shouldn't be too rough to travel over. I think that's where we should head."

Tabitha couldn't believe they were discussing an extended stay. She wanted to go back, now. Tabitha needed time to adjust to the idea. Maybe if someone had told her there was a zipper she could step through that would take her to another dimension or world and she had had a few days to absorb the idea and had had time to prepare adequately for any contingency, then she would have been all over this adventure of exploring another dimension. This business of abruptly getting shoved into another world without any warning, no time to absorb the possible reality and ramifications, no time to properly prepare and then go about exploring like it was a scenic trail off a scenic point along a major highway was too much to ask of her.

Agent Bismarck nodded. "We'll blend in better in a large town. We should have thought to look for clothes in the village. We'll stick out like this. Okay, first order of business, retrieve some local costume."

"I could—" Tabitha began to say.

"No," they said in unison.

A whoosh sounded by her ear and Tabitha felt something tug her hair a second before that something hit the tree with a loud thunk. An arrow quivered in the tree trunk, a few strands of her hair fluttering from the fletching. Agent Ellis immediately grabbed her arm, pulled her down, and dragged her around the tree all at the same time. Tabitha stumbled after him, clutching at her purse with her free hand to keep it from banging wildly or slipping off her shoulder. Agent Bismarck crouched between them and the road until they were covered by the tree then backed quickly after them, still crouched down, searching for the shooter. Tabitha reached up and touched her hair with a trembling hand. That arrow was very real. Someone had actually just shot an arrow at her head and it had missed by a mere inch.

Chapter Five

Tabitha slid farther back, almost hugging the tree. The bark scratched her palms and wrists but she barely noticed. Tabitha felt a warning itch in her back and turned her head. Five men approached from the north across the open meadow and were quickly a short distance away with bows and arrows at the ready. Maybe it wasn't really north. It was *her* north and she was sticking to it. They were dressed in baggy trousers of blue and gray and brown and wore matching almost poncho style coats of shiny scarlet with yellow bands across the chest. They weren't true ponchos because though they looked like they were made from a single piece of cloth with a neck hole in the center their arms were uncovered. A few half-lowered their bows in surprise when they saw her face. The others were staring intently at Agent Ellis and kept their bows up, bowstrings growing taut as they stood and locked on their targets, the two men. Tabitha tapped Agent Ellis' arm, not taking her gaze off the archers.

"Uh, Agent Ellis. Agent Bismarck. We are not alone," Tabitha said.

The two agents looked up in surprise. A voice in the distance barked a command in a foreign language and one of the archers replied in rapid-fire gibberish. Odd, Tabitha thought, it sounded familiar, as if she should recognize what they were saying but couldn't quite catch it. Agent Ellis and Agent Bismarck both reached for their holstered guns but did not draw, instead they stood slowly, moving hands out to their sides away from their bodies, away from weapons. All the archers now lowered their bows but they kept their fingers and arrows at the ready.

The owner of the commanding voice rode into sight, followed by twenty more men on horseback. One of the riders in the rear held the reins of several saddled, rider-less horses. They rode from the west, Tabitha's west. The owner of the commanding voice was clearly an officer. The officer gestured and most of his men stopped while he continued to ride toward them, flanked by two men. The officer rode up to the tree and studied Tabitha and the two agents thoughtfully. A man dismounted and pulled the arrow out of the tree and handed it to the officer. The officer touched the silky strands of Tabitha's hair caught in the trimmed feathers.

He had a blue stripe in addition to his yellow stripes on his poncho overcoat. Even on horseback he was a tall man, lean but not skinny. Gray streaked his hair but he didn't look like he'd reached his fortieth birthday yet. Thick eyebrows framed deep brown eyes. The man's nose was large nose but it suited his face. Tabitha instantly felt that he was someone to turn to when in trouble, an obvious leader, a man who weighed the situation and judged fairly. He gave her a sense of security. Much of the tension left her. This man would help them get home. He would know what to do.

Three men walked into view, from the southwest, where the arrow had originated. They continued past the larger group of men but stopped before reaching the officer and his two men on horseback. The one in the center had his arms lashed behind his back and the two men flanking him held the ends of ropes around his neck. He was leashed. The bound man was the only one not wearing the uniform. The two uniformed men escorting the prisoner gave short brisk bows of the head before reporting to the officer. He nodded as he listened though he was staring off in another direction.

"I don't think I want to be here," Tabitha whispered. The tension was suddenly back but multiplied.

"Shhh," Agent Ellis whispered.

"I think this is bad. Very bad," she insisted. Her stomach felt twisted in knots. None of the men around the trio even glanced in her direction so if they heard her no one gave any sign of it.

The officer barked a question, raising the arrow above his head, his back to the men. The captured man raised his chin in silent response. Even at a distance Tabitha could feel the anger and hate radiating from the man. The captive stood with his legs wide, shoulders back, head back slightly, face already bruising purple along one cheek and eye. He wore loose brown trousers of what looked like either linen or wool and a fitted blue tunic of the same material. He wore his dirty blonde hair in a ponytail at the back of his neck and was clean-shaven except for a bit of facial hair on his chin.

One of the men holding the captive shouted something Tabitha didn't understand and punched the man in the jaw. The man's head jerked from the impact and there was a sharp crack but he held his footing and stared mulishly ahead. Tabitha winced. Her upper lip started to tingle and breathing was becoming difficult for some reason. The officer still sat his horse with his back to his men. The officer nodded and lowered the arrow. He stared in the direction of the village thoughtfully for several minutes, finally nodding as if coming to a decision. He turned in his saddle, leather creaking from the movement and looked the captive in the eyes, then said one word, "date". The other man holding the captive man pulled a knife from his boot and slit the man's throat. The officer spoke again, staring directly at Tabitha. She thought she understood him. It sounded like he said, "King's Justice." Tabitha fainted.

***

Dane heard the officer order the man executed with the one word, death. Tabitha fainted. He was close enough to catch her as she slumped toward the ground. Rather than a catch it was more along the order of awkwardly slowing her descent but he managed to prevent her head from slamming into the ground. Slowly he eased her to the grass. He checked her pulse and raised an eyelid to check her pupil, seeing nothing that suggested anything was wrong with her but fainting, fortunately. If there were side effects from going through the zipper he was lost in knowing what to look for. He gently tapped her cheek with his palm but she didn't respond. He looked up to find the archers poised with arrows at the ready. He felt like he was staring death in the face. This was a new twist. The officer nudged his horse even closer, staring down at Tabitha. Whatever he felt, his face was unreadable.

"It seems she has fainted," Dane said. It seemed obvious but he felt it didn't hurt to call it out.

"Indeed," the officer said. He shifted his gaze from Tabitha to Dane, eyes calculating, curious, and intense. "She do be a purple halo," the officer said. Dane had to strain to catch the man's words and wasn't sure he heard the phrase purple halo correctly. "You have no escort, no retainers, no ladies to bear this lady company. Do ye be rogue or thief?"

Only two choices and neither good, Dane realized. He glanced at Simon. They were in more than an unknown culture. It was an alien culture. They had to tread carefully. Any wrong step or word here could be dangerous.

"She is his wife," Simon said.

That wasn't quite the right answer either. The officer's head snapped up as if he'd been kicked in the chin. The man raised his hand and bent his first two fingers. The archers slowly lowered their bows. Dane glanced at Simon meaningfully. They had to be very, very careful in this situation.

"Wife? What type of man are ye to wed someone with a purple halo? What type of man to travel alone on Tolman Road with a purple halo wife?"

"We are strangers to this land," Simon said.

The officer looked at the agent as if he had just announced the sky was blue. "I am Captain Geoffrey Olin of the King's Men. Ye be in my custody until I can deliver ye to the king. We shall leave it to the king to decide your fate." He turned and barked quick orders to his men to dispose of the body in the trees behind the village and to deal with Ravin as needed. He turned back to Dane. "Ravin be the man who tried to harm the, uh, your wife. Do ye wish the right?"

Dane frowned. "Right?"

"Since I did not know your status when I ordered his death ye have the right to a death."

Dane considered carefully before saying, "You have already satisfied the right."

Captain Olin stared at him then nodded. It was the right thing to say. "Done. Indeed, your speech is foreign. Remember, in this land our customs are the only customs." He looked down at Tabitha. "My men are not allowed to touch her. Can ye carry her into the stead?" Dane nodded. "Good. We shall further discuss your illegal visit in a future time."

Dane considered how best to carry her. If he slung her over his shoulders he could carry her for miles but that wasn't as elegant as carrying her in front of him and elegant seemed a better choice at the moment. He bent and slid one arm behind her knees and one arm under her back. She was heavier than she looked but he thought he could manage to make it into the village. Captain Olin dismounted and walked beside him. Simon kept pace on Dane's other side. The horse's shod hooves clopped quite loudly on the cobblestones. Olin periodically flipped the ends of his reins over the back of his hand. The slap of leather against skin was rhythmic. In another man it could be seen as a nervous tick. Dane suspected Olin used it to help him focus on his thoughts. The officer certainly kept a masked face but he had to be uncertain about them.

"Ye even have a sense of being men of uniform," Olin said. "How came ye to be alone on Tolman Road in alien garb?"

Simon said. "We were set upon by brigands."

Captain Olin snorted. "Shall I call ye liar to ye face but yet there be a touch, nary a smidge, mind, of truth in ye words. Some man truly did do a misdeed to strand ye unprepared. Yet that do not establish the strangeness of your garb."

Dane was quite startled at how astute the captain appeared to be. He glanced at Simon. The man was a veteran agent and they had worked together for years. They had known each other even longer. The man was totally competent and professional, quick to correctly assess situations. Yet every time Simon opened his mouth he seemed to bury them deeper in trouble. Obviously he had picked up on that and was now being quiet.

"We are hardly alone," Dane said.

Olin smiled. "True men of uniform. Yet two men to guard your wife? Now ye do be on foot without possessions nor provisions. Rash that. Do ye not realize her value?" he asked.

"Value?" Simon asked, glancing at Tabitha.

Captain Olin misstepped, then strode more purposely. "When the lady does wake, if she does say one word of denial and I learn ye be indeed rogues abducting her, then ye shall join Ravin as a warning."

"Point taken," Dane said. "But I assure you we are not abducting her."

Olin nodded, slapping the reins against his hand as he walked. "As ye say," he said.

They walked in silence the rest of the way into the village. Dane didn't feel like talking as his burden became heavier. Simon firmly clamped his mouth shut. He regretted not tossing her over her shoulders instead of trying to make an impression by carrying her in his arms in front of him. Simon made a gesture that he would take a turn carrying Tabitha but Dane shook his head slightly, glancing at Olin. It wasn't worth the risk of yet again offending the captain. He gritted his teeth and shifted her dead weight slightly, trying to ease his strained muscles, but it didn't help. Dane would have chosen the first house in the village but Olin gestured to a house farther into the village. Dane gritted his teeth and kept going. Olin led the way inside and Dane followed him to a bedroom at the back of the house.

Dane gently set Tabitha on the bed, noting that Simon had carried her purse and now tossed it on the bed beside her. It was more knapsack than a bag he realized, looking at it for the first time. Maybe she actually had a meteorite in there. It certainly appeared large enough to carry many surprises. Dane brushed the hair from her face and smiled without realizing it. He had a feeling she was going to be one big surprise after another.

Dane had over reacted by pulling his gun on her. He had been so shocked to see her that he had thought she had something to do with his being stranded on the wrong side of a beam of light. Dane hadn't been thinking rationally since finding himself stranded in this deserted village and had had to deal with the concept of having stepped through a beam of light to another world. Yet when she had pushed that gun out of her face he had come back to himself. She wasn't afraid to say it, stepping through a beam of light into another dimension was a lot to absorb and though he couldn't deny the reality of it, adjusting also took its toll on the senses and the mind.

Dane straightened and turned, to find Captain Olin and Simon both staring at him. He could imagine what Simon must be thinking but had no idea what Captain Olin was thinking. Dane strode past them into the large main room. The two men followed, Simon shutting the door behind him. The main room had a large, heavy wooden table and several wood benches and stools. All pieces were worn smooth and had a patina that took generations to generate.

"Are you a history teacher, Captain?" Dane asked. Olin met his gaze. "A quick lesson in your land's customs and history would be helpful. We could start with things that can get us killed. And tell me if this purple halo business is in that category."

Captain Olin stared at him. It was a calculating stare. At last he nodded. "Ye do have a strange way about saying things but I think I understand what ye ask. I'll see what the owners left that's edible and then we shall hold a lecture. I be interested in learning your land's customs as well."

"Wife?" Dane muttered in a low voice to Simon when Captain Olin left the room.

Simon shrugged. "You'll both thank me if we're stranded here. Can you imagine trying to pass yourselves off as brother and sister permanently?" he asked in a low voice.

"Why did it have to be one or the other?" Dane asked in irritation.

"I felt a close bond was the only expedient solution, given the circumstances," Simon said in explanation.

Dane nodded. At the moment however he was thinking keeping his neck intact was more important than pretending to be brother and sister for a few days or weeks. Learning more about this purple halo business was clearly very important. Being married to a purple halo sounded like a potentially dangerous thing. Yet her being a purple halo didn't seem to be a bad thing, just being under suspicious circumstances associated to that purple halo. Captain Olin had been quite shocked to hear they were man and wife. Maybe a purple halo was a high priestess of some local religion or a type of shaman. It could be anything. Maybe Simon was right, he couldn't imagine trying to pass themselves off as brother and sister. One stolen kiss and he might find himself hanging from a gibbet or parts of him being sliced from his body, parts he preferred to keep. Still, the truth seemed a simpler thing. Dane could control any urge to take her in his arms.

They found Captain Olin in the next room kneeling on the floor in the kitchen area in front of an opened trap door. He pulled out two crocks and set them on the floor next to him before dropping the trap door. Captain Olin stood and turned his attention to the cupboards along the wall. A few more minutes of rummaging and he had collected some mugs made of pottery, some cheese, and sausages. Captain Olin tossed a few coins on the butcher block in the kitchen and used a wood cutting board as a tray to carry his finds to the large table in the main room. He went back into the kitchen.

Captain Olin returned, carrying the two crocks. He set them on the table then settled onto a bench at the table. "Water. Ale," he said, pointing to each respective crock. He poured himself a mug of ale, nodding ever so slightly when both agents poured ale as well. Olin unclipped a small bundle from his belt and set it on the table. It was a leather pouch about three inches by five inches. He opened it and slid out a rectangle of thick glass that fit snuggly inside its case.

"This be a field glass so it's not detailed of course," he said. He tilted it so the agents could see his hands through it. Though the glass was clear his fingers were blue through the glass. He handed it to Dane. "A majority are blue. *The* majority are blue. Look at your wife through that."

Dane took the glass in his hand. His fingers were blue when he looked through it but the glass was still clear. Dane stared at the piece of glass for several minutes as he considered what it could mean. Obviously he would look through this glass at Tabitha and she would be purple instead of blue. He got that from what Olin said and didn't need to actually look through it. Yet he would, to satisfy Olin. Dane walked to the bedroom and opened the door. He held up the glass and looked through it at Tabitha. She was purple. He could see it from across the room. Dane turned and looked at Simon. Simon was blue. Dane gave Simon the glass. Simon peered at Tabitha then at Dane and grunted. He looked at Captain Olin through it and handed the glass back to Dane. Dane shut the door and walked back to the table. He studied the piece of glass but could see nothing special or unique about it. Dane examined the wood frame around it. The frame was a laminate that fit snug and seamless around the glass. At last he set the glass on the table near Captain Olin.

"A purple halo be rare," Captain Olin said.

"You mentioned her value," Simon said. "Are people owned here?"

"Owned?" Captain Olin repeated slowly. "Ah, ye mean slaves? I have indeed heard of slavery. Owning a purple halo be like owning the ocean." He nodded thoughtfully. "That is why ye be confused when I mentioned her value. Her value be higher than any monetary value."

"Why are you so surprised we are on Tolman Road?" Dane asked.

"Nothing is beyond this village in that direction," Captain Olin said. "Nothing but men like Ravin. How ye survived your way through them be quite a mystery." He gestured at the piece of glass still sitting on the table. "I took that from Ravin. It be illegal to possess it unless ye have the right. They use it to identify their targets."

"He was hunting in this village?" Simon asked. "And you think we belong to a group of these hunters and we had caught ourselves a purple halo."

"They call themselves Cleaners." Captain Olin relaxed a bit more. "Truly ye be not Cleaners."

"So this village was peopled with purple halos?" Simon asked, frowning in obvious confusion.

"Nay," Olin said, shaking his head. "A purple halo is indeed rare."

A guardsman entered the house. Captain Olin excused himself and went outside with the man. Simon went to the front of the house and looked out through a gap in the shutters. He turned to Dane. "I have a bad feeling."

Dane nodded. "The arrow narrowly missing Tabitha gave me my first bad feeling."

"I think we have to take the risk and investigate but this business with Tabitha is complicating things more than I could have imagined," Simon said.

Dane nodded. "One group seems to see her as great value and the other group wants to kill her. We should stick close to the group who wants to keep her alive." He laughed and downed his mug of ale. "Although it's an easy choice since they don't seem prepared to release us anyway."

"You've had time to think of the implications of having a doorway to another dimension," Simon said. "We have to find out what is here before making any action."

"Agreed," Dane said reluctantly. "I would prefer to have taken her back first if it had been possible but if she vanishes and we return I suspect we will not survive long." He took a long drink from his mug. "We don't even know yet if we can get back. Both of you keep forgetting that. She's putting a lot of faith in having something that will open the zipper. Sounds to me like it was something Thomas did."

Simon leaned over the table, elbows on the heavy wood, gaze on Olin's back. "If they aren't aware of the zipper we can't be the ones to introduce them, even if it means not getting back. We don't know anything about this place. So they use bows and arrows. We don't know that they aren't just out on some maneuvers and have some arsenal of weapons beyond our understanding."

Dane rotated the rectangle of glass between his long, tapered fingers. This little piece of glass felt like technology beyond bows and arrows. "Agreed," he said.

"And we don't know if Thomas is sitting in his kitchen with a gun pointed at that sunroom," Simon said. "She might just have something. Thomas was damned surprised to see us come back out of that first zipper. Nasty place." He considered the inhabitants of the first zipper. He nodded. "Done. We investigate before returning."

***

Tabitha woke lying on a bed in a darkened room. She stared at the wall, disoriented at first. She was afraid and she didn't know why she was afraid. Something bad had happened. It must have been a dream. It had to have been a dream. Yet she knew it wasn't a dream. There was just enough light filtering through the crude shuttered window to see a stark room with stone walls. The mattress was stuffed with feathers and a few poked her bare skin where her shirt had ridden up while she slept. The final proof that it wasn't a dream was when she turned her head and she saw Agent Ellis sitting on a stool next to the bed watching her. Then Tabitha remembered. Her stomach twisted in a knot. They had killed that man, right in front of her, without any warning.

"You're awake," Agent Ellis said.

Tabitha lay still. "I saw them kill a man."

"Try not to think about it," Agent Ellis said gently.

"How can I not?" she asked, sitting up.

"He would have killed you. If Captain Olin's men hadn't stopped him he would have tried again."

Try not to think about it he said. It was all she could think about. Tabitha didn't think she would ever get that image out of her head. It didn't matter that he might possibly have tried to kill her. They had slit his throat without any warning. She would try not to think about it. Tabitha hadn't really had time to consider that she had been less than an inch from being skewered by an arrow. Her limbs started to tremble. She would try not to think about it.

"He tried to kill you and the captain passed judgment and carried out the sentence on the spot. Not what we are used to. We need to be very careful while here."

"You think we'll make it home?" Tabitha asked.

Dane smiled. "Of course we will. I have no doubt."

Tabitha didn't believe him. He had doubts. She didn't have any doubts though. Tabitha was convinced that she had in her possession the key to open that zipper and return home where she would convince herself that it had all been a bad dream and go back to her normal life. All she needed to do to get home was to get back to the hill and go through the zipper.

They sat in silence for several minutes. Tabitha tried really hard to not think about that man standing there in the bright sunlight, so arrogant and angry and then so abruptly spurting blood from a gaping wound across his neck and collapsing in slow motion as the life left him. His arrogance had faded with the blood leaving his body, leaving an empty, lifeless man. The bound man had not even flinched when that uniformed man moved the knife to his throat. He had to have seen it coming. Yet the prisoner remained so arrogant and angry. Tabitha would have to concentrate on something else to push that image out of her head and thoughts.

"So what language do you think they are speaking? It sounded familiar yet I couldn't quite place the accent," Tabitha said, thinking about how she felt like she could almost understand the officer when he spoke.

"It's old English and heavily accented," Agent Ellis said.

"That was English? I didn't understand anything they said." Wait, she had understood the words King's Justice. Spoken just before they had executed that man. It had been her only warning and since she hadn't known what it mean it had been no warning at all.

"Give it time. You'll get it." Dane sounded confident.

Tabitha nodded automatically but didn't feel confident that she would ever understand what they said. It shouldn't matter anyway. They were going back through that zipper as soon as possible.

Tabitha did not intend to be here long enough to give it time to understand the heavily accented English. The zipper had opened by something she had, not by Thomas accidentally opening it again. That had to be true or they were trapped here. The thought of being trapped here turned her stomach into knots.

Tabitha glanced around the room. They were in a bedroom on the main floor of one of the bigger houses. The bed was a rough-hewn frame of split logs with a mattress resting on rope strung between the bed rails with a rough wool blanket and an armoire against the opposite wall. It even had a door. They were quite alone and private. She couldn't hear anything from outside the room so she assumed that normal voice levels wouldn't carry out there either.

"What happened?" she asked.

Agent Ellis pulled his stool closer. "He supposedly killed one of the villagers. The victim was hung up on a post, like a scarecrow. These are the King's Men. It seems they have the authority to carry out their justice on the spot." He spoke matter of factly. He noticed that she was still quite upset and his voice softened. "It's definitely a different culture. This is not the United States. It took us a long time to get where we are, which can be easy to forget."

So much for not thinking about it. "You were a history major, weren't you?" she asked, guessing.

He nodded, tried to smile, failed, and shrugged. "Understanding history is understanding human nature."

"You condone this?" Tabitha asked in surprise. "You don't know he killed anyone. We don't even know he was the one who shot the arrow at me."

"What gives you the idea that I condone it? I am trying to make you feel better," Agent Ellis said. He bowed his head and ran his fingers through his hair. Dane stood abruptly and paced the room. "We are in a different land. What's done is done. Take it as a lesson that this land is very different than ours. Learn from it. Mistakes here could be costly."

Tabitha considered his words. He was right. They knew nothing about this land. She knew enough about history to know that growing up in America in the twentieth century was a sheltered life of security and rights and that it had taken serious struggling to reach that point, which she now took for granted. Tabitha nodded. "You're right. Where's Agent Bismarck?"

"Convincing them we haven't abducted you."

Tabitha laughed, causing Agent Ellis to glance at her in surprise. "Sorry," she muttered. "No, it's not hysterics. My first encounter with him was convincing him that I hadn't been involved in abducting you. Ironic. It's just ironic." Tabitha swung her legs over the bed and sat up, automatically running her fingers through her hair. "So do these zippers take us back in time? First the Vikings and now a medieval English village."

"This isn't England. I think we're still in Minnesota," Ellis said. He rubbed his chin with his thumb in thought. "You went through another zipper first? How did you get back?"

"We just backed up and ended up back in the sunroom," Tabitha said. She glared at him. Had he really not listened to what she had been saying before they had been so rudely interrupted by being attacked?

"Do you think Thomas kept the doorway open?" he asked. Tabitha shook her head. "Are you sure?" he insisted.

Tabitha shook her head again. She was certain he had been standing right there when she had discussed this with Agent Bismarck. "He was absolutely stunned to see us back there. That's why I think I might have something that will open it again." Tabitha pulled her purse onto her lap. "I found something called a tektite at the site and made beads out of it. I didn't think about it at first. Daniel said that it was the chemical composition or structure of the meteorites that opened the zippers."

"Tektite?" Agent Ellis stared at her purse in amazement. "You made beads out of tektite? Do you realize how rare tektite is?"

Tabitha held out her wrist to show him the watch band she had made and forgot to mention that it was made up of multiple tektite beads when he made his surprised exclamation. Startled, Tabitha looked up at him, words abandoning her thoughts. He knew what tektite was. Tabitha had had to look it up on line when she had found it because she had no idea what it was. Indeed, it was extremely rare.

Making beads seemed like a good use of a rare item. What else would she have done with it?

"I know it's probably the melted sand and dirt from where a meteorite hit. Pretty much just space glass, I guess. I am only hoping it works. But it has to." Tabitha thought about the pendant around her neck under her shirt but decided to keep that information to herself. It was enough that she was sharing the rest. Tabitha rummaged through her purse and pulled out a mint tin that she had decorated with polymer clay. She flipped open the lid and held out the tin to show him the contents. "Or this."

Agent Ellis brushed her fingers with his as he touched the tin without taking it from her. Tabitha felt a jolt at his touch and sucked in her breath. If he felt the same he didn't show it. Dane was very quiet as he studied the pieces of glass nestled on tissue, leaning closer to see. Tabitha could smell him. He smelled of wild grasslands and leather.

"It looks like something is in one. What's inside?" he asked at last.

"A zircon," she said. He raised his head slightly to look up at her. They were very close. She had the sudden urge to feel his lips with her finger, to follow the contour of his full lower lip. He had rough stubble forming a shadow covering his jaw and cheeks. She resisted the urge to touch his cheek to feel how rough it would be. She swallowed. "Like cubic zirconia but different."

"It's green," he said, staring into her eyes and not the zircon. "And heart-shaped." He cleared his throat and moved back, releasing his hold on the tin. "Not many heart-shaped tektites I'm thinking."

Chapter Six

"I ground it down," Tabitha said. She grimaced.

It had been the first one and she wasn't totally happy about how it had turned out, which was why it was in the tin instead of hanging on a chain back at home. The metal encasing the crystal was amazingly hard to work with. Tabitha had also forgotten that it was in the Altoids tin and she hadn't meant to tell him about it. It wasn't that she didn't trust him. It just felt better to keep it to herself, for now. Tabitha had already considered a theory that maybe what she had in her possession might be a bit more special than Daniel's meteorite keys.

Daniel had said one key for each zipper yet if what she had on her from the meteor shower had managed to open the first zipper, the one into the Viking tent and her tektite was from the meteor shower with the meteorites that opened the middle zipper, then that meant that she could have something that opened more than one zipper. For some reason Tabitha was convinced that it was the tektite with the zircon that worked on more than one zipper. Tabitha was hoping the bits of tektite would open this zipper but didn't think that they would open multiple zippers without the added zircon. It was just her theory, of course. For some reason she had not wanted to share that information. Not yet. Tabitha just had a feeling that once they got back to their dimension the FBI would have a great interest in these zippers and anything related to them.

"Somehow I think that's the key," Agent Ellis said, gaze dropping to her chest. He looked up again quickly. "Once Thomas reasons it out he'll be hot to get his hands on it. And you know he's thinking about it. I can picture him staring at that empty room off his kitchen, considering, drooling to get his hands on you to find out how you opened that first zipper. A master key to unlock them all."

Tabitha stared at Agent Ellis in surprise. The thought had crossed her mind that it could open more than one zipper, true, but she was amazed that he also considered it. He didn't seem to pay attention to her half the time, so why had he caught that bit of information? "Why do you say that? That it could unlock them all?"

"Well, you believe that this opened the first zipper, something from the same meteor shower as the meteorite that opened the second zipper and you're hoping this zipper opens as well. Thomas said they all have different keys. So it leads one to believe that it can open many. Or at least you hope it can open more than one. We still don't know if it will work on this zipper."

Of course, she had forgotten that Daniel had given Agent Ellis information before shoving him through the zipper as well. She would have to be careful around him. He didn't miss much even if it seemed he did. Suddenly she was anxious to find out if it worked. She jumped to her feet. "Let's get Agent Bismarck and go back up that hill."

"Whoa. What's the rush?" Agent Ellis said. She stared at him in surprise. "I mean, since we're here it would be nice to see what here is."

Tabitha stared at him. They had slit that man's throat without any warning. Why would Agent Ellis now want to stay in such a place? She chewed on her lower lip. Actually, he hadn't been in a rush to go back from the start. Tabitha seemed to be the only one determined to get back through that zipper. If Tabitha wasn't so determined to go back home maybe she would understand this need to stay and explore. It was difficult for her to think beyond getting home.

"Couldn't we go back and if it works you can come back and explore to your heart's content?" Tabitha asked. She didn't add the comment that she was thinking, come back with a few hundred heavily armed marines but not her.

"There hasn't been time to sort through all the options and implications of this," Agent Ellis said. "First, what if Thomas is sitting back in his living room pondering how you could have escaped the first zipper and concludes that you have a key? So he keeps his eye on that room until satisfied that the first one was a fluke. Second, we can't exactly march up the hill with our escort, open a beam of light, and expect to calmly walk away. There would be a lot of explaining to do on a return trip. Third, we need to know if this dimension poses any threat."

Tabitha sat back on the edge of the mattress. "You're right. All I've been thinking about is getting home. We could walk right back into Daniel's arms. Insane, dangerous arms."

Tabitha worried about Snooze being abandoned. He would be all right for a day or two but hopefully someone would think to check on him before too long. It was frustrating to be so helpless when she had responsibilities. She might have already missed the start of her workday. Hopefully someone from the FBI would call her workplace. They would have to know soon enough that she had disappeared with Agent Bismarck. It was disorienting that they had stepped into the zipper late in the evening and stepped out into broad daylight. Did that mean that time passed while going through the zipper or that the dimensions were just off in time?

What Tabitha didn't say was that even if they managed to get past Daniel, a feat she trusted him to do, who would take the key from her and what would they do with it? Tabitha couldn't imagine the federal government just letting her walk around in control of a key to unlock the entrances of other dimensions or worlds, or whatever they were. Technically the tektite belonged to her but she didn't know the details in possessing something which could threaten the safety of the world and somehow thought the federal government would decide that it had the right to confiscate said item. One thing Agent Ellis hadn't mentioned was what the FBI would do with the knowledge of zippers to other dimensions. He said he had to be sure this dimension wouldn't be a threat but who was going to make sure their own dimension wasn't a threat to this dimension?

The door opened and the officer entered the small room. Olin studied them thoughtfully from the doorway. He was an impressive sight, very rigid and aloof, filled with pure self-confidence. No posturing. Captain Olin was a man in charge, who had no doubt that he was in charge. Though Tabitha has seen him order a man's death without the slightest hesitation she still felt a sense of trusting him with her life instead of fearing him. It didn't make sense. He was a wolf. Tabitha wasn't such a fool as to think that she could walk up to some wolf and pat its head. Tabitha gave herself a small mental shake. How odd, she thought.

Tabitha nearly jumped out of her skin when the captain touched the wall and warm light filled the room. What sort of world was this where they rode horses and used bows and arrows yet had electricity wired into the stone huts of a small village? Agent Ellis was right, it certainly wasn't medieval England. Her curiosity was waking. but she still only wanted to go home. What else would they find in this land?

Captain Olin spoke. Tabitha strained to understand him. He spoke slowly and Agent Ellis listened, his face tightening for a moment then settling into a mask. Tabitha could not understand anything the man said. When Captain Olin finished speaking Agent Ellis nodded once. Agent Ellis turned to Tabitha.

"The day grows short. Captain Olin says we will not reach the city before dark unless we leave now and ride hard. Can you ride a horse?" Agent Ellis said.

"The city? But we can't leave now," Tabitha said. "We have to, uh, perform that one task yet tonight."

Captain Olin obviously understood her. He said something, bowed his head in a curt bow, and then left the room, shutting the door behind him. Agent Ellis stared at the door thoughtfully.

"What did he say?" Tabitha asked.

"It shall be as our lady requests. We ride at dawn."

"So we aren't prisoners, right? See, that proves it," Tabitha said. Agent Ellis looked uncomfortable. "We aren't prisoners, right? We haven't done anything wrong."

Agent Ellis grimaced. "Well, possibly."

"That means we have to try this tonight."

Agent Ellis shook his head. "Unless you plan on opening that doorway in front of an escort it has to wait. That is, if they even allow us back to the hill. And you're forgetting Thomas."

Tabitha tapped her finger against her lips thoughtfully. "Does it matter? If they see? A handful of men? It's like an old English UFO. A shining light and strangely dressed strangers vanish." She looked back up at him. "What do you mean if they allow us back on the hill? Why would they stop us?"

"I don't think it's a good idea," Agent Ellis said. He opened the shutter and looked out the window. "Is that what you want? To go right back without even trying to learn more about this place?" Ellis asked.

"They killed a man," Tabitha said, closing her eyes. "No trial. No hesitation."

"Yes. A criminal, but yes it felt brutal. It's a different culture."

"I'm not prepared. I like to be prepared," Tabitha said. It sounded weak even to her own ears but it was the truth.

"Sometimes we have to go with the flow," Ellis said.

"What do you know that you aren't telling me?" Tabitha demanded. He looked so uncomfortable that she clutched her stomach in concern. "What?" she asked, barely able to breathe.

"We told them you are my wife," he said.

Tabitha stared at him, stunned, then laughed in relief. "That's all? You had me scared there."

"Yes, well, our being married seems to be a complication as well."

"I'm confused. Why would you even tell him we are married?"

"Because they were going to use me as target practice for escorting you. Until Simon said you were my wife. Then they decided that it was the king's right to kill me."

Tabitha stared at him. "You do understand, that makes no sense?" She frowned. "Who's Simon?"

"Agent Bismarck."

"Oh, yeah," she said. Tabitha rubbed her temple. It had been a long day. "And since we're married it might be helpful to know your name."

"Dalton. But my friends call me Dane."

Tabitha frowned. Oh, yeah, he had introduced himself in the art store. "Well, *Dalton*, you already said your life is at risk. What if they take us somewhere and kill us all? I would rather try getting back even if it means we leave them puzzled. We don't even know if it will open. We can't leave here not even knowing if it opens."

"And what happens if they do know what a zipper is and when the light beam shows up they take your key and we're still stranded? Now they have the key to our world," Dane said, turning to her. "We need to be careful."

"There's being careful and there's being paranoid," Tabitha snapped. She hated that he continued to use logic to argue with. Tabitha hadn't considered that someone would simply take away her key. She studied him. "It's something else. Something big. Why else would you be so hesitant to at least try?"

Dane laughed. "It's not a different world. It's Earth. In fact, we're still in Minnesota."

"You say that like you know that for certain."

He nodded. "Yes."

"Dalton, what happened after I fainted?" Tabitha asked, her voice hard.

Dane stood and paced the room. He found it humorous that she not only called him Dalton but made a point to let him know why by stressing the word every time she said it. He began to talk, telling her what had happened in the time since she fainted. Tabitha's eyes widened more and more as his story unfolded.

***

Tabitha listened to Dane without interrupting even once. Her mouth opened and shut several times when he was talking about a purple halo but she managed to hold the words inside. He had skipped some details during his narration, such as Simon and him agreeing on the plan to investigate first but she didn't need to know that. "And then Captain Olin returned to the room and asked me to check on you," Dane said.

Tabitha stared at him when he was done. She stood and walked to the shuttered window. Dane had partially opened it, just enough to see the back of the house. A neatly plotted vegetable garden lay directly in her line of sight. Weeds had begun to grow but it had been well tended before the owners fled and the vegetables had a good hold and the weeds were still small.

"Purple halo?" she asked. "What?"

"I don't know," Dane said with a shrug. "I thought it better to wait and let it play out."

"What sort of place is this? Where they look at halos around people?"

Dane's eyebrows rose and his patience again grew thin. "I'm pretty sure I'm in the same darkness on that as you. If we want answers we will have to investigate, won't we? This is why I've been saying that we need to stay here and learn what we can."

"We have to try," Tabitha said, staring out the window. "Even if we just see if it opens and we don't step through. I have to know."

"We can go to the city. Lull Thomas into thinking we are trapped and of no concern and then try later," Dane said. He paused and his voice changed. "Have you considered what this means? Access to other dimensions. We need time to evaluate the situation."

"You're FBI agents. Can't you go in guns blazing?"

Dane sighed. "He's going to see the zipper open. If he's waiting with a gun, well, not so simple as going in guns blazing. And we don't know if you have anything that works. Besides, we're in protective custody. Or haven't you noticed? We'll go with the flow for now. Cooperate and go into the city."

"But what if we can't get back here?" All her fear and stress came through in that small worried statement.

Dane stepped up behind her and put his hand on her shoulder. "It'll be all right. The city isn't that far. We can find our way back. Even if they throw me in prison you can still make it back here."

"You think they'll throw you in prison and you still want to go?" Tabitha asked in surprise. It made sense. It was his job to protect the country. This could be a threat. If he could be brave she could be brave. His hand on her shoulder gave her strength. Tabitha nodded. "Okay." She walked over to the bed and picked up the tin holding the pieces of tektite. "Take these and give one to Simon," she said, handing two pieces to Dane. "If at least one of us gets away we stand a chance of being rescued."

Tabitha decided not to argue further. She had no intention of going to the city and possibly being executed because someone looked through a piece of glass that made her look purple. Tabitha would face Daniel with a gun before she would allow them to put her in some cage or whatever it was they planned on doing to her. If Dane and Simon wanted to stay they could stay but she was doing her best to get back. At least this way they had a fair shot and she wasn't abandoning them.

Dane nodded and slipped the pieces of tektite into his pocket. He noticed that she kept the one with the zircon inside but he didn't comment on it. It wasn't possible to know what actually worked to open the zipper and though he found it hard to believe that a piece of melted sand would do the trick he would have originally found it impossible to believe that a piece of rock had worked to open the doorway to another dimension to begin with. Maybe she had managed to open the first zipper with what she had.

He glanced at her over-sized bag. "Are you sure you don't have a meteorite stashed in there that you forgot about?"

Tabitha smiled. "Or maybe the ones I took to Daniel rubbed off magic dust and transformed my purse into a key?" Her smile dropped and she grew serious. "So what is this purple halo business? Does it mean I'm to be sacrificed to a volcano or a favorite alien pet monster beast?"

Dane shook his head. "I haven't figured it out yet. I don't think it's a totally bad thing though. For you." He walked to the door and paused before opening it. "Are you hungry? Do you feel up to meeting our friend Olin?"

He turned back from the door and put his arms around her. It was a purely comforting gesture and Tabitha felt more of the tension ease away. It felt good to feel his arms around her and she rested her cheek on his shoulder. He felt solid and warm and she could hear the steady thump of his heart beating in his chest.

"We'll get through this," he said, gently rubbing her back. "It's been a shock to all of us. I'm not in the habit of pulling my gun on beautiful women. I apologize for that. I was more distracted than I realized until you pushed that gun away. I think you've shown strength in a situation that makes veteran agents tremble at the knees. We just have more practice in not showing it."

Tabitha closed her eyes, letting the comfort of being in his arms flow through her. Beneath the crisp shirt his chest was rock hard. It felt good to be in his arms. He rested his chin on top of her head for a moment and adjusted his arms to pull her a little more closely.

Warmth flowed through her. It was worth stepping into another dimension to find this, she decided.

"This makes you tremble at the knees?" she asked against his chest.

Dane laughed and Tabitha felt the vibration through her cheek. "I had almost a full day to come to grips with it and yet when I saw you I was so shaken I pulled a gun on you. For which again, I'm sorry, by the way."

Tabitha nodded, face still pressed against his chest. This was where she wanted to stay. She wouldn't mind staying in this dimension if it meant more time with Dane. Tabitha had to reach deep inside for the strength to step back but she did, straightening her shirt automatically. "It's all right. Let's get out there."

They went into the adjourning room together. Simon was studying the field glass Olin had shown them. He looked up when the door opened and held up the glass. Simon was so startled when he saw the two through the glass that he almost dropped it. He frowned at Dane, carefully tucking the glass into its carrying case. Olin was just outside the door, talking to some of his men. As always, he left the door slightly ajar. Dane gestured at the table and Tabitha walked past him to look at the assortment of food spread out on the table. There was still cheese, bread, and some sausage on the cutting board. A canvas bag held mottled green and red apples and baby carrots still coated in dirt fresh from the garden. She glanced at the food a bit skeptically.

Tabitha sat down on one of the benches and cut a bite-sized piece of cheese. Her eyes lit in appreciation when she tasted it and she sliced off several larger pieces. "Where did the food come from?" she asked.

"Olin scrounged around the kitchen and had his own supplies also," Simon said.

"They must have greenhouses to get carrots so early in the year," Tabitha said, brushing dirt off a small carrot.

Dane kept an eye on Olin's back and pressed the piece of tektite into Simon's hand. "It's from the same meteor shower," Dane said.

Simon nodded and studied it for a moment before he slipped it into his pocket after a quick glance. "A lot smaller than that rock Daniel Thomas had," Simon said. "So this is what you think will work?"

"We each have a piece. Just in case," Dane said. "If it doesn't work alone, well, I just hope we don't have to find out."

"Agent Bismarck, er, Simon, I want to try it now but Dalton is convinced that Daniel is watching to see if we open it again. Do you really think he's sitting there with a gun in hand waiting for us?"

Simon glanced at Dane, then shrugged. "Maybe. The important thing is to discover what we can while we're here. A few days to investigate then we go back. If we can."

Tabitha grimaced but didn't argue. Dane watched her while she ate. Her face was very expressive. He found it mesmerizing to watch her think through their dilemma, imagining her wading through various scenarios, aware each time she had a bright idea that lit her face, then discarding of the possibility by the subtle nose wrinkling and occasional shake of her head. Twice Tabitha got caught up in her thoughts to the point that she froze, staring off into space. Then she would blink and go back to eating like nothing had happened. Dane found her fascinating. It wasn't just that she was amazingly beautiful. There was something else about her that drew him to her.

Maybe Tabitha was right, Dane thought. Maybe they should first at least see if what they had would open the zipper. If one of them could open it but didn't step through and did it quickly enough to not draw Thomas' attention they would at least know if they had a ticket home or not. He had every intention of investigating this new world before returning but knowing they had an exit plan would make a big difference if they ran into trouble. Even if Thomas saw the zipper open, if no one went through he would have no idea what happened.

Dane told himself that it wasn't that he was going against his own gut instinct and training and risking this to make her happy. It was that if Tabitha was right, they should know if they had a back door when dealing with what lay ahead. Thomas would have to be sitting right in front of the room, staring at the right location to see the small flicker that would occur if this key worked to open the zipper.

"I'll do it," Dane said. "I'll just see if it works and come right back."

Simon stared thoughtfully at Dane then nodded his head meaningfully at Olin's back, visible just outside the door as he talked to his men. "And how do you propose getting by them?"

"I can do it. If I'm caught I will just say I was going to find something my wife dropped." He turned to Tabitha, who was gulping water after swallowing a piece of sausage wrong at the exact moment he referred to her as wife. "Are you all right?" Tabitha nodded. Hearing Dane refer to her as his wife caught her off guard. "Do you have something in that super-sized bag of yours that I can use as an excuse?" He turned back to Simon. "I only have to sneak out. I can walk right back in if necessary."

Simon studied both Tabitha and Dane thoughtfully, his considering gaze staying on Dane in the end. "And if Thomas realizes we have a key?"

"He won't. I will only hold it open just long enough to see if it works. He would have to be sitting in a chair staring at the exact spot to see that brief flare. Even then, as long as we don't go back through he won't know what is going on. This is a new zipper for him. Thomas might put it down to something unique about this one. He's convinced there's some residual effect, right?" Tabitha had gone into the bedroom and returned. She handed him a comb. Dane felt the urge to give her a kiss for good luck. He resisted. "He won't even suspect a thing and we'll know if these things work."

"You're taking a big risk," Simon said, shaking his head. "I still suggest waiting a few days, give Thomas some time to relax his vigil. It's an unnecessary risk."

Tabitha watched their byplay with a thoughtful look on her face. Dane could see the wheels turning in her head though. "What do you mean, you have to investigate anyway?" she said, popping a piece of sausage in her mouth ever so casually.

Simon glanced at Dane before answering. "We have to find out if there is any risk in this dimension before returning."

Tabitha nodded thoughtfully. "And this is important why?"

"So we know if there's a risk," Simon said patiently.

"I suppose someone has to do it," Tabitha said. "What would this risk be? Something to national security?"

"Yes, exactly," Simon said even while Dane shook his head to warn him not to agree.

"I suppose you agreed to this already?" Tabitha asked in a warm voice, a light smile curving her lips sweetly.

"Of course," Simon said. He might have said more but Dane started talking over him.

"Of course not," Dane said quickly. "It's just that now that we're here we need to know facts, gather information, formulate a plan."

"Have you intended all along to explore?" Tabitha asked, face flushing.

"We're going with the flow, remember? I'm pretty sure we discussed this," Dane said patiently. "We can't make a mad dash to the zipper, guns blazing, take out Thomas in a shootout, leave you there, and then come back to investigate. Maybe before finding out about this purple halo dilemma it would have been an option. Now it's not."

"You could have just said that," Tabitha said, face flushed in irritation. "You could have just said the two of you already made up your minds and that is that. Instead of trying to pretend you're only considering it."

Dane studied her, not sure why she was suddenly upset. There was always one way to smooth over an argument he did not know the cause of. "I'm sorry. I just didn't want to upset you even more."

Tabitha rolled her eyes. She was still irritated but chose not to continue the argument. "Why did you carry me into the village? Why not just wait a few minutes for me to come to?"

"I'm going now," Dane said, glancing out the door at Captain Olin to make sure he was still occupied. He had no intention of getting into any prolonged discussion with her over something that was already done.

Instead of going back into Tabitha's bedroom he hurried up to the loft and picked a window facing the rear of the house. Within minutes Dane crawled out of the upstairs loft bedroom window. The house had no doors or other windows at the back. As he suspected and hoped, there was no guard at the back of the house. Dane hung from his fingers for a moment then dropped to the ground and rolled, freezing while he counted to ten. There was no outcry, no curious head showing up. He stayed low and ran into the trees. It didn't take long to be out of sight of the house and deep into the trees. He continued to keep a sharp eye out for any of the King's Men who might still be patrolling for any of Ravin's cohorts.

At the edge of the trees, halfway up the hill, he crouched next to a tree and studied the situation. Dane could see where the zipper should be because the grass was well trampled. He had marked the tree next to him when he had come through earlier so he knew the right direction to look. Though Dane felt the need for haste he waited several minutes before darting out of the cover of the trees, staying as low as possible and still managing some speed. Patience was a job requirement, either a natural trait or quickly learned. When he approached the area of trampled grass he hesitated, unsure of what to do next. Dane clenched the tektite in his fist and made a sweeping motion, keeping his arm stretched out as far as possible. He stepped up the hill, swung his arm, and then stepped farther up again, repeating the process.

Dane was up the hill, two steps beyond the trampled grass, when the beam of light shimmered into existence. Silently counting to himself, Dane took a moment to study it. In the sunroom it had been bound by the confines of the sunroom so he was surprised that it only went about eight feet up from the ground. For some reason he had expected it to go sky high. He swept his hand away before he reached ten and within a few seconds the light vanished.

What do you know, Tabitha was right. It was a strange feeling to know that the small bit of glass in his hand worked to open the zipper. On the one hand it was a relief to know that they did indeed have a way back. On the other hand it was still a bit surreal to think that they had traveled through a zipper into another dimension. The implications excited him beyond belief yet made him very wary. There was no way of knowing what lay beyond this small village in this dimension. He opened his palm and studied the tektite. It was more valuable than the biggest diamond back home. It was more valuable than all the diamonds back home.

Tabitha had a fortune nestled on Kleenex in a modified Altoids tin and who knew how many more pieces of the precious stone. This little piece he held opened the zipper so it didn't take much and that roughly heart shaped stone in the tin could be cut down to several pieces the size of the stone he held. Captain Olin's words came back to him. "Do you not know her value?" Indeed, he was starting to get a better understanding. Which, of course, meant Captain Olin already guessed her value.

Realizing he was spending too much time out in the open he crouched, glancing around him warily, then carefully hurried back into the trees. He took in his surroundings, watching for any movement, any sign that he was no longer alone. He studied the tree he crouched next to. Not satisfied, he studied the next tree, noting its position to the zipper. The trampled grass wouldn't be a permanent signal to find it again. He wanted to be able to find it in a hurry, not by having to wave his arm over half the hillside. He felt the need to be quick but also the need to think ahead as he studied yet a third tree before deciding it offered what he needed.

Tabitha felt the tension knotting her stomach. Before stumbling into this adventure she believed she would have enjoyed such a grand adventure, stepping through a beam of light into another world. It was too fanciful to let her curiosity pass it up. It would be something in a book that she would have enjoyed reading about, sitting curled up in a favorite oversized chair, shutting out a rainy day for the adventure of imagining a world reached by stepping through a beam of light. It wasn't so interesting now that she was here.

For some reason she only felt the strongest urge to run back to the safety on the other side of the beam of light, even if it meant facing Daniel ready to shoot them if they stepped back through that zipper. Tabitha had never felt homesick even as a child but she realized that this was what it felt like. She was homesick after just a few hours of being there. Tabitha frowned. Actually, she had started feeling homesick once they walked back to the sunroom and while they were standing on the hill right after coming through the zipper and though it had faded it suddenly started up again now. Maybe it was stress and not homesickness.

Knowing that Dane could be risking his life because she had pushed him to it ate at her as well. It wasn't as if she had told him to sneak out a back window even though he could be killed. She had been so happy when he said he would do it but then as the two men talked and she noticed their serious expressions it had hit her how much danger he risked. Tabitha had thought it a simple matter to just go to the zipper and go back home. If he got hurt doing this she would be at fault. He wouldn't have gone if she hadn't pestered him into doing it.

Simon had his complete attention on Olin just outside the partially opened front door. Tabitha didn't understand why her plan to simply tell the King's Men that she wanted to go to the hill wouldn't have been a better idea than Dane risking his life running around when he was supposed to be under guard in the house. She didn't care what Captain Olin and his men thought when the three of them simply walked through a beam of light and vanished. She would be safely home and that's what would matter.

Tabitha glanced at Simon again. She did what she always did when she was nervous or afraid. Or bored or excited, for that matter. Tabitha dived into mindless chatter. "So, you and Dalton know each other well?" she asked.

"Yeah," Simon said, gaze locked on Olin's back.

"He seems nice. For someone who's first action at seeing me was to put a gun to my head." Tabitha seemed as surprised as Simon that she had said that. She shrugged. Well, it was true. "Do you think this is Minnesota still also? An alternate timeline? It could very well have been a different future if anything in our history changed. Alexander living to fifty. Hitler dying in childhood. A child surviving childhood who died in our history and went on to do something major in life."

Simon glanced at her, then turned his attention back to Olin. Tabitha crumbled a small piece of bread absently as she considered the possibilities. She was talking to herself more than to the federal agent but she felt better pretending that she was talking with him. Tabitha knew that Simon had a personality because he had shown it after they had found Dane on the road but he seemed to have lost it again.

"We've really only had tremendous technical advances in the past sixty years or so. How old is the car? A hundred years? But there weren't road networks in the States to support travel by car a hundred years ago. They still used cavalry in the first world war. A hundred years is really a short time. I wonder what other changes we'll find? No cars but electricity. So do they have discoveries like that piece of glass that fills a need we never had?"

An idea struck her and she frowned. "Do you think we have counterparts here? Do you think we'll find other dimension us'es?" Suddenly her curiosity was overpowering her homesickness.

Simon glanced at her. "Us-es?"

"As in us but not us. Other versions of us."

"It was a challenge," Simon said.

"What?" Tabitha said in confusion at the abrupt change in topic. "What was a challenge?"

"Dane carrying you into the village. It was a challenge Olin gave him. He had to do it."

"He gave him a challenge? Dalton sort of skipped that part." She wrinkled her nose. "He actually gave him a challenge to carry me into the village?"

Simon sighed. "It was a subtle challenge."

"Ah," Tabitha said. "A guy thing." She had been eyeing the rectangle of leather on the table for a while and reached over and picked it up to look at it. Tabitha slipped it out of the case. "Oh, this isn't glass. Feels like a resin." She held it up over her head to stare at it through the overhead light. "It's a filter."

"Filter?" She suddenly had Simon's complete attention. "What do you mean a filter?"

"Like 3D glasses? See, it's a resin with several layers of some type of plastic or paper sandwiched between," Tabitha said. She scrunched one eye shut. "It could be thin glass in between. Colored glass."

"Are you sure?" Simon asked.

Tabitha tapped the field glass with the side of her thumb, mostly using her thumbnail. "It's tacky, not smooth like glass. I'm just not sure what's layered inside. Look, you can see the colors of the edges."

Simon took the offered field glass and studied it, occasionally raising just his eyes to look at her over the field glass. He was clearly not seeing what she was seeing and he couldn't decide if she was making it up or he was just unable to see it. Simon raised the field glass so he could look at it up at the light and when he saw the hair thick edge of color that could be something embedded in the resin he muttered, "I'll be damned." He looked over at Tabitha. "How did you spot that? Even believing it was there it's barely visible."

Tabitha shrugged. "I'll bet you can tell a model of a gun with just a glance and a whole lot more if you got your hands on it. I work with beads, stone, glass, metals, and a whole lot of stuff. Resin simply isn't as hard as glass. It's common to surround items, including paper, with resin. So I looked. That's all."

Simon straightened and quickly set the field glass on the table in front of him. Olin had turned and was walking back toward the door. He stepped inside, gaze going immediately to Tabitha. "Ah, ye are better. Where be your husband?"

"Looking for my comb," Tabitha said, able to understand most of what he said. It helped that she had expected the question to come. "You are Captain Olin?"

Olin nodded but frowned. "He left this house? Unseen?"

The door to the bedroom opened and Dane stepped through. He walked across the room seemingly oblivious to Olin's hard stare, handed Tabitha a comb, and settled onto the bench next to her. He sliced a piece of sausage and popped it into his mouth. He looked up, as if suddenly realizing that everyone was silent. Olin stared at him. Simon stared at Tabitha and Tabitha was staring at the tabletop.

"What?" he asked innocently.

"I misunderstood," Olin said slowly. "When your wife said looking for her comb she must have meant fetching your comb." He glanced at the now open bedroom door meaningfully. "It did not occur to me that ye needed privacy to fetch a comb."

"Is it a crime to leave this house?" Tabitha asked, face flushed. The man was more observant than anyone had a right to be. Dane rolled his eyes when she defended him and gave away that he had left the house.

Tabitha caught the rolled eyes and wrinkled her nose. "You're covered in dried grass from where I lost my comb."

Captain Olin reached over and plucked some dried grass from Dane's jacket, at the shoulder. "Only if ye be caught doing something ye shouldn't be." He dropped the grass purposely on the table. "It be too late to ride to the city tonight but be too early to retire, even for an old man like me." He grinned when he said that. "Would ye care for more history lessons? I must confess, I am most eager to learn of your land as well."

Tabitha picked up the comb and ran her thumb along the tines. The sound was a slight whirring, much like playing cards in a bike's wheel spokes. She didn't like knowing that she was being held as a prisoner. This was even worse than sitting in that drab office being interviewed by Agent Bismarck.

"Why do you hold us prisoners?" she asked, looking up at Olin.

"Ye be in protective custody," Olin said.

Tabitha bit back a laugh of surprise. Captain Olin seemed to mean it. She glanced at Dane, thinking about what he had told her. She glanced at the field glass still lying on the table. According to them, there were people willing and eager to kill just because of that piece of resin giving someone a purple hue. Tabitha knew she should be relieved that there were other people willing to protect her because of that same purple color but she wasn't. Dane also glanced at the field glass but she had no idea what he was thinking.

"So what is so special about purple halos?" Tabitha asked.

Captain Olin stared at her thoughtfully for several minutes in silence. "How can ye not know? Ye speak heavily accented English but it be still English," he said. "Ye would have discovered long ago. As young as five or six be average."

"Well I do not know," Tabitha said. She saw Dane wince but she didn't care if she was tactful or not. She simply wanted information. "It seems to be pretty important here and since I'm supposedly one of these purple halos I'd rather know."

"Very well," Olin said. "There was a time when people with inherent talents were persecuted. Queen Ana intervened. After the War of Deeds these lands were settled with people with talents who would have faced trial in the homeland. The halo was discovered by those early settlers."

Tabitha stared at him. He hadn't said anything to clarify a purple halo. All he had said was that the Spanish Inquisition and Salem witch trials seemed to have been avoided in this world. Maybe that was what he said. "There are people here who can perform magic?" she asked. Simon snorted. Tabitha ignored him, gaze locked on Olin.

"Magic? No. Talents. A gift perhaps," Olin said. "Only the ignorant believe in magic." He realized what he had said and bowed his head. "I apologize if ye believe in magic."

Tabitha felt frustrated. She glanced at the field glass again. "Different colors for different talents?"

Olin shrugged. "That is an interesting theory. In truth only few have existed."

"So what is a purple halo?" Tabitha asked. He was not answering her question.

"Rare," Captain Olin said. He obviously sensed Tabitha's frustration. It was hard to miss as she was grinding her teeth. "An ability to see details, perhaps? An ability to see possibilities in the blink of an eye. An ability to see from different angles? I do not know. I am not a purple halo."

"That's it? People are killed because they are intelligent?" Tabitha asked in disbelief.

"Intelligent? Many without purple halos are intelligent," Olin said. "It is something ye should know, not me."

"So you don't know?" Tabitha asked in surprised disbelief.

"It's complicated," Olin said, throwing his hands out to his sides. "I shall find ye someone who can explain it. I cannot."

"This land ye come from," Olin said, settling onto the bench next to Tabitha, across from the two agents. "Tell me of it."

Dane and Simon exchanged glances. Tabitha went back to flicking the comb tines with her thumb and staring at the table. It was Dane who finally spoke. "It is called Minneapolis, in a land called Minnesota, which is part of a bigger land. A democracy ruled by an elected president. Simon and I are special agents for the country to protect its laws."

Olin nodded as he thought about what Dane said. "This bigger land, is it part of United States of America?"

"A large part," Dane said slowly, uncertain how to proceed.

"And this United States is ruled by a president which changes every four years?"

"Well, four or eight," Dane said. "And ruled isn't exactly the right word. The founding fathers wanted to keep absolute control out of the president's hands, in order to keep it from evolving away from a democracy. Washington refused to take the first offer because he didn't want to change one sovereignty for another."

"Yet, the current United States is only twelve states on the east coast, ruled by Washington's descendants, so this idea of his passing the rule to others every few years is a bit stretched for me," Olin said, nodding.

"Washington's descendants?" Dane asked, taken aback.

Olin nodded again. "And you did not travel along Tolman Road. You came from a hole in reality?" All three stared at him. Olin smiled at their surprised reaction. "Years ago a man came to the city with a similar story. He was not believed, of course. He was quite surprised to learn that the name of the city is Minneapolis."

"This man, is he still here?" Dane asked, leaning forward eagerly.

"Indeed," Captain Olin said, a smile almost lifting one side of his mouth.

They talked for many hours, each side trying to dole out information carefully, then warming to a topic before retreating to careful bits of generic information again. Dane was especially interested in the history. Olin professed to not being a scholar but he still knew quite a bit of general history. It was difficult for them to get much detail from the other as they were both being careful to judge what the other man knew before speaking. Tabitha lost interest somewhere between the crusades and the burning of the great library of Alexandria and completely tuned out the conversation at the library of Alexandria. Apparently the library was doomed in both worlds.

The thought grabbed her. What if a zipper led to a dimension where the library at Alexandria had not been destroyed? Daniel had said there were more zippers. He had a map to keep track of them, so that meant many. Tabitha potentially had a key to open them all. What a grand adventure it would be to find a dimension where the library of Alexandria still existed. Slowly the excitement at such an idea faded. The problem with adventures was that they were dangerous. It all sounded fun and exciting until being faced with it in reality. Tabitha remembered those hard Viking faces at the first zipper. She now understood why Daniel was so afraid to step through those zippers himself. The Vikings would have been enough to keep her from trying another zipper.

But what if a prepared team of crack agents visited each world? There to protect her, of course. If they let her. They might simply take away her key. That thought made her frown. Tabitha would keep her heart pendant to herself at all costs. It was hers and they couldn't have it. Not just because it had taken many hours to grind down the tektite. She wasn't about to let anyone just take it away from her. Within the safety of such a team she would look forward to exploring all these worlds. Tabitha wrinkled her nose. Maybe. It was still far more interesting to read about it from the safety of her oversized chair in her living room with her cat on her lap. She hadn't thought of herself as such a coward before.

Tabitha had driven across the United States and Canada alone without fear. She had traveled to Europe alone and though she had been uneasy about that she had pushed doubts aside and embraced the experience. Tabitha wondered why this was having such a horrible impact on her, then remembered Ravin. Yes, she had never had to worry about people shooting at her with arrows in Europe or about seeing someone in Canada executed right in front of her eyes without any warning.

Really, now that she gave it thought, it made her angry that people thought they could scare her. Well, no they weren't trying to scare her. They were trying to kill her and that had scared her. They hadn't succeeded yet. Tabitha didn't like feeling scared.

Suddenly Tabitha realized they were talking about her. She blinked and looked up and across at the men at the table with her. Olin said, "It be good for a woman to fill a man's hands, though I was not so confident ye'd make it this far."

Red flushed Tabitha's face all the way to her ears at realizing they were talking about Dane carrying her into the village. Instead of being sensitive to Tabitha's embarrassment Olin seemed to find even more delight in knowing that he'd made her blush. "Newlyweds, eh?" he asked, laughing heartily and slapping his knee. Tabitha glanced at the ale mug, wondering how much he'd consumed. The mug was full and she hadn't seen him refill it but she didn't know how much they'd been drinking before she came out of the bedroom. Olin didn't seem drunk but he sure seemed to find her discomfort amusing.

"Why the stigma about touching a purple halo?" Dane asked.

Olin laughed out loud. "Stigma? No. In the years immediately following the Original Settling times were quite rowdy. During a wild party one of the King's Men grabbed an uncooperative woman who had consumed her fair share of liquor and her neighbor's share as well. The King's Man dunked her in a horse trough to help speed up the sobering process. Turns out she was the king's advisor. From that day on it has been law that no King's Man may lay a hand on a purple halo."

"Not even if she was choking?" Tabitha asked.

Olin shook his head. "Not for any reason."

"What if they were married?" Tabitha asked.

Olin shook his head. The ghost of a smile teased his mouth. "A very chaste marriage, indeed."

"What if she told him to touch her?" Tabitha asked.

"She is like a three-year old, this one. Yet not," Olin said, clearly delighted with her persistence.

"She doesn't like being talked about like she is invisible or not present," Tabitha said, raising her chin, eyes flashing in irritation.

"She is delightful and not at all invisible," Olin said, looking right at Tabitha. "Ye hang onto a topic and won't let go for anything, worrying it and fretting and wearing it down, yes? And in the end ye emerge with knowledge everyone else has missed, yes? I know another just as you."

"What is the penalty if he does?" Simon asked, trying to steer Captain Olin back onto topics more relevant for his knowledge.

"King's Justice," Olin said. He looked around at their blank faces. "It is up to the king. The King's Men always answer only to the king."

"That's what you said when you, when, uh, before Ravin," Tabitha said.

"Yes," Olin said turning back to Tabitha, gaze boring deep into her eyes. Tabitha met his gaze.

Dane looked between them. They were still having a stare down. He cleared his throat. "So, was Ravin a King's Man?"

Olin purposely ignored Dane's question, choosing to steer the topic back to more history. He seemed especially fascinated with the concept that the United States stretched from coast to coast. Tabitha couldn't help but wonder how much harm there was in telling him anything, though she felt he already knew what they were telling him and they were just confirming things. Or at least he knew the stories well. Tabitha wondered how much Captain Olin believed of what was being said at the table. She knew that if someone came up to her while sitting in a coffee shop in downtown Minneapolis and started telling her that they came from another dimension where Minneapolis was ruled by a king she would have a tough time believing them. No, Tabitha amended, she would not have a tough time believing them, she wouldn't believe then at all. Tabitha would probably give the person telling such tales a few dollars and hope they found help for their mental illness.

"This man who came from a hole in the air, can you tell me more?" Dane asked. "His name?"

"Pederson. Hans Pederson."

Simon and Dane exchanged glances. Tabitha noticed and saw that Captain Olin noticed as well. They knew this man. Or at least his name meant something to them. It bothered her to think that Dane knew something about the zippers and this world but acted like he knew nothing. She had believed him in the bedroom that this was all new to him yet he seemed to recognize the name of Olin's zipper traveler. It never occurred to her to consider that they knew the name in connection with Daniel Thomas.

Chapter Seven

Tabitha shook her head in an attempt to clear it. There had been too much going on and the day was long. Back home it would be the early morning hours instead of late evening. Maybe she would think more clearly after some sleep. Even if she didn't think more clearly in the morning she still needed to sleep now. Tabitha was tired of feeling paranoid, tired of feeling scared, and tired of second guessing everything going on around her. Some sleep would clear the clogged functioning of her brain. It felt like her thoughts were just going in circles.

Eventually Olin bid them good-night, telling Simon he could bunk with the men, giving the newlyweds some privacy. At the door Simon turned his head and glanced back at them. Dane rolled his fingers together and nodded his head. Simon's eyes widened slightly. Dane nodded once more, put his hand inside his jacket where an inside pocket would be, then patted the spot. Simon nodded and shut the door behind him.

Tabitha watched the exchange with rising excitement. "Does that mean it worked?" Tabitha asked.

Dane nodded. "That little piece of glass of yours worked. We have our way back home. Once we investigate this side of the zipper."

It felt like a hundred pounds lifted off her shoulders. Tabitha felt the release of tension and realized that feeling trapped had been tearing her apart. Knowing that she had a way home took away the driving need to run immediately for the zipper. Tabitha stood and stretched. Her legs and back were stiff from sitting on the bench. "What do you plan to do? I mean once we get back? I know you want to investigate things here first. What impact to discover new worlds exist through a beam of light? Do we have the right to keep it a secret? Do we have an obligation to share it?"

"All good questions," Dane said, slowly. He ran his fingers through his hair. "It's only fair to see how things go here in the next few days before we start considering the consequences when we get back."

"I'm surprised you discussed our world so openly with Captain Olin," Tabitha said.

"He already knew," Dane said. He covered his mouth against a yawn. He had not slept since the night before being pushed through the zipper and it was catching up with him. "It establishes trust in us when we confirm what he already knows."

"Daniel has a map. That means someone has known about it but kept it a secret," Tabitha said. "He said most are in buildings. Hmm... I wonder if there's like a secret society or something?"

Something Daniel said about her tickled her memory but she couldn't place her finger exactly on what he had said. Something about *them*, being one of them. When he had said she was smug she had sort of tuned out the rest of what he said.

"First we have to evaluate the situation here," Dane said, only half listening to her.

"You keep saying that," Tabitha said. An idea struck her. "Do you think Olin is just being polite to three people he thinks are insane? Or does he already know about the zipper? And maybe that secret society? You know who that man is. The one Olin mentioned."

"This man might be the man who Daniel stole the map from," Dane said. "The house belonged to Hans Pederson before Daniel put it in his name."

"What makes you think Daniel stole the map?"

"Who would just give it to him?" Dane asked in surprise.

"But he didn't have the key to this zipper until he got my meteorite. And if this other man has the key why did he stay?" Tabitha said in protest.

"Thus the need to evaluate the situation," Dane said slowly, purposely. "You remind me of a Jack Russell terrier. You dive right in and start shaking things with your teeth before you even know what it is you're shaking."

Tabitha almost stuck her tongue out at him. Finding out that the tektite worked as a key to the zipper had filled her with energy again.

She suddenly had so many questions that they threatened to burst out of her all at once. Tabitha chewed on her lower lip. She was tired. He was tired. They would have time to discuss all her thoughts in the morning.

"I suspect we'll have an early start," Dane said. He gestured to the bedroom. "Shall we get some sleep?"

"Oh," she said in surprise. She hadn't considered that they'd be sharing the same bed.

Tabitha stared at the bedroom door. The thought of sharing that bed with Dane started the warmth spreading up her cheeks. It wasn't that she was a prude but they were strangers really. Snuggling down for the night with a handsome stranger who was her pretend husband felt a bit awkward. When he had put his arm around her he had been comforting her during an extremely traumatic, shocking time. Crawling into bed with him was not the same at all.

"Sure," she said. Tabitha swallowed. "I hope I can sleep after all this, uh, excitement."

"I can help you fall asleep," Dane said as he shut the bedroom door behind them.

Tabitha opened her mouth then shut it. She felt like a fish. All sorts of ways he could help her fall asleep flashed through her mind. It didn't help matters that all those ideas stirred even more ideas.

"There's a nursery rhyme my mom used to sing to me," he said. Dane put his hands on her shoulders and gently guided her to the bed.

"Nursery rhyme," she muttered.

Dane chuckled. Gently he began to massage her shoulders, moving toward her neck, then back out again. It felt amazingly good. Dane pulled her closer to him, all his movements slow and steady. He lowered his head so that his mouth was near her ear. Tabitha felt the soft whisper of his breath as he spoke.

"Did you have something else in mind?" he whispered.

"This seems to be working well," she said in a low voice. Her knees felt a bit wobbly for some reason.

Dane continued to work her shoulders, his long fingers easing away all the tension she hadn't realized she had. When he stopped and stepped back she stumbled and almost fell backwards. He cleared his throat.

"Sorry. I, uh, well maybe a nursery rhyme would be safer," he said.

Neither said anything for a moment. Tabitha took the first step to the bed and Dane followed. They both crawled onto the bed and lay stiffly next to each other. Any relaxation she had gained was wiped away by the knowledge that he had felt the same pull. The best thing about his hands on her had been that all thought fled. There was only feeling. It was good to not think right now.

Tabitha cleared her throat. "Uh, I'm waiting for that nursery rhyme."

Dane was silent for a moment. The room was quickly darkening as night settled. Tabitha stared at the wall, not wanting to move even her head. She was aware of him. She could feel his warmth. She could hear him breathing.

When he started to sing she was impressed with his deep, rich voice. "Rub a dub dub, what a drub. Bedtime has come and yet there's the sun, barely over the edge. Come morning you'll be snoring because you're fighting sleep."

Tabitha burst out laughing the second he finished. She rolled onto her side and half sat up, leaning on her elbow. "You made that up." Tabitha could barely see him but she could see his quick grin.

"You don't know my mom," he said. Dane chuckled. "Someday I'll have to tell you about my parents. So the nursery rhyme didn't work. I guess we go back to other methods."

He ran his finger along her curved side, from hip bone to just under her arm, then across the curve of her breast. Tabitha leaned closer, lowering her head at the same moment he reached up. They kissed tentatively at first, a gentle brush of lips against lips. Then Dane slipped his hand behind her head and pulled her closer, deepening the kiss.

An abrupt, loud knock on the door startled them out of their relaxation exercise and Tabitha just had time to straighten her shirt before one of the King's Men opened the door and hit the light switch. They both blinked against the sudden light. Any doubt she had about looked tousled vanished at the startled expression on the man's face. He quickly averted his gaze to a spot along the far right wall. He cleared his throat. Tabitha automatically used her fingers to attempt to smooth her hair.

"Ye wanned oside," the man said. As an afterthought he added, "Now."

Tabitha didn't understand. She glanced at Dane. He understood immediately her need for a translation and said, "We are wanted outside. Now."

The man bowed once and exited the room, leaving the door open. Dane sat up, adjusting his clothes. "So much for resting tonight," he said.

Tabitha slid off the bed and headed for the door. Dane followed at her heels. Outside the house there was no sign of Simon or Captain Olin. A short, hard-faced man who was as wide as he was tall approached them. He walked stiffly yet with a spring to his step, a result of being so muscular. He gave Tabitha a quick nod then gave his attention to Dane.

When he spoke Tabitha couldn't understand a fourth of what he said. She had begun to understand most of what Olin said. Now she realized that he must have been making an effort to be understood. This man shot off his heavily accented words at rapid-fire speed. She noticed that Dane even appeared to struggle to grasp what he said. Eventually the man stopped and Tabitha automatically looked to Dane for the translation. Dane nodded thoughtfully before turning to Tabitha.

"I believe Thomas has decided to visit. He is armed and definitely hostile. He shot a King's Man and escaped."

"Escaped?" Tabitha's gaze darted everywhere. "Is the man he shot all right? Did he go back? Why would he shoot someone? That means he came armed. Did he come to shoot us?" Tabitha paused to breathe. "The man he shot, is he all right?"

Dane shook his head. Tabitha felt bad that someone had been shot. A niggle of guilt twisted inside her. It wasn't her fault. Tabitha wasn't responsible for Daniel's actions. Yet, if she hadn't pushed and pushed Dane to find out if the tektite worked to open the zipper that man would not have been shot. Daniel must have been watching, just like Simon and Dane had said he would. He must be feeling desperate to have come through himself without knowing what he would find. She remembered how timid he seemed about stepping into the unknown.

Daniel must be feeling quite desperate to come through without knowing what he would find on this side. If they made it back out alive he would be in serious trouble for kidnapping federal agents and his secret would be out in the open. Tabitha assumed it was kidnapping when you pushed someone through a hole in space believing they couldn't get back out. It had to be legally the same as shoving someone in the basement and locking the door. He must be desperate. Desperate men were irrational men and dangerous men.

"Simon and Olin are hunting him now," Dane said, staring off into the distance as if he could see through the trees and buildings.

"Sergeant Harris here has a small detail left for your protection. He would like you in a different house. One more easily guarded."

"Simon? With Olin?" Tabitha muttered.

Sergeant Harris glared at Dane, then nodded, apparently satisfied that he understood what had been said. He gestured toward a house across the courtyard. Tabitha took a step then stopped. "My purse," she said, remembering that she had left it in the bedroom. "I need my purse."

"I'll get it," Dane said, turning to go back into the house.

The muscle bulging sergeant shook his head, blocking Dane with his arm. He issued a command and one of the uniformed men jumped to attention and then ran into the house they had occupied. He returned within a very short time, holding Tabitha's bag out in front of him with two fingers like a dirty diaper. It seemed a man carrying a woman's purse was distasteful to men in any dimension. She rescued her bag and slung it over her shoulder.

The sergeant gestured and they followed him to a smaller house set apart from the others. No one would get near this house without being seen. It was smaller as well. There was a main room and a loft. There were only two windows, one in front facing the street and one on the side of the house. There was no electricity in this house. The sergeant left them a lantern and went outside. He returned in a short time in the company of another man carrying the food from the first building and the two settled at the table.

Dane and Tabitha were left standing without any more attention. If either had stepped toward the door their guards would have been quick to stop them from leaving but they didn't feel the need to get to know them as Olin had. Tabitha realized that she would have to heed nature's call and wondered if there were outhouses in the back. She said so to Dane in a low voice and Sergeant Harris promptly pointed to the kitchen.

Though Tabitha was impressed with his keen hearing she didn't think he could have heard her correctly and pointedly said she needed a latrine. The man scowled at her and got to his feet, gesturing for her to follow him. There was a small door off the kitchen and inside was a toilet. It looked odd, even odder than some she had seen in Europe, but it was a toilet.

"Doesn't look like we have privacy the rest of the night," Dane said in a low voice when she exited the bathroom. "Go on up and try to get some sleep. I'll be up in a bit."

Tabitha nodded and climbed the steep stairs to the small loft above. There was no door to separate the room from the open stairs so the men's voices drifted up. Tabitha was weary to the bone but didn't think she would be able to sleep. First, it was a strange bed. She always had trouble falling asleep on strange beds in unfamiliar surroundings. That the bed was a pile of straw slung across a wood frame on rope instead of a nice, thick mattress on a box spring compounded the alien feel to it. Second, she had so much to think about. Stepping into another dimension without warning where there was an immediate attempt on her life followed by the decisive execution of the man who had tried to kill her was a lot to take in and process. Now Daniel was running loose waving a gun in the air and shooting people. It was all quite overwhelming. Tabitha fell asleep the second her head touched the mattress.

***

Daniel paced. He walked three steps into the sitting room, around the sofa, back into the hall, took five steps, turned on his heel and did the same route in reverse then looped again. Sweat ran down his back, channeled along his spine but not from pacing. Sweat glistened on his forehead and ran down his temples. Every time he rounded the sofa he stared up at the empty sunroom.

He felt like he should run, hide somewhere as far from this house as he could get, yet he couldn't bring himself to abandon all hope. When the attractive woman and her suit-clad companion had stepped out of the first zipper he had been too shocked to think coherently and in his panic had simply pushed them into the newly opened zipper. In reflection he admitted it had been a good reflexive action on his part that had probably saved him from sitting in a cell right now. The suit-clad man was a dangerous man and too powerful for Daniel to control the situation face to face.

When they hadn't come back out of the new zipper his relief nearly overwhelmed him. His hands trembled when he pulled the gun out of the console table drawer. He set it on the table and began pacing. How had they gotten out of the first zipper? It had blinked into nothing immediately after they had passed through. He had picked up the new rock to look at it when suddenly the zipper flared open again and they had come back through, literally backing out of the zipper. If they hadn't backed out but had come out facing forward he would never have been able to push them into the neighboring zipper.

Daniel had had no choice but to push them into the middle zipper. He had wanted her in the first zipper. But how had they escaped that dimension?

Daniel picked up the gun in his right hand and the new rock he had acquired from Miss Anderson in his left hand and approached the first zipper, the one on the far left in the sunroom. He put the rock all the way through the space it existed and nothing happened. Of course nothing happened, it was the wrong key for that zipper. He exchanged the middle zipper's rock key for the key for the left zipper and approached the center zipper. Again, no response when he swung the wrong key through the middle zipper's location. There was no response because it was the wrong key.

So how did Miss Goody Two Shoes and her suited man open it? Daniel returned the key to the glass case and set the gun down on the table and paced. Even if she still had a meteor from the meteor shower it shouldn't be able to open the left zipper. And they hadn't returned from the middle zipper. It made no sense.

Daniel had heard stories, stories that he attributed to wishful thinking on someone's part because he had never found evidence of any truth to them. One key to open them all couldn't exist. He stopped pacing and stared at the sunroom. Or could it? Did she have a key that would work on them all? The sunroom remained empty. Daniel shook his head. If she had a key they would be back through by now. If she had a key he had to have it.

Daniel paced. There were still some things that he didn't know, of course, like why meteorites seemed to be the best choice to test. Not all meteorites worked either but nothing else he had found himself had worked at all. The other keys he had taken he had no idea of their source. There was a porcelain dog statue that opened a zipper in Washington, DC. It had crystal eyes and semi-precious stones embedded in a ceramic color around its throat. He had not dared taking it apart to see if the eyes or collar decorations were what actually worked, not willing to risk breaking some association between the pieces and losing the use of the key.

Daniel had been nineteen when he had learned about the zippers, fresh in his first year at university, still young and confident in his greatness. The first year at university had been a shock. He was used to being the smartest person he knew, had never considered anyone his equal. He had grown up in a relatively small town and no one came near his level of intelligence. Then suddenly he had been plunged into a new environment where he was surrounded by intelligent people, some as intelligent as he. Daniel could not bring himself to admit any could possibly have been even more intelligent. It had taken him the full year to realize that there were other smart people in the world.

It had started in this very house. The old man who lived here had been rumored to have very expensive things and be rather feeble and not so alert. The previous owner liked to entertain young men and was said to be quite generous. Daniel had watched him through the window first, trying to decide whether he wanted to step into the role of companion to an elderly man. Night after night Daniel would creep into the backyard and settle into position next to a shrub and watch the old man sitting at a desk scribbling notes and studying books into the late hours of the night. Occasionally the old man entertained into later in the night and then Daniel was careful not to get too close to the house until everyone had gone.

The night he had actually snuck into the house he had experienced the most fear he had ever felt in his life. Daniel was confident the old man was safely asleep in his bedroom upstairs but there was the chance he would wander back downstairs unexpectedly, though he hadn't yet in all the nights Daniel had kept watch. It was wondering what the old man was working on so intently that gave him the courage to try the side door and push it open when he discovered that it was unlocked. He wore tennis shoes and they made no sound as he carefully walked down the hall to the study. Daniel shut the door before turning on the light.

What he found kept him coming back night after night, waiting until the old man went to bed and then sneaking into the study to review what the man worked on so diligently. At first Daniel thought the old man must be insane but he saw a careful hand in all the notes. He hadn't decided yet what to do with the information when things moved out of his hands and when the dust settled he was in possession of the house and its contents.

Daniel paced. He didn't dare leave the area where he had a visual on the sunroom. How had they opened the first zipper? Did someone from that world possess a key? Daniel grimaced. He was so distraught that he had slipped and thought of it as another world. It was the same world. It was a different dimension. Daniel used the front of his shirt to wipe the sweat from his face. Had they found a way to him at last?

It had been twenty years since he had taken possession of this house and its secrets. His worse fear was that they would find him yet as the years had passed he had managed to settle into thinking it wasn't possible. He was safe. If they were going to find him they would have done it already. First a year had passed and then another and he had even forgotten about them. Now the anxiety resurged and drove him into a nervous frenzy. So Daniel paced anxiously, afraid to leave the zipper in case it opened again and afraid to be there if it did open.

Not different worlds at all. The zippers opened to different dimensions of the same world. The zipper in the Denver house opened to a world where the area hadn't been settled yet. Daniel had bought titles to the land in that dimension containing every historic gold and silver mine that produced the highest volume of metal and the result was that he had a vault in the basement of the house he had built in that dimension filled with gold bars and precious gems. Daniel had been so excited at the wealth that he hadn't planned on how to transfer it to this dimension but had eventually figured out the gold and gems. That was the first economic windfall. Others had come his way as well. Many financial windfalls had found their way to him and he had gone looking for even more.

Now Daniel realized he hadn't planned well for an escape contingency. He was too scattered. What had seemed like a good idea at the time now seemed ridiculously stupid. Daniel didn't have the time to consolidate his assets. He had thought he was being smart in not keeping it all in one place, smart in not keeping it in this dimension. Daniel had felt secure. His only worry was the IRS questioning the source of his income so he hadn't wanted his wealth in this dimension. Daniel just didn't have time to collect everything. If he had to hide he didn't know which dimension he would relocate to either.

If they had found him he wasn't safe. If they were truly capable of what the old man had written in his notes then if they ever found him he was dust. The old man had taken the zipper from them. Daniel had the maps. The maps were important. They didn't just show the location of the zipper. They showed when it was safe to use them as well as which dimension opened to which dimension.

There was a zipper in Venice which if he used it and traveled to London and opened the zipper he'd step into the zipper he'd step into this dimension's London but if he opened the neighboring zipper in London and traveled to Barcelona none of the zippers opened to this dimension. The maps showed him which routes to take and how to keep from getting lost in the zippers. His biggest fear was wandering too far and never making it back to his home dimension. The map detailed the connections. So if he used the zipper in Barcelona while in that dimension and turned right into the next zipper in Barcelona he'd be back in his home dimension. Yet if he went to Barcelona now and stepped into that same zipper he would be in a dimension where the world was in an ice-age.

At first he'd been so certain that they'd find him but eventually he had relaxed, thinking that they'd never find him because the old man must have had zipper-hopped. It was the only explanation he could reason out and so many years had passed that he'd slipped into relaxing his vigilance. Daniel had never known for certain the old man's origin zipper. There was no X marked on any map. The old man had lived in this house yet the left zipper was the Stengarlds dimension and the right zipper was a nondescript dimension quite similar to base dimension. There had been no key to the middle zipper until Miss Goody Two Shoes showed up with her meteorites. The middle zipper was marked on the map but with no hint or clue to its contents or a key. Convinced that the old man had come from the middle zipper Daniel had looked everywhere for a key, even testing any object he could find though they weren't logical, such as figurines and even a feather duster on a whim once. The old man had not had a key to the middle zipper so he could not be from the middle zipper was Daniel's conclusion.

Daniel wiped his face with his shirt again. He still owed the Stengarlds a woman. They would be angry that one had appeared only momentarily and would think he'd pulled her back out. The arrangement of supplying them with women had been necessary at the time. Daniel had come up with the idea while hanging upside down by one leg over a raked bed of coals. That was when he had decided to purchase a gun and learn how to use it. Daniel could have promised the women and not delivered but he needed access to that dimension. It was the only route to access yet another dimension, the land with technology advanced beyond base dimension technology.

Daniel went to the fridge and opened it wide, standing so he could still see the sunroom. All the pacing and stress had made him hungry and though he felt he couldn't eat his stomach growled ominously and he felt slightly light-headed. It was necessary to eat something to silence the hole in his stomach. He grabbed a packet of lunch meat and a chunk of cheese and slammed the fridge door shut. Daniel resumed his pacing, eating the meat straight out of the package. He tossed the wrappings on the counter. When he finished the meat he gnawed on the block of cheese.

The man with her had been hard core something. Probably Bureau. Too hard core for a cop, Daniel decided. Neither had known about the zippers. They had been too confused and surprised. Besides, if he had been one of them Daniel realized he wouldn't be standing in the house alone contemplating the situation. Daniel nodded his head. So that meant the woman had a key. She had a key that opened the left zipper. Why did she have a key that opened the left zipper but not for the middle zipper when she had found the meteorites that worked for that zipper?

Daniel tossed the plastic wrapper from the cheese onto the counter. He suddenly realized he was too far from the gun. Daniel hurried to the console table and picked up the revolver. His hand shook less than it had been. Food was helping. Daniel went back to the fridge and opened the door. He glanced at the contents before looking up at the sunroom. He pulled out a bag of hot dog buns and shut the fridge door. Daniel ate the buns plain, as is, as he paced.

At first he thought he had imagined it. He was so tired from hours of pacing that eventually he settled onto the couch. His head bobbed a few times and he shook his head briskly from side to side to clear the cobwebs. That was when the center zipper flared to light. Daniel stared in disbelief for several seconds before accepting what he saw. He'd lost the gun. No, he'd set it on the console table again. Even as he reached for it the zipper blinked shut. Daniel pointed the gun at the zipper, hand trembling. Daniel frowned. Why hadn't she come through? He watched and waited, gun in hand pointing at the zipper until his hand trembled so badly he had to lower the gun to the arm of the couch.

Daniel sat and thought for a long time, staring at the sunroom, evaluating every minute since Miss Sorority Girl and Mr. Suit stepped into this house. She had a key that opened multiple zippers. The realization stunned him. That was the only logical explanation. He needed that key. Not only could he not risk her having it but he wanted it. One key. Maybe it opened even more zippers. Maybe it opened all the zippers. The thought of one key to open all the zippers filled him with so much excitement that he almost couldn't breathe. No more lugging around all the keys he would need. Some were small and portable but some were awkward to carry around with him, like the porcelain dog statue. He had to have that key.

Daniel picked up the new meteorite and walked with purpose into the sunroom. The center zipper flared to light. He took a deep breath, squared his shoulders, and stepped through, gun in hand. Just as the sudden downslope of the hill had caught Tabitha and Simon off guard, Daniel was caught off balance and almost fell flat on his face as he came out of the zipper. He stumbled to his knees then rolled to the side. The zipper flared out. Daniel lay on the grass, chest heaving but otherwise immobile. It only took a minute before the sound of voices drifted up the hill and he knew to expect company.

Chapter Eight

Something woke her. Tabitha lay still, instantly alert that something was out of place. The room was dark. She could feel Dane's warmth and hear his breathing. He was fast asleep so it was not his coming to bed that woke her. Someone coughed. The sound came from the corner of the room. Heart pounding, Tabitha slowly raised her head to look in the direction the sound had come from. The room was shadowed but she could still see that the corner was empty. Dane stirred while she was digging in her purse for a flashlight.

"Did you hear it?" Tabitha asked.

"I heard something," he said.

Dane sat up and took the flashlight out of her hand, then got off the bed and did a detailed search in the corner where the sound had come from but shook his head. "If there's a speaker I can't see it." He clicked off the flashlight and sat down on the edge of the bed. "Even if this house was big enough to hold a secret passage, which it isn't, who would need a secret passage in the loft of a hut?"

"Could it have been an echo from below?" Tabitha asked.

Dane shrugged. "Hard to believe that but there doesn't seem to be another explanation."

Tabitha stared where darkness hid the shuttered window. "A different world," she whispered. What if there was another zipper right there in that room? It was strange to think that someone could step out of thin air with no warning. She shook her head. It couldn't have been another zipper opening or they would have seen it.

Dane looked at her sharply. "What?"

"You asked what world this is. It's a different world. I have a feeling we need to always remember that."

Dane nodded. He settled back on the bed, locking his hands under his head with his elbows pointing toward the ceiling. "You're right. They're just men like anywhere else. It could be easy to forget we aren't home." He paused before saying the last word, as if he had to search his mind for the right word.

They managed to fall asleep again but Tabitha had disjointed dreams and woke bleary-eyed to a room only dimly lighter with dawn. She lay still for a few minutes, thinking. A feeling of curiosity tickled her mind. It could be an adventure. It could be a glorious adventure beyond her wildest imaginings. Well, it was already beyond her wildest imaginings. They would ride to the city that day and there she would find her answers. At the back of her mind she would still rather go home first but she was gradually coming to realize that this could be the grandest adventure of her life. Tabitha had had time to absorb the situation and the urge to go right back through the zipper was fading. Tabitha had stepped through a beam of light into another dimension, another world, a land where rules were different. It was a grown-up cattle drive. It was a grown-up barge ride down a river into the unknown. How could she not take advantage of the situation and explore?

Suddenly Tabitha was impatient to get to the city. She would just pay careful attention along the way to make sure she could get back on her own again if necessary. Tabitha felt in her pocket for the tektite that she kept in the Altoids tin, the one with the zircon inside. It might be a good idea to take out some insurance and hide a piece here, near the zipper, just in case something happened along the way which resulted in misplacing her possessions. Tabitha looked around the room thoughtfully. Then again, what if there were people living here again by the time they got back to the village? How would she explain needing to get inside their bedroom? She needed a secure but accessible hiding spot. But where?

Tabitha ran her tongue over her teeth as she stepped out of the hut into a briskly cool morning. Though she had dental floss and had used it her teeth were sorely in need of a good brushing. The quick sponge bath in the latrine had not really left her feeling refreshed either, just slightly less grungy. Hopefully they would be able to clean thoroughly once they reached the city. No one had discussed what they would do for toiletries and fresh clothing while embarking on this exploration of this dimension. They would be at the mercy of someone's generosity because they had no money for this dimension either.

There was already quite a bit of activity in the village's common grounds. Several King's Men were saddling horses and checking packs. Captain Olin was inspecting the hooves of a horse when Tabitha spotted him. A King's Man was holding the reins to three horses. Captain Olin checked the hooves of all three horses, occasionally scraping the dirt from inside the hoof with a knife. He dropped the last leg and straightened, sliding the knife back into a holster on his belt before gesturing at Tabitha to join him.

Captain Olin handed Tabitha the reins to a dapple gray mare. "Some of my men need to stay behind with me to watch the area for a time. Ye be borrowing their horses," he said. "Her name is Dahlia."

Tabitha stroked the mare's velvety soft nose, being careful not to tickle her. Horse's noses are remarkably sensitive. It impressed her that he knew the mare's name and had felt it important enough to share the information with her. "Hello, Dahlia," she said. The mare's ears pricked forward at hearing her name.

Captain Olin handed the reins of the other two horses he had been inspecting to Simon and Dane. Simon gave his horse a baleful glare. The horse stood docile but its ears kept flicking forward, sideways, backwards and it was rolling its eyes at Simon. Dane stood with his back to his mount, reins in his hands, studying the area around them but mostly interested in watching Captain Olin.

Dane looked very thoughtful. They had not found Thomas so Captain Olin had decided to leave men behind to keep searching and to guard the area but he wanted to get them to the city without any more delay.

Tabitha leaned toward Dane. "Is it sensible to send us away?" she asked in a low voice.

"Sensible?" Dane asked, clearly confused.

"Is that how the FBI would handle it?"

Dane frowned thoughtfully. "Well, it makes sense to control the situation. Getting civilians out of the way is the first step, yes." He studied her thoughtfully. "Do you think differently?"

Tabitha shrugged. "Nothing makes sense. I thought you'd know if it made sense."

Dane nodded. "You feel guilty, leaving to what you perceive as safety while these men stay to deal with Thomas, an armed and dangerous lunatic who you feel responsible for turning loose on this world."

"Did you get a degree in psychology?" Tabitha snapped. Dane grinned. The thing was, he was right. She knew that she wasn't responsible for Daniel's behavior. Yet she couldn't help but feel that it was her fault that he was here. Putting as much distance between them as possible sounded wonderful. It wasn't as if she could do anything about him, so staying made no difference.

"First of all, he had the knowledge of this place. Second, you have no control over his actions. You're the victim here. Do you think you could solve the problem by turning yourself over to him? It would make no difference."

Tabitha nodded. It sounded good coming from Dane but she still felt what she felt. If she had done things differently none of this would have happened. If she hadn't taken the meteorite to him he wouldn't have had it to open the zipper. If she hadn't gone back to his house with Agent Bismarck they wouldn't be trapped in this dimension with Dane's life being threatened due to a made up marriage to her. If she hadn't talked Dane into trying the key to open the zipper Daniel wouldn't have known that they had a key and wouldn't have come through looking for them. So, no matter what Agent Dalton Ellis said to her, she knew she was responsible for a lot of what was going on around them.

Tabitha led her horse to a mounting block in the center commons and climbed into the saddle. The stirrups were too long and one of the King's Men adjusted the length once she was mounted and then visited Dane and Simon to check their stirrups once they were mounted. Tabitha squirmed a bit in the saddle. It wasn't like a Western saddle with its high cantle and large horn yet it wasn't quite like the small, flat English style saddle either. It felt good to be in the saddle even if it was an unfamiliar saddle. She hadn't ridden in years.

Captain Olin had already vanished without a formal farewell, leaving them and their six man escort in the yard. The King's Men were very thorough, checking and rechecking the horses and tack before mounting and settling into place around the trio. Though the six men ranged widely in height and build, their expressions were cut of the same cloth, very determined and serious.

Two King's Men led the group out of town, with two men flanking them and two men bringing up the rear. Watching poor Simon bounce on his horse's back, struggling to keep from sliding off, Tabitha wanted to tell the King's Man that a one man escort would have been enough. They wouldn't be outracing any escort. Dane settled into his seat like a veteran rider. The group picked up the pace once they were out of the village. The gentle canter actually seemed to help Simon and he settled into his seat. Settling in this case meant that he gripped the saddle with both hands, arms rigid, reins dangling but stayed center in the saddle this way. Tabitha's over-sized purse bounced against her side. Tabitha slid the strap over her head and pushed it in front of her.

It wasn't really possible to hold a conversation while they cantered along the cobblestone road, the shod hooves ringing quite loudly. This left Tabitha to her own thoughts. She was off on an adventure. It had gotten off to a rocky start, true. Who would guess that there were zippers to another dimension? Not her. Multiple zippers existed, actually. Daniel Thomas had stolen that knowledge from others and stolen those twelve houses from others. That meant that others had known. Or knew. Daniel Thomas was a lunatic but he pushed people through zippers instead of killing them. That meant that whoever he had stolen from was probably still alive somewhere in another dimension.

Tabitha periodically checked her surroundings. She had to be able to find her way back to the village. So far the cobblestone road wound its way through relatively featureless terrain. Following the road back would be the simplest way to return but she had to stay sharp in case she had to find the village overland. They were traveling northeast out of the village. Well, her northeast. Tabitha still didn't know if she was right or not about which direction was which. Miles raced by as the sun climbed. It was still early morning. The feeling of homesickness faded with each passing mile.

So, if Daniel pushed everyone through zippers, she wondered if he had pushed everyone through who had known about the zippers. That seemed likely. She wondered where. So many questions popped up. His little note in the meteor case had listed Dallas. If he pushed someone through in Dallas was it the same world as this? The Vikings had been only two or three feet away from this dimension in Daniel's sunroom. Daniel had also said that he had twelve houses and that there were zippers in public buildings. Yes, a person would need a map.

Tabitha looked over at Dane. He looked nice riding on a horse. He rode well, relaxed in the saddle, settling in with the horse's motion instead of fighting against it. His long, lean legs were angular, all hard planes and muscle. Dane didn't have the same shaved haircut as the first two agents she had met and it was just long enough to wave in the wind as they rode. The sun brought out threads of copper threaded in the dark brown. She hadn't noticed before how wide his shoulders were or how capable and strong his hands gripping the reins were.

Tabitha shook her head. It wasn't a good idea to get mixed up with feeling things for him she shouldn't be feeling. There was no denying that there was a mutual attraction but it wasn't a good idea to let it get personal. A bond forged in adventure was doomed to fade into nothing once the adventure's adrenaline faded. She was sure she had read that somewhere. Tabitha had other things to concentrate on. Dane distracted her, made her brain forget to work, and worse of all, he brought to the surface some hidden frustration from deep inside her that she didn't understand. Yet being with him made her feel safe and secure as well.

Tabitha had dated her fair share of men, some creeps and some genuine great guys who just hadn't inspired the feeling that they were the one. It had been a few years now since she had met anyone who perked her interest enough to date him. Tabitha did a mental count. Wow. Two years since her last date. She hadn't done it on purpose. There had been no conscious thought to stop looking for her soul mate. It had just happened. First one project then another project sucked up her time and before she knew it years had passed.

Watching Dane as they cantered along a cobblestone road in another dimension surrounded by men wearing uniformed yellow ponchos who held them in protective custody because some group was trying to kill her she was pretty sure that now was not the right time to get romantically involved with a man. Sure there were sparks flying but when the adrenaline of the situation slowed back to normal would they feel the same way? As much as she would like to pursue a relationship with the man she decided that it wasn't the right time. He was off limits. She would be off limits. They would be off limits. Dane would just let her down and hurt her and go his own way anyway. The last thing she needed right now was the distraction of a budding relationship and dealing with the rejection when it didn't work out, which she knew it wouldn't work out.

They had ridden for nearly an hour and the escort had slowed them to a walk to give the horses a break when Dane edged his horse up to her. "Everything all right?" he asked.

"Actually, yes," she said, meaning it. "How about you? Are you learning anything important yet?"

Since they had done nothing but ride that morning there had been nothing to learn. He nodded and shrugged. "I guess. You sure you're all right? You haven't said anything for over an hour. You sure you're all right?"

"I just don't have anything to say," Tabitha said. Her chin rose. "I can be quiet sometimes, you know."

"Aha," Dane said, giving her a sideways glance that spoke volumes on what he thought about that concept.

Suddenly there was a shout and one of the escorting King's Men flanking them slumped in the saddle. Within seconds chaos reigned.

The steady whoosh of arrows combined with thunks, shouting, and a screaming horse. Men poured out of the trees, some on foot, some on horseback. Only two King's Men were still sitting upright in the saddle. Seeing the number of attackers surrounding them they pulled swords from scabbards attached to their saddles and dropped them to the ground. This world's version of yield, obviously.

Dane had moved in front of her protectively when the attack began but as they were surrounded he and Simon maneuvered their horses so that they sandwiched her between them. Tabitha felt the blood pounding in her ears. Tabitha was really coming to hate this world. Her fleeting sense of adventure had evaporated. The government could take her key. She didn't care. If she escaped with her life she was going home and never going through a zipper again.

The attacking party encircled them but did nothing more. One man stepped up and slit the screaming horse's throat. Tabitha shuddered. She felt ready to break into tears but fought the urge. The ring of attackers parted slightly and a young man and an older woman stepped through on foot. The woman grabbed the reins of the horse Dane rode and looked up at him, then Tabitha and finally Simon.

'You will come with us," the woman said bluntly. "Cooperation is appreciated."

"We'll explain everything but first we must get to a place of safety," the young man said more warmly, glancing at the woman. "You must trust that we mean you no harm."

Tabitha almost blurted out the obvious but managed to hold her tongue. No harm? They had harmed two men and killed a horse. Obviously they felt that harming King's Men meant nothing. They had to be mother and son or related closely somehow. The woman was tall, blond, in her forties, wearing old, worn Levi jeans and spoke with a slight Georgian accent. No heavy Old England dialect coming from her cold, narrow lips. The young man was of a height with her, in his twenties, and wore khaki cargo pants and a blue hooded sweatshirt. They had the same square jaw and droop-lidded blue eyes. They were normal!

"Who are you?" Simon asked, in his coldest agent voice.

The woman gave him a tight smile. "Your new guardians. Do we have your cooperation?"

"Numbers guarantee cooperation. Unless you mean to let us go now that you've liberated us," Dane said.

"Good," the woman said. "We'll make better time if you're not bound."

The line of men ringing them parted again for a man on horseback leading two horses. The woman ignored the last half of Dane's comment and the two swung up into their saddles and rode closer. "We must not waste time." The woman looked over her shoulder and barked some orders. Tabitha edged her horse closer to Dane. The young man might be trying to be polite but the rest of the group stared in open hostility. Two leering men made a joke about her many uses on a blanket. The woman in charge glared at them and they fell silent but once her back was turned one of the men made kissing motions at Tabitha. Then leering man noticed Dane and whatever he saw there stopped the hassling and he melted into the crowd. The group quickly split into several groups, all heading out in different directions.

Simon and Dane exchanged glances and nodded in some form of silent communication. Simon rode slightly ahead of Tabitha to her left and Dane dropped to a position slightly following her on her right. The remaining group around them numbered about twenty people after the split. The woman in charge rode in the lead. They rode back along the cobblestone road for several miles then ten people continued on the road while their group left the road, heading south. Tabitha was impressed. It would take a miracle for Captain Olin to find their route out of all the groups. Quite effective. She studied the area they rode through, worried about finding her way back. They rode for over an hour before slowing and entering a copse of trees.

"You may dismount,' the young man said. "Rick will keep an eye out. We're high enough to see anyone approach in time to escape."

Tabitha slid out of the saddle, grimacing when her feet hit the ground. Horseback riding was a muscle stiffening experience for someone who didn't spend a lot of time in the saddle. Around her everyone else was dismounting as well. Simon's face was almost comical when he dismounted and attempted to use his own legs. No matter how good of shape someone is in, riding a horse when not used to it brings an awareness of muscles otherwise silent.

Dane frowned as he looked around. "What is the plan?"

"Introductions," the woman said. "I am Kate. This is my nephew, Jackson. Rick is out watching for pursuit. These are James, Cal, Erin, and Robert. Now you. Who are you and how did you get here?"

"Agent Dalton Ellis," Dane said. The woman actually winced.

"Agent Simon Ritter," Simon said. The woman sighed. Tabitha made a face at Agent Bismarck. She knew he had made up Bismarck but he could have told her his real name once they found Dane.

"Tabitha Anderson," Tabitha said.

"Ah," Kate said, showing interest. The woman nodded. "You stumbled into the weasel." At Tabitha's confused look, Kate said, "Daniel Thomas."

"You know about Thomas?" Tabitha was dumbstruck.

"We have to go," Rick said, emerging from the trees.

Jackson frowned. "They found our trail already?"

"They're almost to the ambush spot. No sense risking it."

"You can open the zipper?" Kate asked Tabitha. Tabitha didn't know whether to answer or not and hesitated. "We know you're a purple halo," the tall woman said, leaning over Tabitha in an almost threatening manner. Jackson touched her elbow and she eased back slightly.

"That's a purple halo?" Tabitha asked in surprise. "It's the key making me purple?"

Dane grimaced. The woman was just too blunt and honest for her own good. Tabitha just told them she had a key, a key that they were willing to kill for and didn't necessarily have anything to do with any purple halo. Until Tabitha blurted out that she had a key no one in this group had actually known it.

"We have no time for this," Rick said. "You ride. He could send out scouts to follow each trail. I'll stay behind and keep watch."

Kate nodded. "It's true, we have little time now. I was hoping we'd have more time with him occupied at the village. We'll have to discuss more later."

Tabitha's legs protested when she mounted her horse. Her stomach grumbled in hunger. Tabitha kept her discomfort to herself. Staying alive seemed to be more important. Of course, if she didn't eat soon she would simply fall out of the saddle but she decided that if they could do it she could do it. They rode east out of the trees. Gradually they turned north. Eventually they reached the cobblestone road again, following it east only a few miles before turning north again. At least they still seemed to be heading in the direction of Minneapolis, Tabitha realized. The pace slowed, more for the horses than for any other reason. Horses could only be pushed to such a hard pace for so long.

Jackson passed out pieces of beef jerky and flat bread and they ate as they rode. Tabitha smelled the beef jerky first and tried to take just a small nibble to taste it but bouncing along on horseback made it difficult to be delicate so she took a healthy bite on the side of her mouth and tugged until she managed to pull off a piece with her teeth. Other than being overly chewy it tasted quite good.

Tabitha didn't see how Captain Olin could possibly find them out of all the groups leaving the ambush site and after all the backtracking onto the road. She wasn't sure yet who was the best group to be with either. Just because these people seemed to be rescuing them and seemed to be from the normal world didn't mean they were any safer. Tabitha wanted to know if this was the group Ravin belonged to and if they weren't, did that mean yet another group would be attacking her. They knew about the key. They knew about the zippers. They knew about Thomas.

Tabitha sighed. It wasn't likely that they were going to just let them go, so they weren't any different than Captain Olin. What was it with these people and their need to be guardians to them? First Captain Olin had said he was protecting them and now these people said they were protecting them. If Kate's group was protecting them from the other group, Olin's group, that meant that someone was trying to hurt them that they needed protecting from. So which group was actually doing the protecting and which group was actually doing the something they needed protecting from?

Kate decided at last to make camp along a river bank, the steep sides offering some protection. The sun was near the horizon and Tabitha felt ready to fall out of the saddle she was so exhausted.

Under other circumstances she would find the setting of the campsite quite beautiful and calming. Years of rising and falling river levels had leveled out a terrace of sorts, easily reached by a natural ramp but not accessible otherwise except by that narrow strip of grassy land forming the ramp. They had a dirt wall lined with trees behind them, the river in front of them, and across the river another dirt wall lined with trees.

When Tabitha dismounted her muscles were stiff and sore, even worse than the first time. She paced, trying to loosen her muscles. Tabitha didn't know if she would be able to mount a horse again in the morning, let alone ride. Cal built a fire between several densely foliaged trees, picking the driest wood possible to avoid creating heavy, dark smoke. Everyone seemed to hold their breath until he had a pot of coffee ready to pour. Tabitha smiled. Some things were definitely the same in both worlds. While the coffee simmered Cal had thrown together a stew. As soon as the stew was done Cal banked the fire.

Tabitha continued to pace as she ate, scooping up the stew with pieces of flat bread. It was bland but filling. No one talked, each concentrating on eating and enjoying their coffee. Rick, the man who had stayed back to watch for pursuit, had been short and dark-haired. Cal was an older man, missing some teeth and heavily lined creases made his face sag. He had a full head of silver hair. Robert was young, even younger than Jackson, with a wide-eyed look about him and thick black hair. Erin was heavyset and at first Tabitha couldn't decide if Erin was male or female. It was when he spoke for the first time that she felt firmly he was male. His face was smooth and there wasn't anything about him that really stood out as feminine attributes nor male attributes. It was quite an interesting assortment of people. Since Erin wasn't a woman that meant Kate was the only woman in the group. Tabitha wondered who they were.

It was Simon who took the initiative. "So you freed us from the King's Men. Does that mean we are free to go our own way?"

"Where would you go?" Kate asked, not looking up from her bowl as she continued to eat her stew.

"Oh, we hoped to visit the city while in the area," Simon said lightly. "Maybe take in a show while were in town. See the touristy spots."

Tabitha stared at Simon. He was making a joke. She hadn't thought he had it in him. Kate didn't seem to find it amusing however.

"I think that means we are no longer the guests of the King's Men but are now the guests of the Cleaners," Dane said. "Would that be a fair assumption?" he asked Kate.

She shrugged. "Since we're going in the same direction it doesn't really make sense to split up at this point." She stared up at him for a minute, eyes narrowed in speculation. "What do you know about Cleaners?"

"Only what the captain said upon meeting, that there is a group in the area called Cleaners."

Tabitha was tempted to tell them that she just wanted to go home, not to the city, but knew it would be pointless. Instead she decided to go to the heart of the matter. "So are you some secret group who uses the zipper?" Tabitha asked.

"The weasel tell you that?" Jackson asked from behind her.

"Not exactly," Tabitha said, looking over her shoulder at him. It was uncomfortable talking to them separated. For some reason she felt Kate was in charge and wanted to direct her conversation to the woman. "But he hinted at a group or organization and said he had to take care of them. Since he pushed us through it makes sense he did the same to you. You're from our world, right?" No one responded to her question. She pushed ahead. "Two things though. He couldn't open this zipper before getting my meteorite so how did you get here? And if all those people Captain Olin talked about have purple halos how come you can't use them?"

"You ask a lot of questions," Kate said. She set down her empty bowl on the ground next to her and leaned back on her elbows, crossing her ankles. "So you gave Thomas a meteorite that opened this zipper? Why would you do that?"

"Uh, because until he pushed us through I had no idea such a thing existed," Tabitha said, getting irritated.

Kate inclined her head. "I guess that makes sense. There seems to be a lot you don't know."

"There seems to be a lot you know that you're not telling," Tabitha said in irritation, though she muttered it under her breath.

"Some mutual trust is needed," Dane said, crouching on his heels beside Kate. "Tell us what this is all about and we may be able to work together to a solution."

"Well, Agent Man, what is your solution?" Jackson asked.

"Knowing what is going on is the first step. We seem to have landed in the middle of something. What have we stepped into?"

"That's an understatement," Tabitha said with a snort. Everyone looked at her, Dane with a grimace, hoping she would choose that moment to be quiet. He was to be disappointed. "Well, we came out of a zipper, to our surprise finding ourselves in another world, and immediately someone tried to kill me. Then this Olin guy holds us prisoner to take to the king for no reason. Then Thomas comes through the zipper trying to kill us. Now you kidnap us and we don't know your intent either. I just want to go home."

Kate and Jackson exchanged glances. "Thomas is here?" Kate asked.

"Olin? He is king," Jackson said at the same time.

Around them everyone started talking at once. Tabitha looked from face to face but couldn't keep track of everyone at once and quickly tuned out all of them. Kate held up her arm and the mutterings died down fairly quickly.

"We need to sleep on this," Kate said. Hearing that Daniel Thomas was on this side of the zipper agitated everyone. "Once we reach Holmstad we'll decide what to do."

Dane gritted his teeth, shaking his head at Tabitha. She always had to open that mouth of hers. Tabitha shrugged. He may feel like she had interfered with his line of questioning but she had learned something important. First, she didn't trust these people. Someone had tried to kill her and unless there was yet another renegade group running around these woods it was someone who belonged to this group. Tabitha was tired of people trying to kill her and kidnapping her. In her way she had given them fair warning. Tabitha didn't trust them and in her mind she had just made that clear.

"So you're not the leader of the Cleaners? You need to take us to someone who can make a decision?" Dane asked casually.

Irritation and anger made Kate's nostrils flare. "You keep calling us the Cleaners. You don't know anything. Keep your mouth shut before you say the wrong thing," Kate snarled at Dane. She glared at Tabitha next. "Our group has changed. Ravin wasn't trying to kill you. If he had been trying to kill you he wouldn't have missed. We want you alive."

Tabitha nodded thoughtfully. Kate wasn't the one who had felt that arrow a mere inch away from her skull. If she hadn't slipped right then that arrow would not have only caught a few strands of her hair but would have hit her instead. That meant that Ravin was a part of this group. That meant that this group was not helping them. She had enough information now to know that whatever their agenda, this group did not have her good will in mind.

It was a miserable night. Tabitha had been given a wool blanket that smelled of horse and wet dog. There might have also been some goat odor mixed in with the rest of the odors nestled deep into the wool. Wearing the same sweaty clothes for the second night in a row kept her chilled all night despite the blanket and she shivered as she tried to sleep. Dane had placed his blanket next to her and sometime in the night he pulled her close to his hard form. Within minutes of being wrapped in his warmth she relaxed and fell asleep for a solid undisturbed hour. Tabitha woke up, needing to relieve herself, and slipped away from Dane. No one challenged her as she made her way to the far edge of the campsite toward the river but she was aware of the guard posted on the natural ramp though she could only see the silhouette of a body.

Tabitha stood on the outskirt of the camp near the river, staring out into the darkness to what she thought was south. Dane and Simon still wanted to explore. Would she be abandoning them if she just left? Maybe not, yet it still felt wrong. They were in it together. They wouldn't abandon her. That was one thing she was certain of in this whole mess. Tabitha moved closer to a tree for some privacy. When she finished she zipped her pants and turned and saw the guard watching her. In the dark she wasn't sure if it was Jackson or Cal. Luckily the dark meant he hadn't seen anything more than that she had had to relieve herself.

Tabitha carefully made her way back to her blanket, snuggling up against Dane's warmth. She woke with Dane shaking her shoulder after what felt like only ten minutes of sleep though the sky was now a slate gray at the horizon, heralding morning's pre-dawn cast and the birds were doing their pre-dawn chatter. They were always so loud the hour or so before the sun rose. It had always been a mystery to her why birds welcomed the day so loudly. They could sleep in if they wanted.

"Five more minutes," she mumbled, pulling the blanket over her head.

"Now," Dane said firmly, pulling the blanket off her.

Tabitha sat up and rubbed the sleep from her eyes. Her head felt like a giant felted ball of wool. It also felt like someone had beat her with a fish bat while she slept. Tabitha stretched protesting muscles. She ran her tongue over her teeth. She could use a shower and fresh clothes. Luckily she still had dental floss and gum in her bag and she flossed while she tried to adjust to being awake. When Dane asked if she had enough to share she handed him a small travel container of floss. Actually, it was the sample floss from the dentist. Whenever they gave her the little containers she stuck them in her purse. They were quite handy.

"Do you have a plan?" she asked Dane, popping some gum into her mouth.

"For now we're relatively safe," Dane said, glancing around. Silent forms moved slowly about the campsite. "I think the best thing is to go along and see what this is all about."

"Of course you do," Tabitha muttered. "We haven't been killed yet."

"That's the spirit," Dane said brightly.

Chapter Nine

Tabitha glared at him. How could she ever have thought he was attractive? He was irritating and annoying and not cooperating in her getting what she wanted. He knew that she just wanted to go home and yet he continued to drag her deeper into this mess. Well, in all fairness, now that the last of sleep was leaving her head more clear, she had to admit that Dane was getting dragged along as well. There really hadn't been anything he could do differently up to this point, except maybe to start shooting his gun at everyone. That probably wouldn't be a good thing.

Kate came and crouched beside them, offering them flat bread and dried meat. "Sorry, no fire this morning. But we should reach Holmstad this afternoon and we'll have a hot meal then."

"Dane here seems interested in adventures," Tabitha said, taking the food. "Me, I'm more the prefer not to get killed type. Everyone here seems to want to kill me. I have a key to get home. I could find my way to the village and just go home and let you people have your adventures."

Kate nodded. "I suppose it's possible. But I can't let you do that."

"Why not?"

"You're right, there is a group who have maintained the secret of the zippers. This one happens to be a secure world, which is why Thomas didn't find the key. Until you inadvertently gave it to him. But first things first. You know the location of the zipper and you have a key. You are our way out of here as well."

"So you're really trapped here?"

"Of course. Didn't we already tell you that?"

"Not exactly," Tabitha said slowly, trying to remember that topic coming up but not remembering it. In fact, everything she said seemed to go against what she had said the night before. Tabitha sort of felt like the woman was just telling her just what she, Tabitha, had suggested as a possible scenario the night before.

"Once we reach Holmstad we can gather everyone and leave together," Kate said. She smiled. "We will have you to thank."

Tabitha nodded as she said, "Okay." Tabitha felt like she'd just had a brush with a used car salesman. Tabitha decided right then that not only did she not trust Kate, she also didn't like the woman.

Kate smiled again and walked over to help Jackson with the horses. Tabitha stared after her. Why hadn't she just said that to begin with? Because it wasn't true. She shook her head. No matter how much she tried, people were too complicated. Lies clouded everything. Lies and secrets. If people were just honest it would make everything so much more straight-forward. Why go farther away from the zipper if their goal was to go through the zipper? It made no sense.

"You don't believe her?" Dane asked.

"Well, it would just make more sense if she had said that from the start," Tabitha said, gaze on Kate as she talked to Jackson. He stood with his head bowed, Kate leaning in close to tell him something for his ears only. "But she didn't."

"You're right. Don't trust her," Dane said. "She's not who she seems."

Tabitha switched her gaze to Dane. "What do you mean?"

"She doesn't belong to a secret group maintaining the zippers," Dane said.

"But she knew," Tabitha said. "She seems quite sincere."

Dane shook his head. "She isn't who she says she is."

"Is anyone?" Tabitha asked, staring at Dane. She turned her gaze to Kate. "No, she does seem quite sincere but I don't believe anything she said just now. She's changed her story three times in the three times she's had a conversation with us. And Ravin missed. He didn't try to miss. He missed."

"If she was with a secret group maintaining zippers she wouldn't need you," Dane said. He looked down at Tabitha, trying to figure out how to say what he wanted to say without upsetting her. "It would be best to not share any information with anyone, even if they give the impression that they know already. For example, it would have been better to not tell anyone that you have a key."

Tabitha nodded. "I know. I forget sometimes that people lie."

Dane scraped his thumbnail against his whisker covered chin as he considered her response. Tabitha always surprised him. Dane forgot sometimes that people told the truth. Tabitha realized that there was something about the scruffy look that made her knees weak. He looked dangerous at that moment. Instead of intimidating her it made her feel quite stimulated. Dane looked down at her with shadowed eyes and she saw something in those eyes, a sharp intelligence with purpose. There were many more layers to Dane than had at first met the eye. Tabitha hoped that it meant he had a plan. It would be nice if someone had a plan.

Dane felt lost as he looked into Tabitha's eyes. Everything around them melted away into the distance. He looked away. "We should get going."

"Why are we still going with her if she isn't to be trusted?" Tabitha asked. "You and Simon could take them."

Dane took her hands and pulled her to her feet. Once she was standing he kept hold of her hands, staring down at her intently. "Trust me, if I could take you back to that zipper and see you to your doorstep and come back and finish this without you I would. But I can't. At this point we can't even hope to get to that zipper without any intention of coming back."

"So it's not just a matter of wanting to explore now?" Tabitha asked.

"We're being held prisoner and to try to escape would mean deaths, possibly ours," Dane said. "That's what you should keep in mind as to what is going on."

Dane kissed her lightly on the lips, pressing light kisses on a path to her ear. While she leaned against him on wobbly legs he whispered against her ear. "Trust me, Tabitha. Trust Olin with your life but not your secrets. Trust Simon. Trust no one else. I don't know what these people are after but they are not rescuing us. They have an agenda that is not with your best interests in mind."

Before Tabitha had time to absorb what he said he stepped back and Cal was standing there, just a few feet away. Cal stared dolefully, coughed, looked away, shrugged to himself, and looked back at them with dour eyes. Tabitha rubbed her chin, already pink from whisker burn. She could feel her cheeks turning pink as well but that wasn't from whiskers rubbing her sensitive skin.

In a low voice meant for Dane but she knew Cal could hear just fine she said, "No more kissing until you shave."

Dane grinned. "Or it grows out long enough to soften up?"

Tabitha groaned. "Don't tell me you are going to grow a beard."

"It's time to go," Cal said. He looked very impatient with the whole intimate moment thing.

Dane nodded. "One more minute." He waited until Cal grudgingly moved away then turned back to Tabitha. "Any chance you have a needle or pin in that giant bag?"

"Pin or needle?" She shook her head. "No. Certain."

"Thought I could make a rough compass," Dane mumbled more to himself.

"Compass? Oh, I'll bet there's one on my GPS unit."

Dane stared at her. "GPS unit? You have a GPS unit?"

Tabitha looked up from digging in her purse. "Well, it won't do any good. No satellites. Which is why I didn't bother using it. But I forgot about the compass. It should be independent of the satellites." She pulled out the slim gray plastic electronic device and slid open the lid. She turned with the device in her palm until the digital compass said north. "Hey, I was right," she said in delighted surprise. She pointed. "North." She slid the lid back in place and dropped the device back in her purse.

No satellites. He hadn't thought about that and even hearing her say it, it was hard to let go of something one took so for granted but she was right, the GPS would be totally worthless. Dane nodded. "Good to know. What else have you got in there?" He peered into the dark mystery that was a woman's purse.

"Um, let's see. My smart phone, of course. Kleenex. Oh, my scanner wand. A tape measure. A digital dictionary. Huh, forgot I still had that. An iPod…" Tabitha was cut off by Kate yelling.

"Time to go," Kate yelled, getting impatient. The leader of this group of Cleaners had already mounted her shaggy dun horse.

"We'll have to take inventory when we get a chance," Dane said, looking at her purse with sudden interest.

Tabitha slung her purse over her shoulder and picked up the wool blanket she had used. She gave it a shake to get rid of the bits of grass and dirt, grimacing when that simple action activated warning nerves along stiff, misused muscles, and walked to her horse. Cal took the blanket from her and shoved it into a saddlebag on his horse. Dane cupped his hands and gave her a leg up into the saddle. For a moment Tabitha wondered if her stiff legs would stretch far enough to reach to the other side of the saddle. They did. She settled into her seat, stretching her legs slightly before slipping her feet into the stirrups. Her heeled boots were ideal for riding. At least she had been able to walk though she felt stiff. If they had another day of hard riding it would hit her with force the following day.

This group didn't want to do the stealing of the key but they would take her to someone who could. What a horrible thought. Tabitha had spares. She could just give them a piece and be done with it. It was simply handing them a gift and saying sharing was good. Tabitha looked around the solemn group. It didn't really make sense though. They hadn't even asked. They didn't really need to ask. All they had to do was point some weapon at her and tell her to hand it over and if she didn't they could just use the weapon and take the key. Tabitha shivered suddenly and goose bumps prickled her arms under her sweatshirt.

Kate had said so matter of factly that once they reached Holmstad they would all go through the zipper. Tabitha shook her head. It wasn't realistic to think they were taking her to some arch villain who would rip the key away from her and then toss her in a pit to rot. Tabitha didn't know why they were dragging them through the countryside but she did believe that if they only wanted the key they now knew that she had, they could just take it from her.

Tabitha patted Dahlia's neck. These same people had tried to kill her. Ravin had belonged to them. Now they were awkwardly trying to be chummy and simply wanting her to help them all get home. It really didn't make sense. Not only was she not able to figure out what made these people tick she couldn't even figure out what they were doing. It was the key. The only reason they ambushed the King's Men was to get the key. Yet they hadn't asked for it or asked to use it, so they must plan on taking it by force. Which meant they were very bad people. She frowned. What had Dane said? Ravin had already killed a man. Ravin had been using the field glass to hunt purple halo people.

While at the village Tabitha had taken the crudely shaped heart key from the Altoids tin and hidden it, the first attempt at grinding the tektite into a heart shaped pendant that was a bit rough. It had been a spur of the moment decision. She was glad now that she had done it. Tabitha still had the better heart key around her neck, unfortunately. She wondered if anyone would realize what it was and take it from her. It was too precious to hide it now along the way, plus she had no guarantees that they wouldn't find it if she tried to hide it now. Tabitha still had her watch band to give her the purple halo so supposedly they would never notice. She chewed on her lower lip. If she hid it she would have to come back for it. The key in the village was her ticket home. The heart key around her neck was personal. It was her work mixed with the ticket back through that zipper. Tabitha would wait and see what happened.

Once everyone was mounted Kate led the way up and out of the riverbank terrace. Tabitha followed, glancing over her shoulder. It had been a cozy hiding spot. The rest followed single file, the horses occasionally having to surge to get up the incline. Kate came to an abrupt halt and Tabitha almost rode right into her. There wasn't room on the small incline for more than one horse. Dahlia swerved around the horse in front her, striving to lunge up the rest of the incline, back hooves slipping for a moment as she almost went off the trail. Tabitha let the mare have her head, trusting the animal to know how best to maneuver past the horse blocking the way. Kate swore and grabbed for Dahlia's reins but missed.

"Away. Away!" Kate yelled.

Cal rode past Kate's other side and grabbed at Dahlia's reins but Tabitha dug her heels into the horse's sides and the mare leaped forward, shod hooves digging into the soft earth as she climbed up and up. Captain Olin and over thirty of his men mounted on horseback waited above them, forming a ring about fifty yards away to block their exit beyond the natural earth ramp. Tabitha grinned when she saw him. It was quite a relief to see that weathered face.

"Ye be well?" he asked, riding toward her.

Tabitha nodded, guiding the mare to meet him halfway. Kate came up beside her and this time managed to grab Dahlia's reins. "No. Ye shall not have her."

Tabitha shrugged and dismounted. It was so simple. It was worth it to see the expression on Kate's face as Tabitha simply walked away. Captain Olin dismounted and clapped Tabitha on the shoulder in greeting. He seemed quite happy to see her. Tabitha didn't even give him a bad time about touching a purple halo. Kate dropped the reins and raised her hands in the universal gesture of defeat. Dane and Simon rode up the embankment behind them. Seeing Tabitha and Captain Olin on foot Dane dismounted and walked up to stand beside her.

"Captain Olin," Dane said, bowing his head once in greeting. "Impressive. I didn't expect to see you so soon. You caught Thomas then?" There was an edge to his voice that made Tabitha look at him in surprise.

"No. He went back through his beam of light. I left two men to guard it. Now that we have ye in hand again we can send them some relief. I had a feeling ye would find trouble again." Captain Olin chuckled

"How did you do it?" Tabitha asked, thinking about the backtracking and separate groups. "It's like you had a marker to us."

"Dahlia," Olin said. "She's a unique horse. With unique shoes."

Tabitha frowned, thinking about it. Then it hit her, of course, a unique pattern to the hoof or shoe. Maybe a scratch or two made with a knife to form a V, or something along that line. So simple, yet so effective. All the group's elaborate running around the countryside to lead off pursuit was for nothing. Tabitha laughed.

"Ye be quite brave," Olin said to Tabitha, gesturing at the men behind her.

Tabitha shrugged. "It wasn't bravery. I was just happy to see you."

Olin laughed, along with his men close enough to hear her and able to understand her. "Indeed. I do believe ye not be aware of the man Alfred disposed of. The man who do draw his arrow in your direction."

Tabitha laughed at his joke. He had a strange sense of humor. She turned to see the King's Men wrapping a bandage around Rick's arm before binding his hands behind his back. Tabitha wanted to believe that Rick had just appeared to the King's Men like he was going to shoot her with an arrow when he really wouldn't but even she was coming to realize that more likely Olin wasn't teasing her. These people were quick to try to kill her for some reason.

The rest of the ragtag group ascended from below, bound and escorted by five of the King's Men. Kate was quickly bound to her saddle and a lead attached to her horse's bridle. Simon nodded approval at the efficiency. Tabitha stood next to Captain Olin and watched. How strange to be so excited to be rescued by the King's Men when just the day before she felt like she was their prisoner and had wanted to escape them.

"We ride now," Captain Olin said. "No road. Too much activity on the road these days."

At least he didn't have the kidnappers killed, Tabitha thought as she mounted her horse. She didn't know what she would have done if he had ordered them killed. They had been involved in the attack on the escorting King's Men but hopefully no one had been killed. They set off through the open countryside.

As they rode closer to the city Tabitha began to recognize the area but it was a vague tickle of something familiar yet out of place. It was amazing how much roads and buildings could define a landscape. Yet she knew where she was and the feeling grew stronger with each passing mile.

When they stopped for a short break to rest the horses and eat a light meal of apples, day old biscuits, and seasoned sausage Tabitha tried to talk to Dane. Since the rescue at the river bank he had been quiet and almost sullen. "So what do you expect to find?" she asked.

"What?" Dane asked grudgingly.

"When we get to the city what do you expect to find?" Tabitha said, hoping to be more clear.

Dane shrugged. "I don't know." He watched Captain Olin who was talking to the prisoners. "What do you expect to find?"

Tabitha glared at him. "Why be evasive? I know you're expecting something. This man you and Olin discussed? Maybe something more?"

"Guess we'll see what we see," Dane said. He took a large bite of his apple, the crunch as his white teeth tore off half the apple cutting off further discussion.

Tabitha fumed. Dane had said not to trust anyone yet she hadn't realized he meant to not trust her. Tabitha didn't understand. They were in this together. How could he leave her out of it? She knew that he was expecting something in the city. He was so determined to get there, no matter who was doing the escorting, when they could have just slipped out of the village the first night and gone back through the zipper. It was because he was so determined to go to this city that they were not already home. Snooze was likely thinking she had abandoned him by now. Tabitha hoped the cat was all right. Someone had to realize by now that she was missing and gone to her house and checked on him.

With everything else going on she hadn't had a chance to give much thought to the fact that life was going on as normal back home. Tabitha had a cat left home alone and she had a job that she hadn't shown up to perform. When she did get back it was going to be hard to explain why she hadn't even called in. Tabitha hoped being shoved into a dimensional doorway called a zipper was going to be considered a legitimate absence. Worse was to think it was possible no one would even notice that she hadn't shown up for work for several days.

Tabitha watched Dane staring at Captain Olin. He looked like a man sizing up his competition. Tabitha remembered how happy she had been to see the captain and grimaced. Maybe married couples didn't act that way and she was theoretically married to an FBI agent who probably had a lot of male pride. Captain Olin had been the hero who had rescued her and she had been delighted to see him. Tabitha forgot about the marriage business of this adventurous ordeal. She probably didn't act like a married woman but since she wasn't married and had never been married she didn't know what the rules should be in this situation.

"Sorry," she said. "I forgot we were supposed to be married. Was I not supposed to be happy to see Captain Olin?"

That seemed to be the worst thing to have said. Dane stared at her. A vein in his jaw pulsed. He threw what was left of his apple with enough force that it vanished in the trees and then turned his back on her and walked away. Tabitha was genuinely baffled by his reaction. Simon approached. Tabitha turned to him in confusion.

"What did I do?" she asked.

Simon shook his head. "Hit a nerve, I'd say. I'll talk to him. Don't worry too much. I've been married twenty-five years. This happens all the time. I knew marrying you two off was the right solution."

Simon was smiling as he followed Dane. Tabitha shoved the last bite of her biscuit in her mouth. Even the food was better with the King's Men. Tabitha stretched her legs and arms until Captain Olin gave the order to resume mounts. She mounted and looked around for Dane. He was an irritating, frustrating man and had no right to look so good that he made the breath catch in her throat at the sight of him. Tabitha may have forgotten to act like they were married but if it was that important to him he should be remembering that they were supposed to be married and act accordingly, not get all sulky and go off in a pout. Dane was standing next to Simon but there didn't seem to any talking going on between the two.

The rest of the ride to the city was uneventful. Several times Tabitha stood in the stirrups to stretch her legs. Oh, she was going to pay for these past days in the saddle. They rode through small farmsteads that grew in number the closer they came to the city. Tabitha looked at the small farms in interest. They looked cozy and stress free. Green vegetables grew in plots near the houses and cows or sheep grazed in small pastures. Geese and chickens made a racket, often drifting into the road and squawking in protest when the horses trotted down the road, sending the fowl running off the road. Some people came out of their houses to see who passed. Some people waved. Some people glanced up then went back to their tasks without a second thought to why a group of riders went by.

As the farmsteads got smaller and the area had a more urban feel Tabitha had the feeling of stepping back in time, yet not exactly.

It reminded her of Europe in many ways, yet not exactly. Horses were common but there were also noisy cars rattling down the cobblestone streets with wooden wheels. The drivers clenched the steering wheel and stared straight ahead as they bounced along. Large draft horses pulled trolley cars full of people yet she also saw some steam powered contraption pulling a flatbed piled with crates and canvas bags. Everywhere there were people walking. Simon pointed out a dog cart, a large, shaggy steel gray dog trotted happily along pulling a giant-wheeled buggy with an elderly woman in the seat.

The King's Men escort drew some attention, mostly people clearing the way, a few stopping to stare curiously. Then they rode past and the people went back to their lives. Tabitha peered around the horses and uniformed bodies, trying to see the people who inhabited the city. Their clothing seemed different but it was difficult to see exactly what was so different. It wasn't quite the feel of European fashion nor was it consistent with a hundred years past in the Midwest. Peering between the bodies of the escort and their horses she could only make out that it didn't feel like she was riding into turn of the century Minneapolis despite the rough shape the growing city was in compared to her modern Minneapolis.

Tabitha leaned sideways to speak to Dane. "Does this seem, well, not right to you?"

"What's on your mind?" Dane asked, glancing around them, trying to see something odd that might have caught her attention.

Tabitha shook her head. "I don't know." She straightened in her saddle. "It feels, well, odd."

Simon had also been studying their surroundings with great interest. "I think it's because we want it to be our world. It's not."

Tabitha pulled her lower lip with her teeth out of habit but quickly released when the jarring of the horse's movement threatened to cause bloodshed. "You're right. I'm convinced it's Minneapolis a hundred years in our past. It feels like it should be newly built and it doesn't feel new."

Simon shook his head. "Not this city. As we ride deeper every building is brick. This city has been here awhile."

"Well, how long does it take to build a brick building?" Tabitha said curtly.

"How many brick buildings in Minneapolis?" Dane asked patiently.

Tabitha frowned as she tried to figure out the significance of what he said. Then it hit her. This wasn't a new and growing Minneapolis, intent on evolving into the city she knew. This was a different city with its own plan and purpose and destiny. The roads were located in different places, the houses were established and not built according to any area of Minneapolis that she was familiar with.

"I see," Tabitha said at last, feeling a bit embarrassed that she had snapped at Dane. "It's not Minneapolis a hundred years ago. It's their Minneapolis now."

"It's like a bad dream," Dane said thoughtfully. "The one where there are extra rooms in your home or where something significant takes place but in the wrong location. You recognize the location but know it isn't right for what's going on."

"That's it," Tabitha said in agreement. She looked around. That was exactly it.

Their escort closed in, forcing the three to ride single file between two walls formed of King's Men riders, eliminating the chance to talk any further. The reason for confined quarters became apparent as they rounded a huge stone building at least seven stories high and two city blocks long. Directly in front of them stood a suspension bridge across a river to an island where there prominently sat a castle fortress.

"Good Lord! A castle on Nicollet Island," Simon declared in awe behind her.

Tabitha felt her mouth drop open in amazement. She couldn't force it shut again. The whole island belonged to the fortress. Stone walls circled the island almost right up to the water. This castle wasn't at all a fairytale castle. This castle was a huge beast towering above its perimeter walls, complete with four square towers reaching high above the rest of the roofs, one at each cardinal direction. A guard post sat at the entry to the bridge, a stone shelter that provided shelter in bad weather. Two armed guards stood outside the post. The guards watched the approaching party but made no move to stop them or even question them.

They were expected, Tabitha decided. Maybe the guards at the bridge felt no need to question uniformed King's Men but they didn't look curious or surprised. The leading horses reached the wood bridge. The rhythmic pounding of shod hooves on the thick timbered floor of the bridge mixed with the roar of water. She hated most large bridges. This one swayed under the weight and movement of the large party of mounted horses. Tabitha closed her eyes then quickly changed her mind when closed eyes made the swaying even more strong. Tabitha stared at Dane's back instead. The crossing seemed to take forever but in reality it only took a few minutes. Tabitha was sweating at the nape of her neck by the time they touched solid ground again and she wiped the sweat with the palm of her hand.

Once they were off the bridge and clattering across the short stretch of cobblestone road leading up to the gates of the fortress Tabitha was able to look around instead of just at Dane's broad back. She was surprised that the island didn't sink under the weight of the stone that made the castle. It was quite an impressive sight. The escort continued through the gate at the same steady pace, passing walls eight feet thick. Once they were through the walls Tabitha glanced back. The gates were stone. For some reason she expected to see wood gates, not stone. They were pulled back on rollers that glistened with grease or oil and she suspected they could close those gates in a matter of seconds rather than minutes.

Captain Olin dismounted in front of massive steps leading up to massive double doors, oak bound by iron. The whole courtyard was covered with crushed gravel that crunched under the horse's hooves. At his gesture the three being escorted dismounted as well. Their four horses were collected and soon Dane, Simon, Olin, and Tabitha stood alone. Tabitha watched the rest of the party ride away, Kate and her group still in the center of the King's Men escort. She wondered what would happen to Kate and her group.

Captain Olin led them up the stairs, where the doors opened by unseen hands. Tabitha's neck hurt from looking up and up, almost tripping several times because she wasn't paying attention to where she walked. It was the most amazing thing she had ever seen, most likely compounded by the fact that it was right here, in Minneapolis. The walls towering above them were constructed of hand chiseled stone perfectly fitting together. The inner walls comprising the living quarters were broken by arched windows and sculptures. The main floor had been plastered and presented a pristine white face but the second and third floors had been left bare. The contrast between smooth plaster and rough, weathered stone made the upper floors appear more formidable, lacking the sheen of civilization. A winged urchin carved out of stone perched above the double doors on a ledge, looking down at them in curiosity.

Tabitha met the cold gaze of the stone urchin. It stared at her without passion, without life, yet it felt like it was looking directly at her. It warned, hunched over, weight resting on one knee, its wings spread out almost as if to offer protection for itself. The day had been pleasantly warm, a typical spring day. The temperature dropped noticeably as soon as they passed through the doors.

"I never thought to see a castle in Minneapolis," Dane said in a low, somber voice.

"This isn't our Minneapolis," Simon said quickly. "We need to keep that in front of us." He shook his head. "Though I'll be the first to admit it's throwing off my equilibrium. So much familiar. So much different."

A man waited in the hall, bowing formally at Olin. He wore a pin-striped suit fit for a formal event. His tie was yellow and more closely resembled a scarf than a tie. Tabitha realized it was a cravat. "The king has been informed of your arrival."

"Thank you, Jarvin. Please check on quarters for our visitors. The suite in the north wing would be good," Olin said. He glanced back at Tabitha. "Their baggage seems to have been misplaced. See that they have what they need."

Jarvin bowed again. "Very good, sir."

Tabitha resisted the urge to smell her underarms. "I didn't think about it before but how are we supposed to behave to a king here?" Tabitha asked, pulling on Olin's sleeve.

Olin paused, looking down his long nose at her. "Clarify."

"Well, do we bow, curtsy, call him something specific, or what?"

"Ah," Olin said. He smiled down at her. He started his brisk pace again, saying over his shoulder. "Don't worry. Whatever you do will be fine."

Tabitha raised her eyebrows. She highly doubted that whatever they did would be all right. They were already under informal arrest for just being there. It seemed that proper manners would offset the first strikes against them. The problem was that she didn't want to curtsy when not wearing a dress and didn't even know if that was appropriate here and she definitely had no intention of pressing her forehead to the floor even if it was considered necessary here. Tabitha could present herself as an equal and get thrown in prison. Mostly though she just wanted to be able to perform the proper manners and it wasn't about getting into more trouble.

A thought struck her out of the blue, startling her so much that she stopped in her tracks. No one in their side of the zipper had been aware of the zipper, yet here everyone they encountered seemed to know about the zippers. This had to be the starting point, the origin. Her side was the outpost. These were the people in control. Tabitha started walking again, hurrying up to catch up with the others. Dane gave her a questioning look. She shrugged.

Tabitha stared at Olin's upright back. He purposely misled them, she decided. He also most likely knew the reason for the purple halo. In fact, the purple halo coincided with detecting keys to the zippers. He had to have known that. Right? She stopped in her tracks again. If they had keys on this side of the zipper they should be able to open the zipper anytime. Kate's group was watching the village but wanted to get through the zipper and did not have keys. Tabitha started walking again but slowly. If they already had keys they hadn't used them. Right? Daniel would have noticed an army going through his sunroom. So obviously this dimension was no threat to home. Or maybe they didn't have a key to the zipper. It wasn't going to be a good thing to have a key. But if being a purple halo meant having a key someone should have a key. Tabitha slowed and stopped again. She was missing something.

"Are you shorting out?" Dane muttered, coming up behind her and pressing her back with his hand to get her walking again. "You keep starting and stopping like, well, like something shorting out."

"I'm thinking big thoughts," Tabitha said. "It's not every day one meets a king in another dimension. Especially when I feel like we're going to be in the wrong."

"How can you say we're in the wrong?" Dane asked but she ignored him, attention on Olin's back as he kept walking.

"Are we allowed to freshen up before meeting the king?" Tabitha asked, hurrying to catch up with the Olin.

"Ye be fine," Olin said without slowing.

"Because it doesn't matter because we're prisoners?" Tabitha asked.

Olin rolled his eyes. "No. Now stop stalling."

"Well, I need to use some facilities."

"Ye waited this long, ye can wait five more minutes," Olin said patiently. He stopped at a door. "Because here we be."

Chapter Ten

Without any ceremony Olon opened the door and gestured for them to precede him into the room. Simon and Dane strode forward purposely but Tabitha hesitated at the doorway. Halfway into the room Dane paused and looked back. She shouldn't be surprised by the room considering that they were in a gigantic castle but it was still overwhelming. It was a large, austere room with a ceiling stretching twenty feet at the walls and arching even higher to the center. The polished wood floor shone from waxing. Tabitha decided that if she took off her shoes she could slide quite a ways with stocking feet. If she wasn't tired and stiff and sore she would have done just that. It was so shiny.

Several blue velvet upholstered wood chairs sat in a semi-circle facing a larger set of chairs placed in the opposing direction on a dais about a foot higher than the floor. There was nothing else in the massive room, just some chairs facing chairs on a dais. The chairs on the dais were somewhat bigger, somewhat more padded. The one in the center had a high backrest with semi-precious stone inlaid to form a pattern. Tabitha couldn't quite tell from where she stood what the pattern was meant to be.

Olin put his hand in the small of her back and firmly but gently pushed her into the room so he could shut the door behind them. Tabitha turned to him in surprise. "What happened to not being allowed to touching a purple halo?"

"In this room I can," Olin said with a grin. He looked much more relaxed than she had seen him yet, maybe even happy.

"Methinks you made up the story about not being able to touch a purple halo," Tabitha muttered under her breath. "Methinks ye have more surprises"

Olin looked confused at her words, clearly not having heard her clearly, then he shrugged and strode further into the room. "Remain standing," he instructed as he walked past Simon and Dane. "Stand in the first row, at the center."

Tabitha took up a position beside Dane. Simon stood on Dane's other side. They stood in front of the semi-circle of chairs facing the dais, each positioned in front of a chair. Olin nodded in satisfaction at the arrangement and stepped up on the dais, where he took a position facing them, standing to the right of the throne.

Then they waited. Tabitha quickly grew restive, shifting her weight from foot to foot. For some reason she had expected this king to be joining them immediately. She didn't care if the man was a king, to her it was rude to keep people waiting. Why did he think his time was more valuable than her time? Well, maybe it was more valuable in this case. Still, she hated waiting. Tabitha wanted this over with so she could focus on other things.

As always, Tabitha quickly became distracted with her own thoughts. A king was about to enter the room, a king whose throne sat in the heart of what should be the sprawling metropolis of the twin cities of Minneapolis and St Paul and all their congested, elbow to elbow neighboring towns. Instead of the great metropolis there was a smaller city, yet a city, a city ruled by a king. Quite a different city. This city would never grow up to be her Minneapolis. She wasn't sure if that was necessarily bad. It wasn't a time difference. The difference was much greater than that.

Tabitha replayed the journey through the streets of this Minneapolis. The staring faces had been curious. Some even looked irritated, like their day had been disrupted and they were impatient to get back to their normal routine, not caring at all what brought a large group of riders through the city streets. The one thing she hadn't noticed was surprise. Tabitha pictured someone clearing the streets of all technology. They wouldn't have to do the whole city, just the route they were taking. The thought made her smile. She pictured someone racing through the street giving orders. Move that car. Cover that helio craft. The idea made her chuckle, totally unaware that all the men were looking at her with varying expressions. How absurd to think that they would have to hide anything. It was just different. That was all.

Tabitha pictured asking the king if she could have a pony. No, she wouldn't. But sometimes it was so tempting to give in to the impulse to say the first thing that popped into her head, just to see the reaction. Sometimes the more serious the situation, the more outrageous the ideas that popped into her head. It wasn't insanity. It was a strange sense of humor that popped out at the strangest times. Imagine asking a king for a pony, like a child asking their parent. It wasn't fear of being thought crazy that kept her tongue still. Rather it was knowing that the joke would fall dismally flat when she had to explain why it was funny.

Tabitha was bored. Standing at attention in some boring room waiting on someone to show, never mind that he was a king, was to her a waste of time. She wasn't known for her patience but rather for her lack thereof. When Tabitha got bored her brain actually kicked into a higher gear. Kate's son or nephew had said that Olin was the king. Well, that would be interesting to see why he would stand there waiting for someone else to not show up if that was true.

First, there was Captain Olin. He had ordered that man's death without benefit of any trial and without any hesitation. He said it was King's Justice. Well, if he wasn't the king who was he to declare it was King's Justice? Olin had taken the idea of their coming through a beam of light between two worlds without blinking an eye yet seemed to not care one way or the other about it. He was a mystery to her yet. Tabitha was starting to think though that he never believed that they were from a different dimension.

Then there were the rebels led by Kate who had kidnapped them in order to use the zipper. Tabitha wrinkled her nose in thought then reevaluated that idea. She didn't know what they wanted, actually. She didn't even know where they were from. In a way Tabitha felt like the people in the Cleaner group dressed like people back home were playing dress up in costumes. Bigger surprise was that Kate and her group not only knew about the zipper but knew about Thomas, even knowing who he was. It seemed like someone here at least knew about the zippers. Tabitha blinked.

That was it. Tabitha looked around the room with a critical eye. Tabitha glanced at Dane. Kate's group knew about the zipper but more than that, they believed in the zipper. They wanted the key for criminal purposes. They were not afraid to kill or harm to get the key. The starting point wasn't her dimension. Thomas had stolen the maps and keys from some underground secret society in this dimension. Thomas had stolen them from someone from this dimension and that's why this group wanted to get to him. They wanted those items back. He was using these dimensions for wealth and power and that's what these Cleaners wanted. Tabitha felt certain she had figured out what was going on and she needed to share that information.

Tabitha hissed at Dane under her breath, trying to get his attention. Dane was staring straight ahead. She needed to discuss this with him but she didn't know what Captain Olin would do if she started conversing with Dane. It felt like she was in church, silence mandatory. Tabitha cleared her throat. Dane remained staring straight ahead.

Everything about that village was staged. She felt it to her core. What she didn't know yet was why they had an empty village under surveillance but she had an idea. Both King's Men and Cleaners were watching that village. How else had they all been there right after they had come through the zipper? It was not a ten minute ride to reach the village from either the mysterious Holmstad or from this massive fortress in the heart of the city, so being at the village was a concerted effort.

Tabitha had to admit that now that she was here in the city it wasn't so bad. She was used to embracing change and was up to spur of the moment adventures and had never considered herself as timid, yet maybe this little experience of stepping into another dimension was so far beyond anything she had ever faced in her lifetime that she had reacted with the need to retreat. No, she thought, shaking her head. When they had been in the village she had been bombarded with the strange feeling of homesickness but since leaving there the feeling had faded.

Tabitha glanced at Captain Olin. He was standing like a rock, dark eyes staring at her with interest. She casually let her gaze shift away from him to the throne he stood next to. How could she ever for even a moment forget that flurried few minutes, the sudden whistle of the arrow brushing just past her face, the subtle tug of hair when it caught a few strands before the thunk of arrowhead burying itself deep into the tree trunk? Her head was a lot softer than a tree trunk and that arrow had had no trouble penetrating the hard wood so would have done some serious damage to her. The quick scramble to relative safety on the other side of the tree trunk had already had her adrenaline flowing even before Captain Olin had raised his hand and given that single word command.

Tabitha glanced at Captain Olin again. He still watched her intently, face totally unreadable. That was when she had first felt the driving need to retreat to the safety of her world, when that hand dropped to signal the death penalty and the soldier had stepped up without hesitation to slit the throat of the man who had tried to kill her. So maybe she wasn't a coward after all. Maybe she simply preferred to be in a relatively safer environment where things made sense. This world created so many questions which she had no answers to that it was making her head hurt.

Olin had lied to her about the purple halo also. Tabitha didn't believe that he didn't know that it was given off by a key to the zipper. So what else had he lied to her about? If a man would lie about one thing there was no reason he wouldn't lie about anything else. He had lied about not being able to touch a purple halo.

Olin knew about the zipper and he knew she had a key, if that was the purple halo. Tabitha was surprised he hadn't just taken it from her. At least he didn't know that Simon and Dane had keys as well. Yet. Maybe that was the reason why no one could touch a purple halo. Her face cleared. Of course, that made sense. These people had rules in place to protect zipper key bearers. Except if he had lied about not being able to touch a purple halo that didn't fit quite right. It was possible she was running in circles and the truth was on a different path.

The wait was agonizing. Tabitha had so many questions. She had so many thoughts. She had so many ideas. Tabitha had no idea how right or wrong she was. Something was bound to escape from her mouth eventually. She just didn't want the wrong thing to pop out. Asking the king for a pony was one thing. Blurting out that she thought they were going to wrest the key from her and invade her dimension was another thing.

"Did they forget about us?" Tabitha asked aloud. Captain Olin shook his head slightly. "It's been hours," Tabitha insisted. Another shake from Olin. "At least an hour?" Tabitha asked.

"It's been less than ten minutes," Dane said in a low voice.

"Is there any reason why we have to be quiet?" Tabitha asked in a stage whisper.

Dane looked startled by the question. He started to say yes without thinking when he obviously realized that he didn't know of any reason why they were being so solemnly quiet. Dane looked up at Captain Olin just in time to see a ghost of a smile playing along the edge of the man's mouth.

"Do ye have something specific ye wish to say?" Captain Olin asked.

"No. But that's never stopped me from talking before," Tabitha said with simple honesty.

This time a smile definitely curved Captain Olin's lips. He inclined his head briefly, as if granting permission. "Then, by all means, feel free to speak."

Tabitha nodded mutely, gaze drifting around the room. She thought she had figured things out but tempered her initial urge to blurt out her findings. He had already lied to her. Though she would like confirmation of her theory she decided that Captain Olin wouldn't necessarily be the best source for that confirmation.

"What? Ye have nothing to say?" Captain Olin asked in amusement.

"Not right now."

Olin laughed out loud. "I thought I could smell something burning. Ye have been thinking again." Tabitha scowled at him but didn't say anything and he laughed again.

Dane watched the pair thoughtfully. He didn't know Tabitha's thoughts on Captain Olin but it was clear that Olin seemed to be quite enchanted by Tabitha. It put to mind his nephew who, having totally destroyed his brother-in-law's lovingly tended flower garden in an effort to grasp a yellow flower in his chubby three-year old hand, had presented the achieved prize quite charmingly to his mother, Dane's sister. The look of horror in her eyes at the destruction had immediately melted into amusement and warmth and even pride as she accepted the yellow bloom from her garden

Godzilla. The look in Olin's eyes now was quite similar to his sister's eyes that day. For some reason Dane had a feeling that Olin's look at Tabitha did not stem from maternal love, however.

What bothered him was that he had the feeling that she returned that feeling for Olin. Tabitha seemed to like Olin. Her face lit up whenever she looked at the tall captain or talked to him. Dane felt that when it came to himself she was the opposite. Tabitha seemed to get angry with him more often than not. She seemed comfortable around the captain. Dane didn't like it.

Two young men in matching elaborate embroidered uniforms stepped into the room through a door beyond the throne. The brightly colored embroidery was so thick that it made the jackets stiff and they moved stiffly. They each carried a staff a head taller than their own heads, glistening black wood almost two inches in diameter. In unison the two pages tapped their staffs on the tiled floor three times. The sound boomed across the room.

"The king. The king. The king arrives," they said in unison once the boom of the banging staffs quieted. "Long live King Royland."

Upon this announcement a man stepped through the double doors. The king was tall, thin but broad-shouldered. He wore brown leather breeches and a heavily embroidered wool tunic. The king was a carbon copy of Captain Olin. Or rather, Olin was a carbon copy of the king, who was definitely many years older than Captain Olin. If the king wasn't Olin's father he was an uncle who he strongly resembled.

The initial feeling of dread that Dane had felt when they had first encountered Captain Olin and his King's Men had faded away as he spent more time with Olin. Now he suddenly felt a renewed sense of unease. It wasn't anything but a feeling without basis yet seeing the older version of Captain Olin approach in the role of king of this land gave him a very bad feeling. What was the point of the captain keeping silent on his relationship with the king? Dane felt the strongest sense of being handled. The question was why. He watched Olin, who was watching Tabitha as she watched the king approach. Whatever Olin saw in Tabitha's face amused him.

An idea started to form but he shut it down before it could grow. He didn't want any preconceived thoughts distracting him from observing and making a logical decision. From what he had seen so far he still didn't know what to think about the status of this zipper and dimension business in regards to the impact on national security. The Cleaners were definitely aware of the zippers. If Captain Olin was familiar with the zippers he didn't seem to care about them very much. In Dane's opinion, the captain was more concerned with the Cleaners than the zippers.

Tabitha's mouth dropped open. Tabitha stood with her mouth open for only a brief moment before managing to compose her features and shut her mouth. Her face settled into a mask of indifference but her eyes took on that faraway look which meant she was thinking quite heavily. The king walked to his throne and sat. He studied the three standing before him and one eyebrow rose.

King Royland settled back in the chair, hands resting on the chair arms. He raised one heavily ringed hand and waved it languidly. "Sit. Sit."

The three sat almost in unison on command. Simon and Dane sat in unison and Tabitha slowly sat and then only perched on the edge of the red velvet chair positioned behind her. Tabitha stared at Captain Olin, her bottom lip caught between her teeth. Then she stared at the king, tilting her head to one side. Captain Olin had said that only the king could order King's Justice. Captain Olin was not the king. Captain Olin was the prince.

The king studied them thoughtfully, looking down his long nose with interest, giving no hint of what was to come or even why they were there. His gaze lingered longest on Tabitha. The pages tapped their staffs once in unison. The sound rang throughout the room. It was definitely an effective method of gaining attention.

"Lord Marlin Benwick, Chief Bailiff," the pages said in unison.

A man stepped through the same door the king had just used to enter the room, carrying a tablet. Lord Benwick was of average height, thick in the legs and had a receding hairline. He looked to be in his forties. He had strong features but looked like a man who was confident in his tasks but not so confident in himself. Lord Benwick only took a few steps into the room before stopping to look back at some unseen disturbance.

"Royland shall hear of this," a deep voice threatened.

"It is Royland's orders," a guard at the other side of the door said wryly. "It is a closed hearing. Now step back."

The doors shut on the sputtering voice and Lord Benwick hurried across the twenty feet of bare floor to stand at the king's side. Captain Olin stood on the king's right side and Lord Benwick now stood at the king's left side. The king lifted his left hand and Lord Benwick handed him the tablet he carried. Tabitha strained to see what the tablet was made of and what type of paper it was. All she could see was leather for the tablet, so assumed leather wrapped around wood, and white paper on top, held in place by a ribbon wound around the whole tablet. The king studied the papers briefly, flipping to a second and then third page, then handed the tablet back to Lord Benwick.

"You stand accused of trespassing on the king's private land. How say ye to the charges?" the king asked in a solemn voice, studying the three accused.

There was a moment of stunned silence as the three absorbed the announcement, each in their own way. Dane and Simon exchanged glances. They had expected something even if they hadn't known what it would be. Trespassing seemed as likely a charge as anything. They had illegally entered a foreign land. They would accept what came and if the punishment was beyond the seriousness of the charge would use the first opportunity to escape. Dane glanced at Tabitha. She was the wild card in their plan, of course. It was too much to hope that she would remain silent and follow their lead and go with the flow.

Tabitha actually looked not unhappy. She wasn't smiling but she was nodding her head to herself as if having come up with answers and it pleased her. Dane grimaced. There was too much steaming around in that head of hers to think that she really had come up with any real answers and solutions. For half of what came out of that mouth she was amazingly insightful and the other half she was so far off the mark that it was clear that she was just thinking out loud.

"As bearer of the key I say I have the right to any path leading to or from a zipper," Tabitha said. "As my escorts these men have the same rights as me."

The king nodded. "So you agree to trespassing on land posted as king's private?"

"No. I agree to no such term. Trespassing. That's not right. We were forced through a zipper." She tilted her head. "There's a village there."

"You are claiming ignorance?" the king asked.

"Ah, you have an excuse to keep anyone away from the zipper this way," Tabitha said. As soon as she said it she grimaced, not having meant to say it aloud.

The king turned to Olin. "You did say she was sharp? I'm not seeing it. Perhaps a bit lacking in fearful respect as well?"

"I do not change my mind," Olin said.

The king nodded. He studied Dane. "You, husband to the purple halo, who has held silent. What say you to the charge of trespassing?"

"I was where I was. If you say it was trespassing on private land then we are guilty as charged. Let's get to the punishment," Dane said.

"Ah, that's better. Someone with sense," the king said. The king steepled his fingers and studied the three before him. Simon's silence didn't appear to interest him as much as Dane's silence had. "Such a sad lack of respect grieves me as much as does the trespassing." Olin coughed gently. Royland glanced over at his son. "Yes?"

"What would you have of us?" Tabitha asked, frustration making her voice sharp. "You know where Captain Olin found us. You know he is the one who brought us here so wherever we were he's the one who took us that route." The king inclined his head once briefly, the gesture so similar to Captain Olin as to be unsettling. "I don't know what kind of land this is but I've had enough and will not tolerate this behavior," Tabitha said.

"Cheeky lass," the king said in surprise. Simon's groan was audible. "But well said. If you were talking to a servant. You, however, are talking to your king."

"That's a good point," Tabitha said, eyes lighting up. "You aren't my king." Seeing the king's face twist in surprised anger she rushed on. "You may be king of this land but since I'm not of this land I'm not your subject."

"She has a point," the chief bailiff said.

"Shut up, Marlin," the king snapped. "So she should be allowed to run amuck?"

Lord Marlin Benwick looked confused, uncertain whether to remain silent as ordered or answer his king's question. In the end he decided that the question was rhetorical and the order to remain silent was the best option to obey.

The king glared at Tabitha. "For now we will suspend sentencing. You three will remain in the custody of the King's Men until I decide what to do with you. That means you have freedom of the island but any attempt to leave the island without an escort will be seen as an escape attempt and you will be dealt with accordingly. Geoffrey, they are in your custody. Next time tell them what you are doing." The king looked at Tabitha and grimaced. "And get her out of that hideous outfit and into some decent clothes."

With that the king stood and left the room, followed by a startled Lord Benwick hurrying after him.

"I liked him," Tabitha said, staring after the departing king. "But I forgot to ask about a pony."

The three men were silent for a startled moment, staring at Tabitha as she stared at the king's retreating back, then all three men chose to not pursue that topic. "What was that about?" Simon asked Captain Olin.

"Why do you even ask?" Tabitha snapped. "Captain Olin has his own agenda."

"Ach, now ye be testy with me," Olin said and smiled slightly. "If ye will follow me I'll find your rooms for ye. Then we'll look into locating your fellow dimension traveler."

The castle was large and Tabitha felt disoriented by the time Olin found the majordomo and handed them over into the care of the tall, somber man. The majordomo was polite if not overly friendly and led them the short distance down the hall to their assigned rooms. He opened a door, the same as many in the long hall, and gestured for them to precede him then he followed. The room was a sitting room with two bedrooms on either side. The majordomo watched them investigate their new lodgings.

"I understand that you have no luggage but Captain Olin has requested proper attire and amenities be provided." The man carefully averted his gaze from Tabitha's pants but looked again and then away again, as if he couldn't resist staring. "It shall take some time for new attire. At least an hour. But the toiletries have been delivered. If anything is missing or improper please make it known," the man said politely. "Captain Olin will join you momentarily. If you wish to clean yourselves before your clothes are delivered there are robes in each bedroom."

The majordomo left without further ado but as he said, Captain Olin showed up only a few minutes later. He rapped once sharply on the sitting room door then stepped inside, glancing around. "I have tasks to do so ye be on your own for a time. Remember not to attempt to leave the island."

"How could you?" Tabitha asked. "What a stupid charge, trespassing."

Olin sighed. "The king's private land is not to be taken lightly. How would it look if we let you off without even a slap on the wrist. Anyone could say they simply didn't know they had strayed onto private land."

"Right," Dane said, realizing that it was a made up charge for an excuse to keep them there. Time to change the subject. "Pederson. When can we meet with Pederson?"

"Is he really a friend of yours?" Olin asked.

"I don't remember saying he was a friend," Simon said. "He is someone of interest."

"Ah, in that case I shall see what I can do to arrange a meeting," Captain Olin said.

"What's wrong with my clothes?" Tabitha asked.

"I suspect ye indeed are not out to shock society," Olin said. "Here women do not dress as men. Perhaps in your land women dress as men and men dress as women but here ye must dress appropriately." He headed for the door, pausing long enough to say, "I shall collect ye for dinner. Until then relax, unwind. It's been a rough past few days." Then Olin was gone and the three were alone in the suite given to them.

"It could be worse," Simon said, investigating their assigned living quarters. "I suspect this building has some dungeons."

"Something is going on," Tabitha said. "They're manipulating us for something."

"Of course," Simon said. "Either of you see a fruit basket? Nice hotels usually have a fruit basket. Though I'd prefer a steak or even a good Philly sandwich, right now I'd take an apple or a banana."

"It's the key," Tabitha said, looking out the leaded glass window. "They want the key."

"The Cleaners do. Olin has his own agenda. He's more concerned with the Cleaners than with a key," Dane said.

"Trespassing?" Tabitha snorted.

"It's a generic charge," Dane said. "Doesn't mean they aren't going to bend some rules to get what they want. It's nothing, Tabitha. Let it drop."

"But I didn't do anything wrong," she protested. "I don't ever do anything wrong. Now I'm a felon!"

"You've just never been caught," Simon said. "I heard you pushed the speed limits and left your surveillance team scrambling to catch up when you left Thomas's place."

"That's not a felon. That's a ticket," Tabitha said. Tabitha had to think about that a minute. "Okay, I forgot about speeding. But I always follow the guidelines for only going over the speed limit by a little bit so that's not really speeding, right?" Tabitha was pretty sure that speed limits were just guidelines and she only pushed the limits when in rural areas. "They want us here for a reason."

"Like using hidden peepholes and false walls to sneak in while we're sleeping?" Dane asked, tapping a few walls.

"Now you're just being paranoid," Tabitha said, though her gaze darted around the room. "So this man Olin mentioned, do you really know him?"

Simon and Dane exchanged glances. Tabitha wished she knew what silent signal they conveyed in those glances. Maybe they were considering the possibility of eavesdroppers in determining what to tell her at that moment. Or maybe they were just considering how much to tell her.

"Well, I'm going to find a library. I would think there'd be a library in a castle," Tabitha said after a few minutes of neither man answering her question. She headed for the door.

"Don't you want to shower first?" Dane asked.

"I have an hour."

"Do you think that's wise?" Simon asked, directing the question at Dane.

After considering a moment Dane shrugged. "How much trouble can she get into reading some books? She isn't much for patience. Books seem safe."

"I wasn't asking permission," Tabitha said. She tried to slam the door shut behind her but it was so heavy it just rolled gently shut with a silent click.

Simon turned to Dane once the door shut behind her. "You're going to get the cold shoulder in bed tonight. Which room are you two taking?"

"I know I haven't been the ideal husband," Dane said, one eyebrow rising. "I've had a lot on my mind."

"As have we all," Simon said. He stretched. "I think I'll take Captain Olin's advice and get some sleep. Hopefully these beds are decent."

Aware that she was dirty and stinky Tabitha didn't wander very far from the rooms they'd been given but she couldn't back down and not leave, though she wasn't sure within a few minutes what the point was that she had been trying to make. It just made her so mad when he used logic on her and she knew that he was right. Wait, no, that wasn't what had set her off. It was how the two men exchanged glances and understood each other when she had no idea what they were silently communicating about. She didn't know if they were keeping secrets or if they were just telling each other the same thing with that glance. Whatever. That could be what the glance meant for all she knew.

Tabitha paced the hall outside their suite. She was sure that she wasn't normally high strung. She felt high strung right then. Tabitha had never even been sent to the principal's office and now she had been sent to the king's office and it was worse. The punishment for being sent to the king's office seemed to be being sent to her room. Tabitha heard voices and footsteps down the hall and darted for the door to their suite before she could be seen. Their new clothes had arrived.

The days passed. For the most part they were left alone. Captain Olin did collect them for dinner the first evening but they were surrounded by a large group of diners and there was no opportunity to discuss anything private. As the king said, they had the freedom of the island and for the most part were left to their own devices. Olin had made visits every night though he hadn't joined them for dinner after the first evening but Tabitha had not seen the king again since the first day.

Meals were served buffet style in the massive dining hall for an hour each morning and an hour at midday. Dinner was served at the table but still quite informal. When diners arrived at the dining room they were escorted to assigned tables, much like a restaurant at home. The meals weren't elaborate dinners but the quality was good and the food could have been served in a four star restaurant back home. The majordomo explained that the occasional state dinners, celebration feasts, or events were more elaborate but nothing was scheduled in the immediate future except for the basic meals. The basic meals took care of the needs of the castle's occupants.

"The occupants are mainly King's Men officers, royal family and some visitors. All the foot traffic during the day is pretty comparable to the capital grounds at home. Clerks, assistants, magistrates, petitioners, and so on," Simon said as they sat at their table for the midday meal on their third day on the island. Lunch that day was hearty sliced beef in gravy, biscuits, a variety of salad greens, a variety of fruit, steamed green beans with red onions, loaves of crusty bread, and several choices of cheese. Both men had helped themselves to heaping plates of everything available.

"The rest of the guardsmen are housed in barracks," Dane said, tearing off a bite of the crusty bread. "Only the officers eat in the castle dining hall. The enlisted men are served in a separate dining hall attached to the barracks. Those with families only stay while on duty. If we really wanted off the island it wouldn't be that difficult with all the foot traffic but I think it's best to wait to see what Olin has planned before going that route."

"Agreed. I think we have what we need. Olin seems to be dragging his feet about producing Pederson," Simon said, glancing casually around the room to make sure they were still having a private conversation. "What are the odds he'll release the scum into our custody?"

"Depends on what role he is living here, I suppose," Dane said, shrugging. "If he's some favorite of the king it might be hard to convince anyone that we have a right to drag him back with us."

Dane nodded. "Even if they were to get Tabitha's keys I don't think there's any immediate threat here. Not from Olin or the king anyway. They've been aware of us a long time. It would be nice to get a map of the zippers so we can keep an eye on them but I don't think that's going to happen. I'm not sure the government here has a map. It seems to be a private matter. I think keeping an eye on the known zipper is enough."

"Or ours," Simon said. He popped a grape into his mouth. "But no one seems to know we have them."

Dane looked up from his place at Simon sharply. "They are still her keys, Simon."

Simon popped another grape into his mouth and glanced around the room again. "It's been mighty quiet since the king put us under island arrest. What do you think they're up to?"

"Something," Dane said in agreement. Simon was talking about the Cleaners and Dane knew immediately who he was talking about. "It was a convenient charge to keep us here obviously. I just don't know what Olin is doing about them while he keeps us on ice. Now that's a dangerous group, no matter that they were all polite smiles."

Simon nodded. "I got that feeling as well. As long as we cooperated they were willing to treat us well but if we had stepped out of line they'd have trussed us up like turkeys and hung us over those horses the rest of the way to their headquarters, no matter how much blood pooled in our heads."

"It's too bad Olin is dragging his feet about Pederson," Dane said. The last thing on his plate was a generous slice of custard pie with blueberries and he almost closed his eyes when he took a bite, it was that good. "Maybe we should try some discreet inquiries about Pederson through other channels."

Simon nodded. "Won't hurt to try. We can't tell her."

Dane looked up from his dessert. "Tell her what? That the bureau will confiscate her keys? I didn't intend to."

Chapter Eleven

"Without the key it's just a wild story," Simon suggested. "I don't think any of us want her running around telling everyone about the zippers and if she had a key she could do unimaginable damage."

Dane frowned. "That goes both ways." He sighed and pushed his plate away, half his blueberry custard dessert uneaten. "I know that the keys are a danger to national security but she's not going to use them."

"You really think she'll keep the information to herself when we get back?" Simon asked in surprise.

Dane knew for a fact that she hadn't said anything more about the other key, the one with a jewel inside, the one cut into a rough heart shape. He didn't know if the keys she had given them worked on more than one zipper but he was certain that heart key did for sure. Tabitha had forgotten that it was in there. Dane could tell by the way she acted when she opened the tin to give him a piece. She had known that there were pieces of the tektite in the tin but had forgotten that the heart key was there. That would be her weak link, forgetting the details or blurting out the information if someone asked her point blank.

Dane knew what they had to do but it rubbed him wrong. Still, it wouldn't do to have a civilian roaming the world with access to zippers that led to other worlds. He had a feeling that Tabitha already anticipated what would happen. He smiled, wondering if she would try to pass something over on them. She wasn't that good at dissembling and any attempt to hide another key would probably last about a day before she blurted the information out to someone. He had seen the Altoids tin. Tabitha knew that he knew the key was in there. If Tabitha held it back the agency would just hold her until her house could be searched and that would be that. It wasn't fair but it was for the greater good. Dane would make sure she was treated well when they confiscated the keys. In fact, he would push for a generous cash compensation. It seemed fair since she would never have need of the keys.

"Thomas will be dealt with and the keys and maps he holds will be confiscated. Hopefully we can bring Pederson back with us," Simon said. "But if we can't at least we'll know where he is."

"I'm looking forward to dealing with Thomas," Dane said with a dangerous smile. He shredded a piece of bread without realizing what he was doing. "I know it's the right thing to do but it doesn't exactly feel right. They're her keys. If we just take them from her is it any different than these people taking them from her?"

"Yes," Simon said. "She'll be back home for one thing. She'll understand the importance of surrendering the key to the Bureau."

"We could go back and not say anything," Dane suggested. "They've existed this long without it being a threat to national security."

"I know you're just tossing that thought out to see what it sounds like," Simon said. "It sounds like a bad idea."

***

Tabitha felt like the old man was watching her yet every time she looked up from her book he was studying his own book. It made it difficult to concentrate. It was bad enough that it was a struggle to decipher the alphabet used in the books and scrolls and tablets she had found in the library. Fortunately it was still English so she could read about half the words. The letters that gave her the most trouble were the Ts, Fs, and Ss but some of the vowels made her eyes wander as well. Tabitha had an electronic dictionary in her purse but she didn't dare pull it out to use with the old man watching her.

After a thorough shower the night before Tabitha came out in a bathrobe to find Captain Olin waiting in the living room part of the suite to take them down to dinner. Tabitha had grabbed the first dress she saw, pulled it over her head, and silently joined the group for dinner. After dinner she had been too tired to venture out of the rooms that night. Instead of going in search of the library she had dropped the cotton sundress on the floor just inside the bedroom door and put on fresh, clean baggy silk pants and top and found a bed and plopped down and fallen asleep the second her head hit the pillow. No feather stuffed mattress in the fortress. Tabitha felt like she was sleeping on a cloud and woke up early in the morning, refreshed and alert if a bit stiff from several days on a horse when she wasn't used to it. Seeing Dane sleeping on the other side of the bed surprised her, mostly because she hadn't known he had come to bed.

Tabitha cleaned up and dressed in a brick red brocade dress. She admired the dress in the floor length mirror. The fabric shimmered and changed colors as she moved. Tabitha left their suite without having disturbed either man. At least she hadn't seen Simon so she assumed he was still in his bedroom. Dane was still sleeping when she left. She had watched him for a few minutes, smiling to herself. It was tempting to lie down beside him, snuggle in for some warmth and sleep away the rest of the morning but she felt driven to find some information about this dimension and a library was the best option she could think of for now. Tabitha stepped into the hall to find a maid waiting for her. The young woman was sitting on a chair and jumped to her feet when Tabitha opened the door.

"I'm to show ye round," the maid said, bobbing her head. "The dining hall first, yes?"

"Oh, thanks so much," Tabitha said. "I'm Tabitha. What's your name?"

The maid's eyebrows rose. She opened her mouth as if to say something then shut it again as she considered how to answer. "My name be Griggette, ma'am." Griggette studied Tabitha thoughtfully. "Ye not be from the neighborhood, be ye?"

Tabitha shook her head. "No, I'm definitely from out of town."

Griggette nodded, accepting that that explained everything. "If ye will follow me, I'll sets ye straight on the ways of things here then."

The maid was pleasant and polite and led Tabitha to the dining hall for breakfast. After Tabitha had eaten, Griggette showed her around the castle grounds, patiently answering a steady stream of questions from Tabitha. Eventually Griggette brought her to the library and then waited near the door while Tabitha perused the spines of the books filling the room. After an hour the young woman came up to her and said that she would be happy to show her back to her room to make sure she could find it again and then if Tabitha needed further assistance she could ask anyone for the north wing and once in the north wing ask anyone to show her which room was hers.

"I think I can find my way," Tabitha said.

Griggette bobbed her head. "Yes, ma'ame. It only took me a week before I didn't get lost too bad. So I do show ye once and then ye can be on your own."

So Tabitha had allowed the maid to escort her back to the suite and did not say anything when she was sure that the maid was going the wrong way and yet they ended up at the right door. She considered finding a ball of string to use the next trip out.

"The hall is tiled in brown and red and your door is the fifth door once the tile starts," the maid said. She stared meaningfully at Tabitha's dress. "If ye wish a dresser ye may pull the bell in your room and one of us will respond." She bobbed again and hurried away down the hall.

Tabitha glanced down at her dress, searching and feeling for missed buttons or some other sign of not having dressed properly. It was a wonderful dress and she had even made a small screeching sound of delight when she first saw it hanging in her closet. There were many beautiful dresses in that closet, all for her use. She looked over her shoulder, twisting and turning to see if anything was out of place. Nothing looked wrong.

Tabitha walked the halls for an hour or two after that to get a feel for the architecture, the skirt of her dress swishing as she walked. The north wing was living quarters and only servants were in the halls that early so she didn't know that she was overdressed for a morning stroll to the library. Tabitha wandered until she eventually had found the library again and had settled in to learn all she could about this world. Tabitha could confidently traverse between the suite and the library now. So far her reading had proven to only be an exercise in translating and not much else. An idea struck her. If it was a library there should be children's books, primers, something defining the alphabet. The Dewey Decimal

System was not in use here however. She would have to get creative but getting creative was something she did best.

Tabitha closed the book she was studying and glanced at the old man. He appeared to be intently reading. Tabitha glanced around the library. Well, she referred to it as the library. It was a large room filled with books but very few people. If she was a child's book where would she be? Somewhere low on a shelf, at a child's eye level.

It took her about ten minutes to find a collection of children's books. She rifled through a few, cradling in her left arm the ones that looked suitable to help her understand the alphabet, such as picture books with words captioning common objects and animals. Tabitha chose the books at random. She already had four books cradled in her arm and she picked up another one, flipping through the pages. What she saw startled her so much that she lost her grip on the book. Quickly she grabbed and caught it before it fell too far, being careful not to tear the pages. Tabitha tucked it into the pile in the crook of her arm, grabbed two more off the shelf without even looking at them, and headed back to her table.

The old man was gone. Tabitha carefully set her new books on the table, arranging them by size. It was a habit. She opened the top book. It was an alphabet book. The first picture was of an apple. The writing beside the apple was clear and easy to read. Tabitha forced herself to turn each page, to note each letter, and to not think about the third book in her pile. Yes, the backwards F extending below the line was actually an S. The S looking letter with a dot was an F. When she reached the last page of the picture book she looked at the original book she had been struggling to read. Her plan had worked but now all she could think about was that children's book.

"Excuse me," a voice said right next to her.

Tabitha felt like she jumped a foot off her seat but it was more likely only an inch or two. She hadn't heard anyone approach. It was the old man. He was of medium height with sagging skin and shaking hands but his eyes were clear and bright and his gray hair was thick and full, a large cowlick standing up in back so like a young boy's that Tabitha had the urge to lick her fingers and try to press it down.

"Sorry. Sorry. Didn't mean to goose ye," he said, bobbing his head.

"I didn't know you were there," Tabitha said, trying to smile to ease his concern though her heart raced. "Can I help you with something?" It was an automatic reaction to offer assistance.

"Ye be a guest of the castle?" he asked.

"Of the castle? Yes. I guess that's one way of saying it."

He frowned, hesitating as he tried to absorb what she said. Obviously the accent was a hindrance both ways. "It's just that most who visit this room I know. I do not know ye."

"Oh, I'm Tabitha," Tabitha said, not certain how to respond. No one had told her that the library was off limits. Maybe that's not what he was saying, that she wasn't allowed in the library.

"Sir," a King's Man said, stepping up to the table. "The king has need of you. If ye will follow me?"

"Of course," the man said politely. He looked back to Tabitha and nodded his head. "Perhaps we shall meet another time."

Tabitha watched the King's Man escort the man slowly out of the library, very respectfully. Alone again Tabitha tried to focus on her book. She hadn't seen a King's Man other than in the dining hall since entering the fortress. How odd that one had materialized out of nowhere the moment the old man started talking to her. She wondered for a moment who the old man was then shrugged. She had no idea who he was.

Tabitha slid the green leather covered children's book out of the pile and admired the cover for a few minutes before she opened it. The feel of rich leather was a luxury long ago abandoned except in rare cases in her dimension, especially for a children's book. The paper here was different as well, ivory or beige in color and had the crisp texture of parchment. The pictures looked like they had been hand painted into the book with water colors though the printing was definitely typescript. The script was difficult to read. Yet she studied each page intently. When she finished she stuck the book back in the pile by size and opened the second children's book.

Having something to reference helped and she quickly adapted to the differences in the lettering. Tabitha had read some terribly complicated calligraphy in the past that was actually worse. Fortunately the words were definitely English and now that she was alone she slipped out her electronic dictionary and looked up words that didn't quite make sense in context and using the origin or archaic use figured it out.

The book she had originally been struggling so hard to read was a manual on business management. Tabitha wrinkled her nose. Tabitha returned the book to its place on its shelf and skimmed the neighboring titles, looking for something more interesting. She spotted the title *The Key to Geological Sites on the Rice* and she grimaced. Then she gave it a second thought and plucked the book from the shelf. Tabitha flipped through the pages and randomly stopped and read a page. Her interest peaked. She flipped a few more pages and read.

The author had a lively tone and commented on thoughts as he physically trudged along the curving Wild Rice River as well as his scientific method and results. The fact that books existed in this dimension on science told her that their worlds weren't so different. The fact that someone felt interested enough in geology to go out and investigate and then write a book told her that people here weren't so different. Tabitha sneezed from the dust covering the book and musty pages. It seemed it wasn't a popular book. No, the people here were not so different at all.

After a few hours in the library she wandered back to the suite. Neither of the men was around. She didn't know what they were doing to fill their time but was sure they were together. She hoped that whatever it was they were doing they were finding what information they were looking for. Tabitha went down to the dining hall and chose soup and some warm, crusty bread for lunch. The buffet had a large pot of soup stock surrounded by bowls filled with meat and vegetables. Tabitha filled her bowl of stock with slivered beef, carrots, barley, and fresh green onions.

Tabitha chose a table and sat by herself, watching the other people in the room as she ate her lunch. She suddenly realized why the maid had mentioned a dresser. She was dressed for a ball, not a sunny, summer day at the office. Most of the people eating in the dining hall looked like they could be from any office lunch room, though again more like a government office. Though the dresses were full length, most were cotton or tweed, or some light fabric. Tabitha suddenly felt self-conscious and hurried to finish her lunch so she could go back to her room and change her clothes.

After changing clothes to something more appropriate, Tabitha headed for the library again. Though it was slow reading she felt like she was making some headway and had learned quite a bit already. She had nothing else to do anyway and the time went relatively fast as she deciphered more and more books. The maid from that morning showed up at her elbow when she was deeply engrossed in a book and informed her that if she would like to prepare herself for dinner she would have an hour if she left right then.

That evening Captain Olin collected them for dinner but once they were in the dining hall he handed them over to the host and wished them good eating before leaving instead of joining them as he had the night before. Waiters immediately stepped up to the table with bottles of wine and trays of a variety of breads. The first course arrived before Tabitha could even finish buttering her crusty roll, three pieces of battered and fried shrimp with a white sauce elaborately drizzled over the pieces. Bowls of mixed greens tossed with a vinaigrette dressing followed the shrimp. The main entre arrived only a few minutes after the salad bowls were emptied, a generous portion of prime rib steak next to a baked potato and steamed green beans. Dessert arrived while the waiters cleared the empty dinner plates, a glass bowl of blueberry gelato with a strawberry on top.

"I need a walk after that," Tabitha said, leaning back in her chair.

"That sounds good. I'll join you," Dane said.

"I'll let you two lovebirds have some private time together," Simon said in a voice that carried. Tabitha wouldn't be surprised if the cooks heard in the kitchen "I think I'll take a short walk in the other direction."

Tabitha walked in silence, thinking about what she had learned in the library that day, letting Dane pick their route. Slowly she became aware of their location. Dane had picked a path leading out the opposite side of where they had entered the fortress. This was the front of the castle. The bridge they had used when they first arrived on the south side of the island was for the King's Men and the courtyard was used for assembly and practice. Now they were on the north side of the castle and it was like another world. A large courtyard spread out before them from the great doorway but this one was green lawn with paved paths and fountains and formal gardens. Beyond the courtyard were more buildings and several foot bridges.

"What's wrong?" Dane asked, slipping her hand through the crook of his elbow.

"What? Nothing," Tabitha said.

"You're quiet."

Tabitha shrugged. "I'm thinking."

There were other people walking along the paths and they nodded at each other in passing but no one stopped them or questioned them or engaged them in conversation. The sky was turning a deep teal in the distance. The air smelled fresh and clean. They may use horses for their conveyance but the result was a lack of pollution. Tabitha enjoyed it very much. It reminded her of stepping into the forest of the Pacific Northwest. She said so aloud.

"Yes," Dane said, taking a deep breath. "I see what you mean. Did you live in the northwest?"

"I have family there, so visited often," Tabitha said. "There's a lot to do there. As far as outdoor activities. Hiking. Exploring. Are you from Minneapolis?"

"Northern Minnesota. I lived in Portland for a few years though," Dane said, picking a path with less foot traffic. "Where does your family live?"

They walked more slowly as they talked, finally slowing altogether when they reached a small alcove with a waist high wall overgrown with vines. The sun eventually set over the fortress wall and neither noticed. The temperature dropped with the setting of the sun and Tabitha rubbed her bare arms as she stared up at the star strewn sky. It was the same sky she had studied several weeks ago before stepping through the zipper, she realized. Though she wasn't an expert on constellations she had been seeing them her entire life and they looked the same.

"Look, the big dipper," she said, pointing out the stars forming the big dipper. An amazingly strong feeling of normalcy washed over her at seeing that familiar shape etched out with stars in the night sky above. "It feels more like a dream. Everything is the same yet so different."

Dane glanced around them, noticing how isolated they had become. "We should get back," he said. Only a few people moved about in the distance but otherwise they were quite alone. "I think it got really late somehow."

Tabitha smiled softly in agreement. Indeed, somehow the time had passed in the blink of an eye as they talked. It felt like only minutes had passed but the night sky and empty park testified to it being more hours than minutes.

When they got back to their suite Simon had already retired for the night. Dane glanced at Simon's closed bedroom door as he followed her into their assigned bedroom. At her surprised look he smiled a small, tight lipped smile. "Don't worry. I can sleep on the couch. I just need some bedding."

Tabitha hesitated only for a minute before deciding. "No. It's all right. There's no reason for you to sleep on the couch."

Dane's eyes lit up. "Really?"

Tabitha nodded. "We should keep up appearances. Though I don't know what difference it makes." She opened a wardrobe and pulled out a blanket, which she rolled into a tube and put on the center of the bed, sectioning the two sides. "This is my side. That's yours."

"Yes, this is quite effective," Dane said, forcing himself to sound cheery. He lifted the bedding on his appointed side of the bed and the blanket barrier slid to the edge of her side of the bed. Dane turned his back and undressed. He usually slept in the nude but hesitated with his hand on the waistband of his boxers, then left them on. There was no point in pushing it. The suite had two bedrooms with a central sitting room and shared bathroom but each bedroom also had a small dressing room with racks of clothes and a small bench. Tabitha had gone into the attached changing room and changed into a sleeveless white cotton nightgown with embroidered purple flowers along the bodice. She was sliding into bed when he turned.

The sight of her in the nightgown took his breath away. Tabitha was oblivious of the impact she had on him. Her attention was on arranging the blanket barrier on top of the bedding. Though she was under the covers from the waist down she was visible from the waist up. She gave it one last pat and looked up. Dane gave her his most charming smile. "Good-night, dear wife," he said before turning off the lights and sliding into the bed beside her.

Dane knew that she had no idea how difficult it was to not roll over and take her in his arms. Parts of him felt heavy as he pictured her in that nightgown and knew that she was less than an arm's length out of reach. They lay there in silence, each lost in their own thoughts. It had been a rough past few days and if either had thought to test their blanket barrier neither realized that they had both fallen asleep within about a minute of each other within moments of resting their heads on the pillows. The smell of lavender wafted gently over their sleeping forms.

Dane was the first to wake. He resisted the urge to pull Tabitha into his arms and instead dressed and went out into the sitting room. Simon, freshly showered, was already there. Dane used the shower and by the time he was done Tabitha was up. She was quiet as she visited the bathroom. The bathroom was interesting, just a small room off the sitting room, pretty much the whole room was the shower. A shower head came out of the far wall with levers below the shower head and a drain in the tiled floor allowed for the removal of the water. It was a simple system.

When Tabitha came out of the shower the three went down to the main dining hall for breakfast. Breakfast was a wide variety of foods; cut fruit, cheese, sausages, ham, pastries, breads, custards, teas, juices, and coffee. They filled their plates and settled at a table.

"I'm going to the library again," Tabitha said. She spread honey on a croissant. "What are you guys going to do today?"

"Finding anything interesting?" Dane asked, eyeing her dripping croissant. He had taken a bowl of fruit, whole wheat bread, and a boiled egg.

"Actually, yes," Tabitha said. "I have discovered that after the initial settling of talents the European governments from many countries used this area as a criminal drop-off, much like England and Australia in our dimension."

"Interesting," Simon said, nodding his head.

"It continued for almost fifty years, up to about a hundred years ago." She leaned forward. "And it was the Vikings who first discovered the area. There was a war between England and the Vikings before England took ownership of Minnesota. It was almost like an insult to turn around and dump the unwanted after a long drawn out war to gain the area."

"How did they contain them?" Dane asked. "Or was the whole country a big prison?"

Tabitha shrugged. "It's not easy reading the stuff." She eyed Simon's plate. "How's that sausage?"

"Pretty good."

"I'll have to try one tomorrow," Tabitha said. She wrapped a piece of cheese around a slice of melon and took a bite. "All the food here tastes so good. You didn't say. What are you going to do today?"

"We'll start with trying to find Olin. He still owes us a visit with Pederson," Dane said.

"This Pederson. Who is he?" Tabitha asked casually. "I mean you seem quite determined to meet up with him. It seems odd that you're so interested in him just because he owned the house before Thomas."

"Just doing our job, following the trail," Simon said.

Tabitha pretended to be interested in finishing her breakfast but she was getting irritated that they still wouldn't tell her why Pederson was so important. She stood. "Well, you know where to find me if you need me."

"Wait," Dane said. "Where have you been spending your time away from us?"

"The library."

"A library?" Dane sounded surprised and interested.

The library drew her each day. Better than sitting in the rooms assigned to them twiddling her thumbs all day. The time went fairly fast as she researched this dimension in the best way possible at her disposal. Both fiction and non-fiction books were the behind the scenes heart and soul of any culture.

Tabitha spent several hours that morning in the library. At lunchtime she wandered down to the dining hall and ate alone. No one had come to find her in the library and she missed her constant companions of the past few days. Tabitha sat in the corner of the dining hall watching the people come and go, feeling like quite an outsider. No one seemed to even pay attention to her. Now that she was wearing clothes that fit in with this dimension she felt invisible.

Captain Olin had supplied a few outfits for each of them. Simon and Dane had been given trousers the same as what the King's Men wore but their shirts were various colors and looked like what the majority of the other men wandering about the castle were wearing. Tabitha had received multiple dresses, skirts, and blouses to go with the skirts. She had also been given various undergarments that she hadn't figured out how to wear. Tabitha had not wanted to ask anyone about how the contraptions worked so they were left unworn. It would be an odd thing indeed to not know how to use underwear. As long as a brisk breeze didn't lift her skirts she didn't think anyone would notice. The dress she chose to wear that day was actually quite comfortable and attractive. It was a rosy pink, the top form fitting and the skirt composed of several layers with slightly different hues of the pink. She wasn't sure what the fabric was made of but it would sell well in her dimension.

That afternoon Tabitha wandered around the castle, needing to burn off some energy and stretch her legs. Though her visits to the library were proving beneficial she was getting burned out and needed a change of pace. The clothes helped her blend in but she still got the feeling that everyone knew who she was. No one was exactly avoiding her but she definitely felt ignored.

Maybe ignored wasn't the right term, Tabitha amended, watching the people go about whatever they were doing. Servants had tasks, nobility had their heads in the clouds. That probably wasn't fair, she admitted to herself. Some of the apparent nobility looked just as focused and determined as the servants as they went about their own tasks. Tabitha could tell the servants from the nobility by their clothes and also because they seemed to move about in clusters. At least the clothes she wore marked her as nobility. They just all had things to do, places to be, normal every day stuff. When Tabitha got bored with walking around feeling like she had a big neon sign over her head saying outsider she went back to the library.

At dinner the three sat alone again. Tabitha had gone up to the sitting room and found Simon and Dane waiting for her before heading down to the dining hall. There was no sign of Captain Olin this night. He had been quite scarce since their arrival at the island fortress. When Dane and Simon had asked for him earlier that day the King's Man they had questioned had said that he was out investigating some incident.

"Busy man," Simon said, watching the other diners. People came and went in waves.

"We should do something after dinner," Tabitha said. "I'm getting bored."

"Can't have that," Dane said. When she made a face at him he said, "I'm serious. I know how dangerous it is for you to get bored."

"We could go for another walk," Dane said.

"You two should take the Romantic Stroll," Simon said. "Last night I saw a nice green park past the most northern foot bridge, complete with one of those flower coated gazebos." He grinned and wiggled an eyebrow. "One of the men guarding it told me all about it. It's so romantic only married couples are allowed to visit it after sunset. I wasn't allowed to go in by myself."

"Cool," Tabitha said. She glanced at Dane who wasn't looking enthused at the idea. "If you don't want to I can go walk by myself. I'm sure I can find something of interest to entertain me. By myself. Again." Dane sighed at the not at all subtle accusation.

"The gazebo has a clear view of the barracks," Dane said. "We saw it when we were down there looking for Olin. That's why he tried to visit it last night. He just wants an evening head count." Dane studied Simon thoughtfully. His partner was definitely up to something. "Let's show him. We'll do the walk and I won't even look at the barracks."

So they walked to the park. Tabitha slowed in awe as they approached the green park. It was breathtaking. The bushes had been trimmed in a wave pattern and woven with ribbons and flowers. Bird cages hung along the path leading to the center of the park, bright patches of color twittering and singing cheerfully. The gazebo sat in the middle of the park, veils of gauze fluttering about it, twinkling lights strung along the columns and encircling the top. The path crossed a stream over a small foot bridge, more ribbons and flowers entwined along the handrail. Two deer and their fawns grazed near the gazebo.

"Wow," Tabitha said.

"Indeed," Dane said in agreement. The sun had not yet set but dusk had fallen just enough to turn the park into a fairyland dream world.

Tabitha slipped her hand over Dane's elbow as they slowly strolled toward the gazebo. Moving slowly felt natural, especially so as not to startle the grazing deer, who occasionally paused to lift their heads and watch the couple. They paused at the foot bridge, stopping to look down at the gurgling water rushing under their feet.

"I'm not sure but it looks like the stream completely circles the park, in the shape of a heart," Tabitha said, standing on her tiptoes in an attempt to see the whole park to confirm what she thought she saw.

"I wonder why they created this?" Dane asked, frowning in confusion.

"Because someone here has a romantic streak," Tabitha suggested.

"I guess," Dane muttered.

"How long do you think we'll be trapped here?" Tabitha asked, staring down at the stream. "I was going to say being held prisoner but that doesn't seem a good term where we're standing."

"No, you're right," Dane said, taking a deep breath. The air was heavily perfumed from all the flowers. "Hopefully not too much longer." He plucked a flower growing near his hand and threaded the stem through her hair. "It is a beautiful cage we find ourselves in though. And what a view."

"You like the view?" Tabitha had to crane her neck back to look up at him. She realized she was holding her breath, waiting for him to say something romantic. Dane was staring at her when he said it was an amazing view, not at the view.

Dane smiled and bent his head closer. He whispered in her ear, "I can see the barracks from here."

Tabitha punched him in the arm. "Jerk."

Dane grinned. "But I only have eyes for you." He pulled her into his arms. "You have to admit, if we survive, it's the grandest adventure imaginable."

"Thanks for questioning if we'll survive," Tabitha said dryly.

Tabitha leaned her head against his chest. When he held her the rest of the world vanished and it seemed no problem existed that mattered. The air smelled of cut grass and flowers. The stream gurgled and tumbled over rocks at their feet. It was possible at that moment to forget that they were in another dimension reached by a zipper in space where people were trying to kill her. Beneath her cheek his chest was iron and that was the solid reality that anchored her.

Dane stroked her hair for a moment. "We haven't made it to the gazebo yet." He took her hand and led her the rest of the way down the path to the gazebo. The multiple layers of white fabric completely hid what was inside the gazebo. They had to peel away layer after lay of white gauze to form an opening large enough to use to step inside.

"Oh," Tabitha gasped when they stepped through the makeshift door. The gazebo was made of white marble. The waist high walls were lined with cushions covered in crisp white linens. A few cushioned couches sat scattered about the floor. White marble columns held the ceiling in place. The gauze draped around the gazebo had been tied back to create a window opposite the entrance, a window screened with a single layer of gauze to a view of the river and outskirts of the city beyond. Dane stepped in behind her and wrapped his arms around her waist.

"Almost makes it all worthwhile, doesn't it?" he said.

"Are you a romantic, sir?" she asked in a light, teasing voice.

"At this moment I feel I am," he said seriously.

They stood for several minutes in silence, appreciating the moment. The sun had set, though the sky remained a deep, rich teal above the lights of the city. Minneapolis was small enough to not create a light globe blocking out the sky in this direction. Since they hadn't seen the actual city at night Tabitha didn't know if it was lit enough at night to create a light globe in any direction. It was a momentary thought that fled quickly. The outside world had no right to intrude on this moment.

Tabitha looked up at Dane, turning in his arms at the same time. The magic of the starlit gazebo flowed into their kiss when their lips met. Magic was the only word to describe what she felt. Warmth flowed through her, warming every part of her body. They began tentatively, exploring the shape and contours of the other's mouth. There was no rush. They had all the time in the world. Time was suspended. The only time was now. The only thing that mattered was the taste of their kiss, a taste of honey and wine.

Both forgot their surroundings. All that existed in their universe was the flood of desire heating their blood, stealing reason, freezing time to only that moment. They were not in a gauze veiled gazebo in the middle of a public park. They were in their own world where nothing mattered but touch and taste and feel. Nothing mattered but the heat generated by their kiss, fanned into flames as the kiss deepened into serious exploration.

Tabitha moaned against Dane's mouth when he cupped her breast in his hand. She needed to feel flesh. Frantically she pulled at his shirt until she could reach the smooth, velvet hardness of Dane's back. Dane pressed her back against the cushion-topped wall of the gazebo, then lifted her so that she sat on the cushions. It was the perfect height when he stepped up to her and she opened her legs to him. Dane pushed her skirt up and out of the way.

"Is it safe?" he asked, pulling back for a moment in hesitation.

"What?" Tabitha asked, brain clouded by the passion coursing through her veins and the heady aroma of flowers. "Oh." She looked over her shoulder. She couldn't see anything beyond the gauze of the gazebo. They were alone. No one was in sight. "Yes. Yes. It's okay."

Chapter Twelve

"Sorry for biting you," she whispered.

"No blood drawn. It's all right," Dane whispered. He kissed her neck lightly, making her shiver.

Tabitha raised her chin to give him access to her neck and saw the gazebo ceiling. It looked like it had no ceiling but opened directly into the universe. She stared in awe at the swirling Milky Way that looked close enough to touch. Dane looked up to see what had captured her attention and was dumbstruck by the sight.

"Wow," Dane said, unable to find any other words.

"It's like we stepped up into the stars," Tabitha whispered.

The distant sound of voices brought them alert once again. Tabitha frantically pushed her skirts down and lowered her legs while Dane stepped back, quickly buttoning his trousers. Tabitha hopped down from the wall and straightened her skirts. Her legs wobbled a bit but she didn't think anyone else would notice. They left the gazebo in apparent composure, Tabitha's arm linked through Dane's arm. The voices belonged to a King's Man and a lady who had just reached the foot bridge. They nodded a greeting then hurried past, on their way to the gazebo.

"I hope Simon isn't expecting company tonight. Once we get back to the room I'm locking us in," Dane said in a husky voice.

Tabitha's legs got weak just at the thought. "Would it look odd if we ran the rest of the way?" she whispered.

Dane chuckled. "As tempting as that is, yes, it would attract attention. We'd better not."

They managed to make it to their rooms without drawing too much attention though Tabitha was surprised that no one noticed that she was walking on clouds. Dane kept a steady pace and she had no choice but to match him though her feet wanted to fly. He didn't help matters by whispering in her ear what he had planned for their next round. Her face was a vibrant red by the time they reached the sitting room separating their bedroom from Simon's bedroom. Simon wasn't around and they slipped into their bedroom and locked the door.

When Tabitha woke in the morning she stretched. Considering the days on horseback that made her muscles protest and then a night of further unexpected physical exertion and hardly any sleep she felt wonderfully alive and relaxed at the same time. Tabitha chuckled, remembering the gazebo. They had almost gotten caught in an embarrassing position by that King's Man and his wife. That would have been awkward. Just thinking about someone catching them in the act made her stomach twist in knots. It must have been the magic of the place because even now thinking about how close they had come to being interrupted she would still do the same thing.

"You look like a satisfied cat who found a spot of sunshine," Dane said, stroking her arm with his finger. He sighed. "I can't think of any real reason to not stay in bed all day as well but we can't."

"Yes, satisfied," she said, chuckling again. If they hadn't visited the gazebo she doubted they would have spent the rest of the night in such activity.

"You're supposed to be trying to talk me into staying in bed all day," Dane said in a light hearted teasing voice. He smiled. "What's so amusing this morning?" Dane asked.

"The gazebo. It was safe but barely. I have to admit I don't really know if I would have noticed anyone right outside the entrance. I was sort of distracted." Tabitha looked up at him through her eyelashes, feeling shy yet daring at the same time.

Dane froze. "What do you mean?"

"We were almost caught. It was quite public actually. I don't care for that sort of thing, being where someone could just walk in on us but you definitely distracted me."

"Hey, you two," Simon said at the door, rapping briskly with his knuckles.

"Tabitha?" Dane said.

Simon knocked again. "C'mon." He rattled the doorknob but Dane had indeed locked it the night before.

Tabitha kissed Dane on the tip of his nose then jumped out of bed. She pulled a slip over her head then grabbed a dress from the wardrobe. Back home she barely paid attention to what she wore and here she paid even less attention but fortunately she now had a maid who set out the appropriate dress on the bench in the dressing room every night so that she never went wrong in the morning. Tabitha had just slipped her arms into the sleeves and raised her arms to drop the dress over her shoulders when a thought struck her. "Oh," she muttered, eyes going wide in the split second before the fabric dropped to cover her face. She stood frozen as the idea hit her and expanded. "Safe," she muttered to herself through the fabric of the dress. She pulled the dress down from her face and wiggled her hips as she pulled it down until it settled into place.

Dane watched her with a bemused look on his face as she counted with her fingers, starting with her pinkie finger and tapping each fingertip to her palm, tapping the tip of her thumb twice and going back to her pinkie finger, slowly tapping two more fingers. The result made her grimace so she counted again coming up with a different number when she stopped at her pinkie finger. Tabitha sank onto the edge of the bed. "Oh, that's not good," she said. She counted a third time then shook her head. "I wasn't thinking. You said safe. I was thinking safe from being discovered in a public gazebo."

Dane ground his head back into the pillow and closed his eyes, emitting a soft groan. Simon knocked again. Dane's groan came again, louder, followed by a small curse. Tabitha felt the glow of her wonderful mood melt away. It was a minor risk. He didn't have to act like someone had shot him. She had friends her age who tried for months before getting results. One wild moment wouldn't do it. Well, three wild moments, she amended. It had been so long since she had been with anyone that she just hadn't thought about it until now. Maybe she should have thought about it by the time they got back to the room but her mind had been on other things. Tabitha frowned, thinking back over the night since leaving the gazebo. She didn't remember thinking at all since leaving the gazebo.

"How can you not have thought about consequences?" Dane asked, sitting up. He raked his fingers through his tousled hair. "Even if I wasn't totally clear in what I was asking you should have considered it yourself."

"Fine," Tabitha said.

She stood and went to the door, yanking it open just as Simon was about to knock again. He barely managed to keep from clouting her between the eyes with his knuckles as he was in the process of knocking. Tabitha didn't even notice. Tabitha ducked under his arm and sailed out of the room. Simon looked past her to Dane, who looked a bit green on the edges. "He all right?" Simon asked Tabitha.

"No," Tabitha said without even looking back. "He found something tough to swallow." She ducked around Simon and walked briskly away.

"Tabitha!" Dane called, jumping out of bed in his natural glory. He grabbed his pants from the floor beside the bed, almost falling at Simon's feet as he tried to pull them on and run after her at the same time. A door slammed in the distance.

"Too late," Simon said brightly. "She's gone. How was the gazebo? Pretty romantic, right?"

Dane scowled at his partner. "Safe means safe, not safe. She's a bloody genius. How can she not know what I mean by safe?" He buttoned his pants and brushed by Simon.

"Go figure," Simon said, shaking his head. He had no idea what Dane was rambling on about but it was more entertaining this way. "You didn't, uh, fall under the spell of the gazebo did you?"

"What are you talking about?" Dane asked, heading for the shower as he talked.

"Oh, didn't I tell you that part? Huh. Thought I did." Simon was grinning so wide his cheeks hurt. "I'm pretty sure I told you only married couples could visit it at night."

Dane turned at the door to the bathroom. "What?"

"Oh, it's supposed to be magic or something, though I clearly remember Olin saying there was no magic here. Married couples visit the gazebo and when they leave there's a bun planted in the oven." Simon held his arms out in surrender when Dane turned and took a step toward Simon, eyes raging. "Hey, I just suggested a stroll. I never thought you'd take advantage of the setting to, uh, set up a bakery." Simon started laughing at the look on Dane's face. "C'mon, it's just a story."

"You're just making that up now, right?" Dane asked. Simon kept laughing but shook his head. "You think it's funny to send us to a fertility temple?"

"Yeah," Simon said, holding his side as he laughed. "It's worth it to see the look on your face. You have to admit, it's pretty damned funny."

"You'll be laughing in nine months when you're babysitting," Dane said.

"Oh, c'mon," Simon said. "It's their urban legend. You'd have to stretch things quite a bit to put the credit or blame on a gazebo. I don't think an urban legend will override protection. You wouldn't be so foolish as to not use protection?" He lost his grin at the expression on Dane's face. "I'm not babysitting. I didn't even change my own kids' dirty diapers. I'm not babysitting."

***

Tabitha looked up in surprise to see Olin standing next to her. He was staring at the collection of books she had on the table. He picked one up and read the title. His eyebrows rose. "Of what interest to ye to read of the constructing of a forge?" He picked up another book and didn't wait for her answer before asking, "And children's books?"

Tabitha's welcoming smile faded. Every once in a while he came across a bit condescending to her. She couldn't imagine why Dane thought there was anything to be jealous about with the man. It wasn't like the man was even interested in her, except maybe as a source of amusement. "Good morning to you, too," she said. She took the book out of his hand. "I didn't know what it was about. I'm having a difficult time reading your world's script. So I thought I'd try the children's books."

"Glad to know ye not be planning building forged cages to haul our children back to your land." Olin visibly relaxed. "I hadn't considered the script being different. So ye be unable to read adult books?" He flipped through the book on forges, cringing when he read a few sentences. It was not light reading nor highly entertaining, yet if one wanted to construct a forge the book provided step by step by step by step instructions complete with dimensions. If Olin wanted a forge constructed he would send for a smith.

Tabitha's eyes lit with fire. "I'll get it."

Olin smiled. "I'm sure ye will. So if ye can't read, uh, yet, why do ye spend so much time in this room with these books?"

"What else is there to do?" Tabitha asked. "How long are we to be held prisoner?"

"Is it prisoner? Rather guest with restrictions," Olin said politely. "A prisoner would not have free run of the island and the comforts of nobility. With so much this island has to offer how can ye hide away in a room with books ye can't even read?"

"What does this island have to offer?" Tabitha asked dryly. Something he said hit her. "There's nobility here?"

"Did ye not realize that when ye met the king?" Olin asked dryly.

Tabitha blushed. Of course, what an idiot she was. Tabitha just hadn't thought about it but it did not make sense that if there was a king ruling the land then there would be nobility. It wasn't actually the United States. Suddenly she brightened. This was the perfect excuse to get her hands on some books and he was going to help her find them.

"Do you have books that explain the laws and lineage and stuff? We don't have nobility where I come from. Well, other countries do but they're other countries. I get confused by order, like viscounts. Are they higher or lower than a baron?"

Olin winced. "It's not vis-count. The, well, never mind. Let me see what I can find."

Tabitha smiled in satisfaction as she set the books on the table in order by size. It used to set her mom's teeth grinding when she pronounced viscount wrong as well. Olin was studying the titles on a shelf she hadn't looked at yet. In just a few minutes he returned to her table with two books and set them on the table. Then he settled onto a chair at the end of the table, his long, angular legs stretched out full length.

"So why spend so much time reading books ye can't understand?" he asked again.

Tabitha glanced at him then turned her attention to the two books he'd brought her. "So the king is your father?" she asked, his face just at the inside edge of her field of vision.

"Aye." He drew circles on the tabletop with his fingertip. "So ye don't wish to answer my question?"

"I did already," Tabitha said. She opened one of the books he'd just brought and grimaced at the sight of even more archaic style coupled with very dry technical writing. Out of the corner of her eye she caught Olin's quick grin flash across his face before he caught himself and quickly settled into a mask of composed disinterest again.

He was relaxed and at ease for the first time since she'd met him. Maybe now would be the time to get some information from him. Her burning questions would have to wait, like how they knew about purple halos and what they intended to do with the key once they somehow wrested it away from her and when she would be allowed to go home. Tabitha was tempted to offer to hand over the key right now in exchange for being allowed to go home but she knew that Simon and Dane would not be happy with that action. Snooze would be a thinning, unhappy cat if someone hadn't thought to check on him. His well being worried her just as much as she wanted to go home.

"So what does it mean to be a prince?" Tabitha asked him, watching him.

The question startled him. He opened his mouth, shut it, then finally said, "I don't understand."

"Well, can you do anything you want since you're the son of the king or are you forced to follow set rules without any choice since you're the son of the king?"

He relaxed again. "Ah. Ye ask if I have freedom. A little of both, I guess. Just like anyone. Some days the job is quite rewarding and other days I'd prefer to be the farmer's son." He flashed her another grin. "I do outrank both a viscount and baron."

"Why charge us with trespassing when you know what happened?" Tabitha asked.

"The king does what the king does," Olin said, voice growing hard. "It's done. Let it go. Your companions understand this."

Tabitha felt the change in his mood but didn't know how to steer him back onto the relaxed path they'd been going down. She picked up one of the children's books and studied the cover. "I think this is about a monster under the bed. That seems to be a universal theme. Did you ever think there was a monster in your closet or under your bed?"

Olin shrugged. "If I did I don't remember."

Tabitha nodded. She was still on thin ice with him for some reason. "I never actually thought a monster was under my bed but I remember jumping into bed as fast as possible in case something was under there." Tabitha set down the book and turned to him. "So how long do we remain under house arrest?"

"Are ye in a hurry to be somewhere else?" he asked briskly.

"Actually, yes," Tabitha said just as briskly. "I also have a life with responsibilities and sitting here cooling my heels puts a large strain on that."

He stared at her, as if just realizing that she might indeed have a life he was taking her away from, then nodded and looked away. "A comfortable cage but still a cage. At least it is comfortable. It is the best I can do for now."

"Look," Tabitha said, leaning forward. "There are too many undercurrents for my taste. I'm the type of person who likes things up front. Some people might say I'm impatient. I say I just like things up front. We have Thomas after us, that group you call Cleaners after us, and you more subtly after us. All because I have a key to that zipper. I don't know who is the good guy and who's the bad guy. So far you seem determined to keep me alive which Thomas and the other group don't. So far that puts you on the list of good guys. Why not just let me go home?"

Olin nodded thoughtfully but didn't speak for several minutes. At last he said, "I am determined to keep you alive. Remember that. Murder and criminal actions are not tolerated. Ye be complicated because ye have so many enemies after ye. Ye think the Cleaners wear uniforms to identify them. They do not. They can be anyone. If I turned ye loose with only your husband for protection ye would not survive to make it home. I am trying to keep ye alive and also catch these murderers."

"You could escort us back to the village," Tabitha said.

"Perhaps that will be an option. But not today." He stood, looking down at her. "Ye ask and ask but yet ye don't listen."

"I listen," Tabitha protested.

"I must get back to my duties." With a smart node of his head he walked away. At the library entrance he paused and looked back. "I had assigned guardians growing up as a child. If there had been monsters under my bed they would have been destroyed before I entered the room." Then he was gone.

Tabitha leaned back in her chair. Well that hadn't gone as well as she'd hoped starting out. She tilted her head thoughtfully. For some reason tilting helped her brain sort through issues. She had even noticed that if she went to bed at night and laid on one side she couldn't think clearly or even not be able to sleep because she kept thinking and thinking but if she turned on her other side, thinking wasn't so important she would drift off to sleep as her thoughts drifted away. She had mentioned the situation to her doctor once during an annual exam and gotten the deer in the headlights stare then the shrug. So maybe there was no medical reason for head tilting during thinking and maybe an ear, nose, and throat doctor wasn't the right doctor to ask about it but she had noticed that a large percentage of people automatically raise their chin or tilt their head when giving serious thought to a problem.

Her tilted head zoomed in on the possibility that maybe Olin's sole motivation really was in keeping her alive. He just had a different method in how he went about it than the authorities would back home. Tabitha would have to ask Dane what the procedure was for dealing with people who had murderous lunatics after them. Her only knowledge was from movies and television and she highly suspected the accuracy of those. Then again, a prince in a foreign land in another dimension might do things differently than the FBI also.

Her next thought was of Dane, the man, not the federal agent. He was clearly the most attractive man she had ever met. She wasn't sure how much his attention to her was acting out the role of husband or genuine attraction. Simon seemed to think there was something going on between them but that didn't mean anything. She already had reason to doubt Simon's judgment. He had thought she was somehow responsible for Dane's disappearance. Tabitha frowned as she straightened her head and rubbed her now stiff neck. In a strange roundabout way she was responsible. She had provided Thomas with the meteorite.

The feeling hit her again, the strong urge to find her way home. She needed the security of familiar surroundings. Tabitha felt adrift, in an unknown element that was too big to absorb. Being in the library had helped ease the feeling of being homesick. Being surrounded by books gave her a feeling of familiarity. Now it wasn't enough either. Even the library suddenly felt alien. She looked around the room. Shelves of books lined all four walls with additional shelving in aisles, much like any library at home. Maps and paintings hung on the wall and a few scattered tables provided a place to read and study. She could be anywhere in her own world in this room. Tabitha tilted her head. She hadn't really noticed before the huge map hanging on the wall above the bookshelves on the wall opposite her. It was a map of the island. Strange that she hadn't noticed it before because it faced the doorway.

"There you are." Dane's voice behind her made her jump.

"Don't do that!" she said in exasperation. He was alone. "I'm still angry with you and actually, I was just thinking about you."

Dane grinned and slid into the chair Olin had just recently vacated. "I like to hear that. That you were thinking about me. What was I wearing?"

"Your FBI badge," she said, meaning she wanted the agent aspect of his attention.

One of Dane's eyebrows rose. "Is that all I was wearing?"

Tabitha's cheeks flared a healthy pink. Now she was picturing him wearing only a badge, not an ID in a bi-fold wallet but a shiny, silver badge and she couldn't decide where it hung on him. The thought of anything hanging just deepened her blush. Tabitha ignored his delighted grin and pulled out one of the children's books from the middle of the stack and pushed it across the table to Dane.

"You should read this," she said. His eyebrows rose when he looked at the cover. She watched him looking at the cover of the child's book, thinking about their bedroom conversation. "I'm sorry. I wasn't thinking. But you didn't have to act like a jerk."

"Did I?" Dane asked, gaze still on the book. He picked it up. "What am I looking for?"

"Just read it and tell me what you think."

Dane frowned at the script yet it didn't take him long to read it. He looked up at her when he finished. "So what? It's just a story in a children's book."

"It mentions the Closers. See where it says the balance is the goal of the Closers."

Dane frowned, staring at the page. "Okay," he said slowly.

"It all makes sense now," Tabitha said.

Dane stared at her in surprise. "It does? From this book?"

Tabitha pulled out several books, opening them to specific pages and shoving them in front of Dane. "They're like Greenpeace of this dimension. They're slightly radical, their full focus is shutting down the zippers because they think it's destroying the fabric of the universe."

"Is there that much of a zipper problem here?" Dane asked.

When he said it like that she wondered if she was on the right track. "Don't you care to know why those crazy people are after us?" Tabitha asked in frustration.

Dane shrugged. "I didn't need to read it in a children's book to know that they're a threat." He closed the books and sat back in his chair. "Look, about this morning, I'm sorry if I overdid the shocking news reaction. It was just hard for me to believe you didn't understand the term safe and that you wouldn't think of consequences on your own."

"That's an apology?" Tabitha asked.

"I've had time to think about it and maybe the circumstances created the misunderstanding. I want you to know that whatever happens I'll be there for you."

Tabitha's temper flared. She had a very long fuse but once it was lit it was more explosive than an atomic bomb. He'll be there for her? Tabitha knew he was trying to be fair. She knew he was thinking he was being a standup guy. She knew that she was going to throw the heaviest book at hand at his head. What Tabitha didn't know was why he felt it was her problem that he had to be there for her.

His gaze darted up over her shoulder and he looked so surprised and stunned that when their visitor arrived at the table Tabitha was prepared for someone. She set down the book she had been about to hurl at his head without him ever realizing he had just missed being in the line of fire. Tabitha wasn't prepared however for what met her sight when she looked up, despite the way Dane had frozen into shock. She thought maybe the old man had returned.

The woman standing behind her was tall with long, red hair that fell in wild curls around her face and down her back. She wore a magenta cape over a teal dress that was cut low to showcase her assets and had a high slit from hem to hip that displayed well shaped legs. The woman would have been a rival to any super model except for the hawk's beak nose that dominated her face. She wore so much jewelry that she jingled and clanked and glittered.

"Greetings. Ye must be the Captain's charges," the woman said with a warm smile. She extended her hand to Dane, palm down. "Is it Mr. Ellis?"

Dane shook off the frozen surprise and abruptly stood before taking her hand, gaining a frown when he shook the offered hand instead of bringing it to his lips to kiss the back of her hand. "Yes. And this is my wife, Tabitha Ellis."

The woman nodded at Tabitha but did not extend her hand to her. "It be most pleasant to greet ye. May I join ye?"

"Please. Sit," Danc said, offering his chair.

The visitor sat elegantly. Tabitha watched Dane staring dumbfounded at the woman for a brief moment before hurrying to take a seat next to her. It made her smile when she realized that she probably had the same bemused look of astonishment on her face, except that she wouldn't be surprised if Dane started to drool. This woman felt bigger than life. Though her first reaction was to be jealous there was really no point in the emotion. Dane had no choice but to be in awe of this woman.

"I be Shonie," the visitor said. Shonie carefully straightened a fold in her dress. "The Captain felt ye should meet a normal element." She laughed at her own words, a delightful sweep of musical sound, not a giggle, not a chuckle, but a sound that expressed delighted amusement. "He did express to me that ye be visitors and have run into Cleaners." She glanced at Tabitha's open book. "Oh, I see you found the Closers there. That's what they used to be called, ye see. But that's just a brief bit. They be too radical for children's tales. Nasty group, them. How they continue to exist in the modern world is a bit muddled. It's an excuse to feed the hate if ye ask me. Keep the zippers closed to maintain balance. What a fairy tale, that. How can grown people devote their lives to such a fantasy?"

Tabitha stared at Shonie in fascination, certain that she hadn't even had to pause to breathe. It was a little difficult to follow her words but overall she caught most of what she said. Well, she caught the words though she hadn't had time to grasp the meaning of most of it.

"I be at your disposal," Shonie said. "Ye must have good memories of your visit. The Captain will take care of the crazy Cleaners so put them out of your mind. Poof! They be gone." She smiled warmly at Dane. "Now, first we shall go for a boat ride on the river. It shall be a bit cozy in the boat with an armed escort but I have permission to pick out the men of the escort so we'll bring no dour pusses. Captain Olin has insisted it must be thus. Tonight we shall attend a concert. It is on the shore across the river actually but there shall be a gathering on this side of the river and we shall hear the music just as well." Shonie abruptly stood. Dane stood also. Shonie smiled at him and put her hand on his arm. "We shall meet at the front steps in the main courtyard in one hour. The invitation is to your fellow traveler as well, of course. He must join us. See ye then."

Then the woman was gone in a flash of magenta and teal and the tinkle of metal, porcelain, glass, and gems. Tabitha felt like she had forgotten to breath and gulped air. No one could ever accuse her of talking too much she decided, not after encountering Shonie. Dane stood staring after the woman with a very bemused look on his face. He sort of sank into his chair. He looked like he'd just been hit by a Mack truck.

"What just happened?" he asked at last.

"We've been invited on a boat ride and a concert," Tabitha said. "It actually sounds all right."

"Better than sitting in our rooms waiting," Dane said. He studied the room around them, at all the books filling the shelves. "I wish I had known about this room sooner. Would you mind some company over the next few days?"

"It's an open library," Tabitha said. "Have you found your mystery man yet?"

Dane shook his head. "Captain Olin has been elusive. No one else seems to know anything about him when asked."

"He's more than the previous owner of the house, right?"

Dane sighed. "If you must know, he's a fugitive. Twenty years ago he was top in the most wanted for trafficking women and we suspect selling them but it wasn't known to whom. None have ever been found since. They simply vanished. He grew incredibly wealthy but we never found his source of wealth. Then he vanished. Daniel Thomas seems to have taken up where he left off. We became aware of Daniel's activity about five years ago but had no proof. They both had confirmed contact with the women but there was nothing at all to tie in their disappearance to Thomas or Pederson."

"Until now," Tabitha said, realization dawning.

"Right, the zippers."

"The Vikings," Tabitha said. "They were expecting someone. Daniel wanted me in that zipper. They must give him something in exchange for the women."

Dane nodded thoughtfully, surprised at how quickly she had made that connection. It had taken Simon quite a bit longer to toss out the thought. They didn't know if that was the only zipper that had been used but it was a start. Most of the victims had been women but it was possible there were men who hadn't been connected to Pederson or Thomas who had made unexpected one-way trips through a zipper somewhere.

"Oh," Tabitha said in surprise. "So when Olin mentioned his name you thought to bring him back?" Dane nodded in agreement. Tabitha frowned. "So why not just tell me?"

"You're not exactly one to be subtle."

"Little you know," Tabitha muttered. Louder she said, "So you thought I'd open my mouth and warn him off?"

Dane shrugged. "Not in so many words. It's not that I thought you'd blurt it out. We just decided that you would have less to worry about if you didn't have to worry about us dragging a most wanted criminal back with us." Dane met Tabitha's skeptical gaze. "Look, telling you wouldn't have made any difference. I'm telling you now out of courtesy. And so you understand the dangers we face."

Tabitha stared at him. "Dangers? Oh, I understand the dangers. The arrow one inch from my head was the first neon sign of many. There's been nothing but danger."

Tabitha picked up another book and opened it randomly, pretending to tune out his presence. She was still angry with him, after all. It was easy to forget that she was angry with him but she was angry. She flipped the page and stared at the wood cutting drawing. A purple halo stood with his family, all three children being purple. Tabitha blinked. How odd that the whole family was purple halo. She read the subtext. Famous scholar Bastion Lacoombe and his family. Lacoombe had discovered the herb that had cured the plague at the turn of the century.

That made no sense to her at all. If holding the zipper key made someone a purple halo it made sense that a son or daughter would inherit the key but not all of them would be purple halos, just the person holding the key. Tabitha shut the book. Dane was right. They were just children's books. Facts were thrown out the window and a children's tale was left in place.

Chapter Thirteen

"**D**oes Simon still have that field glass Olin took from Ravin?" Tabitha asked Dane. He nodded. She stood, rubbing her stiff back. "I need to see it. C'mon." Tabitha put away the books but kept the two Olin had given her and tucked them in her arm. No one had said she couldn't borrow any books. No one had said anything to her about using the library or any rules that pertained to using the library. Tabitha glanced up at the map she had noticed just before Dane interrupted her. "One sec."

Tabitha walked up to the wall, studying the map thoughtfully. She had the oddest feeling that it was important. Tabitha tilted her head. She felt the homesickness wash over her as she stared at the map. Tabitha turned and the feeling faded. She looked up at the map again, gaze settling on the room she had been looking at when the feeling hit her. The feeling surged through her. She moved her gaze to other parts of the island and the feeling subsided slightly. An idea struck her and she brushed it aside. Tabitha mentally noted the room in the castle marked on the map with a squiggle mark that made her feel so strangely. She would have to visit that room if possible. She was still amazed that she hadn't noticed the map before now.

Back in their suite Tabitha took the glass from Simon and turned the glass on Dane. He wasn't purple. He was still blue. Tabitha was so surprised she almost dropped the glass. Dane caught on to what she was doing and interpreted what her surprise meant. "I don't have it on me," he said. "I hid it near the zipper. Insurance."

Tabitha turned the glass on Simon. He wasn't purple. He was still blue. She looked up at him over the field glass. Simon looked back, not certain what she was seeing but sensing that she was puzzled. He slowly reached into his jacket and pulled his hand out with the piece of tektite she had given him held between thumb and first finger. If the key gave someone a purple halo then Simon should be purple and he wasn't.

"Why aren't you purple?" Tabitha asked.

Simon shrugged. "Beats me."

She held the glass over her arm. "I'm still purple. The tektite I gave you worked to open the zipper, right?"

"Yeah," Dane said. He frowned at her and exchanged glances with Simon. Could Tabitha have actually forgotten already that he had confirmed that the tektite had worked? Or was she doubting that he had said it worked? This topic seemed to be pointless. "I said it worked, didn't I?" Tabitha wasn't listening though, her focus was on the field glass she held.

Tabitha went into the bedroom and removed any piece of tektite and stuck the items in her purse then put the field glass over her arm. She was still purple. Tabitha crossed the room to put distance between her and the keys. She was still purple. The key she had given Dane had worked to open the zipper so Simon should be purple because he still held his key.

Dane knocked once and opened the bedroom door. He slipped inside and shut the door behind him, watching her in concern. "Are you all right?" Tabitha nodded but couldn't speak. An idea was forming and she wasn't liking the idea. "Shonie sent an escort. They're here. Should we cancel the trip?"

Tabitha shook her head. "I'm all right. I'll be out in a minute."

Dane hesitated, thinking she was upset with him about keeping information from her. "About Pederson. Maybe I didn't tell you because it seemed so mundane after stepping through the looking glass. But we have to find him if possible. It's our job."

"I'm all right. I'm not upset by that. I'm purple," she said.

"Yes," Dane said slowly, uncertain why that should be of new concern. They were in their current predicament because she was purple. It certainly wasn't new news.

She tossed the field glass on the bed. "Give me just a minute. I'll be right out."

Once Dane left the room Tabitha slipped the jewelry back on, combed her hair, and grabbed her purse. Tabitha wanted answers. She was going to get answers. Then she was going to go home and put all this behind her. Tabitha made up her mind at that moment to move to Arizona and make pottery. No more security with a nine-to-five job. Her current dream was to make pottery and that's what she was going to do. She just had to get back home first. Tabitha had thought she had figured it out, this purple halo business, yet it wasn't the key making her purple.

"You're going to drag that on a barge ride?" Dane asked, looking in surprise at her purse hanging from her shoulder.

Tabitha wrinkled her nose. He was right. She didn't really need to drag it out on a barge outing. She just felt naked without the purse and all its contents but it wasn't necessary to drag the whole thing along with her. Tabitha went into the bedroom and set the purse on the bed so she could pull it all the way open and see inside. She pulled a wristlet from inside the bag and dug around for several minutes for hand lotion, her point and shoot digital camera, and lip balm, cramming it into the wristlet. The wristlet had a long strap and she snapped that onto the metal rings she could wear it as a cross-body bag. Then Tabitha dug into her purse for a hair band and crammed that into the wristlet. Dane stepped into the bedroom to see what was taking her so long.

"You have a purse in your purse?" Dane asked, staring at the small purse hanging across her hip.

"It's not a purse," Tabitha said, shaking her head in amazement. "It's just a wristlet." She picked up the field glass and stared at it in frustration then shoved that in her bag as well. "I thought it was the key. But it's me. I'm what's purple."

"Have you noticed that you are the only one concerned with this purple halo business?"

"That's not right," Tabitha protested. "We are protected guests because I'm a purple halo. Those people tried to kill me because I'm a purple halo. I want to know what it means. I want to know why I'm purple."

Dane grimaced. She was right. "I'm sorry. I'm trying to say that it doesn't mean anything is wrong with you."

Tabitha glared at him, one eyebrow slowly rising. "You think it means something is wrong with me?"

Dane's temper rose and it took effort for him to tamp it back down. "I clearly said that it doesn't mean anything is wrong with you."

Simon interceded, calling out that people were waiting on them. Tabitha took Simon's interruption as the opportunity provided and ended the discussion with *Dalton*. The whole conversation had the markings of a situation ready to spiral into an argument and she didn't feel like going down that road. Suddenly Tabitha had the urge to never speak to him again. Never speaking to him again would solve all her immediate problems.

The boat was a large, lumbering barge. Thick ropes stretched to the shoreline and were attached to a series of pulleys mounted on a wagon pulled by massive draft horses. Tabitha paused to admire the horses. These were Belgians and were almost identical down to their white stockings and blaze foreheads. Tabitha was a bit confused by the complex pulleys on the wagon when it seemed simple enough to just attach some ropes to the harness but shrugged it off. It wasn't the end of the world if she didn't understand how the barge's method of transportation worked, yet she couldn't help but keep looking.

"I wish Captain Olin had told us himself that it was all right to go," Tabitha said, half expecting to see him come charging down the dock to arrest them for attempting to escape.

"His men are here," Dane said. "They wouldn't be here if he hadn't given his okay. I recognize a few."

A scries of docks suggested that there was normally quite a bit of river traffic though none of the other docks currently had any boats tied off. The barge was snuggly attached to the dock and a secure ramp made the crossing from dock to boat very comfortable. Dane gallantly offered his arm and Tabitha slipped her arm around his extended elbow, for appearances sake. A mix of uniformed King's Men and brightly dressed civilians mingled on the dock waiting to board the barge and roughly ten sailors in beige baggy pants and beige baggy shirts were already on the barge, either holding oars or ropes. Once they had stepped onto the barge it was apparently the signal for the waiting group to also board.

The barge itself was more opulent than a barge should have the right to be. More than twenty guests fit comfortably in addition to several legless couches and pillows and benches. A man sat on a dais playing the guitar. Two servants moved about with trays of drinks and food. It turned out that it was Shonie's personal barge. It turned out that Simon was as invisible to Shonie as Tabitha was invisible.

"The horses are the urban power," Shonie said in greeting. She smiled warmly as she stepped up to Dane and planted a kiss on each cheek, smiled woodenly at Tabitha, took Dane's other arm and led him to a couch. "When I travel from city to city I use bargemen. It's either that or cut down every tree between shore and the river. They'll pull us now and then when we come back it's the river doing all the work." Shonie sat and patted the spot next to her. "Come. Sit. Drink."

Dane glanced at Tabitha as he was pulled away. Tabitha smiled and shrugged. Her first impression of Shonie being bigger than life still held true. It wasn't worth making a scene even though she was starting to get irritated by the woman. It was bad enough that she was so obviously clinging to Dane but the outright ignoring Tabitha's presence was what got under her skin. Tabitha waited for Dane to do something, even though she didn't know what he could do without being rude. Tabitha wanted him to surprise her.

"Excuse me, do you mind sliding over just a bit to make room for my wife? If we join you someone is going to end up in your lap," Dane said lightly.

Shonie looked startled for just the briefest moment then smiled politely and slid over so there was room for the couple to join her. Tabitha took Dane's hand and squeezed it in thanks. He had done it so well and, more importantly, he had done it, which surprised her. Tabitha was already forgetting that she was angry with him.

"Everyone will want to meet you, of course," Shone said brightly. "Once Viscount Harmondal is on board we'll do the introductions."

"So you are Captain Olin's friend?" Dane asked.

Shonie laughed her delighted laugh. "Third cousins or something in that order."

A woman near Shonie said, "I believe your husband be his maternal uncle's third cousin by marriage."

Shonie's smile was fixed firmly in place. "Indeed, thank ye Ione. Captain Olin, Geoffrey, was great fun when he was a boy but being a captain has turned him into a dour old man. All business."

"What has he told you of us?" Simon asked casually as he chose a drink and appetizer from the tray presented to him. He remained standing, looking around the barge in interest.

Shonie looked around in surprise, as if just realizing that Simon was there. "Only that ye be visitors and for some reason the Cleaners have used ye for target practice. Though rumor has it that he is looking for a wife. Which doesn't make sense since your wife is already taken. By ye," Shonie said lightly. "It'll be up to ye to tell me more."

"Funny thing about rumors," Dane said, studying the tray of finger food presented to him. "They sprout anywhere about anything." He smiled at Shonie and changed the subject. "Captain

Olin said that this area was settled by refugees from a talent persecution," Dane said. "Were they all European?"

Shone frowned for the first time. "What?"

"The people in this area, did they come from Europe?" Dane asked. "The people in this area all look to be of European descent."

Shonie shrugged. Her fingernails suddenly became of great interest to her. She held out her hand at arm's length and studied them as she talked. "I suppose. To begin with. What is a talent persecution?"

Tabitha watched Shonie with interest, finding her fascinating for some reason, much like a train wreck or five car pile-up. Tabitha was content to sit back and remain silent and watch while Shonie monopolized the conversation and attention. The woman reminded her of someone but she couldn't place who. Shonie clearly had an agenda but it was difficult to tell what prompted the false gaiety and pointless chatter. The woman could be in love with Captain Olin and scoping out what she saw as potential competition, conveniently forgetting that Tabitha was supposed to be already married to Dane. The woman could be after Dane as a potential romantic interest and conveniently forgetting that he was married to Tabitha. She seemed to have a clear aversion to Tabitha. So many possibilities for Shonie's strange behavior raced through Tabitha's thoughts. Tabitha tilted her head. Maybe aversion wasn't the right word. It could be guilt. Yes, Tabitha concluded, it was guilt. Guilt shone full in Shonie's face.

Simon and Dane had managed to get her talking about politics and government though she clearly thought they were pulling a prank in acting like they were ignorant and not like that she was showing ignorance to history. Current affairs Shonie was comfortable discussing however. "The various kingdoms retain their independence though I have heard that some countries in Europe are gradually losing governing power to boards. I suppose the theory being that several heads in accord is more just than one head being responsible," Shonie said in conclusion. Tabitha had missed the first part of the conversation. Shonie drained her glass and reached for another one from a tray held by an attentive servant. "But no more of politics today. It is enough to hear the talk all day every day. That's all they can talk about lately. Lord This or Lady That coming or going. Delegates meeting. You'd think Geoff would be happy to have a burden lifted but it's probably that male pride thing that, well, look, swans."

Shonie obviously hadn't meant to go into personal political observations or discussions during a pleasure cruise down the river. Two swans had indeed floated quite near the barge. The male bobbed and snaked his head as it followed the female.

"So what is a purple halo?" Tabitha asked after a brief glance at the swans passing in the opposite direction.

"Oh, that again. Ye seem to focus on that topic a lot," Shonie said with a tsk tsk attitude. Tabitha frowned. It was the first time she had brought up the topic. "Well, the Cleaners did attack ye and kidnap ye, indeed. Still, it not be healthy to linger on the subject. It be all in the past. All the purple halos be gone now."

"But why did the Cleaners hunt them down?" Tabitha asked.

"Why, because they be dangerous, of course," Shonie said in surprise. She quickly composed herself, smoothing her skirt with her palm. "That does not give a reason to kill people, of course. But everyone knows that purple halos are villainous criminals bending even the laws of nature to perpetuate their evil deeds. And the balance was thrown askew. Everyone knows that the number of stillborns increase the year a purple halo be born. Crops fail when a purple halo reaches maturity."

"I thought this country was founded on escaping blind prejudice and superstitious nonsense," Dane said.

Shonie nodded her head vigorously. "Oh, yes. We are very tolerant of talent. Why I visit a soothsayer once a month for a reading and I've heard there's a coven of witches living only a few hours from the city."

"So being a purple halo isn't a talent?" Tabitha asked.

Shonie blinked. "Oh, no. It be a curse passed from parent to child. That be why the Cleaners got such a bad reputation. They decided not to wait for children to grow up before hunting them down. Fortunately that be a long time ago. Very bad times. It got a little cloudy and there were rumors that people were killed without even any proof of being a purple halo. Neighbors would take a dislike to someone and report them as a purple halo to get the

Cleaners to get them out of the way." She shook her head sadly at the thought. "Now I've heard the Cleaners are trying to find purple halos but not to kill them."

"I thought at first a purple halo was just someone who had a key to a zipper. Now I'm not sure," Tabitha said.

"What?" Shonie asked, genuinely confused.

Tabitha clenched her teeth. She believed Shonie really had no idea what she was talking about and she was getting tired of the topic. Since arriving here she had been trying to discover the underlying truth about a purple halo in order to understand why people were trying to kill her, why she was placed under protective custody. The only people who seemed to have the answers were either trying to kill her or weren't talking.

"So you grew up with Captain Olin?" Tabitha said, so clearly switching topics on purpose yet Shonie looked relieved.

"Yes. Geoffrey was quite a rascal," Shonie said. Shonie chuckled at some memory. "Always getting into some scrape or other. His mother would just laugh at his behavior."

"It's hard to imagine Captain Olin as a small boy with a mother," Tabitha said lightly.

"Do you remember when he be, oh, about seven or eight and found the kittens in the barn?" a short brunette said from behind them. Tabitha hadn't noticed her standing behind the couch and wondered how much of their conversation had been overheard by how many people. "They had fallen through a trapdoor. He be worried they would get stepped on so he took them back up into the loft. Well, the loft be packed full of hay and be dark but he wiggled his way between the bales with four squirming, yowling kittens. Little Eva on his heels."

"That girl went everywhere he went, even into a dark loft packed with hay. What he didn't expect was to encounter a loft full of wild, angry cats and a mother cat who decided he be torturing her kittens. We couldn't see anything but heard the yowling and after only a few minutes he came crawling out of the hay as fast as he could with a big, fat tabby cat after him." The brunette was laughing so hard she could barely finish the story. "That cat was swatting him right in the buttocks and the way he be yelling I think she be using some claw. Poor little Eva fell through the same trapdoor that the kittens had fallen through and broke her arm."

Shonie smiled politely at the story and around them gentle laughter applauded the story. Shonie looked at Tabitha. "Ye look like her, ye know." Shonie quickly looked away, as if she couldn't bear to look directly at Tabitha.

"Who? Little Eva? Who is she?" Tabitha asked.

Shonie said, "She was Geoffrey's little sister, of course."

"Troeble a'ead," one of the escorting guardsmen announced. All of the King's Men looked ahead. Tabitha had gotten used to the more refined speech from the people she had encountered since entering the fortress and it took a moment to register that the man had shouted "trouble ahead." Dane and Simon looked behind the

barge then looked ahead, then scanned the riverbank with very
serious expressions. Tabitha sat still, calmly sipping from her glass
as she stared out at the view visible straight in front of her. A tree
had been cut down over the path running parallel to the river,
blocking the horses' way. The tree had been cut with a saw, the
sawdust around the trunk clearly visible even from the barge.
Tabitha sat back on the couch. If it was another ambush she
wouldn't be at all surprised but she had more important things on her
mind. Tabitha sifted and sorted through all the information and came
up with the only possible conclusion; these people were all insane.

Tabitha sat with her leg pressed against Dane's leg, her arms
crossed under her breasts, gaze on Shonie, who was standing at the
head of the barge shouting at the men on shore. In the end they
simply released the ropes towing the barge and the barge slowly
drifted back the way they had come. The tray bearers picked up
poles and took up stations to keep the barge on course. Two men
were already working at getting the horses turned around in the tight
quarters. Tabitha picked up a cucumber sandwich and nibbled on it.
If she was going to die she wasn't going to do it screaming and
crying. Her hand trembled as she set the sandwich back down on her
plate.

"Can you swim?" Dane asked in a low voice. Tabitha nodded,
feeling the dread settle deep in her stomach. "The water is cold and
the current strong. Are you a strong swimmer?" She nodded again.
"Hopefully we won't need to but be prepared. Only as a last resort.

Understand. Only as a last resort. The only reason I would even consider it is that we're relatively close to shore. Get rid of the dress if you go in the water." Tabitha nodded.

Simon came around to the front of the couch and leaned toward them. "If we get separated head for the village." He straightened and walked to the front of the barge to join the crowd looking toward shore at the tree blocking the horse's path.

Shonie was clearly unhappy when she returned to the couch and plopped back down. "Our trip has been cut quite short."

"Talents," Tabitha said quickly. "By any chance did you make your own jewelry?"

Shone smiled brightly. "How kind. But no. It be my husband. In fact that be how we met. My father was upset at first when I told him I wished to wed a craftsman. I do love to tease Papa. He be not a craftsman at all, ye see. He be an artist. He gave me this one for my last birthday." Shonie fingered a silver bracelet set with lapis cabochons. "But that is not a talent. A talent is, well, a talent. Ye know, seeing the future. Recognizing other talents." Shonie frowned as she was trying to think of talents while keeping an eye on what was going on around them.

"Where I come from talent just means being quite good at something," Tabitha said.

"How…quaint," Shoni said politely. She smiled at the approaching barge captain and listened to his report then turned to

Dane and said, "We shall have that tree cleared this afternoon and try again tomorrow. There still be the concert this eve as well."

The barge drifted steadily back to the island castle with no sign of the suspected ambush while Shonie chattered amicably about various people of interest in her social circle, the coming winter festivities, and her wardrobe. Dane and Simon smiled and occasionally nodded but Tabitha noticed that their eyes were roving, studying the shore, studying the people on the barge, and even watching the river side of the barge. Occasionally someone else joined the conversation but Shonie liked to be the center of attention and monopolized the conversations.

Tabitha lost interest during the topic of Shonie having found the most wonderful dress shop with the most divine clothes and how Lady Fiddleton's boring speech being much more beneficial if she had had the decency to wear something out of this century and should have listened to Shonie's advice and visited the dress shop before getting up in front of all the peers for some boring speech on moving forward instead of clinging to the past. "There she stood, hand waving about looking to the future instead of living in the past and she be wearing a dress from twenty years past and that hair, oh, it be so dated."

"When we get back I'll talk to Olin about Pederson one more time and then we'll leave," Dane said for her ears only. "We know enough to know that your life is still in danger and I don't want to keep taking these risks. If he won't produce Pederson we'll make our own way to the zipper anyway."

"But we're under house arrest," Tabitha said, puzzled. "We can't just leave."

"Don't think Simon and I have been sleeping or twiddling our thumbs these past days," Dane said. He smiled with self satisfaction. "We can get away if needed."

Tabitha looked at him in surprise. To be honest, she had thought they were just passing the time doing nothing. It hadn't occurred to her that they were plotting an escape. Tabitha did know that they felt they should find out if this side of the zipper could be a threat to national security but hadn't given it much thought that they might actually be doing something. She had been caught up in her own internal struggle on being a purple halo.

Dane smiled, as if knowing what she was thinking. He turned back to Shonie before she realized that they weren't listening to her, making appropriate sounds at appropriate intervals. Tabitha purposely raised one eyebrow. He just grinned at her.

Dane was her husband in this world and he acted the part. When they got home he would be the FBI agent again and they would go their separate ways. The thought startled her. Would he really just go away, back to his life before entering this world through a zipper in space? Tabitha didn't even know what his life was before entering this world. Oh, she knew that he was an FBI agent but she didn't know much of anything about his life outside work.

For that matter, Dane had never really asked her about her life outside of this dimension. He didn't know anything about her. They were strangers really, strangers who acted as husband and wife because Simon had thought it a good choice at the time. Tabitha watched Dane thoughtfully. He wasn't that good an actor. Dane couldn't act like he cared if he didn't. There was something between them, something more than acting like husband and wife to keep up appearances. That something had shown itself in the magic of the gazebo.

Her thoughts drifted to how confusing it was to step into a world where she was hunted and even reviled as a purple halo. Tabitha thought Shonie knew that she was a purple halo yet the things the woman had said about what it meant to be a purple halo showed blind prejudice. That the general population had no idea what it meant but still knew about a purple halo was confusing to Tabitha. She wondered how many fairy tales back home had been fabricated based on a sliver of truth and then twisted out of recognition of reality.

How had she become a purple halo? It wasn't because she held a key to the zipper. It was her, not the key. Was it as simple as some hereditary disease? Something subtle and unobtrusive that she had lived with her entire life? Were others in her family purple halos? Or had contact with the meteorites somehow changed her? So if being a purple halo did not mean possession of a key to open zippers what did it mean?

So many unanswered questions motivated Tabitha into doing something to find the answers. Tabitha watched Dane struggle to appear interested in Shonie's self-absorbed chatter. He had said they could go home. Home was where she wanted to be. Wasn't it? Tabitha sat up straighter. She wasn't ready to go home. She still had to find answers. She wouldn't find the answers at home, of that she was certain.

There was one person Tabitha had to talk to before they left. Kate. She wondered if Captain Olin would permit her to talk to Kate. Tabitha saw no reason for him not to allow it but then she wasn't in his shoes and had no way to know what he would or would not allow. That was the really the only thing left to do, she decided. Once she talked to Kate she would be ready to go home. Hopefully Kate would cooperate.

The barge slowed abruptly with a sickening lurch that knocked many of those standing off their feet. Tabitha looked up and around. There was nothing visible at first, then she spotted the chain just below water level. The city was just visible in the distance, the island fortress a white reflection in the afternoon sun. Dane pushed Tabitha off the couch onto the deck, using his body to shield her as he scanned the shoreline.

"What be ye doing?" Shonie asked Dane in amazement, her eyes wide as she stared at him. "I'm sure it's just a tree root. My men will have us pushed off in no time."

"I saw a chain," Tabitha said in a low voice to Dane.

Dane nodded. "So did I."

They came out of the water instead of from shore. When the first few heads appeared at the side of the barge and climbed over the side Shonie squealed and jumped up on the couch, holding her skirts up from her ankles, reminding Tabitha of her mom spotting a mouse. She pointed a finger at Tabitha. "This is your fault!" Shonie then turned to the armed men swarming onto the barge, some already struggling with the armed escort, who were quick to defend the barge once they realized where the attack originated from. "Get off! Get off my barge!"

"That's a good idea," Tabitha said to Dane as she adjusted her purse to a more secure position. "Let's swim for shore."

Dane looked around. All the attackers were climbing aboard from the river side of the barge, leaving it clear to the shore, but the current was strong and the water cold. It wouldn't take long for the cold to suck the heat out of their bodies and make swimming difficult. They could just as easily get sucked downriver and drown before making it to shore. Several King's Men were fighting their way to them, one of them carrying a blanket. He handed the blanket to Dane and gestured to Tabitha then turned back to struggling with a wet invader.

"Tabitha, wait," Dane said, looking more closely at the blanket when he felt the weightiness of the thing.

Tabitha hadn't waited for agreement and even as the King's Men passed the blanket to Dane she was already at the side of the barge. While Dane was looking at the blanket in surprise she slipped over the side, holding onto the edge of the barge. The cold of the river was such a shock that her teeth hurt. Pressed by the river current and held by the underwater chain, the barge twisted. Tabitha let go of the twisting barge, feeling nails break and slivers enter her palms. The skirt of her dress made it difficult to kick her legs but instead of stripping as Dane had suggested she pulled the skirts up to her waist and used the strap of her wristlet as a belt to hold the fabric out of the way of her legs. Setting her sights on the shoreline she took a deep breath and sank under the water. Tabitha struck for shore, staying under water as long as her lungs allowed. When she had to surface she took another deep breath and dove back under water with only a glance to be sure she was still heading in the right direction.

Tabitha was being pulled downriver but she was also making good progress moving closer to shore. The barge hadn't been that far from shore. She felt a sharp twinge in her upper left arm, like an insect bite, but ignored it. When Tabitha surfaced again she was quite a distance from the barge downriver but very close to the shore. She quickly took another deep breath and dove under water again. It was getting harder to move cold stiffened muscles but Tabitha pressed onward.

Water plants tickling her legs told her that she was close to shore at last. Tabitha surfaced, only her head above water. Cat tails grew along the water's edge and she used them as cover while she decided what to do. Tabitha found it difficult to tread water. Her muscles were stiff from the cold. She edged closer to shore and felt immense relief when her feet touched a hard bottom littered with rocks. The river had carried her quite a distance downriver. Attackers had appeared along the shoreline as well now but they were looking for her farther upriver.

There was no sign of Dane or Simon. Tabitha frowned, then looked in the other direction. There, farther downriver, a head bobbed in the cat tails. A hand in the air next to the head gestured for her to get down. The water was slightly warmer closer to shore, shallow and warmed by the sun, but still cold. Tabitha carefully wound her way through the cat tails, trying to be careful not to disturb the stalks, making her way to the bobbing head.

"Dane?" Tabitha called out softly.

"Simon," Simon responded, pushing cattail stalks out of the way so she could see him. "Hush. Any sign of movement on shore and sink. Got it?"

"Where's Dane?"

"Don't think about him right now. Hush."

Easy for him to say, Tabitha thought. Well, that wasn't fair, she realized at once. Simon cared what happened to Dane but he was right in that their main concern right now was staying undetected. The search went on for only a few more minutes before the sound of a large number of galloping horses caught everyone's attention. Heads on the barge turned to stare in unison at the sound of approaching horses, then there was a mad scramble by many to get off the barge.

"C'mon," Simon said, making his way along the cat tails until they were around a slight bend in the river. Tabitha obeyed his command to follow and when he left the water she followed. It wasn't easy. The hard packed river bottom turned to mud that sucked her feet and held her with persistence and she lost a shoe before she made it to dry ground. "Into the trees," Simon said, taking up position behind her now. Tabitha pulled off her remaining shoe after several up-down steps. "Hang onto that. If they find it they'll know we came out here."

Tabitha glanced back, then whipped her shoe out into the river. It landed with a splash then sank from sight. Simon glared at her. She shrugged. Tabitha had no intention of carrying around a wet half boot and no one was going to find it now. Simon pushed past her without a word and took over the lead.

"Any sign of Dane?" Tabitha asked.

Simon shook his head as he sidled through the underbrush. "We'll wait for a few minutes then make our way to the village."

"We can't leave Dane," Tabitha said in surprise.

"He'll head for the village if he doesn't find us right away," Simon said. "If he isn't there I'll get you to safety and then come back for him. You're the one everyone is chasing."

"She set us up," Tabitha said, looking in the direction of the barge thought it was out of sight now. Shonie acting surprised was all an act and she had so clearly pointed out Tabitha as the target.

Simon nodded. Being quiet was important and he must have decided that the only way to keep her quiet was to not answer her questions. Tabitha wrinkled her nose and took the hint. They weren't out of the woods yet. The literal correlation to the old adage almost made her laugh out loud but she managed to keep her laughter inside. Simon led her farther upriver as carefully and quietly as possible until they could see the barge but they remained in the cover of the underbrush. The barge was a large shape with figures crawling all over it. The riders who had passed them on the road while they were still in the cat tails were King's Men, their uniforms clearly visible now. A tow rope had been attached to the barge and it was slowly being dragged to shore.

"Can you see Dane?" Tabitha asked, leaning in to whisper.

"No. Shush."

"Ye are both safe now." Both Simon and Tabitha turned in surprise. The man standing behind them had made no sound. He was just there. Tabitha couldn't decide if it was a more incredible possibility that he had to have been standing there all along in his camouflage clothes and they hadn't seen him or that he had snuck up on them so silently that neither of them had noticed him approaching. Either solution for him to calmly be standing a few feet away from there seemed incredible. "Captain Olin has captured the attacking Cleaners and secured the area. Let us join him."

They had little choice but to obey, noisily exiting the underbrush to reach the road, their escort silently trailing. He wore a uniform similar to the King's Guard in style but of greens and grays that blended with the surroundings. Two more men in the same uniform stepped out onto the road.

"This way," the silent man said, gesturing up the road.

"Military," Simon muttered. "Domestic peacekeepers and military."

"What?" Tabitha asked in confusion. Though she had grown up running around barefoot she no longer had tough soles and walked gingerly on her bare feet.

"They have various branches of service, of course," Simon said, though it sounded to Tabitha like he was still answering his own questions. He looked at their escort. "You anticipated this?"

"Yes," the man said, nodding once.

"We were bait," Tabitha said in surprise.

"Controlled acceleration of an inevitable situation," the man said with a straight face.

Chapter Fourteen

They reached the section of shore where the barge now rested, still quite a few feet out from the bank but held securely by the thick tow lines. The gangplank had been dropped but its end sat hidden in the water. Whoever used it would have to wade up to their knees in water. Several bound men kneeled on the barge, water dripping from clothes, hair, and beards. More men kneeled on the ground near the water's edge, some with knees in the water, some on the muddy ground, their arms bound behind their backs. At least a hundred King's Men moved about the area, securing prisoners and doing what was needed to control the situation. Captain Olin saw them walking along the road escorted by his men and strode forward to meet them. Tabitha noted that he looked quite pleased with himself.

"You used us as bait!" Tabitha said in greeting.

"I see ye be in one piece," Captain Olin, looking her over from head to toe. He looked over her head. "Only two?"

"Still searching, sir," their escort said.

"Bring him to the island when you find him," Captain Olin ordered. He gestured and a carriage pulled up. "Get in. We'll have ye checked at hospital for any damage and get ye sewed up if need be. When we find your husband he'll be brought to ye. Then ye be released in a few days." He looked down at Tabitha with a wry grin. "Sorry, it was the only way. Ye didn't have to go for a swim. We had ye covered. Why did ye not use the chain mail blanket?"

"I don't need any doctor," Tabitha said, teeth chattering. "I'm fine."

"Well, ye will get a doctor," Captain Olin said firmly. "That arrow wound might need some stitches or it might not but it will definitely need proper cleaning."

Tabitha glanced at the torn fabric on her arm. That was why her arm hurt. That had been the sting she felt under water. She didn't care about some stupid cut. Dane was missing. "What about Dane?"

"My men are still looking. Now go."

Two of Olin's men practically lifted her into the carriage. Simon followed on his own power. Tabitha leaned out the carriage window. "The bit about not being allowed to touch a purple halo, that was a lie?"

Captain Olin looked up at her and grinned. "Having a little fun with your husband. Tells a man about another man's mettle, how they react in unexpected circumstances. Though I was surprised that he chose to carry ye into the village, I enjoyed watching him carry ye. Now go."

The horses started off smartly at the touch of the driver's whip, throwing Tabitha back on the seat. She watched the shoreline carefully for any sign of Dane but there was no sign of him. Captain Olin had used them as bait to flush out the Cleaners. Just thinking about it made her so angry. What if his little stunt had cost Dane his life? The thought of Dane hurt or dead twisted her into knots.

"He's a strong swimmer," Simon said, his gaze also on the shoreline as the road's path allowed.

"How about with an arrow in his back?" Tabitha asked. She wouldn't believe he was dead. Tabitha couldn't believe he could have died in the attack.

They rode the rest of the way in silence. They passed the King Men's gate and were escorted directly to their rooms. A doctor arrived within minutes of their own arrival. Tabitha barely had time to change from her wet dress to a robe. The doctor cleaned the wound on Tabitha's arm and did end up applying two stitches to the wound to close it. When he was done he applied a salve and within seconds the burning pain faded into nothing. He gave her the container and told her to apply the salve twice a day for three days. The doctor also instructed her to avoid getting the wound wet when she bathed.

Then they waited. Tabitha paced restlessly, worried about Dane. Then she remembered her bag. Tabitha pulled the wristlet out of the mass of wet clothes and dumped the contents of the small bag onto the bed and sorted through the contents for damage. The only thing she was really worried about was the digital camera. Though the wristlet wasn't waterproof it was made of oiled canvas and had done a good job of keeping out the water, except at one end of the zipper. Tabitha took the SD card out of the camera and studied it and the slot it fit into. It looked dry. There was really no way to know if the storage card had been ruined without reviewing the images on it. She stuck it in her pocket and put in her spare SD card but didn't turn on the camera, deciding at the last minute to let it dry completely before trying it. It seemed that if she left it alone there was a possibility it would dry completely and work. The SD card was the important thing right then.

She had Dane to thank that all the contents of her purse hadn't been ruined or completely lost, since he had talked her into not bringing it. She doubted she could have swum the river while lugging the big purse. He had possibly saved her life by stopping her from bringing the large purse. The thought made her cry. The day turned into evening with no sign of Dane. Tabitha fretted and paced and felt on edge as the hours passed.

"He'd head for the village," Simon said for the umpteenth time.

"You really think he'd go? Not even knowing if we made it?" Tabitha asked.

"We did make it," Simon said.

"Don't go using logic on me," Tabitha snapped. She paced the sitting room. "Why are we sitting here if we're not under house arrest any more?"

"We're waiting for them to find Dane," Simon said patiently. "We should go down before they're done serving dinner."

"I can't eat."

"You will eat," Simon said.

Tabitha did go to the dining room with Simon but only picked at her food. Every time someone entered the room she looked up, hoping and half expecting it to be Captain Olin or at least one of his King's Men to tell them news of Dane. It never was. Eventually they finished dinner and went back up to their suite, where they sat in total silence until it was time to turn in for the night.

That night Tabitha slept alone in the bed and tossed and turned despite an exhausting day. Her body was tired but her mind wasn't ready to let go of the events of the day and the fact that Dane had not been found. Tabitha had already gotten used to sharing the bed with Dane. She missed his warmth. She missed the sound of his breathing. She missed the way the bed shifted slightly under his weight, the resulting slant making her slide up against him. Tabitha wanted to believe he was all right. She wanted to believe that he had climbed out of the river and headed for the village as Simon and he agreed to do. It just didn't seem possible that Dane could slip through unseen with those men patrolling the shoreline.

Mostly Tabitha couldn't believe he had left her. No matter what Simon said, it felt like he was abandoning her if he just took off for the village alone, leaving them behind without knowing their fate. She tried to tell herself that it made sense, in a logical FBi sort of way, but it didn't really make sense to her. So Tabitha tossed and turned and fretted until she managed to tell herself that maybe his going on ahead to the village was the right choice, especially if he thought that they were going there also.

The next morning at breakfast Captain Olin joined them at the table. They had just finished eating and Tabitha pushed aside her almost empty plate when Olin sat down across from her. He looked quite somber and grave. She held her breath, waiting for the bad news she expected him to give her.

"I'm sorry," Olin said. "I should have given ye warning."

"No," Tabitha said, blinking against a sudden onslaught of tears clouding her vision.

Captain Olin shook his head. "They have not found your husband. However, they have not found a body either." He paused when a servant arrived with a steaming plate of food and set it in front of him. Olin ignored the plate for now. Once the waiter retreated Olin continued telling his news. "My men are still searching."

"No body. There's a chance then," Simon said.

Captain Olin nodded then looked back to Tabitha. "That is not my apology. I do feel your husband be a capable man. I be sorry for having put ye through this. Ye be thinking I should have perhaps shared my plans with ye, yes? But it was much more convincing to keep ye in the dark, so to say. I told ye, my objective is to maintain law and order. By flushing out these criminals I have done so. They will no longer harm innocent victims."

"That is what you're sorry about?" Tabitha asked, an edge to her voice.

"If ye had followed instructions ye would not have had to take a swim in the river," Captain Olin said. He took a deep breath. "It was a controlled situation. Perhaps it would have been good to tell ye at the barge. I did not expect ye to plunge into the river."

"Have they gone as far as the village in the search?" Simon asked. "Our plan was to meet at the village if we got separated."

"Ah, no, not so far," Olin said to Simon.

Tabitha used her knife to draw swirls in the egg yolk on her plate. "So we're free to leave then?"

Captain Olin nodded, studying Simon thoughtfully before turning his attention back to Tabitha. "Yes. Tomorrow or the next day. Depends on when I can arrange to provide you an escort to the village."

"Can I talk to Kate before I go?" Tabitha asked. "And Pederson. The man Simon and Dane were asking about. He's a criminal in our world. Can Simon see him before we go? They wanted to arrest him but if they at least can see that he's imprisoned here that should suffice. I assume he's a prisoner here and that's why you put off letting them see him."

"Ah, yes, Pederson. I see. I did not fully understand your interest in him. He is a criminal here as well," Captain Olin said to Simon. "A very dangerous man. He only lives because my father wished to make an example of him. It isn't pleasant but if ye be up to it ye shall visit him this afternoon." He turned his attention back to Tabitha. "Kate. Ye wish to understand why they wanted ye. A criminal's dream come true, escape into another dimension. No one could stop them. I am not yet sure of their complete plans for ye but I do know that ye be fortunate to have escaped that fate. I think that instead of Kate ye would do better to visit with Lord Kempley. He likes to spend his days in the library. I don't think Kate would answer your questions adequately. Or accurately."

Olin instructed her to go to the library to find Lord Kempley so Tabitha made her way to the library immediately after breakfast. Tabitha stared up at the map hanging on the library wall. Dane had to be all right. Simon seemed convinced that he was all right. She heard slow, shuffling footsteps approach from behind and looked over her shoulder to see the old man coming up behind her. He stopped next to her and stared up at the map as well for several long minutes.

"I am Lord Kempsley," he said at last. "You must be Captain Olin's find."

"Tabitha Ellis," Tabitha said. "Nice to meet you."

He smiled and studied the map. "What do you feel when you look at that map?"

"Homesick," she said without hesitation.

"Ah. For each it is slightly different. There be not many left in this world. I suppose there be possibly plenty in other worlds but like ye they don't recognize what the feelings mean, how to use the gift.

Some still stumble onto discovering their talent against the odds while others go their whole lives without ever knowing that they can use the zippers."

Tabitha looked at him, understanding dawning. She looked up at the map and he smiled and nodded his head. "Yes, in that room be a zipper. The Cleaners found tools, of course. Like many criminals they kept it to themselves. Keys and maps. Poor substitutes for the real thing. They went on their cleaning spree before they realized the depth of the difference. The tools are limited. They can force open a specific zipper is all. You can open any zipper, find any zipper, and find your way between worlds. With experience you will find it second nature. But to what end, eh? To what end?"

"The keys are weakening the zippers, aren't they?" Tabitha asked in amazement. "So the original group was almost right." Tabitha had read that the original group was trying to stop the use of the zippers.

Lord Kempsley nodded. "The keys *force* the zippers open while a purple halo naturally uses the zipper."

Tabitha stared up at the map. "How can I feel it from a map?"

He shrugged. "You've probably passed near it so when you see it on the map it triggers a memory." He shook his head back and forth several times. "Or maybe you already see the patterns. I remember hearing that it was a pattern."

"You're a purple halo?" she asked.

"No. But members of my family were. It skipped me. I did know many though. That was a long time ago. The Cleaners started out wanting to eradicate all purple halos, convinced that it would destroy the pattern of the universe and destroy the world to have people opening doors between dimensions," the old man said, staring up at the map as he remembered. "A very long time ago."

"So why do people here know about the zippers but no one at home?" Tabitha asked.

Lord Kempsley smiled. "Be ye sure no one there knows?"

"But I'd never heard of them," Tabitha said.

"Indeed. That does not mean they don't exist. That does not mean others know not of them." He handed her a leather wrapped parcel. "This is for you. I suggest you keep it to yourself. The zipper you are feeling here on the island does lead to your dimension if you need to use it to keep this knowledge safe."

"Keep it safe?" Tabitha repeated as she took the package. "What is it?"

"Notes. Information. It be better for ye to have some background instead of stumbling your way along, yes?" Lord Kempsley put his hand on the package Tabitha now held. "It was my father's. I have no real use for it. Perhaps one day ye could return it to me though?"

Tabitha nodded. "Yes, I shall. But why would I need to take it to safety? Is Captain Olin really not going to release us?"

"My nephew plans on taking ye personally to the zipper ye arrived through. I was considering the reception ye will receive when ye return. If ye have nothing on your person to tie to zippers when ye return that would be for the best."

"I don't understand," Tabitha said, staring at the package in her hands.

"The men ye be with, they are of a government agency who would like detailed information on these zippers," Lord Kempsly said. "So I have been told. I do know something of this land of yours. I believe that my son-in-law would also confiscate such information."

"Ah," Tabitha said slowly. "Your son-in-law is the king?" She looked up at Lord Kempsley, who was smiling at her as he waited. It was a sad smile. The FBI would take her key and whatever was in this package, if it wasn't Thomas waiting for them on the other side of the zipper. Tabitha would indeed be smart to stash this package somewhere safe until she could go through it. An idea struck her. "Would you like to come with me when I try this other zipper?"

Lord Kempsley stared at her in surprise then his shoulders straightened and a sparkle lit his eyes. "Indeed." He offered his elbow. "I would be honored to escort you in this endeavor."

The next morning a message arrived before breakfast that they would be escorted back to the village the next morning and Simon would be allowed to visit with Pederson after breakfast. Tabitha told

Simon that she would be busy all day so if he didn't see her not to worry.

"More trips to the library?" Simon asked. "I didn't see you yesterday either. I even checked the library."

"I was visiting with Lord Kempsley," Tabitha said, a slight flush touching her cheeks pink.

"This Lord Kempsley, he's, uh, who he is he?" Simon asked, noticing the guilty flush.

"A very wise and helpful elderly man," Tabitha said. "He's been able to explain a lot of this purple halo business to me."

"Ah, that's good," Simon said, quickly losing interest. He was eager to meet with Pederson and if Tabitha was busy it meant she was staying out of trouble and out of his hair.

That evening Simon was already at the dining room when Tabitha arrived. She was quiet and answered his occasional question but didn't start any conversations or invite any conversations. Tabitha had visited with Lord Kempsley for many hours and had read quite a bit of the information in the package and it was a lot to take in. Simon enjoyed the quiet for a few minutes then began to worry that she was quiet because she was worried about Dane. "He'll be at the village waiting for us," he said.

Tabitha looked up from her grilled salmon. "I hope so."

The next morning Tabitha was packed and ready to go when the King's Men escort arrived at the suite. The maid had told Tabitha that the clothes were a gift to her and she should take them so she now carried a suitcase as well as her large purse. Simon chose to not keep the clothes he had been given so he had no luggage. Captain Olin was waiting on the steps leading to the parade ground. Twenty mounted King's Men waited with two saddled horses for Simon and Tabitha to ride. Captain Olin chose to say his farewell at the bottom of the great stairs leading into the castle proper. Tabitha stared up at Olin when she realized that instead of riding with them he was staying. The stone urchin crouched just above his head in the view she had. The escort he had promised waited patiently.

"My men did not find your husband at the village either. I be sorry for your loss," Captain Olin said. "I know that it be a poor substitute but know that his loss wasn't in vain. He was a man of the law in your world so he would understand that the result was capturing dangerous criminals and saving future victims. Perhaps there is a chance he survived but I do not hold out such hope or my men would have found him by now." Captain Olin held up his right hand, palm out. "May fair winds warm your back." He turned, then paused and looked back. "I trust we won't be dealing with adventurers from your land. We like the way things be and that's why we keep it this way." That statement was clearly a warning to Simon.

"You have my word we don't intend to come back this way," Simon said.

With that promise Prince Olin turned and went back into his fortress, the captain protecting his realm. Tabitha watched him go until he entered the doors, then turned to her horse and mounted. She looked up one last time at the imposing sight of the castle filling the whole island. There were many secrets hidden in that stone fortress. Simon was still staring thoughtfully at where Captain Olin had vanished into the fortress.

The ride to the village did not take more than a few hours and passed uneventful. Tabitha rode in a subdued mode. There was too much going on in her head for even her to find room for talking. It felt strange to at last be heading home when she didn't know Dane's fate. Tabitha continued to tell herself that he was all right, that Simon was right and he had headed for the village, expecting them to join him there. Dane had a key so if he reached the village he would have gone home when Simon and she did not arrive. Tabitha was convinced that Dane was all right. She told herself every day that he was all right. The King's Men not finding him was a good sign.

Lord Kempsley had filled her head with wonders and answered all her questions and more. It was that information that had her in a near stupor. She could find and open any zipper. Even when faced with the truth of that by opening the zipper on Nicollet Island and going through with Lord Kempsley at her side, it was still difficult to digest mentally.

Simon had been watching her thoughtfully for quite a while. When the village came into sight and she had remained quiet for the whole trip he said, "You're mighty quiet. Everything all right?"

Tabitha pulled herself out of her deep thoughts, startled to see the rooftops of the village in sight. She turned to Simon. "Did you meet with Hans Pederson then?" she asked.

Simon nodded. "He's in prison. With no chance of going anywhere." Simon chose not to elaborate on the conditions Pederson was living under. He patted his chest, where a thick wad of paper sat in his pocket. "He was most cooperative. I have a list of crimes he committed and locations of where he delivered many of the women he abducted."

"The Stengarlds," Tabitha said thoughtfully. She looked up in interest. "You plan on rescue trips?"

Simon looked at her in surprise. "How did you know? About the Stengarlds?"

"Women abducted by both Pederson and Thomas. There has to be a reason. The Stengarlds. It was probably a toll price. So you do plan on rescue trips?"

Simon nodded. "If possible. Now that we know what happened to them we have to do what we can."

"That's good," Tabitha said. "I can help you."

"About the key you gave me," Simon said slowly.

"Oh, the key I gave you, it's yours," Tabitha said. "I know someone will just confiscate them anyway. But I can still help. I just need the list of names."

Simon nodded thoughtfully but didn't say anything. They both knew that she would lose all her keys before it was over. What

Simon didn't know was that Tabitha had spent the day before learning what it meant in fact to be a purple halo. She didn't need the keys but she didn't intend to simply hand them over to the Bureau without any say in it. Tabitha had hidden the rough heart key from the Altoids tin in the village before they had headed for the city. She hadn't intended to collect it before leaving, not wanting to hand over a possible universal key but hearing Simon saying he planned to rescue the women made her have second thoughts.

Tabitha didn't know that it was actually a universal key. The idea that it was a universal key had grown out of not understanding that *she* was the universal key. She had no way of testing it herself either, since she could open anything. The FBI would have the keys and maps from the house Pederson had owned before Thomas stole it from him. Tabitha debated again on collecting the hidden heart key now that they were at the village. There was no proof that it would open more than this zipper. Tabitha stared at the visible rooftops of the buildings as they approached the village.

They rode into the village. Dane stood waiting in the doorway of one of the houses. Relief and delight and anger washed over her at the sight of him. Dane was alive. But he had abandoned her. He was such a remarkable sight to see. Tabitha felt every nerve in her body come to life just at the sight of him. This was love, she realized. This was love. This feeling that washed over her, filling her with warmth, making her feel alive, this was love. The horse jumped forward when Tabitha touched her heels to its sides and they raced into the village square.

Suddenly the village was swarming with camouflaged United States Special Forces. They seemed to materialize out of nowhere from everywhere all at once. Advanced weaponry pointed, clicked, and projected tiny beams of red light and green light all around her. Dane stepped out of the doorway. Tabitha pulled her horse to a halt in front of him and scrambled out of the saddle.

"I brought the cavalry," Dane said.

Tabitha laughed, wiping away the tears streaming down her face. She threw herself at him, wrapping her arms around him. Dane stiffened at first then embraced her. He leaned down and kissed her, which caused an eruption of hoots and cat-calls from the watching men though it was at best a lukewarm kiss. Confused, Tabitha stepped back.

"I was afraid you had drowned," Tabitha said. She punched his arm. "That's for scaring me."

"Took me some time to gather the cavalry," Dane said, forcing a grin. The grin looked very strained. "Wasn't easy to convince my boss. Luckily soldiers are good at following orders so it was easy enough once the ball started rolling."

Simon walked up beside them. "Damned glad to see you, boy. As you can see we were actually on our way home. Call down the boys before we get ourselves an incident."

"I just have to do one thing," Tabitha said. Dane had made some signal and the guns were being lowered and all the flashing red beams and points of light had vanished. She looked around them thoughtfully. It would have been a lot more exhilarating to see the cavalry a few days earlier. Now they filled her with concern. More people now knew about the zipper.

Tabitha slipped away from the men and went into the little house they had stayed the night in the first night in this dimension. She collected the heart key from its hiding place and left the house with the key cupped in her fist. Dane was talking to the King's Men escort, who were looking uncomfortable, though they had not drawn their own weapons. The cavalry had stood down but their very presence was threatening.

"Let's get them out of here," Simon said, watching the tension mounting.

"Time to head back, boys," Dane yelled. He turned to the King's Men officer. "We're leaving. Everyone is leaving now." The officer nodded, keeping an eye on the steady flow in the direction of the zipper. "Benchly, do a sweep to make sure everyone made it to the zipper."

A well-muscled man nodded and headed away at a run. They all walked to location of the zipper under the watchful eyes of the King's Men. It was easy for anyone to see the location because of the trampled grass. Dane opened the zipper by raising his fist into the correct location and the cavalry began to step through quickly.

Tabitha ducked through, concentrating on the heart key clutched in her left hand, startled at what she stepped through to find on the other side. What looked like a command center now filled what had been Daniel Thomas' kitchen and den. Tables, computers and large monitors filled the rooms as well as the personnel sitting at all the monitors. More uniformed men followed her, then Simon, then Benchley. Dane was the last man through the zipper a few minutes after everyone else.

A tall, impressive, ebony skinned man stood watching the proceedings. Tabitha knew before being told that this was the man in charge. He had that aura of being in control. Tabitha stepped to the side and held her left fist against her back unobtrusively. After a few minutes when she seemed to have been forgotten she tried to melt into the background of the commotion but Dane gestured for her to join him with the man who looked to be in charge.

"Tabitha, this is Agent Collin McNamara," Dane said. Dane was even more cool and distant than he had been in the village.

"Tabitha, nice to meet you," McNamara said, taking her hand. His hand engulfed hers as he shook it. "Not sure if you had a chance to catch up. Daniel Thomas is in custody. Agent Ellis brought him in before convincing me to bring in reinforcements. Let's find a place to have a private chat. A lot of noise out here. Simon and Dane, join us."

Hearing that Daniel was in custody was a great relief but why did McNamara need to talk to her? Tabitha looked at Dane in alarm.

What now? Dane took her hand and gave it a squeeze. "Don't worry. It's just a debriefing. I'll be right there with you."

"What about my cat?" Tabitha asked. "Has anyone gone to take care of my cat? And my job? Did someone contact my company to let them know that I was, uh, unable to make it due to circumstances beyond my control?"

Tabitha caught the look that flashed between McNamara and Dane before McNamara said, "Someone has been to your house. Your cat is fine."

Tabitha nodded gratefully. Though she was relieved that Snooze was all right she knew that they hadn't gone to her house only to check on her cat. Once Dane had established credibility to the existence of a zipper they would have gone to her house to search for more keys, she was sure. It didn't seem right but she knew that anything she had in relation to the zipper was going to be forfeit. Or at least noted that she had it in her possession. Fortunately Tabitha had secured everything they didn't already know about.

"This way, Miss Anderson," McNamara said, gesturing down the hall. Tabitha followed him to the study. Simon and Dane fell into step behind her. Another man followed them inside and shut the door behind them. Empty shelves lined the walls of the room. They had recently been emptied. The lines of dust still outlined the shape of what had occupied the shelves. "Agent Paulhus will take notes," McNamara said. Agent Paulhus nodded his head in greeting then promptly pulled a chair up to the desk and opened a laptop.

"First, thanks to you, Miss Anderson for assisting in the identification and subsequent capture and arrest of the man Daniel Thomas. We have reason to believe Hans J. Pederson has also possibly been located," McNamara said.

Simon tapped the bulge of papers in his jacket's chest pocket. "Pederson's confession and location of almost all his victims. He is imprisoned in, uh, another country of which will be named in a future document."

McNamara's eyes lit up. "Really? We can provide closure for all those families?"

"More than that," Simon said, leaning forward. "We may be able to rescue many of them. He didn't kill anyone, just sent them through zippers. There is the strong possibility that we may be able to find them. Or at least let their families know they are alive. It's been many years. But yes, closure." Simon jerked his head at Tabitha. "Thanks to her. Olin had put us off and she had a little chat with him and he delivered. He delivered big."

Tabitha watched them without commenting, without even having the desire to speak up. It hit her that they cared. They cared about protecting people. They cared about their jobs. Dane also sat quietly on the couch along the back wall, his face a mask. Tabitha watched him most of all. Now that they were back would he go back to his normal life without her? What part was he going to play now?

"I'm sure the big question now, for many of you, is what next? What do we do with this information? We found several maps and items called keys as well as the locations of houses containing more zippers. What do we do with the keys and maps? Agents have already visited each property owned by Thomas and the contents will be searched if they haven't already." McNamara's attention was primarily on Tabitha as he spoke. "Honestly, there hasn't been time to determine a clear course of action, other than one failsafe. That is to secure all known zippers and thus all known keys to open those zippers."

Tabitha held out her hand and presented the Altoid tin she had been clutching in her fist. She had hidden the tin in the garden and it had rained while they were in the city. The Altoids tin creaked when she opened it. The tissue stuck to the pieces of tektite. Tabitha tried to pull off the stuck tissue, giving the bits of green glass a final brush with her fingers before handing them to McNamara. McNamara placed the keys into a wallet sized metal box. Simon and Dane handed over the keys she had given them. McNamara put them in the box then sealed it in an evidence bag.

"There's another meteorite at my house," Tabitha said.

"Yes," McNamara said, nodding. He turned to Paulhus. "We're done."

Agent Paulhus left the room, laptop half open. McNamara smiled and leaned back in his chair. "The rest is just a matter of getting you back to your life. A press release has confirmed your safe recovery. We're using the official story that Thomas held you captive in his basement. I would appreciate it if you would stick to that story, even with your family."

"I need to know what you're going to do now, about the zippers," Tabitha said. "I know nothing official has been decided but where do you see it going?"

"Nowhere," McNamara said. He smiled his slow gentle smile at her surprise. "It's a simple matter of manpower. Technically we would have no jurisdiction once we passed through a zipper. For our search and rescue we will bend the rules just a bit, since it is American soil. But as far as exploring the other sides of those dimensions? There simply isn't enough manpower."

"So you'll secure the zippers and that'll be that?" Tabitha asked.

"Hopefully. We'll probably treat them like border stations. Small key surveillance to make sure no one comes through into our dimension but it'll end there."

"Won't it fall under the Homeland Security thing?" Tabitha asked.

Simon made a sound, much like a muffled bear. "Tell me how exploiting the land beyond those zippers is the business of Homeland Security?"

"More likely customs and immigration," McNamara said. "As I said, at this point our only intention is securing the sites once our search and rescue has been completed."

McNamara stood. "I need to speak further with Agents Ellis and Bismarck but I'll have someone drive you home. We'll be in touch.

But you need some rest. We'll need a statement from you. Agent Ellis requested that we include you in any future dealings with the zippers."

"Really?" Tabitha asked in surprised delight, glancing at Dane. He sat on the couch, not having said a word the entire debriefing. He gave her a tight smile but still didn't say anything.

"He asked that you be given top security clearance in any projects we undertake with the zippers."

"All security clearance," Dane said slowly. "I said *all* security clearance."

"Right. We will definitely keep you posted on the progress made in locating the victims of both Thomas and Pederson. As for anything else, well, there most likely won't be anything else. Except for your statement. Tomorrow?"

Home. Tabitha was impatient to get home. She hesitated, looked at Dane. Tabitha really needed to talk to him. Dane stood. "If you'll excuse me for just a few minutes, sir, I'd like to say farewell to Tabitha."

They stepped into the hallway. The cavalry had dispersed, leaving the house feeling almost empty, though a few figures still moved about the den and kitchen area and the computer equipment was still set up. Dane stood stiffly, looking down at Tabitha, stilling her initial reaction to slip into his arms for a hug.

"Thanks," Tabitha said at last.

"Thanks?"

"For everything. For the cavalry. For getting me included in the future of the zippers."

"It's only right. They are your keys."

"I see," Tabitha said slowly, though she really didn't see.

Dane held out his hand. 'Good luck. I'm sure we'll be seeing each other again."

Tabitha stared at his hand but didn't offer her hand. It was what casual acquaintances did, shake hands good-bye. "I see," Tabitha said, feeling her face freezing around her polite smile. If she lost the smile she'd break into tears. Tabitha concentrated on keeping that polite smile in place. What was wrong with him? Eventually she took his hand and gave him a lukewarm handshake. Tabitha felt like all the air had been sucked out of the hallway.

"Okay, then," she said, remaining rooted to the spot when he released her hand.

"I need to get back in," he said, using his head to gesture to the room behind him. "We'll be in touch."

"Of course," she said. "Bye then."

Dane went back inside the study on trembling legs and immediately sat back down on the couch. That hadn't gone well. That hadn't gone well at all. He would have to make it up to her later. Dane could tell she was upset, angry even, but he didn't have the energy to soothe her feathers. She would just have to forgive him his lack of an emotional farewell. He intended to see her soon anyway. It wasn't like they were saying good-bye for good.

Simon and McNamara were going over Pederson's confession. Dane could hear them talking but could no longer focus on what was being said. Then Simon's face was hovering over him. McNamara's face appeared next to Simon's face. They were discussing Pederson's victims, Dane remembered.

"Sorry, sir," Dane said, words slurring. "Forgot to mention. Got shot when took down Thomas."

"Damn fool," someone muttered.

Dane tried to smile. It took effort. He thought he managed to smile. "Had to bring in the cavalry."

Chapter Fifteen

Tabitha settled into the car and rested her head on the back of the seat. Home. She was heading home at last. Instead of feeling relief she felt ripped to shreds inside. Agent Ellis had been so cold and distant, not at all what she had expected. Dalton had come back with the cavalry. He had made sure that they didn't just take her keys and push her out the door. Yet he acted like they were merely acquaintances and now that the job was done they were done as well. How could she have been so wrong about him? Tabitha had thought he had feelings for her. If he had feelings for her, then coming back through that zipper had apparently somehow erased those feelings.

Tabitha had thought she had gotten to know him during their time in the other dimension. Dane's change of attitude baffled her. He was pushing her away and she didn't know why. Had it only been the moment? Playing at husband and wife, he had maybe gotten carried away and now that they were back in their own world he was realizing that things had moved too fast in the wrong direction? Wanting to slow things down didn't explain the cold, distant way he had said farewell. It did no good to guess at what he was doing, she told herself. All she could do was go by facts. The facts pointed to his backing away and holding out his arm to hold her at bay.

Tabitha stared out the car window without seeing the passing houses and buildings. She had lost her heart to him. She hadn't expected it to happen. It had just happened. Now he had handed it back to her. Or at least he had tried to hand it back to her. She wasn't sure if it worked that way. Maybe that's why her heart hurt so much.

The car pulled up to her house and Tabitha stared out the window for a minute without making any move to get out of the car. Home. How long had she been gone? It felt like a lifetime ago but realized it had been only roughly over a week. Her house welcomed her back. It was the one place she could ease her hurting heart. Tabitha had learned long ago that keeping busy with her projects helped push away pain born of disappointment.

Tabitha thanked the driver and stepped out of the car. She walked up to the front door, pausing to dig through her purse for her keys. An agent followed her to the door and set her suitcase on the steps. Tabitha had forgotten about the suitcase containing all the clothing she had obtained in the other dimension. The King's Men must have passed it on to the FBI Dane had brought to rescue her and someone else had managed to get it in the car. The suitcase was a large leather satchel. It was lumpier than she remembered when she had packed it. Someone had gone through it. The car sat idling behind her until she was inside and turned on a light. A gray ball of fur streaked down the hall towards her at a run, talking the whole way. Rrrr-itt. Snooze didn't meow, he talked. Snooze dropped to the floor at her feet, rolling onto his back, then his side, rubbing his face happily against her foot, talking the whole time. He had missed her.

Tabitha smiled as she scooped him up into her arms, rubbing her cheek on his silky soft head. It took ten minutes of loving and assurance before Snooze lost his frantic need to display his happiness at her return home but he continued to talk to her as she checked his food and water then litter box. Food and water bowls were both half full and the litter box had only one clump so someone had been checking on the cat and seeing to his needs. Someone had brought in her mail and piled it on the kitchen table.

Tabitha wandered into the living room, scooping up Snooze again when she almost tripped on him because he was right under her feet. The rrrr-itt settled into a steady purr that vibrated his whole body with a steady thrum. The melted glass in her stained glass display case had been moved but all items were all accounted for. If she hadn't marked the positions with a piece of hair there wouldn't have been any evidence that they had been moved. Of course when she had set up the display case she had been expecting Thomas to invade her house, not the FBI. The rock from Oklahoma had been moved as well but was still there.

The workshop was next on her return home tour. It didn't look like anything had been touched. Tabitha set Snooze down on the workbench and pulled out the bin with the meteorite. It was gone. They were very, very good. She kneaded Snooze's back, from his head all the way down to the base of his tail. Snooze was so happy he flopped down on the work bench, right on top of a basket of tools. Tabitha smiled as she rubbed his tummy. It wasn't easy to feel down when a happy cat was in a loving mode yet she still felt oddly empty inside. Tabitha picked up Snooze and righted the basket then picked up the pliers, metal files, and awl that had been dumped out during Snooze's affectionate display.

First order of business was a shower and getting into her own clothes. She locked Snooze out of the bathroom when he tried to sneak his way inside with her. It didn't work well to allow Snooze in the bathroom with her. He loved the bathroom but the last time she had let him remain in the bathroom while she showered he had discovered flushing the toilet.

While in the shower Tabitha realized that she didn't even know that what time of day it was or what day it was. The time alignment between dimensions was off and made it disorienting. She had to call her boss. She had to call her family. Tabitha had to figure out what she was going to do about Dane. She had wanted to tell him about her discovered talent, what it meant to be a purple halo but he had been so distant and aloof that he was unapproachable. Also, Thomas' house had been rather chaotic and not the right place to have that discussion.

Clean and smelling of her favorite soap and shampoo, wearing a favorite pair of jeans and an over-sized, deep green hooded sweatshirt embroidered with a picture of a wolf head on the left shoulder, Tabitha slipped her feet into a cozy pair of Chinese slippers and shuffled her way into the living room. Snooze had found a toy, a ball with a bell inside and was batting it down the hall, sliding on the wood floor as he tried to catch up. Life was back to normal for the cat and Snooze was satisfied that it was back to normal.

For the cat life was back to normal but Tabitha knew that her life would be forever changed. Zippers existed between dimensions. That was a startling concept she had barely come to terms with after a week of stark proof. There had been less time to come to terms with the fact that she could open the zippers. Not only could she open the zippers but she could find them to open them. Lord Kempsley had told her that eventually she should even recognize the dimension the zipper opened to before opening it. Also, he had said that she would sense the presence of people near the zipper on the other side even before opening it.

"The dimensions are separated thus," Lord Kempsley had explained, drawing swirls out on paper. "Picture wedges of an orange, but thin. It is where they are close that the fabric of space allows passage between, the zippers. Once you recognize how the dimensions lie in relationship to each other ye will see the possibilities. Knowing the possibilities allows knowing where to look for them."

They had gone through the zipper on the island so that she could bring back her package and heart key without going through the gauntlet of FBI. Tabitha had to go pick them up from where she had stashed them but not just yet. The location where the zipper on Nicollet Island opened in the home dimension surprised her. "What if someone built a wall right over the zipper?" she had asked Lord Kempsley.

"It's not likely. If it did happen ye would feel it blocked. Ye won't walk out into a flooded area or into a solid wall. Ye could walk into a battle or find yourself in someone's private home or in a very public space, however. Ye will learn how to sense if someone is near the zipper. The same thing that allows ye to identify and open the zipper allows ye to use it as a peephole before opening it."

Tabitha called her boss, Susan, first. Yes, the FBI had contacted the company and Susan had been glued to the news so they were aware that she had been kidnapped during an FBI investigation and held prisoner in the basement of a crazy man, along with two FBI agents. The ordeal had been so traumatic that she wasn't ready to come back to work yet. Susan assured her that she should take all the time needed but to keep in mind that there was a large software release coming up in ten days but not to worry about it after all she had been through but there were some project specific items in the release so if she could let a backup person know what they should be looking for that would be great but she should feel free to take as much time as she needed as long as she didn't take too long. She needed a few more days to deal with it. No problem. She could hear the curiosity in Susan's voice while they talked but she really wasn't up to talking about any of it, not even the cover story.

When she got off the phone she turned on the television, turning to a news channel for the date and time. Next she called her brother, to test the water. Maybe the news had only been local. She had no intention of getting her family into a frenzy if they didn't already know about the kidnapping. As she listened to the phone ring she saw the story flash on the news channel, two FBI agents and a woman had been held prisoner in the basement of a man suspected in the disappearance of several people. The prisoners had been discovered and released and Daniel Thomas was in custody.

The coverage had obviously been recorded earlier because the team of Special Forces was just leaving Thomas' house behind the reporter. The reporter caught one of the hard, flacked jacket covered men as he was leaving the house. "Can you tell us if the agents have been released?"

"All three missing persons are safely in Bureau custody," the man said, smiling for the camera.

'The man, Daniel Thomas, is in Minneapolis Medical Facility. Is there truth in that he's saying he didn't abduct them, just pushed them into another dimension?"

The flacked jacket man laughed. "That would be funny, ma'ame. Guess that's why he's in the loony bin."

Tabitha smiled. Even the reporter's tone indicated that she was asking because she had to ask but didn't believe it for a minute. It was unbelievable. The following questions were the normal inane, non-thought provoking questions the media had become notorious for. What did he think would be the impact of having two FBI agents kidnapped by one man? Would the FBI do a complete overhaul of their investigative process now? Should the local police have been involved? How could trained FBI agents be held captive by one man?

The phone connected to voicemail after the allotted eight rings and Tabitha listened to her brother's voice mail message, waiting for the beep. She left a brief message, just to say that she was home and all right. Her thumb was still on the phone from pushing the end call button when the phone rang. It was her mother.

"Tabitha. Oh, Tabitha. Are you all right?" her mom asked, tears already in her voice.

"Yes. So you heard?"

"Heard? We've been frantic."

"I'm all right. I literally just got in the door a few minutes ago. I don't know what the press reported but I'm all right. Everything is all right."

"Come home. Your dad is on his way to your place right now. He's been staying with Jimmy. He'll bring you home."

Home. Being with her family right now sounded good. Tabitha sighed. "I wish I could but I can't. Maybe in a few days when things settle down. The FBI still has questions and I can't leave Snooze again so soon."

Tabitha was on the phone with her mom for quite a while. She brushed over her experience, not wanting to lie to her mom and not ready to talk about it yet. She preferred to listen to her mom talking about normal life. She noticed that the answering machine was blinking a frantic beat, probably everyone looking for her when she vanished. Her mother's voice was comforting and she felt a lot of tension easing away. When her dad and brother arrived at the house she said good-bye to her mom and handed the phone over to her dad so he could assure her mom that she was indeed in one piece. The rest of the day passed fairly quickly as her house filled with friends and family.

When her dad was settled in the spare bedroom and her brother Jimmy was on the couch Tabitha was finally alone in her own bedroom. She was actually glad that they hadn't wanted to leave her alone that night. It was comforting to have them there. It helped keep her mind off the fact that she hadn't heard from Dane all night. Once Tabitha was in bed she tossed and turned for hours. There was too much on her mind to fall asleep though she was totally exhausted.

In the morning Tabitha would call McNamara and ask to visit with him. Tabitha would have to tell him that she could open any zipper without a key. Well, more correctly, she was the key. Tabitha didn't want to tell anyone but she didn't know how to do what she had to do unless she told McNamara. So Tabitha tossed and turned instead of falling asleep, trying to sort out all the events and possibilities. The thread dominating her thoughts was Dane. What was she going to do about Dane? Had it been a short term fling? Was he going to just walk away? Should she just let him walk away without a word? What if Dane thought she was the one walking away? If she told McNamara that she was the key would the FBI lock her up somewhere as a potential risk to the country? It made for a restless night.

***

"Stubborn goat," Simon chided.

"If I had told I'd been shot I wouldn't have been able to lead the cavalry to the rescue," Dane said.

"Yeah, well, that little move nearly cost you your life," Simon said. "Internal bleeding. Infection. All sorts of nasty things."

"How long have I been here?"

"Eight days."

Dane's eyebrows rose. "For a little graze?" Dane asked in surprise. He grimaced when he moved. "Okay, not the brightest thing I've done. Tabitha?"

Simon shrugged, looking across the room. "Keeping quiet."

Dane almost laughed at the expression keeping quiet but it hurt too much and he froze until the urge to laugh passed. Eight days and Tabitha hadn't been to see him or called to see how he was. That didn't fit her. Something was wrong with that but the drugs clouded his thinking."

"The Thomas house. Any movement on that?"

"Thomas hasn't been as cooperative as Pederson was but we found a journal he kept. Rather haphazardly. There are some vague entries about the Stengarlds getting a blonde or a brunette." Simon got up and paced. "McNamara has something up his sleeve, some plan to rescue these women but it's proving to be more difficult than expected. I don't like it. Red tape is getting in the way. Well, the Stengarlds are getting in the way and it's the red tape making it impossible to just mow over them."

"You think he's handing it over to another agency?" Dane asked. It was harder to stay awake and he shook his head to clear it.

"I don't know. That's not what it feels like. It's going to be hard to keep those zippers quiet. Once those victims start coming back through it's going to be damned hard to explain where they've been. There's a reason why the Stengarlds have such a high demand for women," Simon said. "We made one exploratory reach into the zipper and immediately retreated. Thomas seemed fascinated with their culture and wrote more about them in his journal than any other zipper. They held him captive for a short time, in order to gain his cooperation to continue Pederson's arrangement. It's a harsh land. Did I say harsh land? Brutal. Just for that Thomas should be given the electric chair." Simon's mouth tightened in anger. "It was what he intended for Tabitha when he pushed us through."

Dane nodded. The drugs in the IV were kicking in and he felt himself drifting away. Dane felt himself thinking about saying words but the effort to talk was just too much for him to manage. The last two times he had seen Tabitha he had given her no reason to think well of him. He'd have to make it up to her. Tabitha in the hands of brutal men treating her like nothing roused his anger but he lost the struggle and fell back to sleep.

***

Tabitha sat across from McNamara in his office, studying the objects lined up neatly across his desk. Those were the keys located in the other houses owned by Thomas. It had been over a week since the return from Dimension Olin. That was how she now referred to that world, Dimension Olin. Over a week had passed since she had seen or heard from Dane. Tabitha had even called his listed number a few days after not hearing from him and he hadn't answered or returned her call. She had called twice. Tabitha felt like she should have left it at once since she had left a message asking him to call her back yet she went ahead and called a second time and Dane still didn't return her call. Simon had called but she hadn't listened to his message. Tabitha hadn't been ready yet to deal with the FBI. She had some things to work out on her own before confronting the FBI. Keeping busy helped keep her mind off Dane.

Though Tabitha normally didn't wear much make-up she had taken great care to cover the effects of several more restless nights and the tears that had finally allowed her to sleep. Tabitha felt like she had lost something important in her life, the biggest thing to ever enter her life. Dane. He had been so cool and distant immediately after the return and then he had walked away and cut her out of his life without a word. It hurt. Tabitha deserved better than that. Dane at least owed her a good-bye.

Tabitha had collected her package from its hiding spot at the bus depot and spent several days studying the documents Lord Kempsley had given her before investigating the zippers in person. Tabitha had also tucked her better version of the tektite heart into the package of papers before stashing it in the bus depot locker. Between going back to work and working with the zippers every spare minute Tabitha was kept busy. Every time she walked through her front door she immediately went to the answering machine and checked the machine but though there were usually messages there was no message from Dane and she would go to bed without even listening to the messages.

Tabitha had contacted McNamara because she wanted to know their plans for the zippers. She remembered that McNamara had said once that it was to be purely a search and rescue mission. Tabitha had originally intended to contact him the day after the return but then had gone a different route, investigating for herself what options she could give them. It had been a risky undertaking and the result had brought her back to McNamara with the hope that the FBI would cooperate.

"Your intentions with the zippers," Tabitha began to say. That felt awkward. She took a deep breath. "What are you going to do with the zippers?"

McNamara watched her, noting the hesitation. It was a question he had asked himself many times. There were no laws dealing with jurisdiction for this situation. So far he had kept the information to only those already in the know. If he had his way he'd turn his back and forget their existence once all the victims were rescued. Once he reported it higher up the ladder it would be out of his control. For some reason he was reluctant to let it go out of his control just yet.

Even the search and rescue had not gone well up to this point. Their one incursion into the Viking dimension had sent them into a hasty retreat. The men waiting on the other side had not waited to talk. They had immediately attacked the intruders into their world. Two of his men were in the hospital but luckily no one had been killed. Orders had been to only use enough force to defend their selves and because of that limit they had been quick to retreat. The Vikings were not "ask questions first" type of men. These Vikings were "attack first then maybe ask the questions" type of men. Most of the Thomas victims had gone through that zipper and unless they were willing to go in with the intent to slaughter their way through the tent surrounding the zipper they were stuck cooling their heels for now. Some of the men were ready to go in guns blazing but McNamara wouldn't allow it. A few bruises and concussions due to a training exercise could be brushed away. Dead agents or Marines could not slip under the wire unnoticed.

Since McNamara wanted to keep a low profile they had not yet explored any zippers in other cities. In addition, the other locations

Pederson had named were not so easy to locate and identify keys for. It was taking time to go through what information they had, made slower by his desire to keep limited those who would have knowledge of the zippers.

McNamara steepled his fingers and leaned his elbows on the desk as he watched her. He noted the heavy make-up and shadowed eyes. McNamara was a good judge of character and body language. Tabitha clearly had something important to discuss but she was wary, distrustful. Tabitha would need some assurance from him before she disclosed what she had churning inside her head. He decided it would require his being up front with her regarding the Bureau's position on the zippers.

"So far we are treating it as a search and rescue mission," he said. "We have no further plans." He sighed and sat back in his chair. "Hell, what a bombshell. To be honest, I've kept this whole thing under wraps. If I have my way we'll find the missing people and toss away the keys."

Tabitha nodded thoughtfully as she considered his words. Suddenly she straightened in her chair, the worry and fatigue melting away. "Okay. If you're willing to do that I will help."

"What's that?" McNamara asked in surprise. He hadn't seen that coming.

"If you'll give me all the keys you've collected and allow me to dispose of them I will help you get to all the dimensions with the missing people. I, uh, I have a map as well."

McNamara frowned. "I have to tell you, we tried the piece carved into a heart and despite the reported possibility that it could be a universal key it only opened the one zipper."

"Yes," Tabitha said. "Did anyone step through once the zipper was open?"

"Why do you ask?"

"It only opens to the Dimension Olin and we said we wouldn't return with the intention of trespassing."

"No. No one went through." McNamara noted her relief. Simon had also made it clear that it would be considered an invasion if they went through that zipper again. There was no valid reason to visit that dimension, yet when McNamara had held out that heart-shaped key and the zipper had flared to light it had been tempting to step through, just to experience it.

"I know a back door into the Stengarlds zipper. I can get you in without going through the men guarding the zipper from the sunroom. In trade I want all the keys you've collected."

McNamara laughed. Tabitha patiently waited and McNamara sobered. "Oh, you're serious?"

"You don't need the keys and I have learned that the keys are more dangerous than just being in the wrong hands. I can get you through any zipper needed to rescue those people."

"You can get through any zipper? Without a key? Or do you have a universal key after all?" McNamara asked.

"I can get through any zipper needed. Can that be enough?" Tabitha said.

McNamara nodded his head as he considered. "I can't just hand over the keys," he said, waving his hand over the collection lining his desk. "They are the only way we have to find those missing people."

"I would advise that you tell your men to not wash or shave in the days between now and when we go through. You'll need appropriate clothing as well. It'll take time to locate these women. It's been five years since Thomas sent the ones through, that we know about. Twenty years since Pederson sent his last one through? But there could be some between those times. And Thomas said he sent people through new zippers." Tabitha sighed as she considered the prospect of the huge task of locating all those people. "But it's the Stengarlds we have to deal with first."

"You're serious?" McNamara asked in surprise.

Tabitha nodded and stood. "I went in to scout around." She shuddered. "It's not safe for a woman alone. So we need each other in this." Tabitha paced as she thought. "No deodorant either. They believe the dirt protects them from parasites and germs. The men you send have to blend. It is a world where standing out gets you noticed. Getting noticed is not what we want." Tabitha stopped pacing and looked up. "Have you been to the mall lately?"

"The mall?" McNamara was having a tough time keeping up with her direction of topics.

"Let's go. You can pick up clothes there. You'll need them later anyway. You strike me as the type of guy who has to take care of things himself so you can help dispose of the keys when we go back."

"Go where?" he asked in confusion.

"The mall," Tabitha said. "There's a zipper at the mall that leads to the dimension of the Stengarlds. A back door. I think they only know about the one because the others aren't guarded."

McNamara stared at Tabitha. Go right at that moment to the mall to step into another dimension where a team of his men had failed to get through, with this small confusing woman as his only backup. Initially it seemed like a very bad idea. McNamara studied her and thought about what she had been saying. Tabitha had already gone through, he realized. Tabitha had gone through, come back, and was willing to go through again. Finally he nodded and stood. McNamara locked his office door since he didn't want anyone wandering in with all the keys sitting on the desk. He gave his assistant the heads up that he was stepping out and to not allow anyone into his office while he was out.

When they reached the mall Tabitha led him to a store that specialized in costumes. She picked out outfits for both of them and they went into the dressing rooms to change. They were fair quality costumes, simple linen pants and rough wool pullover shirt with a fake fur vest for him. The shoes were just fake fur wraps around his ankles to cover his loafers. Tabitha chose a long prairie style wool dress and the same fake fur wraps to cover her ankle high Bjorn boots. McNamara paid for the costumes and asked the clerk to hold their clothes while they continued shopping. The clerk's eyebrows rose but he smiled and said they'd be behind the counter for them when they returned. Dressing up as Vikings to stroll the mall wasn't very common obviously. McNamara followed Tabitha as she led the way to the other side of the mall and into a large foundation store. She ducked into the receiving room and after a quick glance around to make sure no one was around stepped up to a shelf holding returned clothes and a zipper flared to light.

"After you," she said, waving him through.

McNamara hesitated then stepped through. They stepped out into a twilight rural setting. The change in time was definitely disorienting. So too was stepping into a grassy hollow lined by trees where the Mall of America should be. Tabitha immediately crouched, looking all around them before slightly relaxing. She pointed. In the distance was the faint shadow of buildings, a good two miles away.

"That's the closest village. I don't recommend that we explore any further though," Tabitha said, eyes constantly darting around their surroundings.

"You're afraid, aren't you?" McNamara asked. Tabitha nodded, attention focused on watching for any movement. "But you're willing to come back here to rescue these women?" He was surprised.

"It's the only way." Tabitha looked around them nervously. "I just wanted you to see. Can we go back now?"

McNamara nodded and they slipped back through the zipper, which Tabitha opened with a wave of her hand again. In the blink of an eye they went from twilight in a rural location to the half-lit storage area of a department store in the middle of the day. For some reason McNamara had the urge to feel his limbs to make sure he was in one piece. No one was in the storage area but when they left the receiving room there were several employees standing together talking. The pair got a startled look when they exited the receiving room dressed in skin and wool costumes. McNamara didn't pay attention. He was busy planning their course of action.

"Agreed," he said at last after they'd collected their clothes. "With some terms. The keys wait until everyone is rescued."

Tabitha shook her head no. "No, they can't wait. If you use the keys it puts stress on the zippers because they are forcing them open. Imagine the zippers weakening and anyone being able to cross through. Or worse. Who knows how many times Daniel already used them? Do you really want to risk that?"

McNamara's eyes widened. "How do you plan on disposing of the keys?"

"Taking them to a dimension where they don't work and tossing them in a pile of rocks where no one will give them a second glance."

"Damn. So simple." He shook his head, trying not to think about how well that plan would actually work. The keys would be gone. But that was her intent. It would solve his problem also. "You'll need to work for me. We agree that this will take time so you won't be able to hold down another job while doing this. You'll be hired as a consultant."

"Simon and Agent Ellis will be involved also?" Tabitha asked casually.

"Of course. It's their case," McNamara said, holding the exit door open for her. "Simon has been working it all along. If Dane makes it out of the hospital alive I'm sure he'll be involved in future rescue missions but not this one."

Tabitha stopped in her tracks and looked up in surprise. "Dane is in the hospital?"

"You didn't know? Ah, you didn't know."

"I didn't know," Tabitha said.

"It's been plastered on the news. I'm pretty sure Simon tried calling you."

"I haven't seen the news since the first night we were back," Tabitha muttered, more to herself. She almost laughed with relief. Dane hadn't called her because he was in the hospital. Then it hit her. If Dane was in the hospital this whole time, that meant something serious. "Is he all right? Why is he in the hospital? Why did you say if he makes it out alive?"

Chapter Sixteen

Tabitha listened to the nurse mutter about macho men who thought they were superman. The nurse added that he'd be fit to leave in a day or two but then only to go home and finish healing. Tabitha tried to be patient while she waited for the nurse to look up the room number. All she had asked the nurse was the room number for Dalton Ellis but hearing that name had set up the grumbling tirade from the woman. Tabitha wondered if she should have called first so that she could have gone straight to the room without stopping at the nurse's station. The foolish man had been shot and ignored the wound in order to lead the cavalry back to her. Foolish. Yet she smiled. Tabitha bounced on her toes, impatient to see him.

"Room 234," the nurse said at last, looking up from the monitor.

"Thanks!"

Tabitha smiled so wide that her cheeks hurt as she walked down the hall looking for the right room. The floor was like a maze with confusing signs with arrows pointing out vague directions for clusters of numbers. She walked down one hall and had to backtrack when she saw that the numbers were increasing above 250. Then she saw that the right hall was marked by numbers and arrows on the corner walls of the corridors that seemed to match the numbers on the doors better than the signs on the walls. There was construction going on, which added to the confusion. A woman walked past briskly, knowing where she was going. Tabitha slowed in surprise when the woman walked ahead of her into room 234.

"Hi, Beautiful," Dane's voice said. "Where's Tommy?"

"I know how much you like to see him but he's with a sitter this time. I wanted to be able to focus on you, not chasing after a four year old."

Tabitha heard Dane's warm chuckle before she felt the blood freeze in her veins and a roar like the ocean in her ears. Her feet continued to walk on their own until she stood outside room 234. Tabitha waited at the door, staring at the beige curtain partially blocking the view into the hospital room so that she could only see the bottom half of the bed and the woman's back as she leaned toward the patient lying in the bed. Tabitha wanted to continue into the room but for some reason her feet refused to move another step. There could be an explanation for a stunningly beautiful woman making herself at home in Dane's hospital room, of course. The woman was sitting on the edge of the bed, not the chair.

"I get to play nurse for a few days when you get out," the woman said, laughing. "My dream come true."

Dane made groaning noises. "I still have scars. You do not have the nurse gene. Put me out of my misery now."

The casual intimacy and warmth made Tabitha feel like an eavesdropper on an intimate moment between two people in love. Tabitha took two steps backwards then turned and hurried away, almost running down the hall. She stopped before she reached the nurse's station. This wasn't right. The man she had come to know couldn't be married already or involved with someone else. Dane would have told her. He wouldn't have cheated on someone else with her. Tabitha had to know the truth. She couldn't just run away without giving him the chance to explain. Tabitha turned back and forced herself to walk back down the hall to room 234.

When Tabitha reached the room she stepped inside without giving herself the opportunity to change her mind. The woman was checking the moisture in a foil wrapped potted plant. She looked up at Tabitha and smiled. The physical resemblance to Dane was startling.

"Hello," the woman said. "If you're here for Dane he's out again already."

Tabitha stepped further into the room. She had always intensely disliked hospitals, especially hospital rooms. Dane was lying on his back sleeping. He looked awful, pale and scruffy with shadows under his eyes, yet she had never seen anyone who looked more beautiful. Tabitha drank in the sight of him like a tall glass of cool water on a July day in Texas. It was so good to see him.

"I'll stop by another time," Tabitha said, though her feet were rooted to the spot.

"I can tell him you came by," the woman said. "I recognize you from the news. Tabitha, is it?"

Tabitha nodded. "I've been busy. A lot going on. I just heard today he was in hospital."

"I'm sure he'll appreciate it," the woman said. "He drifts in and out. They're keeping him sedated so he stays put until they're ready to release him. If you want to hang around a bit he'll wake up eventually."

"I can't stay. Have to be somewhere," Tabitha said. She took a deep breath of hospital room air. The disinfectant smell mixed with other unpleasant odors meant to be eliminated with the disinfectant was too much. "I'll come back later."

The woman nodded. She was too polite to ask but she looked like she was dying to ask something.

"Hey," Dane said, struggling to wake up. "Tabitha?"

Tabitha warily approached the side of the bed. "Hi you."

"Decided to visit after all?" There was no rancor in his voice, only pleasure that she was there.

"I didn't know you were here until McNamara told me a few hours ago," Tabitha said. "How are you? The nurse said you'll be going home in a day or two."

"Tough as nails. But not bullet proof."

"I need a coffee," the woman said, heading for the door.

"Wait, Cass. Tabitha, my sister Cass. Cass, my wife, Tabitha."

"Wife?" Cass and Tabitha said in surprised unison.

Dane grinned. "Got used to saying it. Iz nize."

After that bombshell he promptly drifted away again. Tabitha turned to his confused and curious sister. "They told our captor that Dane and I were married."

"Huh," Cass said.

Tabitha grimaced. Without going into detail it wasn't possible to explain and she wanted to explain but she couldn't explain. So she kept quiet, which wasn't easy for her to do either. How could she explain that to everyone they had encountered in another dimension Dane had assumed the role of her husband when the official story was that Daniel Thomas had held them prisoner in his basement. There was no explanation for why they would pose as husband and wife in the basement of a lunatic.

"Yes, well, I have to go," Tabitha said. "It was nice to meet you."

"Nice to meet you as well," Cass said. She smiled her big smile. "I hope we will meet again."

"I think so," Tabitha said, finding a sudden liking for Dane's sister. "I really think so. I just can't stay or I would. I had to sneak away from work to at least say hi. I have to get back to work but I can come back tonight. I just had to see him. Bye."

Five days later Tabitha wrinkled her nose as she watched the rescue team assemble in the huge garage. Two black vans were parked inside to transport the whole team to her back door zipper at the mall. Tabitha wore a shapeless wool dress and had not combed her hair for two days. She already felt itchy. Though she had told McNamara that the men should not wash or use deodorant since they started planning this she hadn't been able to go that long herself. The room smelled like they had followed instructions though. They had also found a seamstress who had managed to make real clothes accurate for what they needed instead of relying on costumes from a costume store.

McNamara entered the garage, followed by Dane. Dane winked at her as he followed McNamara behind the screens in the corner of the room designated as a dressing area. A few minutes later they emerged costumed as Vikings. McNamara walked over to talk to one of his men while Dane came over to stand next to Tabitha.

"Are you healed enough for this?" Tabitha asked, worried that he wasn't. Dane still held himself stiffly though he looked much healthier.

"Sure. No problem. I'll stay in the background, let the big boys play rough," he said lightly. His gaze shifted to the canvas bag she carried. "What's that?"

"Most of the keys," Tabitha said.

Dane's eyebrows rose. "You're giving them to the Stengarlds?"

"No. They won't work for this zipper, so I'm leaving them on the other side."

Dane frowned. "So how do you know about this "back door" zipper? And how can you open it if these keys don't work on it?"

"I'm a purple halo, remember?" Tabitha smiled at his frown. McNamara joined them and she turned to him. "Have you figured out how we're going to get all these men dressed like this, smelling like this, into the Mall of America?"

McNamara nodded. "Piece of cake."

"Where's Simon? I thought he was going to be here also," Tabitha said, looking at the scruffy faces surrounding her and not seeing the agent.

"He got called away on another case that was too urgent to wait," McNamara said. "He'll come back in when he's done with that task."

The signal came and all the men stowed their gear in the van and climbed inside. They drove to the mall and entered the store's delivery entrance. It was past closing time and the staff who would normally be working were all out of sight. They saw no one as Tabitha led the way to the zipper and opened it. The team quickly passed through. Tabitha followed last. They were in the rural hollow, pre-dawn making the sky gray. Once again it felt like stepping into the past though it wasn't the past.

"This time there are several villages," Tabitha explained to Dane. "The first one is about a mile away."

Dane nodded. "I read the info you gave McNamara."

"Okay, men," McNamara said. "You know the plan. Two groups. We meet here end of day. First run is strictly recon. We need locations before we start anything. Dane, you'll be staying here with Tabitha. Stay out of sight."

"There's at least fifteen miles between here and the zipper inside the tent with the waiting party," Dane said, looking off at the village in the distance. "That's a lot of terrain to cover in one day on foot." He turned to Tabitha. "You came here already, didn't you?"

Tabitha nodded. "Just a small group to get a rough map. No one went near the villages. I had to get a feel for the, uh, land."

"You can help Tabitha with the keys," McNamara said as the other men moved out in their designated directions. He gestured to the bag of rocks Tabitha held. "First step is to make sure none of these work on this zipper."

Dane eyed the bag warily. "What are you going to do with them?"

"Well, Tabitha wanted to toss them in a rock pile but that's too random of FBI protocol. We'll test each rock to make sure it doesn't open this dimension's zipper and then we'll bury them. Since the geography is the same in each dimension I have located a secure spot not too far from here."

"Let's see that," Dane said, reaching for the bag. Tabitha gave it to him.

Dane walked through the zipper's location twice without triggering it. "Looks like nothing in here works."

McNamara frowned. "That was simple enough. All right, let's head for the spot I picked." He pulled out a GPS locater, frowning when it didn't work. McNamara looked up at Tabitha. "I know, I know. Habit."

Tabitha took the bag back from Dane. It was heavy but she knew that to do what she had to do she had to be in possession of the keys when the moment came. Tabitha knew where she had to go. Dane fell into step beside her while McNamara trailed behind. Tabitha kept alert to their surroundings. Despite the presence of the two men this dimension gave her the creeps. They had walked less than half an hour when Tabitha spotted the river. This was what had given her the idea of bringing the keys to this dimension and dumping them.

Tabitha paused, looking down at all the rocks lining the river bank at this location. Once she did this the keys would be gone, unavailable. It was the right thing to do. She knew that it was the right thing to do. She felt a bit uncomfortable getting rid of them forever though, for some reason.

"Nice view. You've been mighty quiet," Dane said, staring out at the view.

"What? Oh, just thinking," Tabitha said. She opened the bag, pulled out a key and looked at it. It was a porcelain dog with crystal eyes and gems in its collar. She raised her arm and hurled it into the river. It hit with a soft plop.

"What are you doing?" McNamara yelled.

"Disposing of the keys," Tabitha said, tossing a second key. She hadn't even looked at it before throwing it.

"But I was going to bury them."

"You said I could dispose of them. That was the agreement."

"That looks like fun," Dane said. He reached into the bag and pulled out a rusty nail with a wire coiled around it and whipped it into the river with gusto. Dane grimaced the second the key left his fingers. "Crap. Doctor might have said no baseball for a few months." He clutched his side in obvious pain.

"I think someone's coming," McNamara warned in a low voice.

Tabitha shivered. She tipped the bag, sending the remaining rocks skittering down the rock-covered bank, a few rolling into the water with a soft splash here and there. She looked up at Dane. "Don't do anything rash."

Dane frowned then quickly grinned. "As you wish."

Tabitha scowled at him, convinced that he was mocking her. Dane was in no condition to take on any of these Stengarlds if things went badly and from what she had seen they tended to move in groups when outside the villages. Tabitha would trust him to know how dangerous these men were. She hoped he trusted that she knew these men better than he did. She just didn't think he would define something rash in the same way she would define something as being rash.

The intruders were two men. Tabitha felt some of the stress leave her when she saw that it wasn't a larger group. They approached the trio confidently. Both men were shorter than McNamara but of a height with Dane. Tabitha had their interest but they eyed McNamara warily. Both men wore leather breeches, leather vests over wool tunics, and shaggy facial hair that covered their necks. Tabitha stepped closer to Dane, putting her hand on his arm. One of the men pointedly stared at her. His stare turned into a leer when he saw how uncomfortable he made her.

"Drowning rodents?" one man asked, jerking his head at the bag Tabitha held.

"Collecting wildflowers," Dane said, picking off imaginary dust from his sleeve.

Both men laughed. They waved and kept walking. Tabitha stared after them in amazement. Dane continued to study this sleeve as if the two men walking past didn't matter enough to draw his attention.

"How did you do that?" she asked in awe when they had passed out of hearing range.

"Do what?"

She waved her hand in the air. "That! Whatever it was. I thought for sure they'd start a fight."

"They decided the odds weren't in their favor, I'm sure," Dane said. He glanced up finally. The men were still in sight but moving away at a good pace. "Let's not stick around for them to find some buddies."

They walked back in the direction of the zipper location. Tabitha felt vulnerable and exposed. McNamara was sullen and silent. His elaborate plans for disposal of the keys had been whisked away with one shake of Tabitha's wrist. Tabitha was impressed with how well Dane had diffused the situation and went through the scene over and over in her mind. Dane seemed to understand how the minds of these men worked, something she still couldn't wrap her mind around. Tabitha noticed McNamara sulking.

"The agreement was that I'd get to dispose of them," Tabitha said, watching McNamara. He just shook his head, not saying anything. "Feel free to go back and collect them if you want. If you can find them."

"You've gotten yourself a harsh woman, Ellis" McNamara said, shaking his head. "Leaves me no room for argument."

Tabitha felt her cheeks warm. It felt strange to be referred as being Dane's woman. It felt nice yet it felt odd. She glanced at Dane through her lashes. He stood there with a pleased grin on his face. "If you had buried them someone would have noticed and found a pile of items important enough to bury and kept them without knowing what they are. This way they vanish in plain sight. Quite efficient."

"As I said, no room for argument." McNamara studied their surroundings, already putting it out of his mind. "We need to set up a camp away from the zipper in case we do get more visitors."

"I'll look around," Dane said.

"No. I'll look around," McNamara said. "I shouldn't have let you come so soon."

"Right there," Tabitha said, pointing ahead. "C'mon." Without waiting for an argument she headed for the likely location. After a slight hesitation including exchanging meaningful glances the two men followed her.

The area was cozy. They had the zipper's location within sight. Trees ringed the north side. To the south large boulders lined a gentle, grassy slope. Dane nodded grudgingly. "Good spot."

They set up camp by McNamara pulling out his communication system anticipating the scheduled contact from the two teams. Since satellites were not available in other dimensions they had to go old school with radios. They had brought backpacks with supplies, including some small tents but waited to set them up in case they had to move out. While Dane and McNamara tested the radio equipment, Tabitha found a boulder with a flat top and settled down in a crouch, her legs drawn up so that she could rest her chin on her knees. It was the perfect spot to catch some sunlight. The view was amazing. In their dimension this land was covered with a super shopping mall and miles of high speed interstates and exits that were almost long enough to be considered roads themselves and parking lots for the massive volume of shoppers. In this dimension the land was open, green, and beautiful.

Dane came up to stand beside her, leaning against the boulder so his hip rested on it. "When things calm down we should have dinner," he said.

"I'd like that," Tabitha said, looking up at him with a smile.

"I know the perfect spot. Do you like lamb chops?"

Tabitha's eyes widened. "Very much. I love lamb chops. Sounds great."

They were quiet for several minutes. Tabitha felt more relaxed than she had since the business started with the visit to Daniel Thomas to see if her meteorites had a monetary value. It felt real now, whatever it was between her and Dane. Sure they had carried on as husband and wife, in all ways, but until he asked her out on a date she felt uncertain what was between them. This step back into normalcy was necessary. Dating defined what was between them. It wasn't enough that McNamara referred to her as Dane's woman or that they had told everyone in another dimension that they were married. McNamara could think what he wanted and the married lie was a lie. The simple act of Dane asking her out on a date gave definition to their relationship. She realized suddenly how much she needed definition.

She looked back out at the view. "How do you think it's going? Do you think they'll find any of the women right away?"

Dane thought about it before answering. "Let's wait and see what the scouting mission learns." He shifted his body around so that he was partially sitting on the boulder but still able to see her. "Why are you doing this?"

"What?" she asked, pulling at a piece of grass growing near her feet at the edge of the boulder.

"Why are you doing this? Risking yourself for women you don't even know."

"Someone has to. They deserve to be rescued. I'm just glad the Bureau is willing to help. I don't think I could have done it on my own."

"You would have though, wouldn't you?" Dane asked.

"Well, I would have tried. Well, I did try," Tabitha admitted grudgingly. She wrinkled her nose at the thought, staring in the direction of the village out of sight beyond the knoll. "I couldn't do it. It feels less scary having company in my corner." Tabitha shivered, thinking about her attempt to learn the location of the women by herself. She looked up at Dane. "I know I'm a coward. I tell myself that this way they will be rescued all the sooner. If I had done it myself it would have taken years and I'd have died of a heart attack from the stress."

Dane stared at her in amazement. Several emotions battled inside him. Fear, that she had come into this land by herself, putting herself at risk. Pride, that she had the gumption to attempt to rescue abducted women in a land populated by warrior men who treated women like chattel. Anger, that she would attempt to do this without turning to him for help first.

"I can't begin to imagine the courage it would take for a woman, a civilian, to venture into this land knowing what you know about it. You did the right thing to go to McNamara," Dane said. He took her hand and kissed her palm before looking up at her and saying with absolute conviction, "And if you ever do something so foolhardy again I will skin you alive."

"Promise?" Tabitha whispered in delight. She had never heard more beautiful words out of a man's mouth.

"I'm here for you, Tabitha," he said in a low voice. "I can't bear to imagine if something happened to you. I'll bet you didn't even tell anyone what you were doing, did you?"

"This from the man who forgets to tell me he was shot," Tabitha said, arching her eyebrow as she looked at him.

"Okay. Okay. We're even." He leaned over and kissed her cheek. "I'd prefer to taste those lips but that has to wait," he whispered, glancing at McNamara.

Tabitha nodded, feeling the same way. As much as she wanted to get feel his lips on hers it wasn't the right place and it took a lot of effort to resist. She wasn't done with their discussion either. "But you do this sort of thing all the time, right? Put yourself on the line to help people."

"Sometimes. Not all the time. If necessary. But it's my job and I've had training," Dane said. "You haven't."

"That's a good idea," Tabitha said, brightening. "I could use training."

Dane rolled his eyes. "Or you could not go into situations where you're putting yourself in danger." He sighed as he realized that she was not going to slip back into a life without zippers and the unknown dimensions that they opened into. "Or we could look into some basic training for you."

The day passed without any sign of the inhabitants of this dimension. The two teams made their check-ins with McNamara on schedule. Tabitha was getting restless and bored. It wasn't in her nature to sit idle all day. Knowing what lurked out there kept her from following the urge to explore however. So she did what was first nature to her, she talked.

"What are they doing?" she asked.

"Who?" McNamara asked, attention still on his equipment. The man definitely loved his gadgets.

"The teams. How do they plan on finding the women? They can't exactly go in and start asking, can they?" she said. Dane and McNamara exchanged glances. Tabitha groaned. "Is that the plan? To just go in and start asking questions?"

"They'll be subtle," McNamara said. "They know what they're doing. When they get back with their information we'll work out a detailed plan of action. This is strictly recon. Any sign of trouble and we're out of here, let things settle before taking any action. We don't want to put these women in more danger."

Tabitha pictured the men who made up the teams being subtle in asking about women who came through a zipper of light against their will and it created a wave of despair in her gut. She had thought they were just going to observe the villages from a distance, not walk in without a clue about the culture of this land. Daniel Thomas had not gotten into any detail in his notes other than that after the results of his initial visit he had been willing to risk abducting women to send through the zipper to meet their demands rather than risk a second encounter without their favor. Dane suspected what she was thinking from the dumbfounded expression on her face.

"Now isn't the time to question tactics," he said. "We did our homework, Tabitha. Besides reviewing pictures, each man has personal information on these women. The plan is to get into the villages and have the women approach them."

Tabitha was confused. "How are they going to do that?"

"Imagine if I came into a village where you were being held and I mentioned that I have a cat named Snooze."

Tabitha's eyes lit up. "It would get my attention."

"My brother Jared tied a feather to Snooze's tail."

Tabitha's eyes widened and she visibly relaxed. "I get it," Tabitha said, nodding. "They use information from the women's life to get their attention while that information wouldn't mean anything to the rest of the people around them. Okay, that's subtle. Very subtle."

It was evening when the first team quietly slipped their way into the camp. A few minutes later the second team came in without a sound. The two team leaders joined McNamara while the other men settled down and pulled food out of backpacks. Tabitha walked over to the team leads and McNamara so she could hear what they were discussing.

"Three of the women are in one village," a team lead said. "Karen Thieland. Mindy Thompson. Judy Candoli. We weren't able to talk to any of them and I'm not sure how we're going to extract them without warning them first. They got our message but that doesn't mean they'll be ready when we go back in."

"Once we pull any of them out the locals will be on the watch and the same tactics won't work for any future recons," the other team lead said. "Raiding is common and we had to be very low key to not gain suspicion. We located one woman, Sandy Olson. She almost gave it away. I'd say she's pretty desperate to get out of there. We did get a chance to tell her to stay put until we could get back. Hopefully knowing we'll be back will keep her level."

The first team lead nodded. "It won't take them long to start talking about it. One of the women almost gave it away but another woman caught on and was sharp enough to calm her down. But how long before someone gives us away without meaning to? They're civilians. They're scared. They're desperate."

"I'll have to do it," Tabitha said. "And we'll have to do it tonight yet." They all looked at her. "You find them. I'll extract them." The word extract felt awkward on her tongue.

"No," Dane said. "It's too dangerous. These men know what they're doing."

"But if you leave them until you find all the women the locals will know it's you once you rescue any of them," Tabitha said to the team leads. They were the ones she was trying to convince. "If I do it they won't suspect you."

"We rotate out different teams," Dane said.

Tabitha shook her head, noticing that one of the team leads had also shaken his head slightly. "We have to keep this quiet and bringing in more teams means more people who know which means risking it getting broadcast."

"No more teams," McNamara said in agreement.

"It would be even better if you could be in the company of some of the locals when these women go missing," Tabitha said, thinking ahead. "An alibi."

"How the hell do you plan on waltzing in and waltzing out?" Dane asked angrily. He shook his head. "No."

"I need help getting into the villages but once in I need to work alone," Tabitha said. She turned to McNamara. "They only see women as property. They're not on guard for a woman walking into a village. They will be on guard for a group of men skulking about a village in the dark. If anything happens to me you can come get me when you get the others. We need to try it this way first."

"How do you plan on getting them out?" McNamara asked.

"No," Dane said firmly.

Tabitha looked up at him. His concern touched her but she knew that she had to do this. If the women felt help was so near but had left they might do something rash. If the teams went in and forcibly rescued the ones they had found so far they would be marked and not be able to freely move about to find the rest. Tabitha wanted to reassure him that she wasn't being rash but didn't want to tell him in front of all these men that she was going to be careful because she was in fact terrified.

"You know I'm going to do it no matter how many times you say no," she said to Dane.

"I know," he said, grimacing. "But I'm not going to like it, no matter how many times you ignore my protests."

Tabitha smiled. It was an almost sad smile. She turned back to McNamara. "I'll let the women figure it out. They know the locals better. If I go in I can talk to them." She closed her eyes and concentrated. Yes, there was a zipper to the east of the villages. Silently she sent a thank you to Lord Kempsley for his packet and all its wonderful information. It would require some zipper hopping but it would work to lead searchers in the opposite direction. "I need your help, Dane."

Dane wavered. He knew that she was going to do it regardless and she was giving him an out by including him. At last he nodded.

"Maybe one more man and then the rest should head west so they're in the opposite direction when the women are discovered missing," she said, nodding to herself. That should remove suspicion.

Tabitha stood at the edge of the village. Tabitha couldn't see Dane. That was good. He was supposed to be out of sight. She walked into the first village like she belonged there but kept her head down. The woman Tabitha was looking for was standing outside a hut washing dishes but she was staring out into the growing darkness beyond the village with a haunted look on her face. Her concentration was definitely on what she had learned that day about possible rescue more than on doing dishes. Tabitha stepped up to her without the woman even noticing her.

"Sandy?" The woman jumped in surprise. "Calm," Tabitha said softly. "We're going to walk out of here like we have the right. Okay?"

Sandy nodded. She trembled like a leaf but managed to keep her composure. Sandy picked up a woven reed basket and headed out of the village, stopping near the edge to pick up some branches. Tabitha realized what she was doing and whenever Sandy paused they both picked up a few branches before straightening and moving a little farther away from the village. No one paid any attention to them. They continued out into the night.

"We have a friend joining us then we'll walk awhile," Tabitha said as they neared Dane's hiding spot.

Sandy whispered a soft "okay" and when Dane joined them tears ran down the woman's cheeks but she was silent. The three set off briskly for the next village. About halfway there Sandy remembered the basket for kindling and asked softly if she should bring it with or set it aside. "If I leave it here hopefully someone will find it and use it. It's a nice basket."

Tabitha considered. "I can carry it if it's heavy," Tabitha said. "But it might come in handy and we don't want anyone to find it just yet so we can't just drop it along the way."

Sandy nodded. "It's not that heavy. I was just wondering."

Dane grew thoughtful. "We could give it to someone in the next village and have it returned to your village if you'd like."

Sandy sighed in relief. "Yes, that would be a good idea. It's just that Brigget made it herself and it took her a long time."

Tabitha felt bad that she hadn't caught on to Sandy's real question from the start. She was very impressed that Dane had. He had a real talent of empathy. Tabitha felt the zipper just outside of the next village. It was late and they were tired from hurrying in the dusky light to reach the next village. Tabitha's eyes felt strained from staring at the path in front of their feet in little light. Fortunately the next village was only a few miles from the first village so they had nearly reached it in only an hour.

The closer they came to the next village the more Sandy's legs trembled until she could barely walk any longer. Tabitha skirted south to take them right to the zipper, which helped give renewed strength to Sandy's legs. Dane wasn't happy when she said the two would have to wait there for her but he knew that Sandy couldn't wait by herself. Her original plan had been to have them wait on the outskirts of the village and then all come to the zipper but she could see what it was doing to Sandy to head back to what she saw as the lion's den.

The next village was about the same as the first except it was larger, more buildings, more activity. Tabitha studied it for a few minutes to determine her next step. It didn't take long to spot three women clustered together at the edge of the village, near one of the outermost buildings. A small blonde woman, a tall blonde woman, and a dark haired woman. Unfortunately they also had the attention of one of the men sitting by a fire pit sharpening an axe with a whetstone. Tabitha waited in the near darkness, crouched next to a tree unmoving except her heart thumping wildly in her chest.

Further into the village a large group of men sat around a large bonfire, laughing and drinking. The single man at the small fire pit glanced up repeatedly from his axe as he brushed the axe with a long, slow stroke of the whetstone. Tabitha sat frozen, watching the man with the axe and the three women talking in agitated, low voices. Finally he set his tools down and got to his feet with a heavy sigh. He approached the three women, who grew silent when they saw him.

"What's wrong with her?" he asked, pointing to the small blonde woman the other two were comforting.

A slender woman with black hair faced him defiantly, hands on her hips. "She heard Bandal bragging he was going to steal a woman he saw today. She's afraid that if he does she'll go to Markly."

The man grunted in surprise. Then he laughed. "Bandal's a fool." Still chuckling he went back to his axe. He reached down and picked up the axe. He glanced back at the three women again then laughed and shook his head before joining the larger group at the bonfire, the women and their problems forgotten.

Tabitha edged her way toward the women. Being seen was part of her plan but it didn't make it any easier and she would avoid it if possible. The slender brunette spotted Tabitha right away and nodded once, very calm and confident. She leaned down and whispered in the tall blonde's ear. The tall blonde nodded and went into the nearest building without even glancing behind her.

"Karen?" Tabitha asked tentatively when she was close enough to be heard in a low voice.

The brunette nodded. "Mindy is staying. We're ready to go."

The two walked boldly out of the village and into the darkness in the direction Tabitha had come from. Tabitha followed, having to trot briskly to catch up and take the lead. They reached Dane and Sandy without incident. Tabitha could sense the zipper or she'd have never found them in the dark. Any last bit of light had fled. Tabitha opened the zipper and they stepped through in single file with only the barest hesitation. It was dark in this dimension also but in the distance there was the glow of light over Minneapolis that indicated that it was a big city here. Power lines were visible against the teal sky as well. Sandy's eyes widened and she ran to a power pole and hugged it.

"I'm free! I'm free," she cried.

Tabitha wanted to give her time to relish the realization that she had escaped the nightmare she had been living but in truth they weren't done yet. "We have to do some walking to reach the next zipper," she said.

"Where's the third one?" Dane asked.

"She's staying," Karen said. She looked around them. "Are we back?"

"Almost," Tabitha said. "We're safe but we're not completely back home. We have to go through a few more zippers," she explained. "Beams of light. I didn't want to lead them to the other zipper in case they started watching that one also."

"We have time to rest a bit first," Dane said. Tabitha opened her mouth to argue then changed her mind. She was so focused on rescuing them that it was easy to ignore the exhaustion and forget that it would benefit them to take a breather and rest for at least a short time.

They found a spot to settle down until it was light enough to walk to the next zipper. The grass was dry and once they were sitting it was tall enough to block the cool breeze. While they waited Sandy and Karen talked about their captivity. Mindy had been torn about whether to take the opportunity to go home or stay because she had a good man who treated her well and she had fallen in love with him. Mindy didn't want to take his sons from him, which meant she had to stay or abandon her children. She chose to stay. Mindy had refused to look at who was rescuing them so she could honestly say that she hadn't seen the others leave.

"Bandel actually loves her also," Karen said. "He treats her pretty well. They have two sons and she wouldn't leave without them and she couldn't take them from him. Judy has two children as well but there was no question of bringing them." Judy's eyes filled with tears and she looked away, crying silently.

"Bandel?" Tabitha asked in surprise.

Karen smiled, a crooked, mischievous smile. "Grot thought we were all nuts. What better way to get rid of a man than to try to drag him into a relationship issue he sees as complete foolishness, eh?"

"I also left a child," Sandy said in a low voice. "He's four now. A carbon copy of his father. I haven't seen him for a year. Not since his father traded me to Yorden. His name is Stravic. I called him Steven."

Tabitha shivered. The hairs on the back of her neck tingled. She turned to Judy, who had yet to say a single word. "Did you also leave a child?" Judy shook her head.

"Brock had her tongue cut out," Karen said, putting a hand on Judy's shoulder. "She talked too much. It irritated him."

Tabitha felt sick at that information. She reached out beside her and found Dane's hand. He squeezed her hand with his comfortingly. As the sky lightened Tabitha and Dane sat holding hands as they listened to the women talk about the treatment they had received at the hands of the men in that dimension. Mostly Karen talked. Sometimes Sandy contributed to the conversation but was mostly content to stare at the definitely more modernized dimension coming to light around them. The one positive piece of information was that Karen knew the locations of all the women who they were looking for. They didn't marry, marriage was not part of their culture. Women belonged to the men. Karen had belonged to a man who kept track of the women who came from Chanja's Tent.

"Chanja's Tent?" Dane asked.

"We all went through Chanja's Tent," Karen explained. "He exchanged the women for favors or payment. So he kept track of where they went."

Chapter Seventeen

Once it was light enough to see they started walking. They came to a road. It was paved asphalt. For a moment it seemed like Sandy considered dropping to the road and kissing the asphalt. A farmer came along from the east in a battered red pickup truck, puffs of blue smoke streaking out behind the vehicle. He slowed down, then pulled over on the shoulder and offered them a ride. They all gratefully climbed into the truck bed, heading west.

"Where are we going?" Dane asked.

"I'm not sure. I need to see a map," Tabitha said.

Dane tapped on the rear window and asked the driver if he had a map. The farmer nodded and dug around on his seat for a minute then passed a tattered state map back through the sliding window. Dane helped hold it down on Tabitha's knees as the wind whipped it around so she could study it. Everyone watched her very intently.

"Two miles north of the next town," she said, nodding to herself.

"That takes us back to our world?" Sandy asked.

Tabitha shook her head. "It takes us near the site of our camp back in the Viking dimension."

"We're going back?" Sandy asked, panic and fear rising in her voice.

"Just long enough to step into a final zipper that will take us home."

Sandy looked around them. "This place seems safe enough. I could just stay here."

"We're almost there," Tabitha said. "They'll be looking for you to the east. We're going to come out miles to the west. They might not even realize yet that you're missing."

"They're not stupid," Karen said, a hint of worry creeping into her voice.

"No one thinks they're stupid," Dane said quickly. "In fact, we're going about this with the belief they're highly intelligent and skilled. Our tracks lead east."

Karen nodded thoughtfully. "I'll trust you."

The farmer pulled to the side of the road at the edge of the town they needed. Dane handed him the map back and thanked him. The farmer tapped the brim of his hat and once he saw they were all standing on the road he pulled out onto the road and drove casually away. All three rescued women stared after him with various expressions. It would take some time to adjust but they were clearly eager to be able to rejoin their real world instead of the nightmare Daniel Thomas had pushed them into.

Everyone was tired but they still walked quickly in the direction of the zipper Tabitha felt ahead. "This is it," Tabitha said. They stood in a cornfield. Just to the east a pile of boulders lined a gentle slope at the edge of the cornfield. She looked up at Dane. "It'll be all right, won't it?"

Dane nodded. "Let's do it."

Tabitha opened the zipper and attempted to step through first but Dane beat her to it. Tabitha grimaced and followed him. Dawn had only grayed the sky here. In the distance torchlight bobbed to the east of the nearest village. The FBI agents were just within sight in the campsite. Tabitha sighed in relief. It wasn't that she had expected to step into a full scale battle but that actually was exactly what she had expected. McNamara spotted them and gave a signal. The teams jumped to attention and as the rescued woman stepped through the zipper they were greeted by the sight of armed FBI agents on alert to their surroundings.

"I suggest we all return," Dane said. "We have new information that will speed up the search better than any teams remaining and searching." His gaze was on the bobbing bits of flame light in the distance. "Let things settle down and come back another day."

"They'll know the only women taken were from Chanja's Tent," Karen said.

"Don't argue with him," Sandy said. She stepped forward. "I want to go home."

"I agree," Tabitha said. "We all go now. With the information from Karen we can do this much more efficiently."

"Agreed," McNamara said. "All right, men, make it look like we've never been here and let's move out."

They stepped into the Mall of America, startling several employees when a group of oddly dressed, dangerous looking men suddenly appeared in the stock room. Sandy and Judy both immediately broke into sobs of relief. Karen was made of sterner stuff but she was also clearly overcome with emotion. McNamara made a call the second he was through the zipper and by the time they all reached the exit and stepped out at the loading dock several vans were waiting for them.

Judy turned and threw her arms around Tabitha for a bone-crushing hug, then ran to the nearest van. Karen and Sandy also hugged her and thanked them all then joined Judy. Karen turned and came back. "The costumes your men are wearing. They mark them as outsiders. You'll need to know the insignia as well as what furs which rank can wear."

"I've acquired rooms at the Holiday Inn," McNamara said. "You'll be able to clean up and rest and we'll debrief you there." Karen nodded and hurried to join the others in the van. McNamara turned to Dane and Tabitha. "The other vans are heading back to the warehouse. I'll see you bright and early tomorrow." McNamara then hopped into the front seat of the van and it immediately pulled away.

"Bright and early tomorrow?" Tabitha muttered. "I could sleep for a week." Both Dane and she climbed into the same van and settled into their seats while team one climbed in with them. "Is this what you do all the time?" Tabitha asked, weary and drained from the stress more than from the long night.

"Rescue women from another dimension where they're treated like valuable livestock? No, this is the first."

"I mean the face danger part."

"Is that why you wanted to pull out?" Dane asked gently.

"No." Tabitha shook her head. She closed her eyes and leaned her head back against the wall of the van. "Hearing those women. It was real. The danger to them was real. What if I messed up? It would be my fault if something happened to them. I had to get them out of there. And I couldn't blindly stumble around trying to find zippers. What if I had opened one right in the village?"

"I understand," Dane said. "You've been very brave, Tabitha. What you are doing is very brave."

"Karen is right. They'll be on to it very quickly. We can't wait around too long. Or we should wait until the attention fades. I don't know. I just don't know the right route. It makes my head hurt."

"Don't think about it now," Dane said. "It's not on your shoulders. We're all in this together."

Tabitha nodded but her thoughts were troubled as she stared out the van's back window at the houses, cars, modern roadways, and buildings passing by and fading into the distance. "We take so much for granted," she said in a low voice.

"Ma'am, that's the point," one scruffy, body odor scented special forces man beside her said.

Tabitha sat up and turned to look at him. "What?"

"That's why we do what we do. So the average citizen can go about their life without fear."

There was a low mutter of huzzahs throughout the van from the former Marines. Tabitha smiled.

"We'll bring those women home," a voice promised.

"Are you up for dinner tonight?" Dane asked. "I'm thinking just some take out and then crash."

"A girl has to eat," Tabitha said lightly. It did feel good to be home. Tabitha was so used to being on her own all the time that it wasn't always easy to remember that she wasn't alone any longer. She was part of a team and she had Dane at her side. It felt good. It felt right. Tabitha leaned against Dane and rested her head on his shoulder. Together they would rescue the rest of the women no matter how long it took and then face what other adventures came their way.

www.ingramcontent.com/pod-product-compliance
Lightning Source LLC
Chambersburg PA
CBHW071159250626
47159CB00001B/135